The Canaries

Paul August

For Christine and Alex…

Prologue

Cold Water Drowning

March 11th 2015: Gardell Martin, a 22-month-old child from Pennsylvania, fell into an icy river with a water temperature estimated to be 34F. Things only got worse from there. Very quickly, the little boy was swept downstream for a quarter mile until he washed up on a grassy knoll. He had been in the frigid water for almost 30 minutes before a neighbor found him. Upon arrival at the Evangelical Community Hospital in Lewisburg, PA, the toddler had no pulse and his body core temperature was 74F. After performing CPR and warming his body for twenty minutes, doctors detected a pulse. CPR and warming continued for 2 more hours until the child woke up. Six days later, the boy was discharged to go home with his parents, talking and smiling with no neurological damage.

May 28th 2015: A 14-year-old Italian boy, identified only as Michael, jumped off a bridge near Milan into a canal. He became trapped under 7 feet of 58-degree water for 43 minutes. He required extensive life-saving efforts and didn't become conscious until 13 days later. Discharged after 37 days and neurologically intact, he could still speak the four languages he spoke before his accident.

May 20th 1999: One of history's most notable cases of cold water drowning involved a Swedish skier named Anna Bågenholm. In 1999 at 19 years old, she became trapped under a layer of ice for 80 minutes. While trapped, Anna found an air pocket that allowed her to breathe for forty minutes until she suffered cardiac arrest. After the rescue, she was diagnosed with an extreme case of hypothermia. Her body temperature was measured at a frighteningly low 13.7 degrees C (56.7F). This was one of the lowest temperatures ever recorded for a human being's core. More than 100 doctors and nurses resuscitated her over nine hours. She awoke ten days later paralyzed but did fully recover, eventually. Today she is a Senior Radiologist working at Tromso University Hospital, where her life was saved.

Approximately 240,000 people die yearly from drowning, making it the third leading cause of unintentional death worldwide. In the US alone, between 3,500 – 4000 die annually. The primary reasons for drowning include the inability to swim, diving or falling into bodies of water (lakes, rivers, oceans), bathtubs, in-ground pools, not wearing life jackets and alcohol overconsumption. Males are twice as likely to die from drowning than females.

When a person is drowning or has drowned, it oftentimes goes unnoticed, contradicting the perception depicted in television and movies of someone calling for help. When a person drowns, their body stops receiving oxygen and suffers from hypoxia (oxygen deprivation). They can then slip into a coma, suffer a seizure, and eventually experience brain death. All of these conditions typically occur within 4-6 minutes of drowning.

There is, however, an exception to those rules.

When someone drowns via submersion in cold water. Numerous cases throughout recorded history have shown amazing occurrences of children, adolescents, adults, and infants slipping beneath freezing waters for long periods to drown, only to be resuscitated and suffer no neurological damage or physical side effects. The younger the victim, the better the odds of surviving a cold water drowning.

The reasons are not entirely understood, but it's believed it is because young people have a smaller ratio of body mass to surface area than adults, causing them to suffer hypothermia quicker and to a greater degree. Their bodies slow down the brain's metabolic rate quickly, protecting it from harm. Additionally, there is a condition called the diving reflex, activated by fear. Blood is immediately directed to the heart and the brain to prolong survival and limit damage to the central nervous system.

Surviving a drowning in cold water can happen. There are many heartwarming, cold water survival stories. The human body's natural will to live, combined with the heroic efforts of medical staff, EMTs, and ordinary citizens, give hope to drowning victims.

When witnessing a cold water drowning incident, citizens should immediately call 911 and request help before attempting a dangerous rescue that could worsen matters. Most of today's EMTs are trained in cold water drowning and rescue techniques. The EMTs will try to stabilize the victim and transport them to a healthcare facility where they will hopefully survive and live a long life to tell their own incredible story of survival.

Part One

"Every day is a renewal, every morning the daily miracle.

This joy you feel is life."

Gertrude Stein

Chapter 1
Shangri-La

If she were granted only one wish, it would be to have her sister back - alive and well.

The doorbell rang and Kim jolted in the leather chair as if an electric shock had gone down her spine. It happened every time. The amygdala gland inside her brain would initiate a hyperarousal response flooding her body with adrenaline. With her heart rate spiking and pupils dilated, Kim was ready for fight or flight. When you live with extreme anxiety, every minute of every day, the doorbell ring is damn intrusive. As far as her body was concerned, something terrible was about to happen.

The sound triggered her ever since that morning ten years ago when the police rang the doorbell. They rang it over and over and over again.

She turned towards Brad and found him staring at her. "What?" he said. "I'm not expecting anyone at four o'clock on a Friday afternoon. Go see who it is."

"I'm in the middle of something," she continued typing on her MacBook Air laptop.

Brad snickered and then imitated her in a high voice, "Honey will you see who's ringing the doorbell? I'm scared there's a grizzly bear or a flesh-eating zombie waiting to devour me."

"Knock it off, Brad."

"Go see who it is, for Christ's sake. I pay all the bills around here. The least you can do is get the door now and then. Besides, you need to practice conquering your little anxiety problem, Kimmy dear."

"Why can't we get one of those doorbells with a built-in camera? You know, to see who's out there from our phones?"

"Because having guts and intestinal fortitude means we don't need to spy on people just because they're ringing the doorbell. Grow a pair and see who it is, will you?" He shook his head and then returned to reading his self-help book, You Arc A Badass.

She stared at him seething and muttered, "Asshole."

The bell rang a second time, and Kim jolted in her chair again. "Fine!"

Slamming the laptop closed and tossing it on the chair made her feel better. Tidying her white blouse and then tucking her long black hair behind her right ear, she walked down the hall toward the perfectly decorated foyer as she hummed Bobby McFerrin's Don't Worry, Be Happy under her breath.

The condominium they lived in was expensive. Travilah, Maryland, was about as upscale as you could get, and Brad wanted to live there to feel that he had arrived. As a successful Business Development Manager for a large chemical company and supplier to big pharma, he was paid north of two hundred grand a year. Brad owned the condo or, more accurately, paid its mortgage payments while his beautiful girlfriend lived with him and paid for the utilities and groceries. And she did all of the cooking.

Brad often played king of the condo by specifying where to position everything. That included the Ethan Allen living room furniture. Kim had deferred to his decorating taste until she moved her favorite chair to the opposite side of the room one day to better view the varied species of birds that fed off berries from a holly shrub outside the window. Brad came home and erupted at the change, insisting she move the chair back to the exact spot it had been.

Bird-watching was one of her passions, so Kim stood her ground and refused. A nasty argument ensued, resulting in a cold war lasting for three days. It was one of their shorter arguments, which had become more frequent lately. She could still remember driving in her car to call her friend Janey for comfort and telling her she was just about ready to make an exodus.

It hadn't always been this way. Kim first met Brad when he was selling new chemical compounds to a scientist at her company. One of her scientist buddies made her aware of Brad's interest in her, and a first meeting led to a first date which led to another. Kim thought they were an unlikely union; he was the extroverted sales representative, and she was an introverted clinical lab technician. But Kim was taken by Brad's kindness and generosity. He would arrive early for their dates with her favorite flowers, chrysanthemums.

He brings them every time!

She didn't care that Brad was seven years older than her. He was still handsome and tall, with brown hair and a friendly smile. In only six months, she felt they had achieved serendipity, and when her roommate bolted for the west coast, Kim accepted Brad's invitation to move into his place. She was finally happy even though a private storm raged behind her façade.

Kim opened the door to find an Asian woman, who she guessed was in her mid to late twenties, standing alone. Her shoulder-length black hair had a stylish bob cut, and she smiled a little too cheerfully. Her outfit could be described as wholesome, as if the Gap or Banana Republic were her favorite stores. Kim gave the stranger a dubious grin as she stood holding the door handle, poised to shut it as soon as possible.

"Can I help you?" Kim asked.

"I was actually hoping I could help you." The stranger smiled demurely as she held out her hand to shake. Kim noticed Chinese characters tattooed on her wrist.

"What do you mean, help me?" Kim shook the stranger's cold hand with reluctance.

"I was wondering, do you have a few minutes to discuss Jesus Christ?" Her eyes were a shade of ocean green that Kim had never seen before.

Is she pushing the holy savior wearing fake contacts?

"Um, well, no, thank you, I don't. I mean, with all due respect, we're not religious. I'm not interested in donating or anything." Kim fumbled for the right words as her hand squeezed the doorknob.

"Oh, I'm not asking for money. I want to discuss our Lord and Savior with you or anyone else here. He can help ease your pain. Do you have any pain in your life? Most people live with some pain or discomfort. Understanding Christ can help with that."

Kim's cheeks flushed red, and goosebumps pebbled her arms. Her anxiety level was now in the caution zone with the awkward intrusion from this random stranger who insisted on asking personal questions.

This is why I hate answering the door!

She felt her face contort and then gathered some composure.

"I'm not in any pain, miss. Neither is anyone else here. Thank you for stopping by. Have a nice day now." Kim began closing the door.

"Perhaps your husband or partner would like to talk for a minute? Faith is a person's personal decision, and I can speak to him individually if he would like."

"How would you know if I have a husband or a partner?"

"You said *we're* not religious, so I assumed someone else lived here. Does he have a moment to chat?"

5- The Canaries

Kim looked toward the ground to hide her red face. Her anxiety levels were now in the danger zone. Done with fight, it was time for flight. “Again, we’re not interested. Have a good day.”

She slammed the door in the woman’s face.

Pulling back the side window curtain, Kim watched the stranger walk up the street. Something was weird. For one, her stiletto high heels didn’t go with the rest of her modest appearance. And why wasn’t she stopping at any other houses?

“Who was it?” Brad asked as she plopped back into her chair, letting out a sigh.

“I don’t know. Some girl who wanted to talk about Jesus Christ and ease our pain.”

“What’d she look like? Was she hot?” he asked without looking up from his book.

“What kind of question is that to ask the woman you live with and supposedly love? Is she hot; seriously!”

“My bad. Sorry about that, babe.” Brad backpedaled.

“She appeared to be modest, I’d say.”

“Jesus Freaks, did she leave you with a pamphlet or something?”

“Now that you mention it, she wasn’t carrying a single thing. She was on foot. I didn’t even see a car.”

“Wait till she knocks on the Murphys’ door. They’ll sic that shepherd on her.” Brad chuckled.

“The weird thing is she didn’t stop anywhere else on the street. Wonder why she picked our place?”

“Get a job,” he muttered, taking a pull off his Beefeater and tonic.

Kim was back in her favorite chair, loving how it fit her body and grateful the whole ordeal was over. Turning her head, there was a glass of 2007 Sassicaia along with four slices of Comte' sitting on a plate next to her. She smiled at him, but he didn't notice.

This is what we have become. He's condescending and rude to me. Then he tries to redeem his bad behavior with a glass of expensive wine and a few slices of French cheese.

It was getting old. Back when Brad traveled more for his job, it helped her cope, but lately, he was always home. Inside her head, one of her favorites played, *You see it your way, and I see it mine, but we both see it slipping away.*

Kim opened her laptop again to the presentation for the upcoming meeting. Brad had just made himself another drink and stood by her side.

"What's the project about, babe?" he suddenly had an interest in her work.

"Huh? Are you seriously interested?"

"Wouldn't ask if I wasn't," Brad said, still backpedaling.

"Okay, well, I'm finishing off a PowerPoint presentation that's loaded with graphics and data to prove a hypothesis that a unique enzyme we've run tests on in the lab can be used in conjunction with synthetic opioids to allow them to bind with chemicals through catalytic actions and thus increase their efficacy."

"Wow," he said. "Now that's a mouthful."

Kim giggled, "Well, the team and I have done months of research. Plus also all kinds of experiments and two clinical trials."

"Didn't you tell me Geneltex was number one in opioid manufacturing?"

"We're right up there. Number one in synthetic opioids, at the very least. We manufacture versions of Fentanyl and Methadone for other drug companies so they can put their brand names on the bottle."

"No offense, babe, but the subject matter's kind of dry. Guess that's why I saw the navy blue business jacket with the white blouse and short skirt hanging on the closet door. The power suit never fails."

"A bit jealous, are we?" Kim said, looking out the window to see a goldfinch land on the bush to nibble on a berry. She knew that soon enough, the temperature would become cold. The leaves and berries would fall from the bush, and the birds would leave. But in the Spring, they would all be back. She loved nature in any form. Park ranger would be her dream job.

He waited to answer. "Should I be?" he asked.

"No, Brad. You should not," Kim answered with confidence.

The truth was more than one of the scientists had inquired to Janey about Kim's availability, but no one had asked her out. It didn't matter; she'd committed to team Kim and Brad. Her flag was still planted in their camp, for now.

Leaning back in her comfy chair, Kim closed her eyes to draw in a deep breath through her nose and hold it until she slowly let it out through pursed lips. Her therapist had recommended the breathing exercise. It calmed and centered her. She shut out all the other thoughts in her mind and focused only on her breathing. But there was one distraction she couldn't ever shut out. Grace's face always appeared. There was no shutting her out. There was no forgetting what happened.

The breathing was a big help, but she needed something more. Kim walked into the bathroom and locked the door. She pulled out a plastic container from the secret hiding spot. There were several pills that were already crushed up and ready. Flipping on the bathroom fan to mask the noise, she took out the straw. A tiny line of pink powder would do. Leaning over, she accidentally knocked the container on the floor, scattering the powder. Freaking out, Kim grabbed a cloth to wipe it into a neat line. Blocking one nostril with her finger, she snorted it off the floor. The residue was cleaned up, and everything put back while she felt disgusted with herself.

Kim knew it was repulsive, but the effects of the synthetic opioid she stole from work kicked in instantly. Flushing the toilet, she fixed her hair in the mirror.

"What are we doing this weekend, babe?" Brad asked as she came back into the room. He was making his way toward the kitchen where the gin was located.

Kim felt the euphoria from the drug immediately. Suddenly happy again, the anxiety was gone for a while.

"I told you last week, Mum's moving into her new place at the senior housing community up in Crawford, New Hampshire. I'm getting up early to drive there and help her unpack. I'm staying the week, remember?"

"Oh, that's right, shit, I forgot. Me too?" Brad yelled from the kitchen as he clinked ice cubes into the tumbler and poured in some more gin.

"No, I told you she's got movers doing the heavy stuff. You're off the hook, lucky man."

"You sure?" he said.

"Yes, I'm sure." She appreciated his kind gesture. He knew he wasn't going in the first place. He had always been sweet to Mum. Despite recent behavior, that alone earned him points.

"Phew! Well, that's a relief," he said. "I have a busy week at work coming up. Then I have to help Paul pull his boat out of the water this weekend. Season's pretty much over, although you wouldn't know it today; scorcher out there."

Kim changed the topic, talking louder for him to hear. "The wholesome girl; she asked to speak to you, but I told her you weren't interested. You can thank me later."

"Figures, if they can't get one, they go after the other. What was her pitch?"

"Christianity, I guess. She was Chinese, so I thought there'd be a connection between us being of the same ethnicity. But she was too pushy. I couldn't get rid of her fast enough."

"Pushy? Chinese?" His attention peaked as he stared out the window at the neighboring condominiums. "How'd you know she's Chinese and not Korean or Japanese?"

Kim laughed, "Asians can tell each other's country of origin in a second. She did have unique Chinese characters tattooed on her wrist that I found interesting. I just Googled them, and, get this; they mean perfect one. Talk about loving yourself!"

She returned to work on her laptop, typing away as Brad stared straight at her. He walked back into the kitchen to pour more gin into his drink and then returned to his chair.

A shock had gone right down his spine.

Chapter 2
Urgent

The river couldn't be heard from the peaceful silence of Mum's backyard. It was secluded and shady back there, a little slice of heaven. Maples and birches approaching peak foliage splashed vivid displays of orange, yellow, and red across the blue sky and pine forest canvas. It didn't feel like autumn. Indian summer prevailed, peaking thermometers into the low nineties.

Helping her mother unpack and organize, Kim felt optimistic. New beginnings gave her hope for the future. What memories would be made in this new house that was yet to be called home? The tediousness of emptying each box became fun as Kim and her mother commented on each item's origin or history within their family. They chatted and gossiped as mothers and daughters tend to do. Before they knew it, two hours had elapsed.

"I just realized what time it is," Mum said, looking at her watch. "I have to stop by the realtor's office to sign the last of the ownership papers. Why don't you take a break, sweetie? The movers put the Adirondack chairs in the backyard. Have some ice water and cool off for a bit. I shouldn't be too long."

Kim happily agreed with Mum's proposition and dragged the light blue chair into the shade to rest and use the time to meditate. Pushing off her sneakers by the heel, she felt the cool blades of grass run between her toes. Leaning her head back, Kim began meditating. Deep breath in, four, five, six, hold, and slowly exhale one, two, three. Now repeat four, five, six, and exhale. Focusing on a white birch tree that grew amongst a group of pines, she repeated her breathing. "Feel as if the air you draw in is being delivered to your entire body," her therapist told her.

The sweet, musky odor of fall filled her nose as random images entered her mind. She let them float by, passing no judgment. It was peaceful, with an occasional nature noise heard and accepted. A caw from a distant crow, or geese flying overhead in a V formation made her smile. Her anxiety was floating away like the perspiration drying from her skin.

Faint at first; the voice appeared in her ear like a dream. "…elp!...umbody!..."

Mediation on hold, she sat upright in the chair. Kim cupped her hand to her left ear. Am I hearing things? Another crow cawed and flew off erratically. Then, complete silence again.

Just my imagination.

Back against the chair and relaxed, she began her deep breathing. But the muffled cries for help floated around her again, this time clearer, "Help...Please!"

Damn! Should I call 911? The realtor had mentioned a trail leading to the river.

"It's a nice nature trail. A little over a mile walk." The realtor had explained that it led to Souhegan Rapids and that sometimes the kids swam down there when it was hot out. "They horse around like teenagers like to do."

Okay, it's got to be the kids swimming and messing around.

She leaned back into her chair and heard silence for a full minute. *Yes, silence. Besides, if anyone needs help these days, it's me.*

"Help! Somebody! Please!" It was undeniable now.

She shoved her feet into the New Balance Runners and shot out of the chair where she had been relaxing only moments before.

The Souhegan River ran fast with rapids that roared over boulders, fallen trees, and limbs as it meandered its way through miles of dense forest to the confluence of a much larger river, The Merrimack. Miles of trails ran alongside both rivers and throughout thousands of acres of wilderness. None of the trails had markers or navigational aids, leaving the locals as the only ones who knew where the paths led.

Her feet pounding against the dirt, Kim kept her eyes on the terrain so as not to trip along the tight and winding trail. She flew down the path, arms and legs pumping, her long hair flowing straight behind her. There wasn't a second to take in the sight of foliage or a bed of green ferns providing lush ground cover. The ninety-degree heat and higher elevation hit her like a wall. She struggled for air as sweat poured down her face. It had been less than a mile, but it felt like three. Kim burst through a thicket of trees and greenery to see the churning rapids of the Souhegan River.

A boy stood by the rushing water, no older than ten. Waves crashed against boulders and logs as she bent over with both hands on her knees, trying to catch her breath. A frayed rope dangled from a mighty limb above the water.

"What happened?" Kim shouted over the roar of the rapids.

His eyes were wide, face filled with terror, "My sister, Julie! She fell off the rope and went straight into the river! She never came up!"

Reaching around to slap her pockets, Kim realized she'd left her phone in the house on the charger. She scanned the area and saw no houses or people, an isolated wilderness.

No phone, no people, no help. Great!

"How long?" Kim yelled as she kicked off her running shoes.

"We got here about an hour-"

"No!" she cut him off. "How long has she been under?"

"Like, I don't know, ten minutes? I can't remember!" Tears streamed down his cheeks.

"Do you have a phone?" she asked.

He looked puzzled and tilted his head, "Ahhhh, No?"

There was no time to weigh the options. There was only one. Kim knew she would have to dive in and find Julie to get her out of the river, but it scared the shit out of her. She could feel her fear and anxiety peaking. There was no time to deal with it, so she psyched herself to the task. *Kim, you've always been a swimmer. You got this!*

Poised at the edge of the rock, she positioned herself to dive into the lagoon. The water would be freezing; she knew that. Rivers always were, and besides, it was October. Her warm body would seize up the second she hit the water, stung by the bite of the cold.

She looked at him. "Okay, listen to me. Stay here and keep yelling for help. If you see anyone, wave them over. Tell them it's an emergency!"

There was a ten-foot drop from the boulder into the waters below. She paused with eyes closed and prepared herself. The first breath was drawn in, filling her lungs as her chest expanded until she exhaled. Kim took in a second breath and then a third. Her high school swimming coach's voice boomed inside her head. He would always ask her the same question before she stepped onto the platform. "Kim, can you do this?"

Her answer never varied, "Just watch me."

She opened her eyes and dove.

Kim always remembered her first experience swimming in a river. Her cousin Scott lived near Chapel Brook Falls in Ashfield, Massachusetts, and she had been invited to spend the week. It was mid-summer, and temps were in the nineties. When he challenged her to dive off the dock into the Deerfield River, she had no idea how frigid the water would be. The shocking cold was like a slap across the face. To this day, she remembered surfacing to scream at him as he stood on the dock laughing.

Bracing for the same shock she felt that summer, Kim descended through the air. Years of daily laps in a heated, Olympic size pool maintained her swimming abilities. But an underwater rescue in frigid water was a far cry from that.

Kim plunged headfirst into the water. The cold was devastating as every muscle and tendon seized up. Thrashing and kicking her arms and legs randomly, she struggled to swim. Instinct took over, and she dove downwards with her eyes wide open. The reality crossed her mind that this girl named Julie was, in all probability, already dead.

The visibility became murky as she reached the bottom depth of twenty feet. Feeling the current pull her away from the spot where Julie went in, Kim held onto a submerged tree and swiveled her head from side to side, searching for her. Following the current, she swam deeper into the frigid darkness and pinched her nose to clear her ears. Visibility was less than five feet as she looked all over for Julie. The waving of long auburn hair in the current caught Kim's eye. She swam to her. Julie was young, twelve or thirteen, Kim guessed. Finding her was only the first step. The girl's eyes were closed, lungs filled with river water. Kim assessed the problem. Julie's foot was wedged solid between two huge boulders. Kim's lungs were desperate for air as she gripped the young girl's ankle and yanked up with all her strength. It wouldn't budge. From several angles, Kim desperately tried to free her again and again.

I have to surface!

She pushed off the bottom and shot to the top like a cork. Her body flew out of the water as she screamed in relief and inhaled fresh air. Julie's brother was doing his job, holding his hands around his mouth and calling for help. Kim gave him the thumbs up and yelled, "I found her! Her foot's wedged!! Keep at it!"

She took in three more deep breaths and went back down again.

Dammit, this water's freezing!

Reaching Julie for a second try, Kim pulled up on her ankle, but it still wasn't moving. She grew frustrated, yanking her leg in every direction without success. Work used up her air faster, and it was almost time to surface again. *No! C'mon!* She was developing hypothermia and decided this would be her last try. Self-preservation had to rule.

Kim recalled a phrase they said in the lab at work. If, at first, you don't succeed, try the opposite. She grabbed Julie's leg with both hands. This time, she shoved it down instead of pulling it up. A cloud of debris floated up in the water, and Julie was dislodged. Kim wrapped her arms around Julie's lifeless body and bolted toward the surface. With her air completely gone, Kim was positive she'd drown before they reached the top. The sun was shimmering through the water above like a bright light at the end of life. As the last air bubbles left her mouth, Kim looked down and noticed a small tattoo on the back of Julie's neck.

The lotus flower. A sign of rebirth. It's beautiful. Will that be the last thing I ever see?

They exploded onto the surface. Kim fought to take in air while staying afloat and keeping Julie's head above the water. Shifting her position, Kim placed Julie onto her shoulder and performed the side stroke until they reached the shore. She dragged her onto the riverbank but needed help lifting her to the dry rocks above. Dripping and exhausted, Kim looked around for Julie's brother.

But he was gone.

Chapter 3
Wanted Dead or Alive

The horseshoe rotated along its long axis, flat and horizontal, spinning like a metallic Frisbee as it made its way through the bright October sky. It made a whirling sound, and it was obvious there would be damage if it were to hit something.

Unfortunately, it did.

"Milt Logan. I've had it with you! Turn round and head out the way you came in!" Nick yelled out just before the horseshoe landed with a thud against his windshield, splintering it into cobwebs. It ricocheted off the white Ford Explorer, to land at the owner's feet.

Milt stood next to his vehicle staring at him in disbelief, "You just…you just broke my goddamn windshield!" He stared in amazement at the spider web of cracks on the safety glass.

"Nick Caldwell, you *will* be paying for a new one!"

The tall, lanky young man with a shock of curly blonde hair stood with hands on his hips as Milt charged straight toward him.

"You listen here, son," Milt looked up at him being shorter in stature at five foot nine. Sweat drops formed underneath his crew cut and then ran down his face. Pulling a handkerchief from his pocket, he wiped his brow and then lectured the young man. "What the hell is your problem? I worked with your dad for twenty years, and he never threw a darn horseshoe at me."

"He threw you a lot of business loans at you, though, didn't he?" Nick retorted.

"Yes, yes, he did, and I serviced those loans. But here's the thing, son. Your dad made his payments on time."

to go by. He'd lost his mother to breast cancer at age eight. The only other person Nick thought might be familiar with how Gus ran things was Walt, their loyal ranch hand. But he informed Nick that he "didn't know nothin' ‘bout nothing 'cept being old."

Gus had left Nick with a lot of questions and a huge, adjustable-rate business loan at Milt Logan's bank. Making ends meet became a struggle. Not long after his father died, some people approached him about a side business selling high-performance horse feed called Equine-Pro to horse ranchers all around New England. Nick said no for the first few years, but they persisted. A year ago, he jumped at the opportunity for the side hustle. He still came up short, so Nick pocketed some money bartending a few nights during the week at a downtown pub, The Rising Son.

Walt sat on the fence watching the entire episode between Nick and Milt Logan. He'd been Gus's right-hand man for twenty-four years. As Nick approached, he studied the young boy he had seen develop into a man and tried to offer some friendly advice.

"Hey, cowboy, you catch more flies with honey than you do, vinegar."

"What you know, old man?" Nick adjusted his Stetson down to block out the sun as he walked towards the barn.

"Just saying…" said Walt.

"Bet you know a lot about flies, old timer."

Walt yelled some final advice, "I don't know much, but I know one thing, you need him more than he needs you!"

Walt looked around at the farm he'd worked at for so long and harkened back to better times when Gus had the place running like clockwork. They'd breed and train five or six Arabians a year and sell them for twenty to thirty grand each. They had a beauty years back named Turk that went for fifty grand! A large vegetable garden was always growing, and there was a chicken coup with a dozen hens all laying eggs. He hopped down from the fence to head back behind the barn to work on his project. Groaning, he felt a pain shoot up the side of his back.

"Sucks gettin' old."

Inside the shady barn, it was at least five degrees cooler than outside in the midday sun. Nick's mood drastically improved as he approached the stall and opened the gate. He stood back as the stallion walked out and came to him.

"Hey Cracker, how you doing, buddy?" He kept his tone soothing as he rubbed the animal's head while maintaining eye contact. Cracker acknowledged with a nod and a low-pitched guttural sound as if to say, "Good to see you too, I think."

Nick knew how to talk to horses. It was people he had problems with. Cracker was the strongest Arabian he'd ever seen. Still just a colt at nineteen months of age, Nick was pushing the horse's breaking schedule by at least six months, maybe a year. He needed the money now, not later. At the Caldwell Ranch, horse breaking meant getting the Arabian to the point where a new owner could ride it. Then it was sold for lots of money. The old-fashioned and cruel style of horse breaking where the animal's spirit was broken had been, for the most part, discontinued over the years. Gus had called what they did horse-making, not breaking. Both father and son used far more gentle methods and trust-building. They'd both heard all the fanfare in recent years about horse whisperers; "a bunch of bullshit," Gus said.

Fiery and independent, Arabians had to be worked carefully. In some ways, they were like people, each horse communicating through body language. The way they dropped their lower lip or flicked their tail was the language they spoke. A relationship was built by convincing the animal that the rider was the trusted alpha. That was their version of horse whispering.

As Nick groomed Cracker, he leaned against him, showing affection. Cracker's personality verged on bipolar at times. One minute affectionate and playful, the next crazy as hell. Still, there was a special connection between this man and horse that had been magical since the beginning.

Yesterday had been the first day he accepted the bridle and bit. Today was day two. Nick stayed within sight so as not to spook him. Taking the bridle, he slid it over the animal's head past the small white star on his crest. "There we go, fella" his voice was low and calm. He put the metal bit on Cracker's lips, and the horse opened his mouth to accept it with some hesitation. Cracker immediately threw his head upwards, let out a neigh, and then shot it back down, causing the apparatus to fall on the ground. "Easy boy, easy," Nick said. He ran his hands up and down Cracker's long head and neck for several minutes. Picking the bridle off the floor, Nick cleaned it off with a rag and then reached over to a nearby jar. A skinny brush full of molasses was used to slather the bit with the sweet substance.

Holding the bit up to Cracker's nose, Nick let him smell it. His nostrils flared as he moved his front legs to whinny. "You like that, don't you, boy?" He slid the apparatus over the colt's head again and inserted the molasses-coated rod into Cracker's mouth. His lips clasped around the sweetened metal licking and slurping with approval. Nick clipped a ten-foot rein to the bridle and led him out of the barn to the pen to begin walking him in clockwise laps. Today he would stop during every lap and yell "Halt!" teaching the horse his first commands.

He could feel his tension subside as they circled in mundane laps. There had been many moments of stress trying to run the show himself. Small successes like this one felt good. He looked back at Cracker and then up to the heavens and smiled. They'd gone twenty laps and practiced several commands as the hot October sun warmed Nick's back. It felt good even though the temps were out of place this late in the year. He welcomed the long and cold New Hampshire winter coming right around the corner.

Fall Out Boy blared from the rear pocket of Nick's jeans. *So light em up up up, light em up up up, I'm on fire!* Cracker whinnied, rearing back on his hind legs to yank the rein out of Nick's grasp and gallop across the pen.

"Smart move, head case!" Nick yelled as he pulled out the phone without stopping. The alarm was a reminder it was noon and time to go. Walt was back sitting on the fence and having a smoke break.

"Gotta deliver some feed to the Hanson Farm," he said "Take him around for a few more laps, ya? If he gives you any shit, stick him back in his stall."

"Sure thing," said Walt. "What time you back?" He could be inquisitive.

"Don't know, hour or two. Don't wait for me," Nick said, walking away.

"Okay, gotcha. Pickup's gotta full tank; filled it yesterday," Walt called out.

Nick yelled back over his shoulder, "Takin' the Quad. Just got a couple of bags. Goin' down the trails; cooler in the woods."

Nick finished tying down the bags with bungee cords and settled into the ATV's hot leather seat to feel the heat through his jeans. He turned the key and pulled in the left clutch lever before he pressed the ignition. The Suzuki's engine roared to life, and he kicked his boot down to engage first gear. He took off like a shot and headed towards the northwest trail that ran through the woods.

The trail ran right past the Souhegan Rapids.

Chapter 4
Staying Alive

The sweat ran down Kim’s forehead and stung her eyes as the muscles in her arms ached with fatigue. She'd just finished a round of chest compressions and had begun another.

"...24, 25, 26, 27, 28, 29, 30." She leaned back, taking in two deep breaths of fresh oxygen, and then placed her mouth on Julie's to transfer it into her lungs. She kept repeating the procedure again and again, frantically trying to revive her.

No luck.

Paralyzed with indecision, Kim was tentative. *Should I run back to Mum's and call 911? Wait! I think her door locks as soon as it's closed! Dammit! Anyway, I can't just leave her here!*

She stood up and looked around to see if anybody was in the area, perhaps taking a hike.

“Help! Help!” Kim shouted as loud as she could. *What the hell happened to the brother?*

Indecision plagued her. *I should run back to Mum's and get my phone to call 911. But what if a bear wanders by and devours her?*

Kim looked down at the beautiful young lady whose skin was turning gray. Julie was just twelve and could be mistaken for a young Mila Kunis. Small in size, she had her whole life ahead of her. Grace would have been her age had she lived. Both girls would miss out on first dates, senior prom, driving a car, and all the joys that life has to offer. Kim crouched down to Julie's mouth, hoping to hear the faintest whisper of breath.

Nothing.

She was close to leaving the land of the living.

"Why won't you wake up for me, sweetie?" Kim pleaded with her. She brushed several strands of wet hair from Julie's face and placed her hand on her forehead. "Jesus, it's ninety-five out, and you're a block of ice."

Kim utilized the basics of a CPR class that was given at work two years ago. That was all she knew about saving lives. After she pulled Julie's body up onto the rocks, she applied her training as best as she could remember; three sets of thirty chest compressions followed by mouth-to-mouth breathing. Why wasn't it working?

"C'mon, kid, wake up!" Clap, clap clap, she slapped her hands together right in front of the unconscious girl's face.

"Stubborn, huh? Okay, break's over. Another thirty, here we go… 1,2,3,4,5… 25, 26, 27, 28, 29, 30."

"We've been looking for you, Charlie. Where've you been and where's Julie?" Ashun asked him. Charlie had panicked and fled through the woods, trying to find someone to help. Ashun and Winger weren't just friends with Charlie and Julie. They helped out the people who were considered their family. They were trackers sent by the family to find the two kids. Charlie told them what had happened to Julie. They listened, and then they ran. They all ran as fast as they could toward the rapids where Julie was clinging to the last minutes of her life.

Chapter 5
Emotional Rescue

Nick's right hand rotated the ATV's throttle downward, gunning the two-stroke engine. It roared and sputtered like a strange animal that had no place being in these woods. The Suzuki King Quad 750 was an older model with impressive power. Painted in military camouflage, the machine flew down the trail toward its destination spooking wildlife and leaving a cloud of blue smoke in its wake.

The trail took a sharp turn to the right, and Nick leaned his body into it to maneuver around the corner like he was riding one of his Arabians. Turning, he looked over his left shoulder and caught a glimpse of the two people through the trees. *Huh, teenagers gettin' a swim down at the rapids even though there's a no swimming allowed sign, plain as day. So what else is new?*

It was late autumn, and the fallen leaves that filled the trail were thrown into the air like a wave as Nick blasted towards his destination, undeterred by what he'd seen. He had ridden horses, dirt bikes, and ATVs down these trails for so many years he didn't have to think about navigating them. Mental autopilot guided the machine as his mind's eye wandered. He began playing video memories. *Fighting with Milt Logan ain't too smart. Dang it, I better give old Milt a call later.*

His mind continued to wander to thoughts of his father. Always seeking his approval, he wondered what Gus would say about how he was running things at the ranch. *He'd tell me I'm doing everything all wrong, I bet.* Nick told himself to move on. Gus was gone, and that was that.

Nick focused on the trail again. Mid-October, and the foliage colors popped. He never grew tired of their beauty. His mind returned to the momentary visual he'd just seen by the rapids. *One was standing. The other one was lying down. No, wait, the first one was kneeling over the other one lying down. Arms extended down on the other one's chest.*

"Dang, it, they were doing chest compressions!"

Nick shifted his weight to the opposite side of the seat while locking up the rear brakes to put the Quad into a 180-degree power skid across the leaves. He turned the bars and cranked the throttle hard until the machine responded. There was a new heading now.

He burst through the trees, and steered towards them. Downshifting as he approached, Nick dismounted letting the Quad coast to a stop.

Kim paused her chest compressions and looked up in surprise. A ray of hope at last.

"What happened? She drowned, huh? Who is she?" Nick fired off questions.

"Who are you?" Kim stood up, glad to get help but annoyed by his interrogation. "More important, do you have a phone?"

"Yeah, but there ain't a signal round here."

"Can you double-check?" Kim asked as she wiped her forehead with the back of her arm.

Nick pulled out his phone and checked. "Just like I said, no bars and no service." He held the phone up for her to see. "Place is a dead zone."

"Great!" Kim raised her arms in frustration.

Nick looked down at Julie, pale and lifeless. "She went and drowned herself, huh? They ain't supposed to be swimming here. Used to be a sign over there, but now I see it's gone. We could throw her on the Quad and try to find someone that's home down the trail, maybe?"

Kim was crazed with tension and fear, "Look. That young lady; her name is Julie. She was under for a long time. I think around twenty minutes. We have to get her breathing right now, or she'll be brain-dead if she isn't already!"

"I was a lifeguard at Echo Lake, and we brought a few back to life that went under. Let me look at her," Nick kneeled next to Julie to check her pulse on the neck and listened for breathing. He looked at Kim, "No vitals; she's as good as dead."

"I've been giving her CPR for quite a while. Why isn't it working?"

Dark, ominous clouds were covering the sun as they spoke. The wind picked up as a nasty storm was brewing.

He stood back up. “Let's throw her on the Quad and find some help." Nick walked toward his machine as raindrops began falling on them. Kim ran over and cut in front of him, blocking his way. "Look, whoever you are, you said you brought back a few, so get over there and bring her back before it's too late! Please!"

He stared into her dark brown eyes, filled with fear and anguish. "Yes, ma'am," he said, giving her a semi-salute and turning back to walk toward Julie. "Name's Nick, by the way," he said over his shoulder.

He crouched down over Julie again to work on her methodically like someone who'd saved a life before. Positioning himself over her, he straddled her chest. "She's young but probably too far gone by now. Even if we get her vitals back, she's an eggplant."

The rain started to come down heavy, as he put his ear next to her mouth and listened. Straightening up, he took in a deep breath and tilted Julie's head back. Nick pinched her nose, opened her mouth, and exhaled while resting his right hand on the center of her chest. Kim scolded herself for forgetting about pinching the nose. Nick repeated the procedure two more times.

“Her chest ain't risin,” he said.

Nick opened her mouth and looked inside. He stood up, "See the problem!"

Ashun, Winger, and Charlie had found their way back to the rapids. Rain fell as they watched from behind an oak tree thirty yards away. Charlie had to be held back by Winger, or he would run and help them save Julie.

"Let me go!" Charlie's freckled face scrunched up in anger as he fought against him. Small for his age at only four feet tall and, weighing fifty six pounds, he didn't stand a chance. "I should've stayed with my sister!" He was trying to push past Winger, a native Abenaki Indian by blood, and at six foot four, he easily held back the boy. Ashun came to them. "Shhhh, keep it down, Charlie. We want to avoid being spotted by the Normals. They're trying to help her."

She was Ashun, a native Abenaki Indian by blood and partner to Winger.

Winger grew impatient and began putting the pieces of his weapon together. "Normals or not, if those two don't wake her up in a minute, I gotta put 'em down."

"Like hell you are!" Ashun gripped his arm. You don't know how to save someone from drowning, and me neither. I overheard the guy say he's a lifeguard, and they know how to bring people back to life after they've drowned. Julie's got a better chance with them."

"She's gonna die, Ash, if she ain't already. Let's go get her," he loaded the dart into the tube.

"Hold on and stop getting all emotional. Rescue is what lifeguards do, so let him do his thing. Besides, look overhead. Storm's rolling in. I better get the tarp out."

"Okay, they got one minute, and then we move in. Winger aimed at them from behind the tree. I got one loaded and ready to shoot."

29- The Canaries

Ashun stared at Winger with black, piercing eyes. "What did you dip them in this time?"

"It's curare. Knocks 'em out for a while; paralyzes too."

"Unless you dipped them with too much. Then it kills them, right?"

"Yeah, too much curare kills them for sure."

"Remember Marshera's Golden Rule is to save lives, not take them? You didn't forget that did you?" Ashun said.

Winger looked up to feel the rain come down harder now on his face, "We aren't part of those people. We just help them out."

"You're right; we aren't. But these two are. So we abide by their rules, Wing."

Black, billowing storm clouds had crept in like mammoth continents quietly floating above them. The rain grew stronger as the temperature dropped by ten degrees. They could hear rumbles of thunder as the wind picked up. In seconds, they had to take action.

Nick yelled over the wind as Kim's hair whipped across her face. "She's got something blocking her windpipe, and we gotta get it out!"

"What's blocking her?" Kim yelled back. Nick failed to answer, having already positioned himself behind Julie. He lifted her from behind, his arms wrapped around her waist.

"Need a hand!" he called to Kim.

Kim ran over and helped Nick straighten up Julie's body as her matted hair blew upwards from the gale-force wind. Blotches of raindrops pelted down on them as thunder rumbled louder. Nick positioned his arms around her waist, placing his fist just below her abdomen, ready to perform the maneuver.

"We're almost out of time. You ready?"

"You're giving her the Heimlich?"

The wind was howling and pushing them around, making it difficult to stand. Lightening crackled down to the ground from the dark sky, a bolt just a mile away.

"Here goes!" In one motion, Nick jerked his arms up into Julie's abdomen as his legs lunged to lift her off the ground. She was a ragdoll with arms flailing as Kim tried to keep her body upright.

Nothing came out of Julie's mouth.

Rain was soaking through their clothes as they fought for position to try again.

"Again, now!" Nick pulled up under her ribs with all his power. No discharge. A brilliant flash of lighting was unleashed from the heavens, followed by a clap of ear-splitting thunder. Kim dropped to the ground and screamed in fear. Nick looked at Kim over the maelstrom of rain.

"Last try, then we're out here!"

She nodded her head as he counted down, "3,2,1...Gaaaah!" He yanked up into Julie's body with all his power, driving his fist deep into her abdomen. Julie's head snapped back out of Kim's reach as Nick lost his balance. Together, they fell backward with Julie still wrapped in his arms. He took the brunt of their fall as the pair hit the ground and tumbled over behind the rocks.

Kim saw something on the rocks washing away in the rain.

It all happened so fast now. An electric bolt of lightning was followed by an explosion of thunder, right over their heads. Kim ran to Julie. She was on her knees, spitting up water and bile, but she was breathing. Kim held her hair back as she coughed up the last of whatever had blocked her windpipe.

Nick righted himself and scrambled over to them as the rain unloaded in sheets. Kim jumped up and hugged him. "She's breathing!"

"Follow me to the Quad!" Nick shouted. He scooped up Julie and carried her as the storm unleashed. The rain came down harder as Kim climbed on the back of the machine. Nick set Julie in her arms and released the bungee cords to dump the grain bags on the ground. Starting the machine, they barreled down a trail at full speed seeking shelter at the first place Nick could think of, The Caldwell Ranch.

Ashun, Winger, and Charlie crouched under the green tarp as rain hammered down on them.

"We lost Julie!" Charlie yelled over the noise. "How are we gonna find her?"

"Tracks, Charlie," said Winger. "ATVs leave nice, deep tire tracks."

Chapter 6
Cuts Like a Knife

He was Lucious Johnston, and he wasn't one bit worried. There was cause for concern because the stakes were high but so was the payoff. Risk versus reward was the stuff they talked about on Wall Street. But in his case, the risk was low, and the reward very high. The risk was low because he had a system. He had a proven system that would pay lucrative dividends.

He had just given a large sum of money to his friend and bookie, Targa.

"You sure about this dude?" Targa asked. "Lotta bread you wagering here today."

"Yeah, man, I'm sure. The system works, so let it ride; all of it: theirs and mine."

"This system of yours. How's the whole thing work?" Targa asked.

Lucious was happy to brag about his system. "Okay, you swore you'd keep this shit between us, so I'll give you the low down. It's like this, amateurs bet on sports they love, but they're not always the sports you should bet on. They're too damn unpredictable. So step one is to gamble on the basketball. Hoops is for the intelligent gambler, man. Pays great and it's more predictable, plain, and simple."

"Step two is to use a weighted list of crucial criteria to handicap the teams. I created that term by the way."

"What the fuck's these crucial criteria you're talking about, man?" Targa didn't get it.

"It's the engine that drives the system," said Luscious. Crucial criteria includes stuff like home-court advantage and knowing if a team had the day off before the game. Also, looking up which team won their last game or lost it. All kinds of shit like that. Oh, and the refs make a huge difference. Have to consider them. All that stuff is weighted and calculated into my system. I even read up on which stars are getting along with their old ladies and which ones ain't. It's bulletproof, man. I tested it twelve times with small bets, and it paid a hundred percent. I can't lose, man!"

Tweaking and perfecting his system had led to this day when the stars aligned. His system showed every pre-game box could be checked. The contest between The Boston Celtics and The Golden State Warriors would be, as they say in gambling terms, a lock. The game would be played in Oakland, California at the Oracle Arena, the Warrior's home court. The home team had just come off a big win over the Los Angeles Lakers, and they'd had a day of rest. The Celtics, meanwhile, were floundering. Experts predicted they'd have a great season. In reality, the Green were fighting off a long losing streak. Golden State's stars Stephan Curry, Kevin Durant, and Draymond Green were all healthy and happy. They would be allowed to run with abandon while this group of referees would stay busy not calling fouls. The game had more green lights than the starting line of a drag race. The Warriors would destroy the Celtics.

His system said so.

Lucious couldn't believe his luck and went all in. The payoff would be enormous; he estimated as much as one hundred fifty to two hundred thousand. The windfall would set up his daughter Kiley for all four college years. And the best part was the people he borrowed the money from, who happened to be his employers, would thank him for tripling their take.

"What happened, Lucious?" Targa asked.

"Fuckin disaster, man. It would've been better if an airliner crashed through the roof of the Oracle and killed everyone inside. At least that way, I would have had a push."

On that fateful day, the airliner landed squarely on Lucious's head when the Boston Celtics defeated the Golden State Warriors 128-95.

For Christ's sake, it wasn't even close!

Luscious lost all of his money and, even worse, their money. They wouldn't be happy.

Sure, he had been a reliable earner for them, moving opioids, heroin, and coke around New Bedford, Massachusetts. But explaining that he'd lost their money on a basketball game might be challenging. All he could hope for was they wouldn't kill him.

Every month their mule, Topaz, would drop off his supply of drugs to him. At the end of the month, the muscle known as the Volkov Brothers would come by and pick up the cash. He had a good track record, never having been short or late with the money. Topaz was a friend. Luscious was sure he would vouch for him to the Volkov Brothers.

They won't kill me. How would they get their money back?

Still, if the street found out that they let him off with a slap on the wrist, others would take advantage of them. A statement would have to be made. He decided to stop worrying and figured they'd rough him up with a few gut punches and a black eye, maybe a broken nose. He would have to pay it all back along with a healthy vig. They knew him, and he knew them, Boris and Dimitri Volkov from Paterson, New Jersey. Luscious used to kid with them. "Hey, it's the Russian Jersey Boys!" They would all laugh and slap each other's backs. *Good guys, the Volkov Brothers. I'll work out a payback plan with them.*

Over a year ago, she was promoted to manage the New England region. It had been underperforming, and some sloppiness needed to be fixed. There was a new sheriff in town and her name was Lee Chen.

35- The Canaries

The first technique that she introduced to the brothers was ancient but effective. She learned it from her days spent in Yakuza, the Japanese Mafia. They called it Yubitsume. It had been around for over a hundred years but was considered over the top in modern times. She may have been young at just twenty-seven, but she was old school. "It's time to bring back the old ways," she told the Volkov brothers.

When asked why Yubitsume worked better than beating the offender to within an inch of their lives, she would reply, "Bruises and scars eventually heal. The pain will subside. Yubitsume not only makes the sinner atone for their sins, it's also a daily reminder to them and everyone else. They must never commit their sins again."

It was early morning in New Bedford. The Bamboo Butterfly Restaurant was closed. They met in a separate function room before anyone arrived at work. Lee Chen stood in front with arms folded. She wore an expensive business outfit; gray skirt, white blouse, matching gray jacket, and of course, stiletto high heels. Many would consider her pretty if she wore more smiles and less makeup. Luscious didn't expect to meet with the new boss lady that day. He thought that he could work something out with his friends, the Volkovs.

They listened in complete shock as Lucious explained how he'd lost fifty thousand dollars of their money by gambling it on a basketball game. Before Lucious could finish his story, Lee Chen left to go outside and make a call. When she came back in, he noticed her looking at the brothers. While Lucious talked about how he lost their money, the brothers prepared.

A bull of a strong, black man, Luscious played college football for the University of Connecticut Huskies. When he discovered his punishment, he fought them with every ounce of strength, taking on both brothers. He fought until Dimitri got him in a chokehold while Boris pulled out a photo and held it in front of Lucious's face. It was a day-old pic of his daughter Kiley waiting at her school bus stop. He had his Chinese-made QSZ-92 pistol pointed at Kiley's head. "Keep fighting us, and she dies today!"

"I'll fuckin kill all of you if anything happens to her."

Lee Chen approached them. The clicking of her stiletto heels echoed throughout the empty room. It was an announcement of authority. She spoke without emotion, as if what was to happen next was a business transaction.

"Simple as this, Luscious, we have a car down the street waiting to pick her up. The choice is yours. But either way, choose now. If you want to be selfish, we get your daughter, and she is never seen again. You can't hide her from us. Take it like a man Lucious. There has to be punishment. What would the street say if there wasn't? You fucked up, not us."

The thought of them harming Kiley made Lucious explode with a final burst of resistance. He blackened Boris's eye and kicked Dimitri in the ribs before he succumbed to the fat part of a wooden bat that landed five times against his back until he dropped like a fallen tree. Lying on the ground, he sobbed with regret. He had to take it like a man. It was payback time.

Lee Chen would be the one to do it. She liked doing it, saying it was better than sex. Inflicting pain on others was the sweetest revenge for what her father and brother did to her. The transferal of her pain temporarily soothed her inner turmoil.

The brothers followed the ancient ritual precisely as they had been taught. They set clean white linen cloths on the table. Lucious's right hand was placed palm down on the fabric with the small finger extended while the other fingers remained closed into a fist. A second white cloth was wrapped around the hand as if he was having a surgical procedure. Lee Chen looked at the Volkov Brothers to give them a nod of her head. They held the big man's hand in place as he moaned and cursed them for the bastards they were.

Her jacket hid a scabbard that held a Tanto knife. The scabbard had a built in device that allowed her to sharpen the Tanto knife by pumping in and out of the holster faster and faster. As the blade became sharper and hotter from the friction, she became more excited with each pump. Her face turned red, nipples became erect through her blouse. Boris was the stronger of the two brothers. He used his powerful arms like a vise to hold Luscious's hand in place. Dimitri held his Russian-made Grach against the victim's head. Beads of sweat rolled down his forehead as he looked away in the opposite direction. Lee Chen stopped pumping the blade in and out of the holster and raised it high above her head. It was a sign of dominance. Hot from her sharpening, the nine-inch knife was ready to complete its mission. Lucious whimpered in a low tone, dreading what was to come next.

She drove the point of her knife down to the wooden table, slamming its tip into the wood, creating a fulcrum to hold the lever in place. She let out a high-pitched squeal as she dropped the blade down to the table, slicing off his finger with clean precision. Luscious howled in pain like a wounded animal as his severed digit became separated from the hand. He snapped it back to look at the shortened appendage in disbelief. The white cloth that remained wrapped, began turning crimson. Boris took the severed pinky and placed it into a velvet box to be presented to Lee Chen later.

The punishment was finished. She barked out final orders to Lucious for deliverables that he owed her. "You have two weeks, Lucious, two weeks! We know everything about you and your family, so don't try anything. Your credit rating is strong, so you take out a home equity loan on your house and have money ready for our next visit. No more gambling with our money! We will take your daughter Kiley if you don't have money for us in two weeks. You are being monitored, so if you get stupid and call the cops or the FBI, we will kill all your family. Do you understand Lucious? Tell us you understand, Lucious!"

He stared at her glassy-eyed, defeated, and resigned, "You cut off my goddamn finger."

"Yes, of course, I cut off your finger. This never happens again, right? You have a daily reminder now!"

He nodded his head. "I understand," he said, looking at the blood-soaked lined cloth.

She took the last clean cloth and wiped her knife using a small bottle of hand sanitizer in her side pocket. "Boris, you need to help me with something now. Dimitri, you continue to the meeting place."

"We will see you in two weeks, Lucious. Have our money plus another fifty grand."

Chapter 7
Gimme Shelter

The raindrops hammered into Kim's skin, stinging like bees as she strained to hold on to Julie. She wrapped one arm around her; the other gripped a wet handle next to her seat. Julie appeared semi-conscious and breathing but what worried Kim the most was whether she had suffered permanent brain damage from the extraordinary amount of time she had been underwater without oxygen. If only she had known of her blockage and cleared it sooner. It was her fault; everything always was.

Blaming herself was typical. When they got to Nick's house, they would wait until the storm passed and then take Julie to the emergency room. While they waited, they would talk about their pasts. That would be when Kim would slip into the alternate identity she had practiced for years. She was an imposter. As she emerged into adulthood, Kim developed imposter syndrome, an after-effect of the trauma she suffered from Grace's death. Her life was a façade, never revealing her true self. The guilty party is who she indeed was, playing the role of an innocent bystander. A calm, rational, down-to-earth woman with nothing to hide from her past was what society demanded from her. So she adapted like a chameleon to give everyone what they wanted. Fake it till you make it was her motto. Her affluent veneer and effervescent smile gave others the perception that she had it all together; reserved and nice. Kim was friendly in the comforting normality of a Catholic upbringing with enrollment at private schools followed by graduation from The University of Chicago, Suma Cum Laude, with a degree in Botany. The creation of her character included participation in athletic activities like track and swimming. Piano lessons immediately followed athletics. She became a proficient player but could never play before a live audience. Her anxiety provided her with excessive amounts of stage fright.

With friends, Kim gave convincing acting performances in the role of a dear friend. She learned to exchange witty quips and a laugh about a sensitive subject she and a bestie kept secret. New friends left their time with her, feeling that they would soon be accepted into her circle of close friends. But that circle never existed. Maintaining close friends meant sharing personal information and secrets. That could spell trouble when they discovered who she was, the neglectful one who let her sister die one night. Keeping friends at arm's length was a prevention technique she followed with discipline.

Bombarded by raindrops, Kim held Julie a little tighter as they bounced down the muddy trail. The rain had soaked through their clothes, and Kim worried that Julie would catch pneumonia. They had to get her to the ER. Kim smiled as she pictured Julie's parents meeting them at the hospital. They would gratefully thank her for saving their beautiful daughter. But something else caused Kim to worry. Where had her brother gone?

The Quad suddenly slid around a muddy corner of the trail and fishtailed wildly out of control. Nick fought with the machine as Kim screamed in horror; Julie was sliding out of her grasp. If Kim let go of the handle, they'd both fly off. She screamed out, "Nick! I'm losing her!" The Quad skidded back on track at the last second, and the vehicle stabilized. "Sorry!" he yelled to her.

They emerged from the woods into an open field. In the distance was a lone ranch house and red barn, barely visible through the driving rain. Nick gunned the throttle, and the reliable Suzuki responded, sending the three waterlogged travelers toward the open doors of Nick's barn. They pulled inside to hear three horses grumble as he cut the engine. They disembarked to run through the downpour into the ranch house.

All three stood sopping wet in Nick's kitchen. He ran around gathering clean towels for Kim and Julie to dry off as he dug up several pairs of his sweatshirts and sweatpants. They were too big for them, but were dry and warm against their skin. Kim wrung out their wet clothes, and Nick tossed everything into the dryer.

41- The Canaries

The ranch house was well-appointed and decorated with a masculine touch. The eat-in kitchen was large and adjoined by the living room and formal dining room. Warm and comfortable with vaulted ceilings and a western motif, the living room's centerpiece was a giant stone fireplace that rose to the ceiling. Framed photos of Arabian horses the Caldwell Ranch had owned over the years adorned the walls. Comfortable and rustic with exposed beams overhead, the leather furniture and antique tables completed the natural look.

Julie curled up on her side and lay on the couch with a blanket Kim placed on her. She had fallen asleep from the minute she put dry clothes on. Kim sat at Julie's feet, watching her, and thought about all that had happened since running down the trail to answer the cries for help.

Nick gave Kim directions to the bathroom. After she finished and flushed, she quickly checked her look in the mirror while washing her hands. "Ouch," she said under her breath, looking at wet hair resembling a mop blown around by a twister. With no hairbrush, Kim used her fingers, running them through her jet-black hair to move the disheveled spaghetti and find her part. About to turn the knob, Kim remembered something. She shoved her hand into the side pocket of the sweatpants to find a small plastic container with some pink powder in it. She had removed it from the pocket of her wet jeans. A small amount of pink powder was sprinkled into a cup filled with water and then swallowed. Now she was ready to face reality again.

Entering the kitchen, Kim stood still and watched Nick move around the hardwood floors on his knees, wiping up the water they had brought into his house. She felt terrible for having yelled at him when he first stopped by on his ATV. He had come to help them out. And help them out, he did. If it weren't for him knowing that Julie was blocked, she would be dead.

Kim gazed out the rear window overlooking the open field. In the distance, lightning bolts scattered down to the ground from the sky as thunder and rain raged. She felt grateful they were safe and dry inside. The country setting of the ranch gave her a feeling of serenity and calm.

Back to reality, she went over to check on Julie. She was still sleeping on the couch. Kim sat next to her and listened to her breathing. Nick came over and stood next to them. Kim looked at him, standing in his gray-colored sweatpants and a hooded sweatshirt. It occurred to her she had yet to formally introduce herself. She stood up as he was about to speak and thrust her arm out to shake, "Kim Moreno. I never told you my name back there. Thanks for helping me. I should say Julie and me. I don't know how we can thank you enough."

Nick shook her outstretched hand, dismissing her praise. "Not to worry, glad to help. Nick Caldwell, here."

"Your house is lovely," said Kim. "So I guess you're a rancher?"

"Yeah, rancher, cowboy, distributor of horse grain, bartender. You name it. Whatever it takes to stay afloat. How about you?"

"Me? I'm a clinical lab technician for a pharmaceutical company down in Maryland. I'm up here helping my mother move into the new senior housing complex in town. It's not far from that river where you spotted me giving Julie CPR."

"Huh, clinical lab something, whatever that is, it sounds like you gotta be smart. How's she doing?" He motioned his head toward Julie, sleeping peacefully. "She gonna be okay?"

"Strangely enough, she seems alright. Her color's coming back, and I just felt her hands. Her body temp's returning to normal too. She hasn't spoken a word yet, so I'm crossing my fingers. Soon as this thing lets up, we should get her to the closest hospital. They'll want to check her out, test her and look for any neurological damage."

Nick was silent, looking around the room and then over at Julie.

"She might have dodged a bullet with the water temp."

"What do you mean?"

"How deep you find her?"

"Not sure, fifteen, twenty feet down?" Kim said.

"Water was freezing, no doubt."

"You have no idea," said Kim placing her palms on her cheeks. "Couldn't feel my face."

"Yeah, we're looking at forty-degree water temps at that depth. Her brain's in a freezer, waiting for you to come and save her. You brought her up and gave her CPR on the rocks in the shade until I stopped by. We brought her back before her brain thawed out."

"Yes, but she was without oxygen for at almost thirty minutes. That's a long time."

"Saw it on the news a couple of years ago. A kid in Pennsylvania was under for two hours; until they revived him. His body temp was down to, like, seventy. That's damn cold. Saved his brain and organs from damage. Happens now and then, I guess."

"Wow. I wasn't aware. That's amazing stuff." said Kim. They stood looking at Julie sleeping. Kim broke the silence. "I'm hoping she will be alright, even more so based on what you told me. Still, we need to get her to the ER and give the police a call to let them know what happened. I should call them now."

Nick rolled his eyes, "You don't want to get the cops involved."

"The police? Why not?" Kim asked.

"Because they won't do a damn thing."

"So, I guess you're not a fan of local law enforcement. But we do have to let her parents know where she is so they can come and get her. They must be worried sick. There's also the issue of her brother; he disappeared for some reason. The police or somebody should get involved to find him."

"Go ahead; I ain't stopping ya." Nick stared at her. His blue eyes became intense, and he entered the kitchen to open the cabinet. He took out several packages of powdered cocoa mix.

"Makin some hot cocoa; you want some?"

"Sure, that'd be nice." Kim decided to shelve contacting the police for now. She needed Nick's help and wasn't about to pick this battle. Waking Julie and getting her to sip some warm cocoa would help her core temperature until they brought her to a hospital. *We can maybe get her talking and find out where she lives. One step at a time.*

As Nick poured water from the tap into the carafe and set it in the holder to boil, Kim went to the kitchen and sat down in a chair at the counter. "Just you living here? Nice place."

Nick turned from the water as it began to simmer, "Yeah, just the horses and me. We breed Arabians or at least used to. Just got one now named Cracker. Few hens are roaming round the coop out there. Oh, and Walt, our ranch hand. He's worked for my dad for years. Guess he counts as an animal too."

Kim chuckled, "Your parents live here?"

"Neither one's alive anymore," Nick said.

"Oh, I'm sorry. That has to be tough, running this farm yourself."

"Yup, been a challenge at times. But I'm figuring it out one day at a time." Nick employed his strategy to end discomforting questions from strangers. The best defense is a good offense. "How about you? Where in Maryland are you from?"

"I'm from a little town called Travilah. I drove up yesterday to help my mother move in and unpack. It's nice here in New Hampshire; I've never been."

45- The Canaries

Nick filled the three mugs with boiling water and cocoa powder, added some cream and stirred. He found some halfway stale but edible cookies and put them on a plate. "Hot cocoa's ready. Might want to let it cool a bit before you give to the girl. What's her name again?"

"It's Julie. That's all I know, said Kim. She was a goner until you showed up just in the nick of time."

"Well, Nick of time is what they call me around town."

"Seriously?" Kim saw him smirk and shake his head. She felt silly and laughed endearingly. Taking a sip from her cocoa she felt relaxed being near him. She couldn't remember ever meeting someone new and just being herself. For once, Kim wasn't acting like someone they thought she should be.

The cocoa tasted yummy but on the hot side. Julie's would need to cool down a bit more before she brought it over to her.

"So how'd you know she needed help again? Who told you she went under?" Nick asked.

"Her younger brother was calling for help. I heard him from my mother's backyard, ran down the path, and dove into the water to bring Julie up. Then, poof! He was gone. It worries me, her being his sister and all, plus the storm. Where would he go? Is he alright? I don't even know his name come to think of it. He told me Julie's, but I didn't get a chance to ask him his."

"It's Charlie…" a muffled answer came from Julie lying on the couch, still half asleep.

Kim whipped her head to the living room and then to Nick. "Oh my God!"

Kneeling on the floor next to Julie, Kim lowered her head to her face and whispered.

"Julie, my name is Kim. Can you talk? How are you feeling, honey?"

There was a long pause until Julie opened her eyes a sliver. She spoke again. Her lips were the only muscles that moved. "Save us, please. Save Marshera."

Nick stood back from them with arms crossed and a blank face. Kim looked up at him and mouthed Julie's words, "Marshera?"

Nick shook his head.

"Julie, what is Marshera, honey? Where do your parents live so we can tell them where you are?" Kim waited again for an eternity only to see she had fallen back asleep.

Nick went into the kitchen to look out the window and returned to them, "Rain's just about over."

Kim had woken Julie and managed to get her upright. They sat together on the couch. Hoping she would talk again, Kim held the mug for her as she sipped warm cocoa. "Let's get her to a hospital first," Kim said. "I'll call the local police from there to find her parents and tell them about her brother." Marsha? Marshera? Do you know what that is?"

Nick stood and looked at her expressionless, "No idea."

***

They had found another tree to hide behind. This time, it was a giant maple that stood across the front yard from Nick's ranch.

Winger looked up the tree to a limb, "Sight lines are perfect. I'm going up, Ash."

He climbed up and put himself in position for what would happen next.

She looked up at him sitting on the branch. "Rain's all done. Sun's even coming out."

47- The Canaries

Winger smiled as he inserted the last section of the barrel into place. He looked down at Charlie and Ashun. "Time to get our girl back."

"And then she and Charlie can go home where they belong," Ashun said.

"I can’t wait," said Charlie.

Chapter 8
Julie, Do Ya Love Me?

"Rain's completely stopped," Nick said, peering out the kitchen window. "Let's get her over to the hospital right now; I got a lotta stuff to do." He entered the laundry room and returned with a laundry basket and plopped it on the countertop. "Clothes are dry. You two can change up while I bring the truck around front."

As Nick approached the door of his pickup, he reached for his phone. There were four text messages, and two missed calls. Shit! He pulled the Hydro-Blue Dodge Ram pickup around to the front and pulled up hard on the emergency brake handle. As he ran to the front door, Kim came out with Julie. Nick was surprised to see Julie walking reasonably well.

"She's getting stronger," Kim said, walking with her arm around Julie's waist. Nick helped Kim settle Julie into the rear seat of the truck. Kim buckled her seat belt and closed the door.

"You gotta second?" Nick asked as he stood in front of the truck while the engine idled.

"Sure," She closed the truck door and walked over to him.

"Figure we go to St. Joe's; it's the closest hospital. The thing is, soon as we get there, I gotta let you guys off at the ER and then take off. I'll come back for you. I'm late for delivering those two bags of feed I dumped on the ground when the storm hit. Take about an hour. I'll circle back after that. Then I'll bring you to your mother's, okay?"

"Sounds good," said Kim. Don't forget, though, if the doctors release her and I can't get in touch with her family; we should bring her to the police station."

"Yeah…okay. Cross that bridge if we come to it," Nick said.

49- The Canaries

The tube peeked through the red and orange leaves that shrouded Winger. As Nick paused to reach for the door handle, Winger inhaled a lung full of air and unloaded it through the eight-foot blowgun, launching the projectile directly toward its target.

Pffffft …jab. The dart hit precisely where it was intended. “Aaaaach!” Nick shouted as he grabbed the back of his neck to feel the pinch. He looked around, “Fuckin’ wasp!”

“You alright?” Kim called over to him. Nick stood in a daze, staring at the blood on the palm of his hand.

“Think I got stung.“ He looked down to see the dart that had just flooded his body with curare. His voice faded as he fell to the ground. Seconds later, he was unconscious.

“Nick!” Kim ran over and kneeled next to him. “Nick! Wake up!” she yelled in his face. Kim leaned over him, exposing her arm. Pffffft …jab. The next dart hit its target. “Damn it!” Kim felt the sting; like Nick, she reached for the source of her pain and found a dart. Seconds later, she was unconscious too.

“I’ll say this much, you’re accurate with that thing,” said Ashun as Winger dropped to the ground.

“Been practicing on deer and a few bear here and there,” he said.

“Are they still alive?” Ashun smiled.

“The wildlife or these two?” Winger smiled back at her.

“Winger!’ shouted Ashun.

“Kidding!”

Ashun smiled, “Alright, let’s go get Julie.”

Winger opened the driver’s door to turn off the engine as Ashun and Charlie got Julie out of the truck.

"Hi, Jules; how's it going?" Charlie said enthusiastically.

"Alright, I guess," she said. "What happened to them?"

"Blowgun; they'll wake up later," said Ashun. "Right now, we need to get you and your brother home."

Ashun helped Julie stand up. "How are you feeling, Hon?" Before Julie could answer, Winger came from the other side of the truck, having figured out how to silence the engine.

"Can you run?" he asked Julie.

"I can run a little, I guess," she said.

"A little's good enough. I'll carry you the rest of the way. Let's go."

Winger grabbed her hand to run, but Julie pulled it back, "Wait! Are they going to be alright just lying there in the driveway?"

"They'll be fine; we gotta go," Winger said.

Julie walked over to Kim and bent down to put her ear over Kim's mouth and listen for her breathing.

"I don't want to leave them lying on the ground like this. What if the storms come back or a Fisher Cat gets them?" Julie said.

"We should go, Jules," said Winger.

Julie had already walked to the ranch's front door to open it. "Charlie, help me," she called out to her brother. He ran over to help. "Take Kim's other arm so we can drag her into the house where she'll be safe."

They positioned Kim on the living room carpet. Julie put the blanket on her. Ashun and Winger were right behind them with Nick. They set him on the floor, next to Kim.

“They’ll wake up in a little while. Ready to go home?” asked Winger.

“Ready,” said Julie.

“One more thing,” Winger ran over to find the darts on the ground. He picked them up and stashed them in his backpack.

Winger took Julie’s hand, and Ashun took Charlie’s. They bounded across the open field towards the woods and the mountains to deliver them back to their home. It was a remote cave dwelling high up inside Wildcat Mountain, where they had lived for the last three years.

It was a place called, Marshera.

Chapter 9
Walk On The Wild Side

He waited for her inside the air-conditioned cabin of his Audi A8. His friends called it the spaceship, and they should. It cost him close to ninety grand. The location was Ollie's Bakery and Café in Exeter, New Hampshire. It was a breakfast place off the beaten path where they could meet incognito and discuss the problem. His car idled unevenly, perhaps from lousy petrol, or it had adopted the owner's anxiousness. He continued gnawing away on the toothpick in his mouth, scanning the lot for her. The meeting was mandatory. She wanted something from him, and he wanted something from her; don't pull any more crazy stunts. He'd driven the eight and a half hours up the turnpike to set things straight.

Phillips Exeter Academy, the prestigious prep school Brad had almost attended all those years ago, was just a mile down the street. He was ruminating on what his life might have been. Scenarios of graduating from Harvard or Yale ran through his mind. Then he would work for one of the big boys. The fact was, he had been accepted at PEA. That alone was quite an accomplishment considering even today, only fifteen percent of applicants are eligible. He never did attend. The cost was forty-five thousand a year. How would his parents afford it? Miraculously the school told them that Brad had qualified for a scholarship. He was overjoyed at the good news. His life arc would be on a winning trajectory. But then his parents explained their conundrum. A scholarship only covered sixty percent of the tuition bill. They would have to come up with eighteen grand a year plus incidentals. His parents had a strict rule; they didn't believe in loans. So they sat him down and delivered the verdict. "Sorry, son, it's not going to happen, and besides, you don't need a fancy prep school education."

Thanks, Mom and Dad. You're right; I don't need to go to one of the finest secondary schools in the country, where thirty percent of the graduates are accepted to Yale or Harvard. I'll make sure to have a good life. After all, what did Phillips Exeter do for Gore Vidal, Mark Zuckerberg, or Andrew Yang?

Nestled between two cars in a shady corner of the parking lot, he watched the patrons enter and leave. She was late. That wasn't like her. Lee Chen had never been late in the past. But then again, it was none of his business. Don't ask, don't tell was the rule that each of them lived by. They both got what the other wanted from the arrangement. The sex stuff was fun for a while, but that was in the past.

Brad often considered the risk-reward nature of their business arrangement. If he was ever caught, everything would be lost, including Kim. It was necessary to tell himself that it was okay to bend or even break the rules to get what he deserved. And why not? How many billionaires started out breaking the law to grab the American dream? Admiring the likes of Joe Kennedy, Bernie Madoff, and Elizabeth Holmes provided all the justification he needed.

Brad Parkland smiled as he chewed the toothpick and realized he could sell himself on anything as long as it fattened his wallet. His values were fluid.

Tap, tap, tap! She hit the passenger side window with her ring scaring him half to death. His spell broken, he turned to see her waving, head tilted, and smiling. He reached for the button and lowered the window halfway.

"We're going in for coffee, yes?" he asked.

"Well, yes, but I don't want anyone to hear some sensitive stuff I must discuss with you. Can I hop in for a minute?"

She wore her customary expensive gray business suit with a tight, white blouse. The modest, wholesome girl was long gone.

"Yeah, sure," he looked over to his door and hit the unlock button. She opened the passenger door and bounced into the seat. The rear door opened at the same time and a sizeable European-looking man jumped in the back. He wore shades, and a hoodie pulled over his head.

"You've got to be shitting me! What are you pulling here, Lee?"

"It's fine, Brad. Just drive, and I'll explain on the way. Don't try anything; he's carrying."

"Oh, just fuckin great. Is this the way we do business now?"

"We do business any way Mr. Chang tells us to do business. He flew in from Hong Kong yesterday and wants a one-on-one with you."

"I know I'm overdue and owe you guys, but I'm working on it."

"You haven't answered my messages, Brad. I was in the area so I took a chance and stopped by your place, but your lady answered the door. She was so nervous she slammed it in my face, that little bitch."

"Yes, I heard. We've worked together for two years, Lee, and now you're showing up at my condo pretending to be a holy roller while Kim's home. Talk about a Jesus Christ moment."

"Drive, Brad. Stop arguing and head in the direction of Newport, Rhode Island."

"Newport? I just drove up here from Maryland!"

Lee Chen's eyes narrowed in anger as she turned to the back seat and nodded. Her accomplice smacked Brad hard on the side of his head. Cocking the hammer on his pistol, he pressed the muzzle against the base of his neck.

Brad froze and slowly moved his eyes to look at her in shock.

55- The Canaries

They drove, making their way down several back roads and eventually onto route 95 south. It became uncomfortably silent as he checked his rearview to watch the hooded man sleeping.

He had planned on laying into her for showing up unannounced at his place, and now he was on defense. The hunter had become the hunted. It's not every day an ordinary person has a gun jammed into the base of their skull.

"Your friend doesn't have much to say, does he? Is he deaf or something?"

"Bear left up here and stay on route 4 for ten miles towards Newport. I told him not to speak; he's the muscle."

"Tell me again, why are we headed to Newport?"

"I told you Mr. Chang wants to talk to you. He prefers face-to-face meetings."

"We've never met. We've never spoken. So why now?"

"Don't act dumb, Brad. You understand why. He wants to know what the delay is on the API's. I wasn't supposed to tell you that, so you owe me one."

"Right, you carjack me, and I owe you one. Anyway, everything's still the same. My guy says they're tweaking the chemistry to maximize the efficacy in R&D. The API will be ready once they work that out. Shouldn't be much longer."

"You've been saying it shouldn't be much longer for way too long, Brad. Why do you refuse to tell me who your guy is? We could help you out if we knew who this person was."

"Why would I give up all my leverage and let you people go around me and work with him directly? No, he stays confidential. Besides, where's the trust in me? I've delivered the info all along. I have one hiccup, and you kidnap me, which isn't a smart way to do business. Just remember, I'm not a member of your gang, just a solitary contractor."

"You're nothing to us when you don't deliver what you promised, Brad."

"Wow. I'm nothing. This whole thing's gone dark. I'll see what this mysterious Mr. Chang has to say to me. I'll straighten him out."

They drove in silence over the two-mile-long Newport Bridge. Brad glanced into the rearview mirror to see the hooded man still sleeping and not wearing a seatbelt. He considered locking up the brakes to send him face-first into the windshield. Then run for it. But how far would he get? There was no running away from what his life had become. He'd crossed the Rubicon a long time ago.

"Take this exit onto Farewell Street," she said.

"Fare-well Street; how appropriate. Where are we meeting him?"

"We're meeting at Harbor Landing restaurant. Take a right down this street."

As they approached the entrance, the door opened ahead of them. Brad couldn't control smirking at the cliché of two heavy-set, tattooed men standing on either side of the door. He noticed a sign hanging in the window saying "closed." They entered, and he heard the door lock behind them. It was the first time in decades he had been scared.

"Search him," Lee Chen ordered the oversized security guard. He patted Brad down as he looked at him with disgust. His cell phone was found and slipped inside the big man's suitcoat.

"Hey!" Brad objected.

"You will receive it back at the end of the meeting," she said.

They gathered in the lobby, and introductions were exchanged. Mr. Chang shook Brad's hand in the friendliest way possible, as if they were long-lost friends or relatives. "It's nice to meet you,

Bradley." He grinned at him, smiling from ear to ear. This will be a breeze, Brad thought to himself. They'll want some BS status report with updates and promises to deliver what he wants, blah, blah, blah. He decided not to correct him and ask that he call him Brad. The only one who called him Bradley these days was his eighty-seven-year-old mother. Brad profiled Mr. Chang and noted he was a stylishly dressed Asian businessman in a blue suit and dark tie. He was fit, in his forties, with wire-rimmed glasses and jet-black hair slicked straight back, reminding him of a guy you'd pass on the street and never think about twice.

Little do we know of our fellow man.

"I am glad I can put a face to go along with the name that I have heard so much about in conversations with Lee Chen," said Mr. Chang. "Come, follow me. We have a nice table with a view of the harbor."

Brad looked around to see nautical ships, whales, and ropes typical of a waterfront restaurant represented on the walls.

"Is this one of your favorite places, Mr. Chang?" Brad asked.

He placed his arm on Brad's shoulder, "Yes, Bradley, I like to dine here when I make the journey over. What makes you ask?"

"You must know the owners, the restaurant being closed and all."

"We own this establishment and use it for our functions whenever necessary." His face showed a confident smile as they approached the table.

They sat in the windowed corner of the restaurant at a large round table with a white linen tablecloth and place settings for eight. Tourists walked by and glanced in the window, oblivious to the affairs inside.

Mr. Chang sat with his back facing the corner. Lee Chen sat to his left. Brad was placed across the table from them.

"Would you care for something to drink, Bradley?" asked Mr. Chen.

"Water will be fine."

"Are you sure? We have cold beer, liquor, and fine wines from our wine cellar."

"The water will do just fine, thank you."

Brad looked out the window and saw a one-legged seagull standing ominously on the pier. He imagined if the bird could speak, he would say, "I only have one leg, but you're about to lose everyone who ever loved you." Behind the gull, wall-to-wall sailboats were crammed into the harbor. Meanwhile, the vast room they occupied had no customers or wait staff making it appear empty and lifeless.

"Let us begin," said Mr. Chang. I want to discuss the status of the one missing component that we require but have yet to receive. In short, we need the information you have promised us, Bradley. I am referring, of course, to the API or the Active Pharmaceutical Ingredient for Novel Synthetic Opioids. We can only begin to analyze and manufacture new pain relievers in China once you provide the API formularies. They are, in essence, the recipe. Before you answer, let me tell you why this is so important. Novel Synthetic Opioids, or NSOs as we call them, are a new class of synthetics. Previous versions were time-released over twelve hours. The new NSOs will be time-release over a twenty-four-hour period. And *that* is a real game changer."

“I'm aware of the benefits of the new synthetics, Mr. Chang, but…."

He interrupted Brad's story, "Here is our problem, Bradley. The market wants these long-lasting opioids right now, like, today. You are a salesman who sells chemical compounds to several pharmaceutical manufacturers, yet you only have this one source who has not been an asset lately. I suggest you get creative and find other connections at this company besides your contact. Or find another pharma manufacturer. Then you may find new opportunities to provide us with their APIs."

"It's an old marketing proverb that is true; the first guy on the block selling a new product gets the lion's share of the market. Our goal is to be that guy. You have received a healthy advance from us to pay off your source. Therefore, we need an immediate return on our investment Bradley. So I now must demand that you have the APIs to us within two weeks."

Brad could see the sweat beading on his forehead and the intensity in his eyes. People like Mr. Chang were accustomed to getting what they wanted.

"My answer is short, Mr. Chang," said Brad trying to maintain composure. "I can't give you what I don't have. As I told Lee in the car, they're still tweaking the chemistry."

"Enough!" Mr. Chang raised his voice for the first time. "I have heard these excuses before, and they are disappointing. You didn't listen to what I just said." He sat back in his chair and stretched his legs as he took a sip of his water. He turned to look at Lee Chen sitting emotionless next to him.

"It has been my experience, Bradley, that men are capable of amazing feats of accomplishment if they put their minds to it. Look at the Great Wall, the Polio Vaccine, or the Apollo Moon Mission. Demand is the mother of invention, and men can achieve miracles when they have their backs against the wall. Would you agree with this?"

"I can't make their scientists go any faster, Mr. Chang."

He took off his glasses and set them down on the linen tablecloth. "Let's change the subject, Bradley. I have found that a person's relationship with their parents can often affect their performance as an adult. Do you have a strong connection to your parents?"

"My father is no longer living. I am close to my mother, though."

"And where does she live?"

"She lives in an assisted living facility in Massachusetts."

"Do you visit her often?"

"Yes, I do. I visited my mother last week."

"This is good. People should care about their mothers. They give us life and nurture us. I have some updated information for you, Bradley. Your mother is no longer located at Brooksby Village Senior Living Community in Peabody, Massachusetts, as of yesterday."

Brad felt a sudden sting of panic; his face flushed red as he sat straight in his chair. "What? How do you know where my mother is? What do you mean she's not at Brooksby?"

Mr. Chang stared at Brad; his face hadn't changed expression. "I know where she is because she is in a safe house with one of my people. It's not too far from here."

"What? You bastards! You're telling me you kidnapped my mother?"

"I wouldn't say kidnapped, more like she is on loan to us. She is comfortable and safe, I assure you."

Brad stared across the table at Lee Chen. "This is bullshit. Did you know about this?"

Mr. Chang repeated his cliché', "Demand is the mother of invention and innovation, Bradley. It is time for you to innovate, and it is time for me to see a return on my investment."

"Bring her back immediately, or you'll get no APIs!" Brad yelled loudly.

"Quite the contrary, Bradley; if I don't get the APIs in two weeks…well…you get the picture. And it isn't pretty."

"For the last time, I can't create what I don't have!" Brad was standing now with fists clenched in a fighting posture.

"Be careful, Bradley," he held up his index finger to the two large bodyguards as they stepped closer to the table.

"Now you have your demand; the mother of creation. Get creative, beg, borrow, or steal. Just do whatever it takes. You now have a sales goal and two weeks to meet it. This is how America was created. Welcome to America."

Mr. Chang didn't wait for Brad's response, "We are done here. I have another meeting to attend. Please help yourself to anything on our menu Bradley. Or you may leave; it is entirely up to you."

Brad remained standing in defiance and stared at Mr. Chang.

"Good day, Bradley." Mr. Chang walked to the rear of the restaurant.

Brad turned his stare at Lee Chen without speaking. He knew that someday she would betray him.

Mr. Chang stopped and turned back, "Ms. Chen could you come with me? I need to discuss a few things with you. Oh, and Bradley, Ms. Chen, and the other gentleman won't accompany you on your trip back. Do not concern yourself with their transportation. I look forward to hearing good news soon!"

Lee Chen bolted out of her chair and followed her boss into the next room. Mr. Chang had one hell of a new assignment for her.

Chapter 10
Wake Me Up Inside

Nick opened his eyes first. He stared at the vaulted ceiling above him, trying to focus, but it wasn't happening yet. He tried to move his limbs. They felt disconnected from his body. His eyes could move left or right, and he saw Kim lying on her side on the floor, a blanket covered her. Still paralyzed, he tried turning his head by shifting his eyes toward the floor and the ceiling. After several tries, it worked. Facing Kim's back, Nick tested his ability to speak.

"Kim, wake up!" he yelled. She was non-responsive. He wanted to try and nudge her, but his limbs were still out of commission. Slowly, the disconnected feeling was replaced with a tingling, like his arms and legs were waking up from being asleep. He was coming out of it, whatever it was. Next came the fingers; they slowly responded as he opened and closed his hand to bring feeling and sensation back. With each repetition, his hand and arm slowly awoke. Nick could finally move his arm to reach out to Kim and tap her on her back.

"Hey, wake up. Wake up, Kim."

Her eyes opened slowly. She felt nauseous and bewildered. "Can't move anything."

"It'll come back, be patient," said Nick. "Try to move your fingers and your toes first." He could now turn to his side and raise to lean on his elbow. "Keep trying; it'll come. We got knocked out by some stuff in the darts. The side effect is the nerves get temporarily paralyzed."

Kim was moving her fingers, making a fist, and as she started coming around. Within ten minutes, they both were able to stand up.

"What the hell just happened?" Kim asked him. "And where the hell is…." Kim, lost her balance and grabbed the coffee table for an anchor. She got her bearings and ran to the front door to see Nick's truck sitting quietly. There was no one in it. She turned to him and yelled, "Julie's gone!"

"You're shitting me," Nick said.

Kim began to panic, "What is going on around here? Why on earth would someone want to kidnap her?"

Nick sat on the couch, trying to shake off the curare still inside his body. "No clue. I was standing next to the truck when I got hit by the dart. It felt like a bee sting, and I remember seeing it on the ground before I passed out. They must have dragged us in here and put us on the floor next to each other. Then they kidnapped the girl."

Kim's hands were shaking, as she brought them to her mouth, "What does someone want with a twelve-year-old girl? She needs to be in a hospital right now!"

Nick came to her and took Kim in his arms to comfort her. "Let's not panic. Come on, we'll go outside and have a look around."

Both looked around the area by Nick's truck and saw the marks in the gravel, where somebody had dragged them into the ranch.

"So much for evidence. There are no darts on the ground," said Nick. "Whoever nailed us, must have been watching the whole time from that maple." He looked up at the tree overlooking the driveway.

"Let me use your phone, please. I'm calling the police," said Kim. "Julie's been kidnapped. I want them to start investigating this immediately."

"Okay, wait a minute. I don't want the cops snoopin' round here," said Nick.

"What? We are talking about a serious crime, Nick! A kidnapping has happened. And Julie needs medical attention!"

"I ain't got time to talk to the cops. Let's do this, you take my pickup, go down to the station, and talk to them. They'll want a statement and all the information to search for the girl. I'll take the Quad and drop off those two bags I left behind so this guy has some feed for his horses. You come back when you're done with the cops, and I'll shoot home to your mom's."

"I guess that'll work. I thought the cops wanted to investigate the scene of the crime?" Kim said.

"Not the cops in Crawford."

"Alright, I'll go then. Time is wasting away. I have to tell them about her brother Charlie too. He might've been kidnapped first for some reason. I wonder if the ransom note will come to their family or us. Anyway, which way is the police station?"

"Drive out of here on the gravel driveway and then hang a left at the end. Stay on that road for three miles, and you'll see it," said Nick

"Okay, I'll be back as soon as I talk to the police," said Kim.

"Good luck," Nick said. *You'll need it.*

Chapter 11
I Fought The Law

They were back; the horrible feelings of sadness Kim suffered when Grace died ten years ago. Over time she healed by burying the pain deep inside herself. Denial, the first of five stages of grief, was the numbness that filled her. Kim couldn't believe the young girl whose life they had saved was gone. As Nick's truck brought her closer to the police station, Grace's image appeared in her mind, Kim could only think one thing. *It's happening all over again.*

"I would like to report a kidnapping," Kim said. She and Detective John Jacquard sat in a brightly lit interview room with an observation window that faced her. The red numbers on the digital clock hanging on the wall showed 5:05 PM. Kim gave the detective the details of her story while a mini voice recorder's tape heads spun in the record mode. She could feel her anxiety constricting her trembling voice. Pure adrenaline had driven Kim to incredible feats of bravery, but now she wanted to cry.

The Lieutenant passed the box of Kleenex across the desk to her and paused the recorder to excuse himself. Fifteen minutes later, she stared at blank walls as her mind wandered. What would a career in law enforcement be like, she thought? *At least I'd be able to conduct the investigation myself and not sit here waiting for him.* Then she laughed out loud, knowing it would never work. Right out of college, she knew herself well enough to look for a career, that would be safe and without risk. Big Pharma had pursued her after graduation even though her degree was in botany, not chemistry, as it should have been. She even raised questions about their interest in her, during the interview process. The offer came anyway. Somebody in management liked her. They got it right, though, in a short time, Kim became one of the company's top clinical technicians.

Jacquard swung the door open, breaking Kim's daydreams. "My apologies. We're dealing with an opioid epidemic in town. Please, continue your story."

As Kim finished explaining the day's events, he looked at her doubtfully.

He's questioning everything I say either because he doesn't believe me or simply because I'm a woman.

"Okay, a lot has happened here, Miss Marino. Recapping, what you've stated thus far, let's go back to the beginning. Where are you from again?" the detective asked, as he wrote in his black notebook. He wore readers perched on his nose, as he scribbled away. Middle-aged, he wore a denim shirt, tie, Docker pants, and Hush Puppy shoes. Kim thought, he resembled an older and heftier version of the actor Gerard Butler. His face had a perpetual worried look, and he kept his full head of salt and pepper hair styled neatly.

"Okay, I live in Travilah, Maryland, and it's Moreno."

"Right, right, Moreno, sorry. So you're a research scientist with a pharmaceutical company, and you just happened to be up here in northern New Hampshire helping your mother move into a new house."

"I'm a clinical lab technician. I work with research scientists. And yes, I'm helping my mother move into her new place. I want to get over there and finish helping her unpack eventually."

"Right. And your mother's name again?"

Kim was getting annoyed. She had provided the same information once already. He kept asking her the same questions, as if he was trying to trip her up. Every question seemed to be about anyone, besides Julie and Charlie. She understood the detective's explanation about police procedure and gathering every detail, but he could at least show some urgency in finding the missing kids.

"Jennifer Moreno, that's my mother's name. She is moving into the new senior community here in town." She watched him take notes before speaking, "Detective Jacquard, are you going to ask about the two kids who were kidnapped?" She was beyond tired of what felt like an interrogation.

"I'm getting to that, Ms. Moreno. We need to get all possible information about the person reporting the crime. It's standard police procedure."

"Why?"

"Why? Sometimes when a person reports a crime, they are in some way involved in the crime too. You're not from around here, so we need to know your story and how the kidnapping happened. Now, if you bear with me, we will be getting to your friends in a moment. I need to finish collecting all pertinent data. Have you or anyone you know been contacted by the kidnapper or kidnappers? Have they sent you a ransom note in any form, paper, electronics, or a phone call?"

"No! Again, some darts knocked us out, and when we awoke, Julie was gone. Her brother disappeared while I was saving her from the rapids. If I had received a ransom note, don't you think I would've told you by now?"

"Alright, Miss Marino, please calm down. Again, I'm checking the boxes here and ensuring, that I've retrieved all the necessary data to move forward. Now, please tell me the full names and addresses of the two minors who you say have been kidnapped."

"For the last time, my name is Kim Moreno, like the actress, and not Marino, like the football player."

"Right."

"Thank you! Okay, first, there is Julie. I don't know her last name. I assume she lives around here, but I'm not sure. She would be twelve or thirteen, by my estimates. She's small with auburn hair and wearing a green t-shirt and blue jeans. Her brother's name is Charlie. Same thing, I don't know his last name. He's around ten or eleven. I heard him yell for help, ran down the trail, and dove into the river to get Julie. She'd gone underwater without coming up. Her brother had disappeared by the time I pulled her out. Nick and I resuscitated Julie and got her back to Nick's ranch. We were about to drive her to the hospital when the darts knocked us out, and she was taken. End of story. Can you get a few of your guys to start looking for them? Can you put out an APB for them? We're wasting precious time, detective."

"Okay, now back up a second. Nick? Who's he again?" the detective asked.

"Now, his last name, I know. Nick Caldwell. His ranch is close to here. It's…"

"Nick Caldwell? Yeah, I know him. I knew his father, Gus too. He died a few years ago, sadly. How'd Nick get mixed up in this again?"

"Yet again, he was driving through the woods on his ATV and saw me giving Julie CPR. He turned around and came over to help. We were able to get her resuscitated, and then the storm hit. We jumped on his machine and drove back to his ranch in the downpour."

"Why didn't either of you call 911?"

"I left my phone charging in my mother's house when I heard her brother screaming for help. Nick's phone had zero service at the rapids. We wanted to get her to the hospital as soon as the storm let up and then alert the police to find her parents."

Detective Jacquard took off his readers and closed his book to look up at Kim. "You haven't given me much to go on. We have no last names of the alleged abductees and no addresses. The alleged kidnappers haven't contacted anyone with any demands. It sounds a lot like a child custody case. Custodial interference is usually a schedule misunderstanding and a waste of the police force's time and money."

"How do you explain the darts and both of us being knocked unconscious?" Kim asked.

"I can't. I'll run out to Caldwell Ranch to look for evidence and get some answers about the darts. Have a conversation with Nick Caldwell and get his statement, if he's around. You said the darts were gone when you two woke up from being rendered unconscious?"

"Yes, they were gone, and Nick and I saw them on the ground. Look, Detective Jacquard, all I can do is provide you with the truth as I saw it. There's a young girl and boy who have gone missing. That girl needs to be in a hospital ASAP. She had completely drowned and we brought her back to life. But she was underwater for a long time. I was hoping you could put together the puzzle pieces I've given you and take action so we could get her and her brother to see a doctor and then home to their parents."

“I can’t take much action when we’re flying blind, Ms. Moreno.”

“I understand, detective. Neither of the victims spoke much before they disappeared except when Julie said her brother's name was Charlie and then something about saving Marshera. That was about it."

"Did you say Marshera? The girl said Marshera?" Jacquard picked up on the word and reopened his black notebook to begin writing again.

"Yes, she said. "Save us, save Marshera."

The detective scribbled away with a stern look on his face.

"Do you know this place? What is Marshera?” Kim found a puzzle piece.

He closed his notebook again, "Marshera is a well-known name around this town. There are caves up inside Wildcat Mountain, just north of here. There's a hippy colony in the caves where people live or used to live; I don't know anymore. Last I heard, the place was deserted."

Kim suddenly wondered why Nick said he didn't know what Marshera was.

Jacquard kept explaining, "It's an Abenaki Indian name, means a place of healing or something like that. Abenaki Indians used to inhabit this area back in Colonial Times. Some of them lived in the caves back then too. A few Abenaki descendants still live in the mountains and forest up there. There are thousands of acres of backwoods. They're throwbacks to the original Indians, feral, but they don't bother anyone. They live off the grid and the land. Anyway, I'll drive to Nick's to look around and chat with him. Maybe he has some clues. Leave me your phone number in case I need to contact you. You said you're with your mother for a few more days?"

"Yes, at least."

"Do me a favor, don't go home to Maryland without calling me first."

"I have a question for you, detective. Is there a chance Julie and Charlie are up in that hippy colony?" Kim asked.

"Oh, I can't say; they might be. It'll be part of my investigation, one of several I'm working on. I'll call you if anything develops."

Kim walked out of the police station, frustrated. She used to listen to crime podcasts and knew that people had perceptions about the miracles that police seem to perform daily. The reality is those miracles result from hard work spent investigating tips. Information from witnesses or confidential informants is gathered, and the puzzle is put together. The problem is the puzzle is rarely completed, and Jacquard only had a few pieces of the puzzle.

Kim was filled with speculation. *Why was he so blasé about looking for Julie and Charlie? Two minors go missing, and he's more interested in grilling me than finding them.*

Then she beat herself up for not getting either of their surnames. *You're in the information-collecting business.... It's what you do, dummy!*

Kim detoured and found her way back to her mother's house. Her mother's car wasn't there. To her relief, she left the side door unlocked. Her phone, now fully charged, Kim had a missed call from Brad. She returned it, but it went right to voicemail.

Sitting down on a kitchen chair, she stretched her legs out and sighed. Mum had hung up her bird clock above the window over the window. She let out a laugh knowing that all the teasing in the world wouldn't stop Mum from putting up the funny clock that let out a different bird song every hour. It always reminded her of Grace and how she would marvel at the different, hourly bird chirps. That was ten years ago. *Wow, where did ten years go?*

They shared a bedroom. At nine years, and five months older, Grace felt like Kim's living doll. They loved each other more than two sisters possibly could. The details of that night were still blurry and confusing to her. Grace had been screaming from night terrors when her father came into their room to quiet her down. He was visibly upset. Kim was awake, peering out from under the covers. What was he doing to her? Why didn't he lift her out of the crib and lull her to sleep?

"C'mon, Gracie, go to sleep," he said. "Your mother's sick with a cold, and I have to be up at five for work. Just go back to sleep, Grace! Daddy's getting angry!"

I should've told him what Mum always did to quiet her. She would pick her up and rock her in her arms while she sang to her. Why didn't I help him! Why was I afraid?

He left the room for a while and then came back. Magically he managed to quiet her down and put her back in her crib. It seemed, too good to be true.

The next morning the unthinkable happened. Mum came into the bedroom and found Grace dead. She wailed and cried openly, holding Kim's dead sister in her arms as she watched in horror. Her father had already left, on a flight headed to Brazil. Kim called 911 and the police came. For safety reasons, Mum had strict orders that Kim was never to answer the front door. The police rang the bell over and over again. Kim yelled to her mother to go get the police at the front door, but she couldn't stop crying as she held baby Grace. The combination of her mother's out-of-control emotion combined with the police ringing the doorbell and banging on the door left an indelible scar on Kim that never went away. It was a nightmare that stayed with her. Her sister, whom she loved more than anything in the world, was dead.

The coroner's report listed SIDS as the cause of death. However, the report was vague in its conclusion. *The exact cause of death and the contributing factors cannot be specifically summarized.* Things only got worse after the funeral when her father left and wasn't heard from again. The inconclusive autopsy and her father's disappearance led Kim's negative thoughts. She should have helped him with Grace. *Why didn't I get out of my bed instead of hiding under the covers? I could have prevented it!*

A vicious loop of self-blame lived inside her. How could it not?

It was almost six PM; a day of days, Kim thought. Taking in the new surroundings, she realized that her childhood home where she grew up was officially gone. The house where she had done her homework on the dining room table, had friends over for slumber parties, and where her first boyfriend came to pick her up in a fancy tux to take her to prom was sold to a new family that would fill it with new memories.

Kim would take Grace's memory with her wherever she went. It didn't have a house to inhabit. It remained in her heart.

She would put clothes away for a while, feeling guilty for not helping her mother, before returning Nick's truck to him. She left her mother a note on her to-do pad that didn't say much. There was too much to write.

Kim stepped outside and looked up at the crisp autumn sky. The three-quarter moon looked down upon Crawford, and she found herself wishing for her lunar friend to watch over Julie.

Keep her safe until I find her.

Chapter 12
Boys Are Back In Town

Kim jumped down to the ground from Nick's giant pickup truck. Almost 6:30, it was twilight time and getting dark out as she approached the barn to look inside. Cracker was standing silently in his stall. He was unlike any horse she had ever seen; majestic and beautiful. It was dark inside the barn as Kim entered to stroke his muzzle gently. *How are you doing, fella?* Next to Cracker were two more stalls with what Nick called his working horses. Grade horses, he explained, weren't purebreds. They helped with work around the ranch and keeping the Arabians company.

Leaving the barn, she walked outside and looked around for Nick without success.

Where is he? He must be inside the house.

Heading up the walkway to the ranch house, Kim saw him from the corner of her eye. Just behind the barn, Nick was on the ground, flat on his back. His nose was bleeding.

"Nick!" She bolted to his side.

His shirt was ripped open with two buttons missing. Kim gently lifted him. Nick's eyes popped open like he'd just awoken from a deep sleep.

"Kim… what are you doing…how long was I out?" Nick's brain wasn't cooperating yet.

"I just got here. I brought your truck back and saw you on the ground. What happened? It looks like somebody beat you up."

He squinted, trying to concentrate, and then explained, "Cracker, that bad hoss son of a gun. Turned my back on him after fixing his shoe and pow, knocked me right on my crackerbox."

"But Nick, Cracker's in his stable in the barn. How'd you get out here? Your shirt's ripped, and buttons are missing." Nick's account wasn't making sense to her. She had developed an instinct for questioning evidence from her job.

"Oh hell, I must have been dizzy after that nag kicked me. I think I put Crack in his stable and wandered out back here. I'd already ripped the shirt earlier. Got it caught on a nail sticking out of the fence post. No biggie, it's all good."

His explanation satisfied her for now. Horses and ranching were areas where she had no prior experience. "Can you stand up so we can get you inside to clean you up?"

Wrapping her arm around Nick's waist, they made their way into the ranch house. She helped him stop his bloody nose, and then he changed his shirt. They moved to the kitchen, where Kim took up a seat on the stool next to the counter where she had been just a few hours ago.

"You want some ice water or something?" Nick took out two glasses.

"Sure, that's great."

"I ain't got much time here. Gotta get changed up and over to the Son to tend bar in an hour. You should stop by; a good band comes on at nine. The Bacres, good ‘ol classic rock. How'd you make out with the cops?"

"So you're a bartending cowboy, huh?"

"More like a cowboy that bartends," Nick said. He leaned his elbows on the granite countertop to be at her level.

Kim took note of his lanky frame, bushy blonde hair, and blue eyes.

He looks more like a surfer than a cowboy.

"So, I spoke with Detective Jacquard from the Crawford Police and told him everything. He asked more questions about me than Julie and Charlie. It didn't seem like he would take any significant action. Guess it's because I needed more information, like the kids' last names. He thinks it might be a child custody case, but I disagree. He said he would swing by here and look around for evidence like footprints or other stuff left by the kidnappers."

"Oh, that's great. Cop's snooping around. I know Jacquard. Real flannel mouth. Bet you he never shows up anyway. The cops in this town are lazy asses."

"Okay, I get it. You're not a fan. I have a question for you, though. Why did you tell me that you didn't know what Marshera was? Detective Jacquard said most people in town know about that place. Do you know about it or not?" She wondered how Nick would react to being put on the spot.

"Yeah, hell, you got me. I wanted to avoid seeing you get involved. There's been a bunch of hippies living in those Marshera caves up there on Wildcat Mountain for a few years, I hear. Quite a sight; the waterfall runs right through the mountain and that hippy colony place too. I figured Julie and her brother belonged there, and they'd take care of their own."

Kim rolled her eyes and sighed, "I don't know what's going on with people like you and Jacquard. We're talking about a young girl that needs hospitalization. I have no idea what kind of shape her brother's in. They both may be in danger."

"I'm sure they're just fine," said Nick.

"I will be the judge of that," said Kim. "I want to go to this Wildcat Mountain and this Marshera place tomorrow morning. I just need to find Julie and Charlie to put my mind at ease."

"I don't know; I'm pretty busy with stuff around here. It might be best to mosey out to Wildcat in a few days. If we did go, the best way would be on the quad down the trails." He walked over to look at the framed mirror on the wall.

"Shit, people's gonna be asking me who licked me. Screw it." He turned to Kim, "You want a ride home to your Mom's?"

"I'll give you one hundred dollars for a ride out to Wildcat Mountain and back. You're working a part-time gig, so the extra money might come in handy."

"For a C-Note? Sure, why not. Scoot you out there and back in the morning," Nick said.

"Terrific I'll be ready and have your cash by 6:00 AM," said Kim.

“Course, I’m thinking this thing through now,” Nick said. You do know we’re gonna have to hike up to near the summit of Wildcat Mountain? That’s where the Hippy Colony is.”

“I didn’t consider that part,” said Kim.

“So why don’t we make it two C-Notes for the ride and the hike; sound fair?”

“One fifty, and that’s my final offer, Nick. I don’t want to spend any time there. I just want to make sure they’re both alright.”

"It’s a deal," Nick said. I got to get ready for my shift now. Think about coming by the bar later, and we'll talk some recent history about Crawford and how things work here. The name of the place is The Rising Son. It's on Main Street." Nick walked into the bedroom to clean up and change.

Kim closed her eyes and took a deep breath. She felt relieved about taking action to go see the Hippy Colony where Julie and Charlie might live. Then a phrase came to her that she would repeat over and over again.

I'm not going to lose another one.

Chapter 13
House Of The Rising Son

Nick dropped Kim at her mother's and headed off to bartend. As soon as she walked in the door, she smelled the pleasant aroma of a home-cooked meal. The love she and her mother had for each other couldn't be described. It was shown every day in every way. She loved the comfort of coming home to her mother's cooking. It's one of many ways Mum showed her unconditional love and acceptance. Sometimes Kim imagined what it would be like to carry an infant in her swollen belly until the day she would scream in pain to bring the child into the bright world. Imperfect as Mum might be, she was the one who gave her life and sacrificed so much. Years from now, her mother's mind would move toward that of a child from whence it came. The circle would be complete when it became Kim's turn to care for her until the day she died. Ashes to ashes, dust to dust.

"My lord, what a day you had, my dear!" Mum reacted to Kim's telling of all the events. "Here I am, doing odds and ends while unpacking. Meanwhile, you're saving lives and outrunning a terrible storm! I saw your phone charging on the kitchen counter. I was so worried that I couldn't call you. I'm glad the whole episode is over, and you're safe here with me now." Her voice was shaky and hoarse, revealing how tired she was from the day's move. For the first time, Kim noticed she looked a little older. People described her mother as a twin to Meryl Streep, and she couldn't disagree. But today, she was a little less glamorous, with more gray than blond in her hair. Sixty-three wasn't old, despite a few more wrinkles around her eyes.

"That's the thing, Mum, the episode's not over. I'm going to find out what's happening in this town and why no one besides me wants to find Julie and her brother Charlie."

"But Kim dear, don't you think you're better off letting the police handle this matter? You said you met with the detective, and he thinks these two kids live in a hippy colony or something. I'm sure he will investigate and check it out. You don't need to do anything else. Just let the police do their jobs now." Mum held her steaming tea in both hands, sipping it from a Disneyworld Mickey cup she had found at the top of an unpacked box. The movers had placed the furniture into the individual rooms where it belonged. There were still full boxes everywhere that needed to be unpacked and organized.

"Mum, Julie said *to save us, save Marshera.* She and her brother Charlie have to be up there in the mountains. The detective said he would investigate, but who knows how long that would take. He asked more questions about me than he did about the missing kids. There is something he's avoiding; I need help figuring out what it is and even why. The fact that I didn't have Julie and Charlie's last names or other information about them was all he needed. He's not even trying to find them."

"What will you do, Sweetie?"

"Remember I mentioned that guy Nick on the ATV that helped me revive Julie? After dinner, I'm going to shower and head to this pub downtown where he bartends, the Rising Son. He said he has some information about Crawford that we should know," He also agreed to bring me out to this Wildcat Mountain tomorrow; it's just north of here. That's where the hippy colony is. I need to see if they're out there!" Kim's passion caused her to move her hands as she spoke. "Plus, I'm paying him a hundred and fifty dollars. Do you mind if I take a little time tomorrow morning?"

"No, I don't mind, Honey, but you could also just relax here and let nature take its course."

"What's that supposed to mean?"

"It means that everyone has problems that they need to fix themselves. Charity begins at home."

"Oh, Jeez, there you go with your clichés again. What charity did Grace get at home?"

She stared at Kim in shocked silence. "I do not want to discuss your sister, and it's not fair to bring up her name. I'm simply watching out for you."

Kim lowered her head, feeling ashamed.

Just keep sweeping things under the rug, Mum.

Mum rose from her chair, "I'm baking a meatloaf using the recipe that's your favorite. I prepared it earlier today; I was worried sick, about where you were during that storm. I think I'll go check on it." She walked to the kitchen, ending their talk.

Kim covered her face with both hands and then ran her fingers up through her long hair in anguish. She realized she was badly in need of a shower. Ever since the day they lost her sister, Mum had been afraid of her taking on anything dangerous. After all, she was down to just one kid. Growing up, she was helicoptered. Mum ensured that every moment of her adolescence was organized, planned, and safe. There hadn't been any downtime. Every day consisted of scheduled sports activities, piano lessons, and private tutors. Her priority was to tell Kim what not to do and how to avoid any potential danger. The problem was that she never provided any encouragement to go along with the fear she instilled. Was she worried that confidence might give her a license to try dangerous things?

Kim stood up and ended her self-analysis, knowing that her mother was far from perfect, but she always had her back. She would love her unconditionally no matter what.

Walking into the kitchen, she gave her mother a long embrace. "I'm sorry; it's been an exhausting and emotional day. I love you, Mum."

"I know Kimmy, and I love you too."

"Meatloaf and green beans are ready."

"I could smell it the second I walked into the house. I'm starving!"

As they ate, she told Kim, "I have my appointment with Dr. Edmunds, the Oncologist, on Tuesday afternoon in Concord. It'll be a quick checkup to review my last scan. It's up to you if you want to come or not. They said it's a routine appointment."

"Oh, I forgot about that. I'll go with you, of course. What time is it again?"

"Three PM."

"Great, afterward, we can find a nice ice cream place to treat ourselves," said Kim.

The meatloaf was all warm and meaty, with a slice of bacon along the top. They both devoured it and even went for second helpings.

With dishes and pots cleaned, Kim headed upstairs to shower. After the events of the day, the shower felt amazing. She tilted her head back and let the warm water flow over her, washing away the conditioner and the tension. As she toweled off and moisturized, thoughts about the day came back to replay in her mind. It was all so surreal. She would never be able to move on without knowing that Julie was alright. Yes, she cared about Charlie, but something told her he was okay. He hadn't drowned and been resuscitated like his sister. Kim felt something undeniable when she held Julie on Nick's ATV, battling through the storm. She knew she was substituting Julie for Grace, she couldn't deny her feelings.

After blow-drying her hair, she applied a little bit of makeup, a pair of skinny jeans, heels, and a plain white top to finish the transformation. She was ready with just one more item needed. Kim searched through her overnight bag pushing aside makeup, vitamins, and feminine napkins to find the prescription container for Trazodone, a commonly prescribed sleep aid. What was inside the amber bottle was anything but that. The reliable pink powder and pills were retrieved. Kim needed a little artificial courage when venturing to a strange bar to meet a man she barely knew.

She had already cut the 20 mg pills in half. Kim downed one without water.

That ought to take the edge off.

***

The Rising Son was about as honky-tonk a pub as she thought it might be. Black and white photos of the logging era and nostalgic artifacts like old saw blades were tacked to knotty pine walls. A blackboard sign advertising Tito's Vodka read, Hakuna Ma Vodka - It means no memories for the rest of your day, greeted patrons. Kim smiled at the sign and approached the bar.

Nick was working with an attractive woman behind the bar, preparing for a busy night. Both wore the same black t-shirts with gold western lettering in front of a New Orleans-style house displaying the Rising Son name. The house speakers played Tom Petty, singing that the waiting was the hardest part as the band members carried amps, keyboards, drums, and guitars through the side door.

Nick smiled at Kim and gave her a wave as he finished tapping a pour on a Smuttynose IPA. She sat at the end of the bar where there were no other customers and checked her phone. Still, no text or call from Brad, even though she had called him over an hour ago. That wasn't like him. Sometimes he did that; he got so engrossed in his work that he forgot to check in. *Oh well. Time apart is always a healthy thing for us.*

"You clean up good. Perty enough to be a cowgirl," Nick smiled as he slid a menu in front of her.

"It didn't take much to improve the homeless look I was rockin. Your face isn't looking too bad, considering a horse just kicked it. How are you feeling?"

"Borrowed some makeup from her," Nick pointed to the other bartender. "Feelin okay considering. Something to drink or eat?"

"No food, thanks. I'd love a glass of your Pinot Noir."

"Comin right up."

"Chrissy, I'm taking fifteen!" Nick yelled to the other bartender as he walked back to Kim with her vino and soda water for him.

"So where's the Son?" Kim asked, taking a sip.

"Sorry, miss, the sun sets around six thirty in these parts," he said, overdoing his southern drawl.

"I meant the actual son, silly. Is there one?"

"Oh, right, that son. Yeah, well, Bill Spence, the owner, had high hopes for his boy to join him in the family business here, but it didn't quite work out that way. Young Bill lives in Boston. Performs with The Boston Ballet and is a pretty damn good dancer, from what I hear. Christine, over there is Bill's daughter. She's got it all; smart as a whip, athletic, good looking. Even though, ya know, she's not the..."

"The rising son, right? I get it. There's no song named House of the rising daughter. You might suggest he change the name of this place to Father and Daughter, a nice little song by Paul Simon."

"I'll make sure not to mention it to him," Nick said, smiling.

"Anyway, switching subjects, you and I were going to discuss how things work around here. Also, our trip out to Wildcat Mountain and Marshera tomorrow morning if that's still on. How exactly *do* things work around here in Crawford, New Hampshire? Tell me, won't you?"

"Right, it's like this;" he leaned down to her to talk at a lower volume. Here's some recent history about this place. We were limping along around here after the paper mill closed in 05. Lots of folks were out of work, and money was tight. Then 08, 09 came along. That recession that hit the whole world hit this town too. No money was coming in from the mill, and then with the recession, no tourism money was coming in either. After that, Crawford was down for the count. The planning board met day and night to try and figure out how the town could make ends meet. They started discussing bankruptcy. My father Gus was on that committee."

"Wow, that stinks," said Kim.

"Yup, it did. Local businesses started cutting back on hours and laying off workers. Some of them closed for good. Folks were trying to sell their houses and move out, but who was going to buy them? People were stressed out to the max. Then, out of nowhere, the drugs started creeping in, first with meth and then opioids. The opioid addictions went sky high. Kids and even the grown-ups were OD'ing. Businesses that were already hurting went under because someone in the family or the owner got addicted. It seemed like half the town got hooked on painkillers overnight, and it spread like wildfire. Then this giant, Swiss multinational company rescues us out of the blue. Chromel International's the name. It was a miracle."

"How did they do that?"

"The head guy was in town for some reason and liked the place. You know, quaint, little New Hampshire town with a white church and a big steeple. They had tons of cash to spend, and Crawford was a good investment even though everything was crumbling and half the residents were hooked on drugs. So, the investors took ownership of a bunch of the town's businesses. Next thing you know, those places are back open and running. Then they bought a bunch of foreclosed houses and renovated them too. They even helped pay for the new police station and a drug rehab clinic to help folks with their addictions. They only asked to let them do some logging and a little mining of some precious metals now and then."

"Hmm, I've never heard of a big, multinational company buying up a town like that. But then again, what do I know? What did your father have to say about the investors?"

"Well, Gus was all for it. He loved his sayings. Said something like don't be looking at a gift horse in the mouth when that filly's trying to bail you out."

Kim laughed, "My mother loves her clichés' too. So that's great, the town is in good shape thanks to corporate investment. What's your point, Nick? How does what your telling me to affect my mother or the two kids that were taken?"

Nick leaned closer to Kim's face, "My point is that things are good around here again. As I said, the town was run down and talking bankruptcy. These guys came in when things were at rock bottom and bailed us out. The downtown's hoppin again with new stores and stuff. Best of all, tourism is way up again. Campers, hikers, and leaf peepers are coming back. Everyone's property values have gone way up, and they're building some beautiful houses around here that rich folks are buying. People got money to come down here to The Son and have a meal and a few drinks, you know?"

"Yes, well, the whole world did emerge from the recession. But you still haven't answered my question."

"Bottom line's this. If something gets a little weird now and then, live and let live. Do you know what I mean? Turn the other cheek and keep the peace. We don't want to scare away the tourists after getting them back. Same with Chromel, the investors, or anyone else. Why scare these good people away after they did so much for us? Some girl and her brother that nobody knows go missing. Where are they? You know how them hippies are. They come, and they go. Let the cops handle it, or let them hippies worry about their own. You heard the girl talk a little. I'm sure she's fine."

The song lyrics over the house speakers resonated with irony in Kim's ear, as Nick told her the town sees no evil, and speaks no evil policy.

So, so you think you can tell, Heaven from Hell, Blue skies from pain, A smile from a veil. Wish you were here.

Kim smiled and thought her mother might fit perfectly in a town that loved to sweep anything questionable under the rug.

He ended his sermon, and there was a pause as they both looked around to see the patrons begin to fill the pub in anticipation of the band's nine o'clock start. Kim processed what Nick had just told her. It all made sense now. Detective Jacquard had been more concerned with her and Mum than with two missing kids. *Of course he did.*

The band had finished setting up, and the bar was getting busy. "Nick, I know you have to get back to work. The problem is this; you're minimizing what happened. Julie and Charlie didn't just wander off with some hippies. We saved that girl's life. We were bringing her to the hospital, which she needs, when we got knocked out by darts dipped in something. Julie got kidnapped, and we were dragged into your house to be placed on the floor like two sacks of potatoes. How do we know she and her brother aren't in grave danger? These two kids are minors, and they need someone to step up to protect them. I can't just forget about everything for the sake of real estate and commerce. I need to know that they're safe. You brought that girl back to life after being stone-cold dead. Don't you care about her at all?"

Nick stared at Kim for a moment. "It's the girl that's got you worried. So why do you care so much about her?"

"Honestly?" Kim downed the last of her Pinot. "My baby sister died in her crib, sleeping next to my bed, ten years ago this month. She was my angel, and I miss her every single day. They said it was SIDS, but I have my doubts. My father came into the room to quiet her down that night, and I think he may have killed her."

"Your father killed your baby sister?" Nick raised up at her shocking revelation.

"I have no proof, but the thing is, after her funeral, he disappeared, and we never heard from him again. That's suspicious as hell. I was awake when he came into the room that night, pretending to sleep under the covers. He was leaning over her crib, blocking my view. He was really angry she wouldn't go back to sleep. I should've protected my sister. I should've spoken up for her instead of hiding. It's bothered me every day since then. I will not lose another one to answer your question about why I care so much about Julie."

"Julie ain't your sister, Kim."

"Doesn't matter; she needs to be protected until I know she's safe. I know you can't relate, but it's how I feel. And I feel strongly about it, Nick."

Nick paused as his eyes turned from glad to sad, "Actually, I can relate. I told you my dad Gus died a few years back. The truth is, he killed himself."

"Oh my God, Nick. I'm so, so sorry."

"Thanks. But the thing is, I can't believe it. He wasn't down or nothin'. The whole thing made no sense. We were getting along, and the ranch was doing pretty good. Something suspicious happened, I have to believe. If anything was bugging Gus that much, I could tell. Hell, he was my Dad. I went to Jacquard, and he didn't do a damn thing."

"What are you saying then?"

"My father's death was a homicide, not a suicide; that's what I'm saying. I should have been there to help him but, I went and delivered a horse down in Connecticut. It bothers the hell out of me every day too. But there's nothing I can do now. Jacquard and the cops said there was no evidence of any foul play. Lazy bastards," Nick said as his eyes welled up.

Kim could see they had connected, and she slid her hand over to rest on top of his. "You never know. It's probably a stretch, but just maybe there's a connection between Julie's kidnapping and what you think happened to your dad. Assuming we're still on to go to Wildcat Mountain, I'll make you a deal. If we find Julie and

Charlie, and they seem fine, I'll drop it and leave them be. I'll go back to helping my Mum unpack and then go home. But if they're not living in those caves, I'll call a friend from college Sheila Russo. She works for the FBI, and she can investigate. Who knows? She might find a lead to your father's death. Do we have a deal?" Kim couldn't believe she was brave enough to leverage her college roommate, who she hadn't spoken to in years.

“Like I said, I'll take that C note and a half to give you a ride out to Wildcat, perty lady." Nick's eyes and mood went back to laid-back, cowboy again.

She rolled her eyes at his comment.

"Be ready to go at six AM, like we said. I'll pick you up." Nick smiled at Kim, "Y'all have nice rest of yer evening, Ma'am. "

Kim left a ten dollar tip on the bar. The place was filling up quickly as the band ran through a sound check of one of their classic rock covers, Bob Seger's Ramblin Gamblin Man.

As she exited the Son through the lobby, her eye caught a sign on the wall printed on neon orange paper for a place called *The Wildcat Off-Road Playground.* They featured ATV, dirt bike rentals, and Wildcat Falls guided tours.

"Hmm, interesting," she held up her phone and snapped a pic of the sign.

As she put her phone away, she saw a text from Brad. *Hey Babe, I need a favor. Barb wants that recipe for the cookies again. She accidentally deleted the last one. Needs by tomorrow to bake for an event. Why don't you shoot me your laptop PW and I'll grab the file and send it to her? You can change it when you get home. Luv ya, B*

"Sweet man," Kim said out loud. *Any guy that takes care of his mother the way Brad does has to be mostly good.* The problem was her company had just implemented a two-step verification process. She would have to call him when the code was sent to her phone for Brad to log in. Kim recalled Nick's shocking revelation that his father had committed suicide.

So much drama around here. With all his faults, thank goodness Brad's fairly normal.

Chapter 14
Concrete Angel

It all began in Hong Kong centuries ago. They were the Chinese Mafia, commonly known as the Triad. The 14K was a considerable gang derived from Triad. In fact, they were a gang with over ten thousand members that maintained operations on every continent.

She first joined them in Shanghai when her bosses were given outstanding references by her previous employer, a Yakuza syndicate operating in Kobe, Japan. Upon joining the 14K, she moved up the chain quickly. Recently there was an opening that she filled to head up a region in North America that needed her unique set of skills. Her reputation landed in the new country well before her plane touched down at JFK Airport.

A rising star in a male-dominated gang, she was ultra-ambitious. The word on the streets was that Lee Chen was not only intelligent, she was also lethal. Her nine-inch Tanto knife and Glock 43 were calling cards that she wasn't afraid to utilize. May God help you if she wants you hurt, more so if you are male.

Her background was kept confidential, revealed in small parts, and only when she needed to leverage it in exchange for information provided. Those that partnered with her were trusted with secrets and rewards. Those that disagreed with her philosophy were quickly replaced, one way or another. She didn't have to overcome every obstacle using violence. Pleasures of the flesh were sometimes used instead. It hardly mattered to her. Sex was just a biological function like eating. The urge was quickly satisfied, and then it was over. The act was temporary; what was received in return, was permanent.

Lei Chun was born to a dirt-poor family of rice farmers in Hunan Province, China. She was little at birth weighing only 4.4 pounds, so her mother nicknamed her Xiǎo-lěi (Little Lei). They lived in a tiny one-room Yaodong, a cave house dug into the side of a hill. Her father built the house in a makeshift manner. With meager tools and no one to help him, the result was a poorly conceived building with draconian living conditions. The hut had dirt floors, walls, and ceilings. Spiders and other insects were prevalent and Little Lei had to pick them off her body while she tried to sleep.

There was no running water, electricity, or any essential utilities. Winters in the region were freezing, and their single heat source came from a tiny stove that burned low-grade coal. With poor ventilation, the smoke would agitate their lungs and throats. The air outside was hardly an improvement. All the other houses in the valley burned the same low-grade coal pucks, creating a smog cloud that permanently hovered within the village. Their bathroom was outdoors. Not even an outhouse, it had a leaky roof and was open on all sides to access a hole in the ground to squat over. Little Lei learned to position herself carefully, or she might fall in.

Many farmers in the village grew a variety of crops like wheat, corn, soybeans, kaoliang, and of course, rice. Little Lei's father didn't have much land, nor did he possess an ox to help him dig plows. And so her parents only grew rice in the paddies that the entire family cultivated daily. Little Lei remembered eating rice until it came out of her ears.

All of the squalors she endured would have been tolerable, if not for the absence of the one key ingredient essential to make any house a home. Love. Her parents didn't believe in showing their children any gestures of adoration or affection. Little Lei would never feel loved in the house, where she grew up. The Chinese custom was to build mental toughness and prepare children to be responsible for the family's welfare through hard work in the rice paddies. Instead of feeling tough, she felt like an indentured servant. Little Lei soon realized that her life in the dirty little village with a smog cloud hanging over it would be a lonely one.

But then, one day, a miracle arrived. At four years of age, Lei had been too young to notice her mother's secret until a baby sister was placed into her arms. It was the brightest day of her dreary life when she held Ying Yue for the first time. The most beautiful thing Little Lei had ever seen was her tiny fingers and toes; so perfect! She gave her baby sister a nickname, Wánmei Yi (Perfect One), because she was perfect to her in every way.

Her mother told her now that they had two children, there could be no more due to China's strict population control laws. They were fortunate that they were allowed to have two children in their remote region when most Chinese families could only have one child. Little Lei told her mother this law didn't matter, for her baby sister was all she would ever need.

Joy turned to fear and anger when her father reacted to seeing Ying Yue for the first time. He screamed at her mother and slapped her across her bottom as if she were a donkey. "Bèndàn! Bèndàn!" (Stupid Ass), he yelled at her as she could only cover up against his blows. Little Lei had never heard these words before, but she could tell they were terrible words of anger. He stormed out and left them for several days, returning home only when he became hungry.

One day Little Lei made a fantastic discovery when she changed her baby sister's cloth diaper. She called her mother in a panic to show her. "Look at her right shoulder, and then look at my right shoulder!" She needed her mother to tell her she wasn't asleep and having a dream. When her mother looked at both sisters, the dream became a reality. They had matching birthmarks on their right shoulders in the shape of a crescent moon. Overjoyed with this rarity, she couldn't believe how much love she felt for her Wánmei Yi; her perfect one. Her perfect sister.

As time went on, Little Lei and Ying Yue played Chinese games like; cat catches the mouse and four fingers out. Her mother let her feed her sister and teach her things. Little Lei had to wash her diapers, but she didn't mind. Ying Yue was her baby too. She would protect her younger sister and teach her things and learn lessons that older sisters passed down to the younger ones when the time was right. Little Lei was more careful to take care of the few clothes she owned so they could become hand-me-downs to her sister. Finally, there was hope for the future, and it made Little Lei happy. She couldn't ever remember smiling and laughing so much. Two years had passed, and baby Ying Yue had grown so much. She was plumper and healthier than Little Lei ever was at two.

Little Lei awoke one morning in March of 1996, she came to know devastation. Ying Yue had just seen her second birthday. Her mother looked down at her and spoke as her eyes slowly opened. Still too tired to focus or comprehend, she bolted up and begged her mother to repeat what she had said, for it could not be accurate.

Her sister Ying Yue had been taken during the night to Tian, a far-away place high up in the sky. She would never return. "Death and life have predetermined appointments", her mother had quoted an ancient Chinese proverb that awful day. Neither of her parents ever spoke of her sister again. The person that Little Lei loved more than anyone on heaven and earth had died, but her parents gave no explanation for her death. How had she died? Why did she die? It was as if her perfect sister had never lived. There was nothing to remember Ying Yue by; all of her belongings and clothing were gone too. Little Lei was traumatized. Her sadness was deep, and she didn't speak for a year. Words came back eventually, but the sorrow would never cease. Sadness eventually turned to madness and she found herself capturing and torturing little frogs and mice around the village.

Lei would never forget her sister. *The sister of my dreams*, she said over and over to herself, calling out to her at night. The loss hardened her. Becoming hardened was the only way she could cope. Someone took away her childhood fantasy of growing up with Ying Yue.

She became just like her mother. Little Lei showed no emotion anymore. Throughout her grief and crying, she could feel her future begin to take shape.

A year later, she was old enough to notice her mother's swollen belly. She dared not hope for another baby sister, still mourning the loss of Ying Yue. Her parents were overjoyed when her mother gave birth to her brother Zhang Wei. Little Lei refused to hold him when her mother attempted to place him in her arms. Her father was thrilled with his great fortune to have a male child.

Zhang Wei was fed well; he needed to grow big and strong to help his aging parents. And grow he did, big and robust enough to torment his sister when her parents were working the rice paddies. As the years flew by, she wondered where her life had gone. She was now a teenager, and there stood her brother, a young man whose voice had just dropped. They had never been close. Little Lei would not accept him in place of her beautiful Ying Yue. They argued and fought constantly. One day it happened. He raped her and then apologized. She told her mother. They punished her brother with more labor, but she could tell he wasn't sorry. He was to be her father's golden goose. Little Lei felt as disposable as manure.

He continued to physically assault her as he blamed her, saying she sexually attacked him. He looked for any chance to abuse or torment her. Time and again, Zhang Wei tried to rape Lei Chun. Sometimes she fought him off, other times he succeeded. Her parents ignored her pleas. They told her that he would eventually outgrow his obsession with her.

She knew that they needed him more than her. Her only option was to run away. Lei hid food and some clothes behind her bed. Her parents had no money to speak of, but now and then, she would lift a yuan or two from them and hide it. The pig truck came to their village to make deliveries every two weeks. That, she decided, would be her passage to salvation. One day while her family worked the rice paddies, she went to the outdoor bathroom. Xiǎo-lĕi never came back. She had just turned sweet sixteen.

No longer Little Lei, she was now Lee Chen. Her journey had taken her through Japan and then back to Shanghai to join Triad and the 14K. Sometimes she would look back on her time growing up in that horrible place and compare it to where she was today; living in a Brownstone in Boston's Back Bay section, wearing two thousand dollar suits and nine hundred dollar heels. Were they all still choking on that gray smog cloud while she traveled on international first class? Her sister Ying Yue stayed in her heart, a tattoo to remember by was added to her wrist. At times after she showered, Lee Chen would look at the crescent moon on her shoulder, and Ying Yue's face would appear in her mind. Losing her baby sister had left a scar on her soul that would never heal. She didn't want it to.

***

The one-legged seagull had relocated to a pier outside the office window. With Mr. Chang excusing himself, she waited patiently at his desk and saw the bird staring at her, as if he were saying, I only have one leg, but you have no family. She stared back at the damaged gull and finally ran to the window, waving her arms, causing it to fly away.

"Please, sit down, Ms. Chen," he said, having returned.

"Thank you, Mr. Chang."

"I am glad we are done with the unpleasantness of dealing with Bradley. It was to be expected. With pain, there will come gain, we hope. Let us see what he is capable of. Tell me, how is operation Tiger progressing?"

When dealing with adversaries or those who reported to her, Lee Chen was a ruthless leader. But now, in her superior's presence, she was the reserved and dutiful subordinate. Power, intelligence, and wealth impressed and intimidated her. Mr. Chang had all three in spades.

"As my reports have indicated, Mr. Chang, our numbers continue to rise drastically in the northern towns and regions of New

Hampshire and Vermont. Operation Tiger is devouring the small regions we have focused on. My goal is to prove to you that my regions will ultimately become the most profitable. Thank you again for this opportunity, Sir."

"You are welcome, Ms. Chen. It is gratifying to see your numbers so strong. The key is that the Process is working and you are utilizing it. It has worked in other regions, and it will work in yours."

"Who invented the Process?" she asked.

"Oh, The Process is ancient. It has been utilized for centuries by other countries, Ms. Chen. We have enhanced and improved it, but the fundamentals remain the same. If you look in your history books, you will read about what the British did to the Chinese during the opium wars in the eighteen hundreds. They dumped so much opium into China that fifteen to twenty million Chinese citizens were addicts. The drug was outlawed and the emperor destroyed warehouses where it was stored. In response, the British bombarded Canton, until they surrendered and agreed to reparations for the opium that was lost. They also took Hong Kong under British rule as part of the negotiation. So I suppose the Chinese learned the Process from the British. In a small way it is payback to the western world for past misdeeds."

"Fascinating, Mr. Chang. I was not aware of the Opium Wars."

"Yes, and another thing the British taught us was there is no better strategy to increase customer loyalty than addicting them to your products. Just ask the legal companies that make cigarettes and alcohol."

"I agree, Mr. Chang."

"Now, are your people performing to your desires, Ms. Chen?"

"Yes, they are, Mr. Chang. One of my mules, Topaz, has been very productive. He is exceeding his goals and projections. I would like to expand his territory unless you have an objection, Sir."

"I have no objections. It is your decision, Ms. Chen. Before we move on to the main topic of concern, please provide me with a summary of the Luscious Johnson situation."

"He gambled and lost the entire monthly take for his region. I employed the Yubitsume on him. He won't make that mistake again. In addition, he has two weeks to repay the debt, along with a healthy fine added on top. I am confident that this problem has been resolved."

“I have the utmost confidence in you, Ms. Chen. Employ whatever motivational methods that you see fit."

"Now, as for the other reason I wanted to meet with you, Ms. Chen. I have an important project in your area that needs your skill set. This project is getting close to completion; however, it is in danger of not hitting the required deadline. If we miss that deadline, it will cost us a significant amount of money."

"May I ask the nature of this project, Mr. Chang?"

"As you know, we have strategic relationships from time to time. Legal companies employ us to help them do their dirty work. We currently have a project where we are aligned with a multinational company. The project will require you to see it through to on-time delivery, which is arriving soon."

"This sounds exciting, Mr. Chang. May I ask the name of the company involved?"

"The company we are aligned with is a Swiss company named Chromwell International. They are mining a rare mineral in your region. The project has been underway for a year but has encountered several delays. Upon completion, the payday to both companies is worth fifty billion dollars. I cannot discuss any further details. Instead, I will ask that you travel north of a town you may have heard of, Crawford, New Hampshire. You will then contact the Chromwell Project Engineer, Dr. Thomas Foulke. He will meet with you when you are on-site and fill you in on the necessary details. Please drive to that location within the next twenty-four hours, Ms. Chen. You will understand everything once you have met with Mr. Foulke. And lastly, let me also add that you will be lavishly rewarded when you make sure the project ships on time."

She sprang up to extend her hand. "It is an honor that you have selected me for such an important mission, Mr. Chang. I will not let you down," she gripped his hand tightly as they shook.

"You never do, Ms. Chen. This is why I have selected you."

A spring was in her step as she walked through the restaurant. Her high heels clicked louder on the hardwood floor than when she entered earlier.

Mr. Chang had just handed her a golden opportunity to bring her to the next level. The dirty little village that she had run away from was fading in her memory.

That was just fine with her.

Paul August-98

Chapter 15
Mother Nature's Son

The limbs at the top of the trees had joined together to create an opaque canopy that blocked out the sun. It was seven thirty AM, but looked like midnight.

Nick flicked on the headlamp and yelled out over the roar of the Quad to Kim, "Can't see, shit! Hold on!"

He gunned it to get them to their destination sooner. Nick had a long list of to-do's back at the ranch weighing on his mind. Clean the tack, train Cracker, hoe the stalls, deliver grain and change the tractor oil. The list was endless. Searching for a missing girl he hardly knew wasn't a priority, but he had promised Kim, and he would fulfill that promise. Even though she would pay for the excursion, he'd thought about blowing her off. But then he remembered that Gus had stressed to him never to break promises. "A promise is like a Mustang; neither should ever be broken."

"Do you know where you're going?" Kim shouted over the noise.

"Pretty much," he shouted back to her.

"We should've taken a map, just in case!"

"Marshera ain't on a map!"

He knew they were getting close when the trees thinned out, allowing him to see without the headlamp. The trail became steeper, and Nick cranked the throttle hard, forcing them back into their seats as the machine howled to answer his call. Clearance became tight; branches whipped against their legs as they flew by. Kim pulled her knees in behind Nick's to shield her bare legs. *What was I thinking?*

The trail continued on a steep grade as they shot upwards. Nick downshifted, causing the engine to rev loudly. They dropped into a gully and came out airborne. Kim screamed and grabbed him firmly. They landed with a bounce and emerged into an opening with the brightness of a morning sun. He downshifted again and pulled into a small clearing to park. His curly blonde hair sprang back into place as he yanked off his helmet. "That's it for this thing."

Kim dismounted and did a few stretches to work out the kinks from their harrowing ride. She took off her helmet and looked up at the wall of trees and mountainside that shot straight up to the sky. With her eyes closed, her lungs expanded to take in a deep breath, hold it and then release it slowly. She repeated the deep breathing two more times to feel her anxiety return to a normal level.

"Trailhead's over there," Nick pointed at the opening in the trees. "That'll take us to the top of Wildcat Mountain. Wildcat Falls and the hippy colony's up there too."

"There's no sign on the trail. How do we know that goes up to where Julie is?"

"It’s the one; let’s just get going."

"How far do we have to walk?" Kim bent over to tie her sneakers tight. She had worn shorts, sneakers, a sky blue t-shirt, and her red University of Maryland Terrapins baseball cap.

"Five or six miles uphill to the top," Nick said as he clipped the harness on his orange backpack and placed his Stetson hat on his head. He watched Kim tying her sneakers.

"Close to ready?"

"You said the mountain is four thousand feet up. That's less than a mile. Why are we hiking five or six miles?

"The trail doesn't go straight up. It zig-zags and meanders side to side, like all trails do."

"I've never hiked up a mountain before. I've done flat trails mostly back in Maryland."

"First mountain hike? Gonna be a workout, so get ready to sweat." Nick smiled at her from the side of his mouth. "Let's mosey; I got a lot of stuff to do back at the ranch."

"Last question; what time will we be back?" Kim asked. “I told Mum I'd help her finish unpacking."

"Five, six hours to the summit. A lot faster comin' down, of course."

"Oh geez, I better call her and let her know I'm going to be a while." Kim pulled her phone out as she followed him up the trail.

"Gonna be the same as by the rapids”, said Nick. “No signal cause we're in the boonies."

The hike began with difficulty. The trail was steep and stayed that way, with rocks and fallen trees to navigate over and around. New to mountain hiking, Kim did well but began to labor and asked to stop for a water break. Luckily, Nick brought two large bottles in his pack.

He looked over at her to see the drips of sweat running down the sides of her cheeks.

"How’re you holdin’ up? "

"I'm fine. You don't have to ask me that question every time we stop."

"I don't have to carry you back down the hill, but I will if you can’t walk, darlin."

"Not to worry, and I'm not your darling," Kim said.

He smiled at her, and they continued their ascent up the trail.

"Who owns all this property anyway?" she asked.

"You mean the White Mountains?

"Yes, all this forest and trees and mountains,"

"National Forest Service for the most part. Gus told me a few of the mountains are privately owned, though. Course, the Abenaki that lives here claim this whole area is their sacred land. Same with Wildcat and that Marshera place too."

"Detective Jacquard mentioned the Native Americans that live here when I met with him."

"Yup, Wildcat Falls, the mountain, the caves; every place their ancestors lived is still considered their sacred land if you ask them. This area was all inhabited by them till we drove 'em out. The English and French colonists made them all sick. Sure, you heard about colonists having diseases like smallpox and measles; they gave 'em to the Indians, but they had no immunity, so most died off. The ones that didn't moved north. Supposedly, a whole village of Abenaki lived in those hippy caves to hide from the colonists. They were the ones that named the place Marshera."

Kim snickered, "A lot of information from someone who told me they didn't know what Marshera was."

Nicked looked back at Kim. "Live and let live. It's how things work around here."

"Uh huh," replied Kim.

They quickened their pace, pushing up the winding path toward the summit. The trail seemed to disappear, and Kim noticed stacks of flat rocks that rose like little towers.

"What are those piles of rocks for?" Kim asked.

“They’re called cairns; trail markers that lead you to your destination.” Nick said.

"I've tripped over rocks like six times already," Kim said.

"Yep, watch your footing. You turn an ankle, and we have to abort the mission.”

"Understood, captain," Kim said.

The wet spot on the back of Kim’s t-shirt continued to grow as she fought to overcome the opposing forces of gravity, terrain, and heat.

The monotony allowed her mind to wander. One of her coping strategies after her sister died was telling herself that Grace was still alive in some metaphysical form. Perhaps she was in a holding pattern, suspended in the ethers. Was it the Hindus who believed in reincarnation? Saving Julie and holding her in her arms had brought back the same maternal feelings she'd had for Grace all those years ago. Perhaps her sister had been summoned from the ethers and returned to her as Julie. Kim had to remember her therapy and let her sister go. She had to live in reality. Julie was a different person. Still, Kim couldn't ignore the irony. Why had she been the one that was randomly selected to be in the right place at the right time to dive into the river and save Julie? Why was the heartbreak of losing her happening again? Was this some sick conspiracy? Kim decided that her mind operated in strange ways. *Didn't everyone's*?

A return to the present happened when she collided with Nick's backpack. He had stopped to survey the creek that wove its way across the trail and then down the mountain. It was shallow, with a strong current from the massive storm the day before. Water gurgled over the rocks as they looked for a way to cross. Nick spotted several boulders spaced close enough to be used as stepping stones to cross the span. The tricky part would be the last fifteen feet, where a fallen log became a makeshift bridge to dry land.

"How's your balance feeling these days?" Nick asked.

"No problem; lead the way," said Kim.

"I got these telescopic hiking poles in my backpack if you want 'em."

"Just go," she said with a hint of nervousness. "I'll follow you."

Nick would have bounded across the rocks and then walked heel to toe with arms stretched out to cross the log. But with Kim behind him, he slowly took one careful step at a time, boulder to boulder, to show her the way. They navigated across the rocks without a problem. Nick stopped just before the log bridge. Kim looked at the long length and paused. "Maybe I'll take you up on those poles after all."

"Sure thing," he said, whipping off his pack to retrieve them. "Why don't you go first, and I'll follow?" Nick said.

"No, I'll be nervous with you behind me. You go, and I'll follow," Kim said.

"See you on the other side. You got this."

Nick turned to the log and extended his arms to walk across without incident. Standing on the other side, he turned and waited for her.

The poles were helpful. Kim felt confident as she made her way down the log. She planted the poles in the shallow water one after the other until stopping halfway across to look at a long black weed that bent and flowed down the creek. Hypnotized, she watched it wrap around her upstream pole. Attempting to move on, Kim lifted it out of the water to see the reed was really a black water snake. It raised its head to look at her as it slithered up the pole.

"Snake! Oh my God!" Kim shrieked, violently shaking the pole with the snake still curled around it. The reptile dropped into the creek as she lost her balance and plunged her right foot into the flowing water on the downstream side of the log. Things got worse from there. The six-foot-long water snake traveled under the log and wrapped itself around Kim's leg. She lost it, "Jesus Christ, It's attacking me!" She frantically tried to stab the snake with her pole.

Nick was already running across the creek, splashing his way to her. The water gushed around his legs as he reached down to grab the snake by the head to uncoil it. He pulled it out of the creek and heaved it through the air to watch it splash downstream and be carried away by the current.

Kim now had both feet in the frigid water and was shaking. Nick placed his hands on her shoulders, "It's alright. The snake's long gone. Come on, now." He took Kim's hand and waded through the water to dry land. Nick sat her down and gently hugged her. "It's okay now." He gently patted her back as she recovered. "It's just a water snake, and it's gone now. They don't bite. It's fine; relax and breathe."

Nick continued to comfort Kim. She appreciated his caring. One deep breath after another was inhaled and then exhaled as she pulled herself together and wiped her eyes. Then she peeled off her wet sneakers.

"Well, those white sneakers of yours were getting dirty anyway. They needed a good bath." Nick looked up at her and gave his boyish grin, trying for a comforting laugh.

"Be quiet," she said, wringing the water from her socks.

"Now that's better," Nick said.

His boots and her sneakers sat next to each other, drying off in the sun. Kim felt weird about being so frightened and then crying in front of someone she had just met yesterday.

"Dang it, I declare, I have never heard a human scream that loud before 'cause they seen a whip. You got some lungs, girl; I'll give you that."

Kim laughed, "By whip, you mean snake?"

"You know it."

"I hate those things. It wrapped itself around my leg! Gross!"

"You know what my dad used to say about snakes?" asked Nick.

"What's that?"

"Even snakes is scared of snakes."

"Amen," said Kim.

"Okay, we best be moving if we're gonna make it there in a respectable time," said Nick.

He waded into the creek and retrieved the poles before they put their boots and sneakers back on and hiked up the trail to the woods. They squeaked and oozed out water as they continued toward their destination. The path took them into more dense forest for some time until they reached a clearing of a green grass field.

They stopped for a quick water break, and Kim turned to see a ravine with a panoramic view of a mountain range. "What's this place?" Kim asked.

"White Mountain Presidential Range," said Nick. It was a crystal clear fall day, and the thirteen mountains, each one named for a president, were flush with fall colors against a purple backdrop.

"Purple mountain majesty," Kim stared in awe at the natural beauty.

"Yes, Ma'am. Okay, let's keep on. Unless you wanna turn back?"

"What? If that snake didn't stop me, then nothing will," said Kim.

"How much further?" she was growing tired.

"Not too much. We're getting there," Nick said.

It was quiet as they plunged back into thick trees again. Kim felt a bad vibe of fear wash over her as she followed Nick down the trail. She decided to talk to him to alleviate her anxiety. "Sorry again about your father and how he died. What about sisters, brothers, cousins?"

"Nope, small family. Mom's been gone for years, too; dang, cancer got her. Gus was all I had until he went and offed himself. Now it's just Walt and Cracker."

"You said last night you don't know why your dad took his life? Darn it, I shouldn't have brought that up. I'm sorry."

"It's fine. As I said, I'm still trying to figure it out myself. Things were going great at the ranch, and we were getting along just fine. We used to fight a lot, but that stopped a few years ago after I got home from serving in the military," Nick said.

"You're a veteran too? I'm learning a lot about you today."

"Guess you are."

"And thank you for your service to the country," Kim said.

"You're welcome," said Nick.

"Did you serve four years in the Army? Where were you stationed?"

"Marine Corps. Fallujah. Only served two years, though. Got wounded, and they shipped me home. I almost died, but twelve operations later, I'm still here. They gave me a medal or two. Gus was all proud of his boy and stuff. When your kid gets close to dying, you accept him for who he is."

"So you're better now? You're healthy?"

"Yep, we're fine." Nick had stopped. He stood still and listened to the forest.

"What is it?" she asked.

He whispered, "I don't know; I heard something. Could be an animal. It's up ahead."

Kim's senses heightened as she listened. She thought of the Leo DiCaprio movie, The Revenant, and shuddered. "Is it a Grizzly Bear?"

"No Grizzlies in these parts. That's a western bear. It might be a Black. Let's see."

Kim looked up at orange leaves rustling from a breeze that broke the silence. Then it became quiet again. She cupped her palm to her ear and scanned. "I don't hear a thing."

They walked a few more steps and stopped again. Nick listened for the noises, waiting for the animal to appear.

He whispered again, "There's something up there behind those bushes."

Kim's anxiety peaked as she whispered, "How did you get wounded?"

"Sniper," he said, "Shhhh."

He took two more slow steps and then froze in place. The serenity of the fall colors contrasted with her fear. She could feel every nerve in her body flexing.

She turned to her left and saw it in the middle of the forest. "My God, that red oak over there, it's huge. Has to be over three hundred years old." She felt her pulse ratchet down and her adrenaline subside. Nature and trees calmed her. Kim stood admiring it and whispered again,

"The Quercus robur; Think of the history it's seen. It was there before they signed the Declaration of Independence or fought the Civil War. He's like a proud General, surrounded by the smaller trees, his privates. Just standing guard right there, watching the decades go by. Sorry, I was a Botany major, so old trees fascinate me."

"He?" Nick said, still focused ahead.

"Sure, oaks are monoecious. They're both male and female simultaneously."

"Just heard it again," he said.

"Heard what?"

"Sounded like a snort."

And then it happened.

The wild boar burst out from behind the bush like a cannonball charging them at full speed. Nick grew up around animals, but for some reason, he froze. Kim screamed, shocking him back to reality. He turned to her and yelled, "Climb a tree!"

Nick whipped his head back, but it was too late. The beast was upon him. He dove, but the animal slammed into his shin, spinning him around in mid-air like a helicopter. His head bounced off the ground, leaving him dazed as the pig struggled to recover its balance. It looked up to see Kim running through the woods at full speed and chased her instead, snorting and pounding the ground in pursuit. For the first time, Kim was in a real-life fight-or-flight situation. Adrenaline, fully engaged, she flew across the woods, urgently searching for escape options. The vicious attacker barreled through the brush with its stout legs pounding the ground as it closed in on her. Kim could hear snorts and feel its breath on the back of her legs. "No, no, no, somebody, please!" she knew she was about to become its prey.

Nick's words came back to her, "Climb a tree."

And there he was, her new best friend, the General. A long limb extended toward her as if holding out a helping hand. It wouldn't be easy; she would have to jump high enough and catch it with both hands to thwart her attacker. The boar's snout hit the back of her heel just as she lunged with outstretched arms. Flying through the air, she caught the branch as her legs dangled and swung beneath her. The bark scraped the flesh off her palms, causing them to bleed, but she held on tight. Kim pulled her dangling legs up to wrap them around the branch, out of her attacker's reach. The pig snorted and squealed in frustration below her. She shimmied upside down across the branch towards the General's trunk, pulling herself onto an adjoining limb that made for a comfortable perch. Kim righted herself and let out a long sigh.

With bloody hands and scratched arms, Kim looked down at the brown, furry beast below to feel victorious. He wasn't at all attractive; fat belly, pointy ears and a long snout that foraged away on carpenter ants from a rotted log. She hoped never to see the nasty thing ever again.

"You out there?" Kim yelled out to Nick.

"Yeah, I'm out here," Nick yelled, sitting in a nearby pine, looking down at his throbbing ankle where the pig nailed him. "You alright?"

"Yup! Sitting on the General," Kim said.

"General, who?" Nick yelled back.

"The three-hundred-year-old oak tree I spotted earlier," Kim said. "He saved my life from whatever this nasty thing is. He's right underneath me, by the way!"

"That thing is a feral pig," said Nick. "They're like a wild boar and pretty common around here. The pig population's been a problem for the last few years. Any injuries?"

"Few scrapes, cuts, and frayed nerves, otherwise okay. What about yourself?"

"He clipped my ankle pretty good, and it's swellin' up. Otherwise, I'm okay."

Kim looked down again to see the animal moving around beneath her. The hair on his head was black and swept up like a pompadour. "How long do we have to stay up in these trees until Elvis leaves? Yes, I've decided he's a male. No lady would behave the way this pig does."

Nick laughed and yelled back, "So you named him, huh? No idea how long; you let me know when he leaves. He was probably threatened by us."

Nick balanced himself on the branch, pulled up his pant leg to view his ankle, and then rubbed the swelling again. *What was it Gus used to say? No good deed goes unpunished.*

Kim fell fast asleep for a while until her eyes popped open. She shielded them as afternoon sunbeams pierced their way through autumn leaves. A voice came from nearby,

"Hello? Are you asleep over there?" Nick called to her.

Kim tried to speak, clearing her throat, "Yes! I'm here. I must have dozed off." She looked down below to see the pig was gone.

"I think we can head out now," she shouted. "Elvis has left the building!"

Back on track, they hiked down the dimly lit trail while keeping a keen eye open for their attacker. Kim noticed Nick's limp from his swollen ankle. The path was headed toward a bright light up ahead which meant another clearing. *It can't be much further*, she thought.

"How's your ankle feeling?" Kim asked.

"Been better, I guess."

"Don't all cowboys carry six-shooters?" she asked.

"Some do, some don't. Why?"

"Well, in case our nasty little friend tries to attack us again."

"Think he's wandered off for now. I ain't worried about him."

"He surprised us before. He could again."

"Don't usually carry a hog's leg when I'm hiking. Live and let live." said Nick.

"I feel the same way, except when wild pigs are chasing me."

Her eyes adjusted as they emerged from the woods into the clearing. A new grouping of mountain peaks was visible off in the distance. She turned her head in the opposite direction, and her jaw dropped. A flume of white water shot out of the side of a neighboring mountain. It plunged down a hundred-foot waterfall into a pond.

"What is that?" Kim asked.

Nick paused to stare while sheltering his eyes. "Damn, if that ain't Wildcat Falls."

She turned to face him, blocking his view, "You said Wildcat Falls flows through the Marshera Caves. Don't tell me that we…."

"Hiked up the wrong mountain? Sure as hell's looking that way."

"What mountain is this one we're standing on? The one we just hiked six miles up?"

Nick scanned the region. "Gotta be Carter. It's the closest one to Wildcat. They call it The Carter Dome."

"If the Marshera Caves are over there by Wildcat Falls, how do we get from this mountain over to that mountain?"

"Not too damn easily."

She clenched her hands into fists in frustration as she stared at the Majesty of Wildcat Falls, gushing white foam out of the cavity in the mountainside.

Is he a lousy trail guide, or have I been tricked?

"That pond the waterfall drops into flows southwards and becomes the rapids where you dove in to save that girl," Nick said.

Kim stood and stared at the view in disbelief.

Nick had taken a seat on a nearby rock where his backpack and boot were off. He massaged his swollen ankle with both hands.

She walked over to him, casting a shadow, and stood with folded arms.

"You fit to be tied or what?" Nick said.

"What do you think?" Kim said.

"I think we hiked up the wrong damn mountain," Nick rubbed his ankle. "This ankle's a blowout; gonna need some ice to stop the swelling."

Kim remained standing with her arms crossed.

"You haven't answered my question, Nick. How do we get over to Wildcat? How do we get to those caves they call Marshera?"

Nick had opened a small medical kit and began wrapping an ace bandage around his ankle. He looked up at her, squinting, "We don't."

"Why?"

"Because we'd have to hike down this mountain and then up that mountain to get there. The Marshera caves are right near the top, where the falls are. Can't make it; my ankle's shit."

"Are you telling me we hiked up this huge mountain, fighting off snakes and wild pigs in the hot sun for nothing?"

"Hey, every cowboy screws up now and then. Today's my turn," Nick said as he applied the clips to hold the wrap in place. "Somebody ought to put a damn sign on that trailhead so folks know if they're hiking up to Wildcat or Carter. We'll have to make another go at it in a day or two. Right now, I gotta bum ankle here, so we best light a shuck and head back down. I know where the right trail is now. I just messed up today."

Kim was afraid to challenge people. She avoided confrontation like the plague. But she was on a mission to find Julie. "Be straight with me, Nick; you knew this was the wrong mountain. You said you know this area like the back of your hand. We wasted the better part of a day because you're turning the other cheek like you said people tend to do in this town."

He began putting his boot back on. "Not true, what you're saying. I know all the trails that go through these woods here. As far as mountain trails and where they go, that's a different story. I got better things to do than hike up a 4K and waste everyone's time. Like I said, we can take another run at it later in the week." He stood up and put his foot on the rock to tie his boot.

"Did I see binoculars in that backpack of yours earlier?" Kim asked.

"Yeah, you did, but I gotta be getting back," Nick said.

Kim continued to stare at him with folded arms.

“Yeah, whatever; the binos are right here somewhere," Nick dug through the backpack to pull out a pair of large camouflaged binoculars. Kim reached out her hand, and Nick pulled them back. "Five minutes, little lady. My ankle's swellin' up something bad."

"Five minutes it is,” Kim said.

"Hey, watch your step over there and put the strap around your neck!" Nick shouted. Those are Steiner's; they cost a grand!"

Kim removed the lens covers and held the powerful binoculars up to her eyes. It took a few minutes of trial and error to get them in the right direction until the blurry image came into focus. The gushing water spewed from the side of the mountain like it was spitting out of its mouth.

"Where are you, Miss Julie?" Kim turned the lens in both directions and squinted into the eyepiece. There were no signs of life. There did, however, appear to be a small vegetable garden on a flat area by the side of the mountain. Lettuce, cucumber, tomatoes, and peppers were growing. It was a homemade garden. She scanned around the garden and saw something that puzzled her. Zooming out, a trail of white smoke rose up from the mountain's backside.

"There's a homemade vegetable garden planted on a ledge off the side of the mountain which tells me that the caves are not abandoned. Oh, and smoke or something is coming from the back of Wildcat Mountain," she said, handing him the binoculars.

"Smoke? Huh, no idea about that. Maybe some loggin. Never know round these parts." Nick said. "Sounds like our problems are solved. If they're gardening and growing their own food, they gotta be fine. Guess we don't gotta come back after all."

"What? The problem isn't solved, Nick. I didn't see Julie or her brother. Remember what Julie said at your place? She said to save us, save Marshera. Something or someone has to be causing them harm. We need to see if they need our help."

"Well, it ain't gonna be today. I gotta hobble down this here hill."

"How about tomorrow morning at six AM? This time the right mountain?" Kim asked.

"No can do. Have to make the grain deliveries I was supposed to be makin' today. Plus, I need to train Cracker. Look, give me a few days. You can help your Ma with her moving in. I'll get caught up, and maybe Thursday, we'll get you out to Wildcat. The thing is, I need to learn about how to get inside that hippy colony place so you can check up on that girl and her brother. Just letting ya know. We might get there and still not see a damn thing."

"I'll take that chance. Thursday will have to do." Kim said. "Oh, and no hundred and fifty bucks until I see Marshera up close and personal. I'll have some time to research between now and then. Research is kind of my thing anyway," said Kim.

"It's a deal. Let's get crackin'. I need to ice this thing down soon as I get to the ranch."

As they descended the trail, Kim wasn't sure what to think about Nick.

Is he a friend or a frenemy? What is he hiding?

There was something he wasn't telling her. She was sure there was a truth hiding behind that cowboy façade.

The sun warmed their backs, and the resistance was more effortless than hiking up. "Hey, look at the bright side; you hiked your first 4K today," Nick gave her his boyish grin again.

"Would've all been worth it if we spotted those kids," Kim said.

"Not to mention you, tanglin' with a black snake and a wild pig!”

Kim rolled her eyes, "Yeah, what a blast. I can't wait to do it again."

Chapter 16
Baby Come Back

"Well, how are you doing today, Loosh?" It's what he'd called his client and friend Luscious Johnson from the first time they met a year ago. "You can't be dry; it hasn't been long enough."

"Shit, I can't predict when we gonna get a spike and get wiped out, Topaz, my man. All I know is I need products. When you gonna visit me again, brother?"

"I am afraid you're going to have to hold tight till next week. It's been real busy, and tomorrow I'm headed to see some people in Vermont. Then I head home. Sit tight, my good friend," Topaz said.

"Where you going in Vermont, man? My cousin lives in Rutland."

"I am going pretty far north of there. Burlington area. Most likely, I will get down to you by next Tuesday. Will you be alright until then?"

"I'll make do, Topaz. Hey, you talk to the boss lady recently?"

"No, I have not. Why, what up?"

"Nothin', man. Just wondering. See you when you get here, brother. Oh yeah, if you talk, don't tell her we don't use the numbers for ID."

"Not a word, Luscious, my good man. See you soon."

Topaz's phone buzzed several times during his call. He could tell she was in one of her aggressive moods and needed to blow off steam. He tried not to get emotional himself. Best to just let her get all that excitement or angst out of her system. It was a shame they couldn't be together. When they were, he would calm her with his touch. A nice massage soothed the lioness. Then she would become sexual, bordering on a nymphomaniac. When they were together, they dropped all pretension and let their animal passions emerge. She became Lee, and he, Tope. And they were *always* hot for each other.

Company policy dictated they use their assigned three-digit identification numbers when communicating. It was policy and mandatory. He thought it silly from the start, but this was the way it worked, from the lowest levels to the highest ranks of seniority.

Topaz was 118, and Lee Chen was 213.

"Hello, my lovely, 213. How are you doing, my dear?" Topaz said.

"I've been calling you and calling you 118. Where are you?"

“I am in the western part of Massachusetts. I was talking to 122. He's low and needs some product," Topaz said.

"What else did he say?" Lee Chen asked.

"Nothing special; why, what's up between you two?"

"Nothing's up. I'll tell you later. Actually, I won't; it’s better that way. You know, you can call me now and then... It wouldn't kill you, would it?"

"I travel in remote areas, and when I do, there are times when a cell signal is non-existent. We're talking now, so what do you need?"

"What I need is you! I was hoping you could be in town so I could tell you in person that I've been selected to manage a big project for the company. I can't tell you the location, but this will be an amazing opportunity to get promoted. Management has trusted me to get this project to the finish line on time. They believe in me, which is great."

"That's awesome. Way to go."

"So can you come to me today or, worst case, tomorrow? I'm pumped up, and I've been craving your body. I'll make it worth your while, big guy."

There was a pause as he looked at the phone's calendar. "You're still in Boston, right? I can't get to you today, and tomorrow will also be tough. I still have some stops to make. Let me think about options. Yes, I am missing your body as well."

"I'm headed for my new assignment tomorrow. I won't be available for who knows how long until the project is completed. Can we meet as I drive to the location? I mentioned you in a favorable light a few times to Mr. 524. This project could benefit both of us in the long run."

He decided that he had to make this happen. "Very well. Why don't we meet tomorrow at the same motel off the highway that we met last time? Say four PM?"

"Okay, I will see you then!" She sounded as giddy as a schoolgirl.

He found the situation humorous. Lee Chen was a powerful woman in the organization, yet she couldn't wait to see her lover to tell him the exciting news. She treated him like he was her high school boyfriend. Then he remembered her saying she never attended high school.

They would rent the same little motel room and tear each other's clothes off to take full advantage of their bodies in their limited time. Topaz wasn't sure if screwing the boss was such a brilliant idea, but he figured it couldn't hurt as long as the romance stayed intact. She told him that he was exclusive and the only one in her life. He had to think about the best reply before he echoed her sentiments.

When they arrived, he would remember she was the boss, but he was in complete control when they were together and naked. She liked that. There wasn't anything sexually she would say no to. He liked that.

Did they love each other? He kept telling himself no; however, sexual passion often turns into love. As the song says, you fool around and fall in love.

Sex can be an addiction, just like the narcotics they peddled.

Chapter 17
Smuggler's Blues

The earthy smell of old books and periodicals permeated the air, taking Kim back to all the hours she spent in libraries like this one. Scholastically talented, she ate up school research projects. They were completed on time using a combination of online resources, academic articles, and good old books from her hometown library.

The librarian gave Kim a welcoming smile as she entered. With only six people in the facility, it appeared more substantial than it was. A kiosk up front featured Pulitzer Prize-winning novels, both old and new. Sadly, a larger cabinet of DVDs stood next to them. There were plenty of choices for books, but only a few DVDs were left on the shelves. She thought it sinful to have videos of Police Academy 7 within inches of Gone With The Wind, To Kill A Mockingbird, and The Goldfinch. The books sat untouched on a gray metal shelf, patiently waiting for new readers to take in their captivating stories.

"Do you keep some type of town records here?" Kim asked the librarian, who appeared to be atypical as librarians go. In her early thirties, the woman had an athletic build with long blonde hair, a tight-fitting blouse, and extra-long nails. She moved around the desk area, quickly organizing a pile of returned books.

"Whatcha looking for, hon?" she spoke sharply.

"Things like newspapers or any general history about the town during the 2008 to 2009 time frame."

"That's over ten years old. Things like newspapers, town records, and public disclosures would all be scanned on microfilm reels. You can read them on the Microfiche Machine down the back. The papers and documents are on the reels sorted by year. You'll see them. Help yourself, hon. Have you ever used Microfiche before?"

"Yes, I have," said Kim. "It's been a while, but I can figure it out. Is there a computer with internet access as well?"

"There's two back there near the Microfiche. One gets the internet, but it's pretty slow."

"Thank you," Kim smiled awkwardly at her and headed towards the back. As she approached the rear section of the library, she could see it was well-lit, aided by three large windows with a magnificent view of an empty parking lot. A small CRT monitor sat on a beige computer box, indicating it was old. *This might be a frustrating experience*. She was accustomed to the computers in the lab where she worked. They screamed with processing speed and stayed connected to the internet at the fastest data rates possible.

The Microfiche Machine was covered with a clear plastic hood and looked like it hadn't been used in quite some time. Kim decided to start with newspaper and town records from 08 and 09. She lifted the hood off the unsophisticated yet reliable machine to do what she did best; get to work.

She fed the first microfilm spool from 2009 into the viewfinder. It was the year Nick had said the town almost became insolvent and was rescued by mysterious investors from a Swiss Company. Research was right in Kim's wheelhouse. As a Clinical Laboratory Technician, she knew how to search and analyze data to identify notable exceptions. Her research goal was always to drill down deep and extract the true story.

The first news article with information about the town's financial woes came from the Crawford Gazette. The piece confirmed most of Nick's facts at the bar. The region had been hit hard by economic woes. Crawford had two primary sources of revenue, the Berlin Paper Mill, located ten miles northwest of town, and the thousands of tourists that frequented their quintessential New

England Village all year round. Streets were lined with trendy boutiques, unique gift shops, and local restaurants offering all types of local cuisine, like venison stew, fried lake bass, and chocolate mice. The businesses bustled with tourists that lined up to spend their hard-earned money with them. With natural attractions and a location in the heart of New Hampshire's picturesque White Mountain Range, hikers, campers, and skiers from all parts of the country stopped by no matter what season it was. Numerous other wilderness and adventure businesses like zip lining and alpine slides also flourished and grew annually.

Then 2009 happened. It was the year the economy hit rock bottom with a thud.

Crawford's two main sources of tax revenue dried up overnight. It started with financial institutions on Wall Street that oversold subprime mortgages and became exposed, leaving them with trillions of dollars in bad debt. The economy tanked, causing layoffs and unemployment. Over five million people across America became unemployed, and the stock market dropped fifty-four percent. Even people who held onto their jobs stayed home, fearing they might be next. The birth of staycation was born, which meant a massive drop in tax revenue from businesses that were no longer visited. The decimation of tourist-driven income was the first shot to hit Crawford in the chin.

The closing of the Berlin Paper Mill was the second blow to Crawford, putting the town on the ropes and headed for a knockdown. Like other mature paper mills in rural locations, the Mill had been on the brink of declaring bankruptcy for years. Rumors frequently arose about a buyout from a larger mill with an investment to upgrade the plant's machinery. The region would become excited, only to have the rumors fizzle out. In the end, a buyout never occurred, and the stories about the plant closing proved to be the only ones that came true. The shuttered doors meant two hundred fifty people lost their jobs. With so many residents unemployed, local spending in Crawford dropped dramatically. Two knockout punches had nailed Crawford. The town was officially on the ropes.

Kim twisted in her seat and fidgeted with her hair reading about a town in freefall. It was the same town where her mother had just relocated.

When it rains, it pours. Adding salt to the wound, drug addictions and overdoses skyrocketed overnight. Kim found an article in a newspaper, The Manchester Leader, that detailed a report about the spread of opioids in rural towns. According to the paper, Crawford was one of the towns most affected by the spread of deadly narcotics. The police tried to investigate the source of the opioid influx. People bought illegal painkillers by the bucket load, but detectives couldn't find the dealer. The drugs just seemed to appear. Kim felt waves of anxiety as she read the newspaper article. Crawford fought the opioid crisis, but the saving bell never rang. Overdoses and addictions infiltrated the town like a silent disease. Foreclosures skyrocketed on personal property and businesses too. Their once bustling streets turned into a ghost town. Awash in red ink, it became necessary to lay off many police, firefighters, and EMT's furthering the town's erosion.

The Crawford town council met with lawyers to discuss the means to declare insolvency. It was their only option to maintain essential services. "Hell, if Detroit and Michigan can declare bankruptcy, then so can Crawford!" Nick's father was quoted by the paper yelling at one of the members opposed to the move. The vote split down the middle; the final decision was still undecided.

One day, an unlikely fortune fell upon their fair town. White knights driving a black Chevy Suburban pulled up in front of the Town Hall. Representatives from a Swiss international conglomerate named Chromwell International were looking for an investment. Saying all the right things about the potential upside they saw in their lovely little hamlet, the deal came together quickly. How could the Crawford council say no? The town was facing the final, mandatory eight count. And just like that, businesses began getting bailed out with loans that no other bank would lend. Many of the loans were from a Swiss offshore bank. All the investors asked in return was to conduct some limited mining operations in the region for rare industrial metals if their geologists found them. No one seemed to care as long as the stores reopened. One main focus for the investors was a key business; the bank. It reopened with all new tellers, a drive-through lane, and ATMs. The shuttered storefronts slowly reopened too. Their timing had been perfect. The recession began to lift as the stores restarted, and tourists gradually returned. They returned with a vengeance. The investor's final touch was to pay for renovating a deserted building, turning it into a drug treatment center. Crawford was mysteriously saved by the bell.

As Kim read through several town and regional newspapers, she couldn't help feeling that the bailout came at a perfect time. The Swiss investors were intelligent businessmen. They bought at the lowest point of the business cycle, knowing that cycles eventually trend back up.

But why Crawford? Why did this multi-national company focus on real estate and small business speculation in a tiny rural town in New Hampshire? Didn't they have bigger fish to fry?

Kim decided that she needed to find the names of the investors involved in the transaction to search for the real stakeholders. She wrote down the only people she could find involved in the transaction. They were a Mr. Green and a Mr. Schmidt.

The local and regional newspapers eventually became redundant, repeating the same information to promote the bailout's success but not revealing the names involved. She stood up, stretched her legs, and then moved over to boot up the old desktop PC. The speed of the machine and the connection to the internet were brutally slow. The screen slowly displayed information as the computer booted up. Her first search was about the company involved in the bailout. Chromwell International had many different divisions, each having multiple companies under their umbrellas. The internet speed crawled as Kim drilled down and linked her way through every piece of information.

She double-checked and cross-referenced the names of Mr. Green and Mr. Schmidt through search sites like Intellus, Truthfinder, Infotracer, Background checks and even LinkedIn. They didn't exist as part of the Chromwell organization or its subsidiaries. Who were these mystery people handing out millions in cash?

Rubbing her eyes and yawning, Kim leaned back in the chair, thinking it was time to wrap up for the day. She pushed herself to do one more search for a real name.

Finally, there was a break! A supplier that Cromwell did business with was a Chinese Man named Sun Ye Chang. He ran a New Jersey company called NAIL, North American Investments LLC. Kim couldn't identify what product or service NAIL provided to Chromwell. As she read further, there was controversy. An employee of Nail turned whistleblower and supplied the FBI with stories of improper business tactics that pointed to racketeering, extortion, money laundering, and drug dealing. An FBI search of NAIL's New Jersey office revealed nothing incriminating. FBI Agents attempted to question Mr. Chang, but he'd already left on a direct flight to Hong Kong the previous night.

If there was no evidence of Mr. Chang doing anything wrong, why did he take a flight back to Hong Kong to avoid being questioned?

Another item of interest involving the whistleblower came up. A few months after blowing the whistle, he fell off a ladder at home. He broke his neck and died. There was no evidence of a homicide. *Perfect timing.*

Kim decided it was time to call in a favor. She pulled out her phone and called her college roommate, Sheila Russo, the same FBI agent she had threatened Nick to call if they couldn't locate Julie and Charlie. The online article didn't name the FBI agents that searched NAIL. She could be one of them or shed some light on Mr. Chang and his company. Kim made the call and left a voicemail.

To her surprise, she received a call back within minutes. The caller ID on her phone said *No Name*. "Hey Kimmy, long time. How's life?" Sheila asked.

"Life's good, Sheel, you?"

"Living the dream."

"We need to catch up soon. At the moment I have a problem. I'm trying to help some friends, so I left you a message about…."

"Got your VM, and I had a minute, so here goes. I wasn't in on the investigation into Chang and his company. I know next to nothing about it. However, if you do some digging deep on the Web, you'll eventually find that Nail is part of a much bigger organization."

"Do you mean Chromwell International from Switzerland?" Kim asked.

"No, the organization I'm referring to is called Triad. That's all I can say about the investigation. Check them out, and you'll find your info. Gotta go, Kimmy. Call me next week, let's get together for coffee and catch up. Be careful, hon. Oh, and we never spoke." *Click.*

Triad? What the heck is Triad?

She went back to the ancient computer and performed a search. It was all there. Triad; The Chinese Mafia. They were like an international conglomerate of Chinese gangs committing every crime under the sun in all four corners of the globe. Individual divisions and gangs were called cells, like cancer cells spreading throughout a healthy host and wreaking havoc. One of their northeast cells was called The 14K, located in Paterson, New Jersey.

Kim adjusted herself and sat upright in her chair. The Chinese Mafia had her adrenaline surging. Wide-eyed and alert again, she started reading into its history.

Originally they were called San Ho Hui; Triple Union Secret Society; their name morphed into the union of three bodies; heaven, earth, and humanity; hence Triad. In 1949, The People's Republic of China ruler Mao Zedong was informed of Triad and other secret societies' illicit activities. He immediately outlawed all of them, but that didn't stop the growth of the cancerous Triad cells. They went into hiding and relocated operations to Hong Kong. Triad continued to grow, and their cells spread to Taiwan, Southeast Asia, and North America. The USA had always been the prize they most sought.

Interpol were unsuccessful in tracking down Triad's leaders. They lived in the remotest locations in China and used historical titles to distinguish their place in the organization's pecking order. A three-digit number system was assigned to all members of Triad to confuse law enforcement further. All communications between Triad members utilized numbers in place of names. Their top leader's organization chart read like a Chinese history book; The President was called The Mountain Master # 989, the Deputy Mountain Master # 832, the Operations Manager #716, and the Mountain Master's Proxy #651.

Interpol tried to get Triad gang members to flip by busting lower-level gang members. But they would never cooperate with authorities. If they did, their death and their families' deaths were guaranteed.

After distilling all the information, Kim used the same process as in her day job to conclude that Crawford had been targeted. Back in 2009, when the town began having major opioid addiction problems, little did they know they had already been infiltrated. Triad ran its software algorithms for regions and towns hit by economic downturns. Out spit Crawford. That was when the 14K gang put people in place, ready to pounce on the host. They called it The Process, and it began by flooding an already vulnerable town with low-priced opioids to help young and old with the pain of losing their jobs or the loss of their businesses. Once the drugs spread, they caught on like wildfire and sold themselves. The town was already in a financial tailspin and facing insolvency until the day the white knight rode into town. The strategic partnership would serve both entities.

What concerned her now was how Julie and Charlie fit into this puzzle. As far as Kim could tell, there was still a piece missing. Why did these two unlikely groups join forces? Regional drug dealing and small-town bailouts couldn't be the answer.

Julie had said, "Save us, save Marshera." Save them from what? Better yet, save them from who? Who would be interested in some hippy colony in the mountains?

It had been almost three hours. It was time to pack up and head to Mum's to help her unpack. Kim thought about her mother's appointment the next day and became worried. Mum had been in remission from breast cancer for almost four years. One more year, and they would consider her cured. Her scans looked clear, but they never knew when it came to cancer.

First, she would stop at a place that was right on the way. The place was a business named the Wildcat Off-Road Playground. Kim found it doubtful Nick would keep his promise to bring her back out to the right mountain. If she could hop onto one of the scenic rides in the morning before Mum's appointment to find Julie and Charlie healthy, none of what she researched would matter.

That would be fine with her.

Chapter 18
Don't Have To Live Like a Refugee

"Who do I see about the ATV tours?" Kim asked the kneeling mechanic with truly dirty blonde hair, as he unbolted a Kawasaki cylinder head. Taking his time, he looked up at her through the curling smoke of a Marlboro that hung from his lip. "In there," he motioned towards the building, as the ash fell off.

She walked carefully around the detritus of wheels, fuel tanks, and engine parts scattered around the yard. Tucking her hair behind her right ear, Kim nervously walked to the tired building with a blue sign that said office.

It appeared dark inside as she approached the door. The world of off-road machines and motorcycles was so foreign to her. *Maybe Mum's right. I should let the cops handle this whole thing. Who do I think I am; Mariska Hargitay?*

Slowly, Kim pulled open the door to stick her head in while standing outside.

"Anyone here?"

A figure quietly entered the dark room, triggering the motion detector lights to flicker on.

"Can I help you? His voice was a low baritone.

"I'm interested in the 9:00 AM tour tomorrow morning?"

"Sure thing, come on in. Name's Cody Metallak. A pleasure to meet you," he said, walking around his desk to extend his hand. He was a sixty-something-year-old man with long grayish, black hair and an enthusiastic smile. He also appeared to be Native American.

Kim stepped into the office and shook his hand, noticing he was muscular for a guy his age. He wore a long-sleeved black t-shirt that showed an ATV sitting in front of a waterfall with the company name Wildcat Off-Road Playground.

"I'm Kim Moreno," she said, thinking Cody seemed overly friendly but probably didn't get too many unaccompanied women walking into his office. "The tour of Wildcat Falls, are they still having it tomorrow morning?"

He let out a cackle and placed his hands on his hips, "Yeah, I'm sure *they* are, seeing how I do all the tours. Will it just be yourself? Husband? Kids? The more, the merrier."

Kim smiled, "Sorry, just me."

"Do I detect a bit of an accent?" he said. "Where do you hail from, if I might ask?"

"You're right; I'm from Maryland. My mother moved to Crawford, and I'm helping her settle in."

"Well, bring her along!" he suggested enthusiastically. "She'll get to know the area and see the beautiful foliage in northern New Hampshire. Of course, the best part is Wildcat Falls. Majestic and beautiful; I never get tired of it."

"Thank you, Mr. Metallak. I'm pretty sure my mother wouldn't go for a ride in an off-road vehicle. She's getting older. So it'll be just me."

"Not a problem. Hey, tell your mom, welcome to the area for me. Now, I see you're wearing sneakers and shorts. You might want to wear jeans and hiking boots if you have them."

"Sorry, I didn't pack any hikers to wear. Sneakers will have to do."

"Not to worry. You can get away with sneaks; been a warm spell lately, and we don't get too crazy on the tours anyway. Just use common sense. Now, we have two options here, so let me ask; do you have experience driving an all-terrain vehicle, Kim?"

"No, I rode on one for the first time yesterday."

"Okay, well, it's good you told me that because driving an ATV takes a little getting used to if you've never driven one before. So I'll assume you'll be a passenger on my machine?"

"Yes, safe assumption," she said.

"Great, I have a two-seater that you'll find nice and comfortable, so you won't have to worry about a thing. You'll have a separate seat to look at the sights while I drive."

"Being a passenger sounds perfect. I was a bit worried about driving one of those things anyway." He was accommodating and nice. She could feel her goosebumps fade as the fear subsided. She drew a deep breath in and exhaled slowly as the big man continued talking.

"Great; we wear full-faced helmets with built-in communication systems during the tour, so I can give you some history of the region as we ride. A dozen helmets are on the shelf if you'd like to pick one out that fits."

As Kim tried on helmets, she reminded herself that the mission wasn't to be a sightseeing joyride. The goal was to find Julie and Charlie. She didn't care what it took or who she had to coerce. Nick said he didn't exactly know how to get inside Marshera. If Cody was an experienced tour guide, he should know the lay of the land. Kim would press him for helpful information once they got close. She decided she would do this. The tour was only two hours, and she might get lucky finding Julie and Charlie. Then Kim would let the police detective know and be done.

The analog clock on the wall read; 12:12 PM. *Mum's still deep into unpacking and organizing. Better get moving.*

“Do I pay you now? Also, how long does the tour take?” Kim asked.

“You can pay me tomorrow morning, and the tours go about two hours.”

Leaving the office, she got into her car and fastened the seat belt. As she pulled out of the parking lot, Kim noticed the office had already gone dark.

It was like he’d never been there.

Chapter 19
I’m A Believer

"Okay, a few safety precautions before we head out," said Cody. Kim found his presentation amusing. It sounded like the same one he gave to a large group of people about to go on a tour of Wildcat Falls. Fact was, it was just going to be the two of them.

"This is a sight-seeing tour over fairly rough terrain but nothing an ATV can't handle. The trail we're taking is in good shape even after the recent rains. As you may have heard, ATVs can roll over easily, so we'll take it slow and turn carefully. There is nothing to worry about, though. Safety first, I always say. Passengers need to lean into turns in the same direction as the driver. I suggest passengers keep both hands on the safety handles on either side of their seat. I have some gloves if anyone's hands get tired or cold. Our helmets are full-faced with windscreens, so there's no need for goggles. Keep the helmet strapped at all times. The helmets have a built-in com system that will allow you to hear me and me to hear you. It's almost peak season, and the colors will be vivid. Our destination, Wildcat Falls, is majestic. A hundred-foot drop into a pool of crystal, clear water makes for a breathtaking visual. Let's mount up and go have some fun!" Cody smiled and gave Kim both thumbs up.

She thought about the majestic view of Wildcat Falls, as described by Cody. *Yes, I saw it standing on the wrong mountain two days ago.*

Kim’s backpack was stowed in the cargo net. She popped the silver helmet on and tightened the chinstrap. She was pleasantly surprised at how comfortable and padded the seat was on the back of the Polaris Sportsman ATV. Cody bounced into his seat as if he was riding his horse. Touching a button on the side of his helmet, he spoke. "Can you hear me, alright?" He turned his head to see Kim give him the thumbs-up signal.

He pressed a button on the handlebars; the machine's engine growled to a start. Kim could feel the vibrations through the seat and smelled the two-stroke exhaust behind them. A chill ran down her core making her shiver. Being here had felt harmless and even surreal until now. *This was really happening.*

"You mentioned that these things are prone to rollovers, so where is the safety belt? I can't find it," Kim asked, looking down on either side of the seat.

Cody cackled over the com, "ATVs don't have safety belts. They're like motorcycles with four wheels. Not to worry, though; it's a sightseeing cruise. We'll be taking it slow. Just hang onto those handles on both sides of your seat and enjoy the ride."

Kim took three deep breaths and white-knuckled the safety bars.

He gunned it, and they set off, bouncing down the trail. With the added weight of the motorcycle helmet, she felt like a bobblehead doll.

"How far?" she asked.

"Exactly 22.4 miles due north."

You got this, Kim.

She had told Mum earlier that morning there would be a two-hour excursion to maybe find where the hippy colony was located. Kim assured her she would be back in plenty of time to go to her doctor's appointment at three.

They motored down the oft-used trail to be quickly swallowed up by trees flooded with autumn's brilliant colors. The forest became dense and dark until they emerged into brightness and a field cut down the middle by water. The shallow brook was traversed, and they plunged back into the musty darkness of the forest again. She was surprised at how the bouncy trip relaxed her. The filtered sunlight altered the autumn colors from different angles to create a trippy effect. In all its glory, the solitary beauty of flora felt like a religious experience.

"Colors are gorgeous!" Kim said, pushing the helmet's com button.

"Glad you like it. We're at peak, right about now. There are several species of deciduous closer to the falls that I think you'll like even more."

"It's a natural beauty that we take for granted and don't appreciate enough," she said. I studied Botany for my undergraduate degree. Most of these trees look relatively young, unless I'm mistaken. I came upon a three-hundred-year-old oak the other day on a hike."

"Really?" said Cody. "Fantastic. Yes, you're right about the age of the trees. The average age is around a hundred twenty or so. There are a few old-timers still around that were spared, but they're rare."

"What do you mean, spared? Was there a fire?"

"A lot of The White Mountain National Forest is still renewing itself from the deforestation period back in the late 1800s," he said.

"Deforestation? They covered that topic in school, but we didn't focus too much on it. What exactly happened?"

Cody waited to explain as he powered the machine up a hill. Kim closed her eyes and gripped the handles tighter.

"Yes, deforestation and clear-cutting by loggers was big business back in the day. They became proficient at it and removed around fifty percent of all the trees in northern New Hampshire."

"Wow, you've got to be kidding!" Kim said. "What a shame."

"Yes, it all started with the colonization of the area. As more Europeans settled into our area, they consumed more wood for everything. Houses, heating, railroads, and factories; they all used wood. Demand was high, and many people who owned land sold off all their trees. Then they decided to try farming."

"All of these beautiful trees. It saddens me," Kim said.

"Yes, many red maple, white ash, sweetgum, and maidenhair. They even took the pines; the bigger ones were used for ship masts. Thousands of acres were clear-cut and deforested. The area became a mess like a hurricane had blown through, knocking down all the trees and leaving an ugly landscape for tourists to see."

"It's disgraceful," she said. “The colonists should have brought some of their wood and also replanted what they cut down."

"That's the irony of it. Many colonists came here because merry old England had deforested most of their trees. You had to be rich to afford wood. When the poor heard there were acres of wood in the new country, they said it's better to risk the new world rather than freeze to death in the old one. But then they came to the new world and tried to deforest it exactly like they did the old one."

"So, how did it finally stop?"

"Well, people that took up farming figured out that rocky soil and long winters made for a tough life. Many of the farms were abandoned. With all the trees gone, there was a major problem with erosion and mudslides. Thankfully, a senator from Massachusetts named Weeks had a house up in the White Mountains and got federal laws passed limiting the clear-cutting of forests. The law also allowed the US Government to buy up land to stop the decimation by loggers.”

“Nowadays, whenever I hike through the forest and see a stone wall in the middle of nowhere, it reminds me that farmers lived there and all the trees had been taken many years ago."

"I’ve seen photos of those random stone walls in the forest and wondered."

"Now you know," said Cody.

“Trees don't grow back overnight," said Kim.

"You're right. It takes at least seventy-five to a hundred years for a deforested area to renew itself. Of course, it's never like it was before. A lot of the animals perished. Yes, colonization affected everyone. Like my ancestors, the Abenaki of New Hampshire. Many died from measles and smallpox spread by English colonists, that were already immune. The village where my ancestors lived stayed here the longest before finally moving up north to what is now Canada."

"How did they survive catching the diseases?" asked Kim

"They survived by living in the Marshera caves of Wildcat Mountain."

Had Cody just said the Magic word, Marshera?

"Cody, tell me more about the cave place Marshera and your ancestors, please."

"No, that's enough about my family and me. Let's focus on the excursion now."

"Seriously, Cody, I need to hear more about Marshera," Kim said.

With no reply, they traveled without talking. Finally, Kim broke the silence, "Cody, I have something I need to confess to you."

Again, he gave her no reply as they traveled to their destination. The trail became winding as they turned a corner and drove into a clearing next to the water. Cody brought the ATV to an abrupt stop. "We have arrived."

Wildcat Falls roared before them. A massive chute of white water plunged down a hundred-foot drop into an icy pool. Mist drifted off the water to dampen their face shields as they removed their helmets. They stood silently to take in the natural wonder of nature's power and beauty. Kim breathed in the mist and smiled, grateful to see the falls again, only this time from ground level.

"Now, what do you feel you need to confess, my dear?" Cody said.

Kim had yet to decide if she should tell Cody about her quest to find Marshera and Julie. She didn't have a plan, only a need. But then everything fell into place. No one else was on the tour, and Cody's ancestors had lived in Marshera.

"Thing is, I've already seen Wildcat Falls; from the top of Carter Dome mountain two days ago." She told Cody everything, from pulling Julie out of the freezing rapids to her and Nick being knocked out and then Julie being taken.

"I had to come here and take a chance on finding Julie and her brother Charlie. I need to know if they're alright. Especially Julie after what she went through," Kim confessed sheepishly. Cody listened carefully without emotion.

"So you're telling me you didn't come out here for the Falls. You came to save a life?"

"Basically, yes. I'm terrified for those two kids' lives!" She was intense and on edge as she explained her reasoning to him.

"Then you must take your backpack and follow me," Cody said.

"Where are we going?" Kim asked.

Again, there was no answer.

For a mile, they hiked down a trail. Dry leaves crunched under their feet, and cicadas hummed in their ears. "You follow the skinny birches," he said, pointing to the stark white trees that lined the path.

What is happening? Is he taking me to them? It was all going so fast that nervous anticipation grew inside her. If Cody wasn't taking her to Marshera, there was no way she'd have the nerve to go by herself. Her fingertips lightly touched the smooth bark of skinny birch trees as they moved down the trail. The sensory feeling kept Kim in the present moment and helped fight off the increased fear and anxiety she felt with each step. One of the birches seemed to stare at her with dark circles where branches had once grown.

Wherever it is, there is no way I can do this alone.

Besides, she thought, what if Julie and her brother weren't in Marshera? Her insecurity grew with each step. Lack of control was an awful feeling for her.

I want to get my hands on the pink pills in my backpack.

Cody stopped as the trail ended, "We have arrived," he said again. He took off his backpack to pull out a blue LED flashlight and handed it to Kim.

"Take this. You'll need it."

"Where are we going? Aren't you coming too?" Kim asked.

"Follow me," he said. They walked behind a red maple tree and stood before a solid rock wall. Gray granite grew up into the sky to form Wildcat Mountain. He moved further to a secluded corner that was hidden by brush and boulders. Cody looked at Kim and signaled her to come closer. He showed her a jagged hairline crevice in the shape of an eight-foot-tall oval.

"This is an entrance to a tunnel. It will take you to Marshera."

Kim stood facing the stone doorway in amazement. *How would they open it? It had to weigh over a ton. What lay behind it? How dark and cramped would the tunnel be?*

Her heart hammered, thinking about all the possible adverse outcomes.

Standing next to the door, he said, "Watch."

Cody kneeled to rest his shoulder against the door. He pushed against it three times and slid his hand inside a notch near the bottom of the door. He pulled the giant stone and rotated the door open with ease to reveal the inside of a tunnel.

"I can't believe it," Kim said." I didn't know Native Americans built things like this."

"They didn't build it," said Cody. "The door was already here when my ancestors discovered this place. There are several secret doors and man-made tunnels that lead to Marshera. An ancient civilization built them. Marshera is beautiful. When you arrive, your eyes won't believe it."

"Have you ever been inside? Kim asked.

"Yes, many moons ago."

"Will you go with me through the caves and show me the way, Cody?"

"No, I cannot."

"There is no way I can do this myself! Also, I need to get back to my mother's for her…."

"Did you not tell me you came here to save lives?"

"Well, yes, I did, but I wasn't thinking. I mean, how will I get back?"

"I bring tours out here again at noon and five PM. You will follow the tunnel to Marshera and find the two children whose safety you need to ensure. The people of Marshera will lead you to a trail where my ATV will be parked. It is near the Falls. I will pick you up there and bring you back."

"I guess that would work. Let me have your cell phone number," Kim said.

Cody smiled, "No cell phones; don't believe in them."

"But what if Julie and Charlie aren't in Marshera? I'll be risking this all for nothing."

"They are in Marshera," Cody said.

"How could you possibly know?" Kim asked.

"I just do. Leave it at that. You must go now; we are wasting time. Marshera is a mile and a half from this point through the tunnel. You may face some obstacles but be brave and stay the course. Look inside yourself and use your ingenuity and intelligence. Never tell anyone of this entrance. Refrain from telling the people of Marshera how you found your way to them. Go now, and you will find this girl and boy you seek. Good luck on your journey."

"I'm still not sure, Cody! This is scary!"

"You can do this, Kim. Now go, or you'll miss your chance." He began walking back down the trail.

"My chance for what?" she said, stepping inside the door to the tunnel.

Cody turned and smiled, "The restoration of your soul, I imagine."

Without notice, Kim watched the giant stone door slowly close by itself to make a low, resounding thud that shook the floor.

Quickly, Kim activated the flashlight. She panned the tunnel walls to get her bearings. Traces of minerals like quartz, mica, and beryl reflected off the light beam. Resetting the digital mileage tracker on her watch, Kim took three long, deep breaths and then slowly exhaled to begin the mile-and-a-half journey. She still didn't believe she had undertaken the challenge.

The light beamed into the inky, black darkness and dissolved into more of the same.

It's only a mile and a half Kim.

She raised her hoodie over her head and cinched it tight, hoping to form a protective layer against whatever might drop down from above. Gripping the flashlight tightly, she moved slowly forward. It would be unimaginable if she lost her only source of light.

A musty smell filled her head as strange noises filtered in from a distance. Still, she told herself, the tunnel was tolerable for a short time.

It's tall enough to walk upright. The smells and noises are probably harmless.

Before Kim knew it, she'd be at Marshera, hoping to find Julie and Charlie safe and healthy. A moment later, the musty smell was overtaken by the stench of rotten eggs. Water flowed off in the distance. Kim decided she needed to deep breathe to calm her nerves, but the odor became unbearable. She pulled her sweatshirt up to cover her nose and act like an air filter.

One careful step at a time was taken as the beam of the light reflected in all directions. *How did an ancient civilization dig these tunnels without equipment?*

The ceiling gradually lowered, requiring her to crouch down to get through the tight clearance. It was then that the light revealed them. At least fifty hung from the ceiling.

"Oh my God, gross."

Bats are the only flying mammal that sleep upside down, making for a strange and creepy sight. Clustered together, their wings were wrapped around their bodies for warmth and protection. Their feet, strong enough to grasp the rocky surface, clung tight to suspend them for hours while they slept. Brown and hairy, each one was eight to ten inches long. Squeaking sounds came from them as they huddled together in slumber. Kim's pulse raced faster, knowing she would have to crawl underneath them without disturbance. It was the only way.

With the flashlight off, Kim began crawling in the dark on all fours. Quietly, she moved under the sleeping varmints. A memory brought her back to the little girl whose father had found a dead bat in the attic. It was a creepy sight causing her to run away to hide. Now she had fifty live ones breathing right over her head. Her knee landed on a jagged rock, and she winced quietly in pain. The squeaking and clicking noises made her face cringe. She paused to turn on the light and get her bearings. The beam showed the tunnel was taller ahead. She would be able to walk upright again. Another ten feet, she'd be past the sleeping creatures. Something gooey stuck to her left hand. Kim knew it was bat feces. *Ewwww.* She would be past them a few more feet. Then a crucial mistake. Forgetting her backpack protruded up several inches, she began to rise and walk again. Kim felt the contact and froze in fear. A tiny nudge; was it enough to awaken it?

Yes, it was.

An explosion of bats erupted. They swarmed in a frenzied circle as Kim slammed her head into her chest and curled up tight for protection. They flew around her in crazy erratic directions, squealing and clicking. The bats bounced off her body and head as Kim screamed into her chest, pulling the hood down over her face. The swarm continued for an eternity until finally, they fluttered away to leave her sobbing on the ground.

Frozen and terrified to move, she stayed curled up for several minutes. Flashlight turned back on, she stood up, brushed herself off, and then moved forward again, looking at the jagged rock ceilings for any more intruders. It occurred to her, *maybe I'm the intruder?* What else would she encounter before she reached Marshera? Doubt seeped in, and Kim began questioning herself, *Is this me?* She felt a tug of war between her unconditional need to find Julie and her disgust with dark caves and bats. She had to press on. There was no turning back.

The tunnel grew larger until it spilled out into a cavern unlike any she had ever imagined. Mammoth in size, it resembled an auditorium. She pointed the beam to the ceiling thirty feet above and wondered where the stalagmites were. Flowing water could be heard, and Kim stopped to shine the flashlight in all directions. The light reflected off something, and she walked over to see a narrow river streaming through the cavern. It was unlike any she had ever seen. Steam rose from the water as it meandered through the cave. Kneeling, she touched the water with her index finger and then yanked it back. The water wasn't just hot; it was boiling!

Are we sitting on top of a volcano?

Kim raised the beam of light up the wall above the stream to see drawings that appeared very old. There were several along the wall. The first one showed several silhouette figures hovering around someone lying on the ground with a bearskin rug covering them as they appeared to be sick. The second drawing revealed two silhouette figures standing next to a small fountain. One figure held a triangle-shaped bowl under the fountain as liquid drained into it. In the following picture, the two figures were attending to the sick person. One held the person's head up, and the other one held the triangle bowl to their mouth. The last drawing showed the three figures from the previous drawing chasing a buffalo with spears. The sick person was out in front, looking like they had been cured of what ailed them. Kim stood for several minutes, trying to understand the story.

Do they drink the scalding hot water from the stream, thinking it will cure their illnesses? She thought about the clinical work she did at her job working alongside scientists. There were no miracle cures in pharmacology. Remedies had to prove their efficacy consistently in several ways before passing FDA approval.

These drawings look like ancient superstitions. It's time to get moving toward Marshera.

Headed down another tunnel that exited the cavern, Kim was grateful this one seemed to be free of bats. A massive spider web reflected off the light like an abstract prism. Pulling her hood further down, Kim used her arms to clear a path through tangled webs. She felt a vibrating buzz on her wrist from her watch. She had traveled one mile. *Just half a mile further.* Suddenly the ground began to tremble. The vibrations reverberated throughout every wall and surface as if an earthquake had started. Kim lost her balance and fell to the ground. Rubble and silt fell on her from the ceiling. The smell of rotten eggs consumed the tunnel. *Volcanic, Earthquake, or both?*

How unstable is this mountain?

The vibrations stopped quickly and she rose to her feet. "Bring it on. I'm not turning back!"

According to her watch, Marshera was coming up soon. The tunnel became wider and spilled out into another cavern, this one smaller than the last, with one notable feature. A scalding river of boiling water, fifteen feet across, prevented Kim from advancing. Steam vapors floated up from the water, leaving her to shake her head.

Does it have snakes too?

Kim's flashlight scanned back and forth to see the tunnel on the other side of the scalding water that would lead to her destination. She kept scanning until the light reflected off the water, revealing a series of five rocks. They were like small stepping stones that rose just above the water's surface, allowing the river to be crossed if done carefully. The problem was obvious; the stones were small, barely large enough to stand on. But they were far enough apart to require a jump from one to the other. She would have to be agile and precise with her footing. There was another worry. How slippery were they?

She had always been confident in her athletic abilities. Track and soccer both required strength and agility, but there hadn't been any boiling hot water involved. This contest would be the ultimate risk match.

Come in first, and I make it across the creek to find Marshera. Second place gets me third-degree burns and probable death. Nice.

Kim used the same preparation she'd used before diving into the river to save Julie. She would deep breathe three times with slow exhale to calm her nerves. She heard her coach's voice again in her head.

Flashlight aimed at her target, Kim stood athletically and took the first leap to fly through the air and nail the first rock with her right foot. Without hesitating, she aimed the light and pushed off to hit the second rock dead center with her left. Pausing to breathe for a moment while standing on the tiny surface with arms outstretched, Kim raised her right leg and aimed for the third rock. She pushed off again to reach stone number three safely. Another pause and another push-off to nail the fourth rock clean.

"Whooo-Hoo!" She shouted with excitement to hear it echo throughout the cavern. Her flashlight aimed at rock number five revealing it would be the hardest challenge. The distance was the furthest, and the rock was the smallest. Pausing again, Kim drew in a lungful of cool cave air to reset. *Just one more, please.* She visualized the desired outcome, pushed off with all her strength, and stuck the landing. But then it happened. Her foot slipped on a slick patch she had worried about. Quickly Kim jutted out her leg and windmilled her arms in a desperate attempt to regain her center of gravity. The scalding hot water lapped against her foot as it slid off the edge. "No!" Kim shrieked, trying to stay upright. But it was too late. She'd lost it and was falling backward to disaster when things got worse. The flashlight flew out of her hand to smash off a rock and break into pieces, falling into the boiling water. Somehow, losing the flashlight helped her regain her balance. Centered again for a second, Kim slammed her other foot down on the rock to blindly push off and dive through the darkness to land on the riverbank.

But she came up short.

Her left foot plunged into the scorching water as her body slammed on the ground and rolled over in the dirt. She yelled out in pain as the water touched her skin.

Her foot was burned but saved in part by her sneaker and sock. She sat motionless on the ground in pitch black, rubbing her ankle.

Dammit, I made it! I made it!

A second later, she realized her new reality. *Shit! Now I'm blind!*

There was a problem that needed to be solved; Kim had no light to navigate and find Marshera. The problem couldn't be solved when she was in a state of panic. With worry came shutdown, and with calmness came innovation. She continued to breathe deeply and told herself, *you must succeed!*

According to her watch, Marshera should be twenty yards away. She couldn't see her hand in front of her face. No solutions came to mind except action. Mum's sayings always popped into her head. *What did Churchill say? When you're going through hell, just keep going.*

Kim rose up and felt her way forward, left arm stretched out in front of her and right arm touching the tunnel's cold, rock wall.

She found herself singing her favorite tune to calm her anxiety. *In every life, we have some trouble, But when you worry, you make it double, Don't worry, be happy. Now there is this song that I wrote; I hope you learned note for note, Don't worry, be happy.* She whistled in the dark, inching forward.

Would Marshera welcome her with open arms? Probably, she thought. She and Nick had saved Julie's life. *I can't wait to get there. Where is this place?*

Tiring of Bobby McFerrin, Kim switched to the first song that came to mind. "Twinkle twinkle, little star, How I wonder what you are. Up above the sky so bright, That's when you show your light, Twinkle, twinkle little star… She stopped in her tracks. "That's when you show your light? Jesus, of course!"

Kim unclipped her backpack and pulled her phone out to turn on the built-in LED light and chastised herself for being dumb. Her mood was buoyed by the ability to see her way now. The screen revealed twenty-five percent battery left with no service.

She moved forward at a faster pace again and sang out loud, "Twinkle, twinkle, little star..." She moved forward again until the light revealed something strange.

A small opening and then a solid rock wall stood before her. It was the end of the line. She used the phone light and her hands to feel around the rough edges of the granite to look for a door. Nothing.

Where are you Marshera? Please tell me what's going on. Am I lost?

She recalled the oval-shaped stone door that gave her entrance to the caves. Kim held the light close to the wall as she squinted and ran her fingernails over the rough surface, looking for a crack. But none existed. Panicking, Kim went to change the phone to her other hand and dropped it onto the dirt floor. It landed light facing down and cast her back into darkness. She dropped to her knees to feel around for the phone.

It was only a sliver of light, but there it was. Down near the floor and only a few inches long, there a crevice with light. It came from a door.

Finding her phone, Kim held it close to find a hairline crack and followed the oval in the door's shape.

Where's the notch that Cody showed me when he opened the other door?

With the phone battery down to five percent, fear crept into her and squeezed her like a boa constrictor. *Oh my God, I'll be stuck out here with no way to get back!*

Kim got on her knees and used the phone's last moments of light to find a rock. She began pounding on the granite rock door. Wham! Wham! Wham! Wham, the pounding echoed throughout the caves.

Screaming out, she yelled, "Is anybody there? Anybody home? Hello?" Wham! Wham! Wham! Wham! She pounded on the door repeatedly until her arm grew tired. She dropped the rock and slumped down to the ground in exhaustion.

Was this even Marshera? Kim began to question everything.

She felt a jarring behind her back. Something began moving, and she jumped up to see the sliver of light become wider and brighter as the giant rock door groaned and rotated open. Her spirit soared with enthusiasm. He was standing before her, a silhouette of a giant man. He was over six feet tall and built like a linebacker.

"Who are you?" He spoke in a low but quiet voice.

"I'm Kim. Kim Moreno. I'm looking for a girl named Julie. Is she here?"

There was a long pause before he answered, "No one here by that name."

She spoke quickly, fearing he would close the door. "She's around twelve years old with long brown hair. She almost drowned, and my friend and I brought her back to life. Her brother yelled for help, but he disappeared. Then somebody knocked us out and took her. They told me that Julie and Charlie might live here at the hippy colony. Is this place Marshera? I'm sorry, I'm rambling. Please, I want to make sure she's okay," Kim began crying; the emotion taking over.

The giant man was speechless for another eternity, "No one here named Julie." With one motion, he closed the granite door. Thud!

Kim sat in the dark in a state of shock. *Was this place even Marshera? Maybe it was, and Julie had never lived there?*

Sheer panic consumed every cell in her body. She began talking out loud, rambling on, "I never thought it through. What was I thinking? I can't do this! I never could! Cody, where are you? They'll find my skeleton in this tunnel after the rats eat all my flesh!"

Kim sat on the dirt floor and sobbed as she wrapped her arms around her knees and rocked back and forth in the darkness. She was tired, alone, and petrified. *I should have stayed in my safe little life living with Brad and helping Mum unpack. I should have listened to her and let the cops handle the missing kids. I never should have run down that trail in the first place!*

Her phone was now dead. A complete loss of hope enveloped her body. Kim wept and sobbed for several minutes, wondering if she would see her life replay before her as she died alone in a cave sitting in the dark. Mum's voice was in her head, warning her this might've happened using her endless slogans. *A bird in the hand is worth two in the bush; nothing ventured, nothing gained.* They were endless. *If, at first, you don't succeed, try, try again.*

Kim stopped crying, wiped her face with her hands, and started yelling, "You know what? That one actually makes a lot of sense!"

Raw instinct and anger took over. She switched from flight to fight and began screaming, "I know damn well Julie's in there! Cody told me so, and I can feel it in my bones!"

She felt around the ground in the dark to find a bigger rock. With both hands and every last ounce of strength, she pounded it against the granite door. Thud! Thud! Thud! Thud.

"Open this goddamn door right now! I know Julie's in there! I'm not going to die out here in the dark! Thud! Thud! Open up this door and bring me, Julie!" Thud! Thud! Thud!

Kim pounded on the door repeatedly until her voice became hoarse, and her arms grew tired. She dropped the rock to the ground and slumped back down again.

One last feeble shout came out, "Open this door right now! I'm tired, and I'm hungry!" She picked up her phone to see the light flicker off dead.

Her sobs were interrupted by a low scraping sound, and then a heavenly light overcame the darkness to once again reveal the silhouette of the giant man. This time someone was standing next to him.

Julie.

"Hi, Kim. Are you coming inside?"

Chapter 20
Space Oddity

A serpentine road led up the leeward side of the mountain for five miles. It snaked around, winding left and right as it cut through the dense forest that hid its existence. The road ended on a mammoth rock ledge that spanned out from the side of the mountain like a giant lip. Behind the lip was a mouth, actually more of a man-made hole that was cut deep into the side of a pristine mountain. Both of the alterations held a secret procedure that was currently in process. The engineer in charge of the project had overseen and assembled the investments necessary to complete the job. Heavy-duty mining equipment, boring and fracking machines, diesel backhoes, explosives, and laborers were all to be utilized in the effort. The most critical component was a precision hydraulic fracking machine, which needed to create the exact locations for the placement of one hundred explosive charges.

The goal of the dangerous operation was to extract a treasure buried beneath the mountain's surface. It had been there for a very long time. The treasure, also called an asset, was valuable. The transaction that was about to take place had determined the asset to be worth exactly fifty billion dollars.

The mining operation had been in process for almost a year and had fallen behind schedule several times. The people who were footing the multi-million dollar bill were not pleased. Those directly involved in the operation reminded them that no one had ever attempted anything like this. The procedure was technical as well as dangerous. Mining operations for an extraction are supposed to operate on something other than the side of a mountain. Therefore, they had to build an access road and ledge to use as a base of operations. That was step one, and it took six months. Then came step two, when the mining machines were employed to perform boring, blasting, and fracking activities to unearth the prize carefully. Soon setbacks occurred due to broken equipment, weather, and unforeseen obstacles. Time and again, the operation ran behind schedule. It was dangerously close to missing the agreed-upon deadline. If the delivery date wasn't met on time, the deal was off, and the multi-million dollar investment would be lost.

What they sought beneath the earth's surface had begun as folklore. Over the years, folklore morphed into science fiction stories and, finally, conspiracy theories. They originated as far back as 1889 during New England's deforestation period when loggers and lumberjacks noted a sizeable bowl-shaped depression on the leeward side of Wildcat Mountain. The trees and vegetation inside the bowl had grown significantly larger than neighboring trees and plants. The loggers marveled at the heights and widths of the trees just before they cut them down and delivered them to the timber mill. Years later, during the regrowth period, fur traders, hunters, and eventually hikers rediscovered the bowl and noted that within it, trees had regrown faster and taller than the ones outside. Vegetation was five feet high, and a blueberry bush sprouted fruit the size of golf balls. Rumors circulated about the possibility of radioactive minerals, solar alignment, or decaying dinosaurs that lay beneath the crater.

In 1983, a team of scientists, geologists, and students led by Dr. Paul Conti, Professor of Geology and Geophysics at The University of New Hampshire, hiked up Wildcat Mountain to examine the area in question. As soon as they arrived, Dr. Conti surveyed the bowl-like depression and took note of the massive amount of growth that had occurred. He told his team the bowl should be classified as a crater, not a depression. He hypothesized that the crater resulted from a meteorite still buried beneath the earth's surface. They would need to dig down through rocky soil to prove or disprove his hypothesis and reveal the object's composition. Easier said than done, his colleagues warned him. The crater was packed solid with trees, brush, rocks, and boulders, not ideal for digging with shovels. After several attempts at multiple locations, the team found a clear area to begin their research. The first-year students commenced digging in a hot July sun, toiling for several hours until they reached a depth of ten feet. When one of their shovels clanged against the mineral, they knew they had reached what they sought. What they found was exposed for all of them to see. It was apparent this was no ordinary geological find. It was, in fact, the object that Dr. Conti had hypothesized; a massive meteorite was buried beneath the earth's surface.

In the pecking order of space rocks and debris, an asteroid is a large chunk of rock that, just like the earth, orbits around the sun. When a chunk of an asteroid breaks away, it is labeled a meteoroid. If the meteoroid enters the earth's atmosphere, it is then called a meteor and can typically be seen as a shooting star. A meteor that is large enough to survive entry through the earth's atmosphere without burning up is called a meteorite. Meteorites are rare; only about one hundred per year hit the earth's surface. Usually, they're small and harmless, ranging in size from that of a pea to no more than a human fist. The meteorite the team discovered underneath the crater was unique for its size alone. It would have started its entry into the earth's atmosphere the size of a condominium. After its mass had been burned away by entry temperatures of 2700 F, the space rock would be reduced to that of a family-size SUV. The meteorite found its new home by slamming into the side of Wildcat Mountain, creating a massive crater and ending its journey.

In fact, its journey was just about to begin.

The first-year students, or as they called themselves, "Conti's Crew," stood inside the ditch they'd spent the last four hours digging. Several jugs of water were consumed as they wiped their brows and stretched their backs to see Dr. Conti gazing down at them from above. He stood silently taking in the sight of their unique geological anomaly.

"It's bright blue, reminiscent of a gemstone like a sapphire or something," he shouted, looking down on their discovery.

One of the underclassmen diggers looked up from the hole. He squinted in the late-day sun and yelled to his Professor, "It's radiating, Doc!"

"Radiating? Radiating what?" asked Dr. Conti.

"It's radiating heat," said the sophomore digger. "It's hot!"

"Should be cool as a cucumber, buried under all that earth," shouted the Professor.

"It's also pulsating a little, too," a second digger added.

"Come again?"

The first one concurred, "I can feel a pulsating under my feet too. I hope this thing isn't radioactive, or we're all dead."

Dr. Conti looked at one of his assistants next to him, "Don't just stand there! Get the Geiger counter, man!"

Fortunately, there was zero radiation measured after employing the Geiger counter instrument, to everyone's relief. Additional instrument readings were taken to measure its composition. One of the last readings evaluated the meteorite's conductivity. The results were shocking. Not only did it exceed silver, the most conductive metal on the planet, it was fifty times *more* conductive.

Dr. Conti sent a ladder down the hole and descended into it to put a stethoscope on the giant meteorite. "Goddamn rock's alive!" Dr. Conti shouted out and laughed along with the others around him.

The team camped out and stayed for several days and nights to take additional measurements and readings with every instrument they brought. Its size was determined to be approximately twenty feet long by six feet wide by eight feet tall. Rough estimations were that it had crashed into the side of the mountain a millennium ago, leaving a crater with a diameter of two hundred and six feet. The researchers chipped away a dozen samples to bring back to the university and conduct a more detailed and in-depth analysis.

One of the first-year students was ambitious and sought out Dr. Conti to discuss the meteorite's plans. Dr. Conti's opinion was that they would take samples and then backfill the ditch. The ambitious student disagreed.

"Dr.Conti, I believe that the meteorite should be excavated for further study in any one of several fields," said the student.

"It's good to see your passion, son," said Dr. Conti. "But excavation of this type would be costly and dangerous. Besides, there's no current use for the meteorite. So I say, let it rest where it is."

"True, there isn't a specific use for the meteorite today. However, once we begin testing it in various applications, I have a feeling there will be," the student argued his position.

"That's what we have the samples for, son," the Professor said.

"But sir, it would be impressive to show off the meteorite with all of us standing behind it getting our pictures taken. Think of the notoriety for you and the university?"

Dr. Conti waved him off, "Oh, who the hell cares about notoriety? I sure as hell don't. Let that space rock stay where it's been for the last thousand years. It sure as heck isn't going anywhere. That'll be my final recommendation to the university. I appreciate your ambition, son, but it's my decision to make. You can propose digging the damn thing up when I'm dead if you want to. By the way, what's your name?"

"Name's Tom, sir. Thomas Foulke, geologist in training."

The discovery of the meteorite and future research were shared with geologists and scientists from universities such as MIT, Princeton, and Stanford. Its discovery was all the buzz in scientific and geological fields of study. The samples brought back were exchanged with university geology departments and several commercial geological experts. The space rock's mineral composition was unique and contained new elements not previously recorded. A meeting was convened at MIT in Boston, Massachusetts, with top geologists in attendance. Dr. Conti commented on the meteorite's uniqueness and asked the scientists to pinpoint what mineral and element the meteorite most resembled. After several months of analysis and discussion amongst the scientific community, it was unanimously agreed that the meteorite was made up of an isotope similar to the earth's rarest element.

Tritium.

Tritium was best known for being a heavy hydrogen isotope with little to no usefulness in the 1980s. However, several scientists predicted that Tritium would find use in the future yet-to-be-built fusion reactors. Fusion reactors would be the power plants of the next millennium, designed to perform with one hundred percent efficiency while emitting zero waste. Due to its conductivity and molecular structure, Tritium would be a crucial component for fusion reactors.

The meteorite that Dr. Conti and his team discovered was made of an element with a molecular structure far superior in conductivity and durability to Tritium. It could be a key ingredient to building the futuristic power source if and when the time came. Nuclear fusion in the 1980s was akin to science fiction.

The scientific boards classified the meteorite as a metal and decided that the name should be Continuum (chemical symbol NU) after scientist Dr. Paul Conti who led the excavation and made the discovery.

Humanity might eventually need the meteorite Dr. Conti, and his students unearthed that day. After all, Continuum wasn't Tritium; it was Tritium on steroids

The ditch was backfilled to leave everything as they found it. The space rock would lie warm and pulsating ten feet underground in a remote mountain location in rural New Hampshire.

After a time, the buzz about the meteorite faded away, and the local people in the area forgot about it. The space rock was left to slumber for another thousand years or more.

That was until recently.

Chapter 21
Roll With It

Lightning lit up the pre-dawn windows like searchlights from a police raid. Less than five seconds later, a guttural crack of thunder was so loud the sky seemed to rip apart. Repetitive booms shook the structure as wine glasses clinked against each other in the cabinet. She screamed in fright and pulled the covers over her head.

"It's fine, Lee," his reassuring voice was low and calm as he held her tight.

She couldn't respond. Her jaw was seized up tight. It was the one thing in all the world that scared the living shit out of her and caused her to shake physically. On the streets, she was known as the tough chick, but when it came to lightning, a little girl emerged.

He could feel her body vibrate as if every nerve and muscle were hit by the same lightning bolts that lit up the windows. "I'm right here. I won't let anything happen to you."

As the atmospheric explosions subsided, she took her hand from holding his and grabbed his jaw. With lips parted, she kissed him deep and wet. "Topaz, my rock of Gibraltar. You think you're an action hero, don't you?"

He smiled, "Think?"

The passionate kissing continued until she sat up and pushed him over onto his back to straddle him with her naked body.

Afterward, they lay still, locked together and asleep as the rumbling of thunder faded harmlessly in the distance.

They slept intertwined and warm. Topaz woke first at daylight. "Have to shower and head out." The handle squeaked, then the water sprayed. She stayed in bed with her face buried in the pillow; to smell his manliness. Her mind wandered to what new responsibilities might fall in her lap. Then her alarm rang out, and it was time to rise. She sat on the bathroom seat to relieve herself and remembered not to flush.

"Leave it going when you're done," she yelled over the shower.

"Got it."

"Where you headed again?" she asked.

"Vermont. And you?"

"Northern New Hampshire, of all places."

"God's country!"

"Not for this city girl!"

His ride up north along route 89 was smooth and uneventful. When he arrived, it was a shame that he had to wait in the car. After a three-and-a-half-hour drive, he liked getting out to walk around and stretch his legs. Better yet, find a shady spot to sit outside and stare at the locals frolicking in the final visages of Indian summer. They hadn't a care in their little minds.

Lake Champlain was one of God's works of aquatic artistry. He thought about the glorious day and how he might like to find a place to paint the lake's white-capped chop and heeling sailboats as they tacked and jibbed across the horizon. What could their destination be within the confines of a body of water even as large as this? Ah, but it's not the destination as much as the journey he remembered. *Life is a highway. I want to ride it all night long.*

His contact was late arriving, and that concerned him. He didn't worry when a client was late to meet with him. Anyone could be delayed for a variety of innocent reasons. Still, he had to be realistic. Plug was always on time. He bragged about always being right on time. It was something his mother had instilled in him since birth. "When you're late, it's like a slap in the face," he would say. If the calendar said there was to be a full moon, one would expect to see a giant hole in the sky. A sky full of stars without the moon would be unthinkable. That's how it was if Plug was late. And late he was.

Was there a double cross in the works? He let his mind wander a few steps down a dark path but remembered that this was his friend Plug. *Betrayal happens in our business but not between him and me.* There was one other viable option on the table. If Plug was late, Plug was dead. It was an occupational hazard that he had to consider.

He was Topaz. Like the rock, only twice as hard. It was the only name he used when dealing with Plug and his other clients. He would use the three-number code for internal communications, as silly as it was to him. It was the way they did things, and he had to respect that. Even though anyone could find out almost anything in today's information age, there was always some scrap of information online that could be cross-referenced and dug up.

Business was booming lately, and he was being recognized as a top earner for the 14 K's. Soon they would expand his base and pay him more. They even trusted him to collect the money now, saving them an extra trip. Trust was an essential quality in their business. And sleeping with the boss didn't hurt his chances either.

But this was today, and it would be his last stop before heading home. He had arrived early and remained in his pickup truck as the procedure dictated. It was how he had been trained. It was two twenty now, making Plug twenty minutes late. He continued to look and scan the area.

An incoming call; it was his friend.

"Somebody's late for the first time. Where are you?"

Plug's voice came through scratchy and almost impossible to hear. "Oh, hey, man. I'm sorry 'bout that. My guy was late getting to my earlier meet. Why don't you come to my place and we'll do our thing? Barn's open, and I'm grooming Tango. Alright?"

"What's up with your phone? Your voice is garbled. Can barely tell it's you."

"Yeah, yeah, thing's been givin' me trouble. No damn time to fix it. See you soon."

"Be there in five," said Topaz.

He started the vehicle and switched the AC to max. His gut still said something was up, but he remembered he was always alert. He was a worrier, most times about nothing. Topaz pulled the loaded Ruger six-shooter out of the glove box and set it on the seat.

The drive to Plug's wasn't much longer than the five minutes promised. As Topaz pulled up to the barn, he saw the back of Plug's horse. The farmhouse was where they always transacted their affairs. It was an older home that needed a lot of work. It was tucked away in the woods up a long secluded driveway. The remote location was perfect for the delivery of his products. Topaz was the middleman, supplying significant quantities of prescription and non-prescription drugs to the street dealers. Straights only hear about the most popular drugs currently making the news. But there is demand for many legally prescribed drugs that can't be obtained without a prescription. There were several from the opioid family of time-released painkillers; OxyContin (Oxy), Vicodin (Vikes), and the synthetics like Fentanyl (Fents) and Methadone (Dollies). Of course, non-prescription recreational cocaine, heroin and weed were available too. He carried the niche stuff; molly, bath salts, ecstasy, flakka, crokodill, LSD, mushrooms, meth, salvia, and spice. He was a one-stop shop for every dealer's needs.

The scene appeared to be normal, and Topaz put the gun back in the glove box. As he walked around his truck towards the barn's entrance, he found it a little strange that his friend, Freddy Beale

(AKA Plug), hadn't come out and greeted him. He was about as pleasant a man as he'd ever met.

Plug would brag about doing what he did to pay for his equestrian pastime, stabling two flawless Morgan's and riding them daily. The horses displeased Topaz. He told Plug the first time they met that he was scared shit of horses. It was some phobia; any animal larger and stronger than he was, intimidated him.

Topaz entered the barn looking for his associate, who was nowhere to be found. Keeping his distance from his friend's favorite horse, Tango, he called out to him.

"Yo, Plug man! Where you be?"

The horse stood motionless except for swooshing his tail up and down to ward off random flies. A portable boom box was on the workbench next to the horse cranking out Slow Ride by Foghat at maximum volume. Topaz would turn the radio town, but that would require him to get close to Tango. He wandered to the other side of the barn, away from the horse and the boom box, not realizing his cardinal mistake.

"Hey, Plug, you here?" Topaz cupped his hand to his mouth, "And can ya turn the fuckin' music down?"

A second later, the rope dropped around his neck and began to strangle him.

His head snapped back violently as the attacker pulled the cinch tight with his muscular arms. As luck would have it, Topaz's cupped hand temporarily saved his life. The killer yanked his head sideways, trying to get him on the ground to finish him off. Topaz fought for air, his one hand trying to push the rope away from his throat. Off balance and disadvantaged, he couldn't see his attacker but could tell they were smaller in height and weight. He flailed and kicked in all directions trying to shake them, but they stayed glued to Topaz, pulling the rope tighter around his neck. He fought for gasps of air, about to suffocate. The music continued to blast.

Move to the music...We can roll all night . Topaz whipped his shoulders from side to side, grunting and trying to shake the attacker off him. With legs positioned around Topaz's waist, they had leverage, and the rope became even tighter. His face was crimson, the air in his lungs gone. There was only one move left, and it was now or never. He stopped resisting and went limp. Reaching down deep within himself, he mustered all the strength he had left and let his head point up to the roof. Jamming his other hand under the rope, he jerked his body downward with all of his strength to flip the killer over his head and roll him across the dirt floor. The man was stunned by the reversal. Topaz pulled the rope off his neck and flung it aside to walk straight toward the disoriented attacker. A small Bowie knife was slid out of a leather sheath, and he stabbed his attacker three times in the neck.

"No, please," were the man's fading words as the blood spurted out of his neck to the final beats of his heart.

Topaz jumped up and ran around the barn, looking for Plug.

I was betrayed! Nowhere to be seen, he ran outside and opened the door of his truck as a green sedan flew down the driveway, followed by a cloud of dirt. He opened the glove box, surprised to see the Ruger still there. He grabbed the gun. It was too late. The sedan was gone. He glanced at the ignition; his keys were gone too.

"Motherfucker, better not have." The back of his pickup was unlocked. He checked the strongbox storage to see it had been pried open and emptied. *It's all gone. Fuck! All of it!* The drugs and, worse, all the money from the eleven pickups he had made over the past two days. Close to one hundred grand and another fifty grand in dope.

Topaz ran back inside the barn and grabbed the annoying radio, smashing it on the ground, the music finally silenced. The horse neighed as Topaz ran around looking for his friend. He found him in Tango's stable with two bullets through his heart.

165- The Canaries

Topaz returned to the dead man lying in a pool of crimson with arms outstretched. His empty eyes stared at the roof. He searched the man's pockets for evidence, but there was nothing. The dead man's arm had a tattoo of a car on the bicep. Topaz pulled back the sleeve to look at the ink.

It was a Porsche 911, a model also known as the Targa.

Part Two

"The harder the conflict, the greater the triumph."

George Washington

Chapter 22
Our House

Kim stood up from the cave floor to wipe the tears from her eyes and dirt from her pants. She followed Julie and the big man through the opening into Marshera. From high above, a bright light was blinding. Kim shielded her eyes as her pupils tried to adjust.

"Oh, this is Barge," said Julie looking back at her. "He's like our big brother."

"Welcome to Marshera," Barge said softly.

"Thank you," Kim said as her eyes slowly adjusted. She squinted at Barge, trying to see him clearer. He was about eighteen and African American. At around six foot three and three hundred pounds, he looked like he could play offensive lineman for the Green Bay Packers.

Her hand held in front of her face, she looked up to the ceiling trying to make out the light source. It was still too bright to determine from where it came.

"What kind of lights are those? They're almost blinding. Are they LED or something?"

Barge turned to Kim as they walked, "No, the light is from the rocks above. They're translucent and face the southern sun."

"Translucent light rocks? I've never heard of such a thing," said Kim.

"We call this The Lightroom," said Julie. "It's where we grow our food."

With Barge right in front of her, Kim still couldn't see. She stepped aside and stood awestruck. Before her was a giant, open room with granite walls that rose up fifty feet to reach the translucent rock ceiling. In the middle of the room were ten raised garden beds. Spaced evenly apart, lanes were in between each bed for access to cultivate what grew. The beds had walls made of small symmetrical rocks to form a perfect rectangular encasement.

Sized at four feet by eight feet and stocked with a variety of vegetables and fruit trees, the beds could yield fresh produce by the bushels.

"Good lord, this is amazing," said Kim. "I've never seen anything like it. All this is grown with natural light in a cave, no less; it's truly amazing. How many people do you have to feed?" She immediately regretted asking the question, being too forward.

As they walked in between the garden beds, Kim stopped to look at each one examining what had been sown. Spinach, lettuce, tomatoes, carrots, mushrooms, green beans, kale, bell peppers, arugula, ginger, onions, beets, cucumbers, and onions. There were dwarf fruit trees that grew apples, pears, bananas, and cherries. A separate bed had a herb garden that contained parsley, thyme, mint, and oregano.

"Very impressive, indeed. My training is in botany, although I currently work in pharmacology. You've done a wonderful job building these beds."

"What is botany?" Julie asked.

"Botany? It's the study of plant science and plant life," Kim said.

Julie turned to Barge, "Maybe she can help us?"

"Maybe," he said.

"Help with what?" Kim asked. *It sounds like they have a plant problem.*

"We did not build the beds. They were here long before we came to inhabit this place," said Barge. "Julie, I have a few things to tend to. Why don't you take Kim to the Cafeteria for something to eat or drink and then give her a tour of Marshera? There should be time before The Offering."

Julie looked at Kim and smiled, "You said you were hungry. Want to get something?"

"Yes!" Kim replied. "I'm beyond starving." Julie led the way toward the Cafeteria. Kim stopped short and turned to her, "Wait, how are you feeling? Are you alright? Nick and I were trying to take you to the hospital when those darts knocked us out. You were clinically dead before we revived you, and I wanted a doctor to give you a checkup. After we woke up, I went to the police. The detective I met with thought you might live here in these caves. Anyway, how are you and before I forget, how is your brother, Charlie? Is he here? I'm sorry, I'm anxious, and I'm rambling. You can't imagine what I went through to get here. I'm so glad you guys opened that door."

Julie calmly listened to Kim. "You don't have to apologize. I am fine. I feel no ill effects from almost dying. Yes, Charlie is here somewhere. He is also fine. I'm glad that we opened the door for you too. I came right away when Barge told me who was outside the cave. I told Barge you are a friend of Marshera."

Kim was touched knowing that she was now considered a friend of Marshera. "I'm so glad I found you healthy and well."

"Ashun and Winger, they're the ones who knocked you out," Julie said. Winger is an expert with his blowgun. They are both Abenaki Indians and trackers. They found Charlie and me while you were reviving me."

"Do they live here in Marshera?" Kim asked.

"No, they live in a tree fort somewhere in the woods. We don't know exactly where. They stop by sometimes and help us. They're also friends of Marshera. Where is the other man that helped you? Nick?" asked Julie.

"Nick had to work at his ranch and then travel to deliver horse grain. We tried to find you a couple of days ago, but we hiked to the top of the wrong mountain, if you can believe that. What an adventure. We got attacked by this wild pig and a snake too." Grrrsssshhhhhh, Kim shook all over, scrunching up her face as they both laughed out loud. Unexpectedly, Julie reached over and put her arms around Kim to hug her tightly.

"Thank you for saving me." They held each other, and Kim felt her eyes well up. It was the happiest she had been in a long time. Julie's hug made overcoming every bat, pig, snake, and river of boiling water worth it.

"How did you find the tunnel to Marshera?" Julie asked as they walked again. "The mountain has several secret entrances, but they're well hidden."

"I had help from someone who prefers to remain anonymous," Kim answered.

"That is a bit concerning," said Julie.

They walked straight through an adjacent room. Kim took it all in, her head turned from side to side, not feeling like she was in a cave.

"This is the common room," said Julie.

It was well-lit with modern LED lights recessed into the stones. The rock walls were painted a cheerful peach color. Smaller in size with a lower ceiling, it held an oversized couch, chair, and a love seat. They were all made with smooth rocks that fit together perfectly and were covered with thick animal pelts for cushioning. Board games, chess, checkers, and a computer sat on an antique chest. With the lights dimmed and pillows covering the rock furniture, the room felt like a caveman's quad where they hung out. With no one in the room, Kim still wondered how many people lived in the colony.

"Could I ask, what did that man you were with, Barge, mean by The Offering?"

"It would be better to show you than tell you. It happens every afternoon at four o'clock."

"Another question; the police detective said these caves were a hippy colony, but I don't see other people?"

"There are only four of us. My brother, Charlie, and me; Barge, who you met, and then Creen. Charlie and Creen are in their rooms, most likely. That's right; we're all hippies here at the Hippy Colony," Julie laughed. "Actually, Marshera has always been a place of healing."

They turned a corner and entered another open room that looked similar in size to the common room. It was a small classroom. The walls were painted mint green, and there were four school desks in the middle. A large whiteboard hung on the wall.

"This is the learning center," said Julie. "This is where Mother taught us our lessons."

Reaching the end of the room, Kim stopped to look at the ceiling and listen, "I can hear water running in the distance. Did someone leave a faucet on?"

Julie giggled, "It's Wildcat Falls, the waterfall. It flows through the mountain at the end of Marshera in the Falls Room."

"Of course!" Kim said. "Everyone living in a cave should have their very own waterfall!" They both laughed, with Kim feeling more comfortable than ever in such a strange place.

"You make me laugh, Kim," Julie said.

They arrived at the Cafeteria. It was a large room with a long granite table that seated ten people. Kim was surprised to see Marshera had all the modern appliances every kitchen would have. Granite walls were painted a warm, off-white color giving the area a bright appearance. As Kim looked around the room, it suddenly occurred to her; they were in the middle of a cave inside a mountain.

"Where do you get the electricity to power all these appliances?" Kim asked.

"I don't know all the details except for what Mother taught us," said Julie. "There are these flat things called solar panels. They're on top of the mountain, and they collect sunlight to make it into electricity. There's a windmill up there too. The panels and the windmill are connected to a great big battery hidden inside Marshera. It saves up electricity for when it's dark out or when there's no sun or wind."

"Wow, that's cool. Mother? Did you say Mother as in your Mother?" Kim asked.

"No, she's not my Mother. Her real name is Joan. She used to be our caretaker and watch over us. She was our teacher too. One day Rumbles began making the floor shake and vibrate. It got worse and worse until Mother tried to find him to make him stop. But she never came back. We think Rumbles ate her." Julie raised her eyes to look at Kim. They were welled with tears.

"I'm sorry to hear that. That's terrible," said Kim. She wondered who or what Rumbles was.

Julie smiled at her and blinked away the tears to stop discussing the painful topic, "Let's make something to eat."

Inside the refrigerator was a wicker basket filled with several varieties of vegetables. They made veggie wraps on homemade flatbread. Julie poured them glasses of water from a filtered pitcher in the refrigerator, and both sat on the long table to eat.

"Before I forget, is there someplace I can charge my phone?" Kim asked.

"Mother used to plug her phone into those wires on the end of the table," Julie said, pointing to them. "Barge has the only phone now."

Fortunately, the connector fit Kim's phone.

Famished, Kim devoured half of her sandwich in short order and then took a long drink of water before she asked Julie for more information. "You mentioned Mother and then her going to check on Rumbles. Can you tell me more about who this Rumbles is?"

Julie finished chewing and replied, "We started feeling vibrations in the ground and the walls a year ago. We had never felt those things before and figured there must be a dinosaur that woke up because the floor had been shaking badly. Mother said she would find out where the vibrations came from. She went down the Forbidden Tunnel that was supposed to take her to where Rumbles lived. But she never came back. So we figured that Rumbles must've eaten her. Now Barge is our new Mother. He's doing the best he can. He's been here the longest, so he knows almost everything."

"How long ago did Mother disappear down that tunnel?"

"I think it was about eight months ago," Julie said.

Kim sat motionless, holding her sandwich but not eating. "Who came up with the theory that a dinosaur is living in the caves?"

"We all did. The floor was shaking so badly. We figured out that it had to be a big one, like a stegosaurus, with a spiky tail. We read about dinosaurs online on the computer."

"Did Mother not teach you that all the dinosaurs have been extinct for millions of years?"

"Yes, that is what she told us, but she couldn't say where the shaking and the vibrations came from," Julie said.

"Julie, there is no such thing as dinosaurs anymore. Stegosauruses, T-Rexes, and Velociraptors; every type of dinosaur that used to live all over the planet died off. That was millions of years ago. They all went extinct, meaning the species disappeared and won't return."

"What made them go extinct?" Julie asked.

"I believe a giant asteroid hit the earth and caused the climate to change. That was a long time ago. But animals go extinct even today."

"Because of those things that hit the earth?"

"No, not because of asteroids. From what I read, it's due to humans expanding into their territories and wiping out their homes. There is also pollution from people and overhunting them for food, too," Kim answered.

"That sounds pretty bad for the animals, but we can feel Rumbles shaking, and there's no one else here but us, so he must not be extinct yet."

"Let's talk to Barge when we see him and figure it out," Kim said.

"There's something else," said Julie. "You said you know about plants?"

"Yes, I graduated from The University of Chicago with a degree in Botany; why?"

"Marshera has a problem. Rumbles is trying to poison us."

"What? What do you mean by poison you?"

"He's been doing something to our water and food. Right after he started making the ground shake, the water began to taste bad. It made us sick. We think he's been going to the bathroom in the water that feeds our well. That's the water we drink and use for the vegetables in the Lightroom. All the vegetables and fruits we grow in the Lightroom are making us sick too. Oh, and nasty smells are coming into Marshera from the tunnels. It's all been happening since Rumbles woke up."

"The bad smells are something I experienced as I came through the tunnel on my way to Marshera," Kim said. But they are more likely from a geological event, not a dinosaur. Because, again, dinosaurs are extinct. The vegetables look to be healthy. Didn't we eat some of them just now?" Kim asked.

"They grow okay and look healthy, but they taste terrible. If we eat them, we get sick. Don't worry; the food we just ate is from a vegetable garden we planted outside the caves. We grew them using rainwater." said Julie. "Those vegetables don't make us sick. Next month will be November, and it will be too cold to grow vegetables outside. That's why Charlie and I were trying to get the food from the nearby farms."

"I have an idea that could help you guys out," said Kim.

"Seriously? That would be awesome. Would you excuse me, Kim? I'll be back in a few minutes."

"Of course, dear," said Kim.

No wonder Julie and Charlie left the caves to steal food from nearby farms. They're slowly starving to death when not being poisoned by polluted water and their produce.

She looked at her sandwich and thought of Marshera's plight, no longer feeling hungry. Kim wondered what could be causing the tremors, noxious gas smells, and the pollution of Marshera's water. She had decided on her way through the tunnel that if she found Julie and Charlie safe and in good health, she would make her way to Cody and catch a ride back to Crawford. When she first hugged Julie and saw she was fine, her goal seemed accomplished.

But the truth was Julie wasn't safe. Neither was Charlie or the others in Marshera.

I can't leave this place or these people yet. They're kids; starving and in danger.

When Julie returned, Kim was excited to tell her about her idea.

"I have a test kit from when I was in college. It's fairly advanced for its day. We could test Marshera's water and determine what pollutants are in it. That should tell us a lot about the source of your problems."

"That sounds wonderful," Julie said. "But where is this test kit?"

"I'm going to need some help. It's at my Mother's house, and she just moved into the area."

"I'll text her and have her take it out. Hopefully, she can find it."

"Your mother can't come out to Marshera, though, can she?" Julie asked.

"Oh no," Kim said. “I'm hoping to get Nick to do us a favor.”

Kim could tell that Nick liked her by how he looked at her when she visited him at the bar. She had to admit there were some mutual feelings for him too. There was also saving Julie, and they'd had a moment when he pulled the snake off her. He wasn't her type, though. Sure, he was handsome, but he was also annoying with his cowboy-up, turn-the-other-cheek attitude. Brad was far from perfect, but at least she knew him, warts and all.

Kim picked up her phone and looked at the screen. Fifty percent charge, half a bar of cell service. She placed the call, but as expected, there wasn't enough signal to go through. A text message would have to do.

Mum, I'm so sorry I'm going to miss your appointment today. I tried to call you, but there's no service where I am. I made it to Marshera. I'm in the caves and found Julie. There are others here.

They're having major water problems. Tell you all about it when home but prob. won't be until tomorrow. Also, need a favor. Asking a friend to come by and pick up my water test kit from school. Can you find it and give to him? TY so much! I hope and pray for great news from Dr. S.! Love you, K!

She waited for the message to show delivered. Now for Nick. She needed him to bring the test kit.

"Do you think he will do it? Do you think he'll come?" Julie asked.

"I don't honestly know, but I sure hope so," Kim said.

“Would you like to see the rest of Marshera?"

"I sure would!" said Kim. She felt much better after eating nourishing food and drinking a glass of filtered water.

They began walking out of the Cafeteria, and Kim posed the question. "If Nick agrees to go to my Mum's and get my test kit, may he come here to Marshera and give it to me? I'll have to tell him how to find us."

Julie looked at Kim with a concerned face. "No one must know about Marshera or its purpose. We are taught this from the first day we arrive here. Do you believe he can be trusted to keep the secret of Marshera?"

"I'm not even sure if I am trusted. And what is the purpose of Marshera? You said earlier that Marshera is a place of healing. So I take it that this place isn't a hippy colony."

"No, it's not a hippy colony. Mother taught us that we want the people of Crawford to think that. You will know our exact purpose later when we gather for The Offering. You will also know why Marshera must be kept secret. Kim, you saved me, and you will always be trusted."

"Then why wouldn't Barge allow me to enter when he first opened the door to Marshera? Why didn't he trust me? I was all alone in a dark cave, and I needed help. I was frightened half to death!"

"It was my fault. When Ashun and Winger brought us back to Marshera, I didn't tell Barge that you saved me from drowning. I made Charlie and them keep it a secret. Barge was already mad at us for leaving Marshera. When he came to me and told me you were outside in the cave, I confessed to him what had happened. That was when we returned and opened the door."

"Thank goodness," said Kim. "By the way, how exactly did you end up at the bottom of the rapids?"

"We have to ration food. We're always hungry. Ashun and Winger told us about farms nearby and their fields filled with corn, squash, and everything we needed. Charlie and I wanted to help, so we snuck out to find some food. We planned on being back before the four o'clock Offering. The farms had so much to choose from. It was, all ripe and delicious. We only wish we had brought more bags. It was hot out, and when we came to that place you called the rapids, I saw the rope swing and wanted to try it. It looked like fun. That's all I remember until I woke up in the storm riding on that machine with you holding on to me. I was scared not knowing where I was, but I felt safe in your arms."

Feeling terrible sorrow for Julie and everyone at Marshera for their water and food problems, Kim felt her face flush with emotion. Julie and her brother's desperate sacrifice was to find food for the people they lived with. It was so brave. Kim reached over to hold Julie's hand. She realized Julie was a substitute for her long-lost sister, Grace. But she also admired her as the courageous young woman she was. There had to be a way to help everyone at Marshera.

"You need to know something," said Kim. "Nick was a huge part of saving your life. We wouldn't have revived you if it wasn't for him. He got you breathing again. We need him to bring me that test kit. We need to trust him."

“We can ask Barge about Nick coming to us to help. He will want to make sure he can be trusted. Follow me, please."

They left the Cafeteria to walk toward the furthest end of the Marshera Cave. The sound of rushing water became louder with each step. Kim was focused on the surroundings inside of Marshera. Quite simply, they were astounding. The floors weren't covered in dirt. Instead, there was smooth cobblestone packed tightly together that covered every floor. Animal hides were used to cover floors providing warmth from the stones. Ceilings and walls were composed of clean gray granite stone, some painted, and some were natural. They all had separate bedrooms with a few extra ones too. As they came closer to the sound of water, Kim ran her hand along the rough stone wall expecting to feel cold. Instead, it radiated warmth. There were water-filled planters everywhere with white, blue, pink, and red flowering lotus plants.

This place is truly beautiful.

They were almost to the room where the river cut through Wildcat Mountain. Drawings of deer, moose, and bear similar to the ancient images that Kim spotted on her journey to Marshera appeared on the walls. She stopped to look at them.

"I saw drawings like these on the walls of a giant cavern on the way here. Did you and the others create them?"

"The cave drawings are from those who first inhabited these caves," Julie said. “We call them the Ancients. The drawings are all over the tunnels and caves and have been here for over a thousand years," said Julie. "They are not drawings. They’re instructions."

"Not sure I understand," said Kim.

"You will," said Julie.

The last wall held a message. It was written in a language that Kim didn't understand.

Marshera es pehonan otenaw wiya pidjinis stem. Oom inikik mij waam ako mistik gacki kakik ohki necut

"What does it mean?" she asked.

"The words translate to the Golden Rule which we all live by here at Marshera. Mother told us it was left here by the Abenaki who inhabited Marshera during Colonial times. Translated, it means; M*arshera is a place to save lives. Those who come here to heal must never take one.* The Abenaki who inhabited this place lived by that rule too. We believe in those words, and we believe in peace."

"If only all mankind would do the same," said Kim.

Julie led the way until they reached an opening in the wall with stairs that went upwards.

Stairs inside of a cave?

A roar of rushing water echoed throughout the stairwell as it led to a cavernous room. Kim felt moisture droplets on her skin from the river flowing through the room's middle. The rushing waves of water flew down a ten-foot wide canal to blast out of a giant opening in the side of the mountain to become Wildcat Falls.

Kim stood in shock to watch the natural wonder of the powerful force that churned and lapped the sides of the bank as it coursed by them. The water had cut a deep trough several feet down from the ground.

"This is The Falls Room," Julie shouted to Kim over the roar of the water. "We're not supposed to go near the river bank because it's so dangerous. If you fell in, you'd be swept over Wildcat Falls."

"I've never heard of a river inside of a mountain that turns into a waterfall!" Kim shouted back. "Did you say you have tried to drink this water, and it makes you all sick too?"

"This water is clean, but we can't get to it. Mother and Barge told us we should not come up here to get the water. It's too dangerous."

Kim could see what she meant. It would be almost impossible to access the water without being in danger of falling in.

"Water water everywhere and not a drop to drink," said Kim.

Kim felt her phone vibrate in the pocket of her jeans. She pulled it out and read the message. It was Mum.

Hi Honey, so proud of you for finding Julie. Glad to hear she is alright. Your Aunt Rose who I told you lives next town over stopped by. She's working harder than me! I'm fine. Please stay safe and come home to me when you're done helping out. I know where your test kit is. I'll unpack it and wait to hear from your friend. Love ya, M.

Kim smiled, experiencing one of those moments filled with internal warmth when all was right with the world. Her Mum was almost certainly cured of her cancer. Now if she would only hear from Nick, agreeing to come and deliver the water test kit. Never in her life had she felt such a sense of purpose. Never had she felt so needed. After Grace was lost and her father disappeared, she was numb for a year. With her botany background, she could hopefully pinpoint the source of the polluting chemicals and make them well again.

Everything about Marshera was new and exciting. When she first heard about the caves, her mind conjured up the visuals of a dark, dank, torch-lit place filled with spiders. Nothing could be further from what Marshera was. The questions that Julie hadn't answered were what and why? What was the secret of Marshera, and why were these four people living here in this fancy cave? What did Julie mean by place of healing?

What would take place during The Offering that would answer Kim's questions?

Chapter 23
Suspicious Minds

Brad's fingers were a blur, flying across the laptop's keyboard while he entered old passwords used in the past. It was a long shot, but he had to try. Who knew when or if she would call him? His face was intense, like someone trying to diffuse a bomb with only two minutes left.

He had made the long drive back to Maryland with his mother's image floating in the center of his mind as he tried to concentrate. It haunted him with thoughts of her being scared to death in some strange house without her meds or the comforts of home.

They better keep her comfortable and warm wherever she's held.

Rubbing his face with both hands, he tried to stop thinking of how frightened she must be.

Doing everything I can, Mom, hold on a little longer.

Brad shook his head in a flurry, trying one password after another. A cold chill enveloped his body. "Jesus, nothin's working."

He felt a pang of guilt, as he thought about his actions. Kim had been kind to his mother, Barb. After his father passed, Barb was all alone. "One damn man in my life is plenty," she'd said. His mother insisted they regularly visit to take her out for lunch and a scenic ride through the countryside. Kim and Barb discovered that they were both foodies, interested in different varieties of fine food and desserts. They regularly exchanged recipes via email. Barb would email or call to ask Kim to send a recipe for a cookie, cake, or sauce.

The recipes; I can sell her on that angle.

Wait! What kind of asshole am I? Seriously, knucklehead, you get this babe to live with you and not only does she love your ass, she loves your mother's ass too. So then you screw her over?

Brad reconciled his actions with a single sentence. *This will be the last time.* He decided he would go one hundred percent clean after he got his mother freed and back where she belonged. Barb was too fragile to take the stress. *If I get her out of this, I'll never steal another file. But I have to, this one last time.*

The dialogue had to be practiced. He held his cell phone to his ear, pretending to speak into it as if he were on a live call. He practiced the script until it sounded natural.

First things first, he would send a text.

Hey Babe, need a favor. Barb wants that recipe for the cookies again. She must have lost the last one. Needs by tomorrow to bake for an event. Why don't you shoot me your laptop PW and I'll grab the file and send it to her? You can change it when you get home. Luv ya, B

He read it out loud to ensure autocorrect hadn't changed any of the words and then hit the up arrow to send the message. Delivered appeared on the screen.

"Voila! Step one accomplished!" he announced to an empty condo. His back felt a cool sensation from the leather as he reclined.

Brad felt so much better having a rescue plan for his mother. He was a man of action, and action is what he took. It was much better than just sitting there helpless.

His criminal behavior had started with help from his father, of all people. He was only looking for extra money to help pay for tuition and books. His father, Frank, was a Jersey guy and a small-time fence who worked for the Amusos, the region's organized crime family. Frank enjoyed a comfortable standard of living, and he tried to become more important than he could ever hope. So why shouldn't his only son Brad have some pocket change as he struggled through school? A little harmless dealing at the community college would put some jingle in his pocket.

When Brad graduated, he landed a sales gig for a chemical company specializing in pharmaceuticals. He soon realized new jobs require a lot of focus. So he walked away from his side hustle selling coke, weed, and Adderall to classmates. But after a while, he remembered something. Money was what motivated him; so did the juice. He made a call, and the side hustle was back on. Only now, they incorporated his side gig to work in unison with the daytime gig. Traveling around New Jersey and Maryland selling both kinds of chemicals fattened Brad's wallet. One day he called on a new company named Geneltex Corporation. They specialized in research and manufacturing for synthetic opioids. An attractive clinical lab technician named Kim Moreno was working there, and they began dating. Things became serious between them fairly quickly.

One day, sitting at home with Kim, Brad watched her working on her laptop and got an idea. He approached the side hustle people. Would they be interested? They were not, but did have a connection to someone who might. The meeting set, Brad met with their representative, an assertive and exotic Asian woman named Lee Chen. She showed interest but required a steady volume of what he was offering. She gave him a way to make the idea work. Have your girlfriend move in with you, and we will take care of everything. Brad did as instructed. The money would be paid in cash, authorized by Lee Chen's boss in Hong Kong. His name was Mr. Chang.

Voila! Ten grand for each API formulary was big money, and it was so easy! Using the secret camera that Lee had installed in his condo, he could view her passwords as she entered them from her favorite chair. He could even record them using the video option. Some months, he would steal and sell two or three API's from her laptop. Once given to Lee Chen, their mainland China lab would copy the formulas and distribute the drugs through Mr. Chang's network, using his black market channel of dealers. Brad loved that there were never any reports to file or middle managers to deal with. His only contact would be Lee Chen. They worked closely together as business allies and, at times, a lot more. Brad jettisoned the day gig and focused solely on his side gig. The money kept rolling in. Unfortunately, just like his father, Brad spent the money as fast as he made it. No problem, he figured; there was plenty more where that came from.

The process worked flawlessly for eighteen months. But then Mr. Chang began rejecting many of the API's Brad presented to Lee Chen. They were mostly revisions of older drugs. Mr. Chang wanted the new synthetic API's, the NSOs'; Novel Synthetic Opioids.

The market demanded more powerful time-release painkillers. If Brad couldn't deliver them, they would have to terminate their relationship. For a while, Brad captured some API's for synthetics from Kim's laptop until the day her company made significant security changes. They required her to change her password more often. System-generated passwords were issued weekly to guard against stolen intellectual property. Geneltex received reports from Interpol and the FBI that synthetic opioid painkillers were copied by labs in China and sold on the black market.

That was strike one.

Brad's pinhole camera had been the key to his success. He called it his blessing in disguise. It was undetectable, mounted inside the wall plate of a light switch behind Kim's favorite chair. The camera was aimed at an angle that allowed the viewer to zoom in and see Kim's keystrokes as she typed in her ever-changing passwords.

One day he came home to find that Kim had moved her chair across the room to the other side. She wanted to be closer to the window to look outside and see some dumb birds. Brad complained about the interior decorating changes, but she couldn't fathom his opposition. They argued about the matter, but Kim held fast to her birds. The chair stayed, and the stolen API's went. He thought about having a contractor install a new hidden camera in the wall, but it would be too obvious.

That was strike two.

Mr. Chang and Lee Chen were business people and expected a return from their investments. The return on Brad had been over the moon, but lately, he was bleeding red ink. He was afraid to tell Lee what had happened and how he wouldn't be able to steal any information until he figured something out.

To make matters worse, Brad had received an advanced payment to buy a vacation home in Florida. Lee Chen warned Brad that he would have to quickly supply the latest and most potent NSO API's or pay back the money. But Brad had already spent the money. When he failed to respond to her messages, she showed up at the front door of his condo, posing as a religious zealot. During their meeting with Mr. Chang, he knew his relationship with Lee Chen had changed forever. Delivering the goods or dealing with the consequences was what he faced. But he couldn't supply what he didn't have. The stalemate was broken when Mr. Chang ordered the abduction of Brad's mother. Push had come to shove.

***

"Hey, Babe, how's it going?" Brad spoke quickly and acted concerned about her. His voice didn't reveal the truth, which was he wasn't at all concerned about her as long as he retrieved her password and the two-step code from her phone.

Kim had moved to the stairs that led up to the Falls room. Closer to the outside world, her phone still only had one bar of reception. It would have to do. She felt a tinge of anxiousness. She hadn't been away from Brad for this long since they began dating. Kim had to admit she missed him. With all his faults, he was her boyfriend and partner. For the past two years, Brad had been her man.

"You're cutting in and out," Kim said. "I'm … a bad …cation … in…mountains."

"You're where? I thought you were at your Mum's helping her move." Brad said.

"It's…long story…involved saving girl from drowning. …I'm in …cave in…mountains. …to explain …story to you later."

"Yeah, I'll want to hear this one. Think you said you're in a cave."

"Okay, first things first. … give … … password and author… code before … lose you."

"So … goes. It … a-l-c-o-t-t-8-8-8-#. Did you … that?"

"Hold on, I'm entering." Brad wrote the passcode down on a scrap of paper and then entered it into her laptop. "Passcode was accepted, Kim."

"Okay, shoul…ave…auth…code on …phone in a sec…"

"Okay, here go… 2754."

Brad entered the four-digit secondary password. His fingers drummed on the tabletop as his foot bounced up and down. The password was accepted. *Yes*! He clenched his fist in victory.

"Voila, It worked, Babe. I'm in," said Brad.

"Great, the recipes for all food are in … separate file …, you guessed …, Recipes."

"So what is going on, and where are you again?" He badly wanted to get off the call and get the new API's for Mr. Chang.

"Okay, I'll try to … you short version … . I… taking a … break in Mum's yard … heard … for help…" Kim relayed the entire story as best she could.

“What kind of story is this you’re giving me? Brad knew that Kim never lied. He liked to put her on the defense, asserting his dominance. So you’re trying to tell me you’re in this hippy colony place in the mountains now?”

“Yes, … here and…found her. She…fine from what…see.”

“Who is this guy Nick again? What are you doing with him?”

Kim needed to convince Brad that nothing had happened with Nick. The power to prove her innocence to an authority figure required her to overcome her default feeling of guilt.

Managing her extreme anxiety caused her to settle disputes immediately and stop the pain. She would settle his mind right here and now, she thought.

Suddenly the signal was lost, and the call dropped, abruptly ending the conversation.

Chapter 24
Fountains Of Light

Time flew by that afternoon as Kim and Julie talked about a wide range of topics. Kim found her to be a calm, intelligent and curious young woman. It was almost four o'clock and time for The Offering. As they walked toward the room where it was held, a strange sensation passed through Kim's body. It was subtle at first and then grew stronger.

Why are my insides vibrating? Her heart began to hammer as she held out her arm for balance. She looked at Julie. Her voice trembled as she spoke.

"What the hell is happening?"

"Rumbles is at it again!" Julie said. They began walking faster, and then an earthshaking tremor erupted. Marshera shook violently as dirt fell from the ceiling ahead of them. Julie fell to her knees. Kim ran to her, and they clung together, enduring the frightening tremors. It was six minutes of hell before it ended. It was like a switch was turned off. The shaking just stopped.

"That was the worst one yet!" said Julie. "Rumbles must be angry today."

"We're going to talk to Barge and get to the bottom of all this Rumbles stuff!" said Kim.

As they approached the room, Kim recalled her father giving her a ten-dollar bill to put in the offering plate at church every Sunday. This ritual, however, was to be The Daily Offering, whatever that meant. The chamber was smaller than the other rooms she had seen in Marshera. Was it to be a meeting for daily prayer or group meditation? A shiver passed through her. Will they sacrifice an animal? All she knew was that every activity in Marshera was designed to stop at precisely four o'clock in the afternoon for this important event.

The room was dark, lit only by twelve identical white candles in a candelabra made of granite stone. A deerskin hung in the doorway to provide seclusion from all things outside the room's smooth rock walls. Ancient drawings showed women and men tending to vegetables in the beds of the light room. The candlelight shadows danced against the walls hiding and then revealing depictions of life in the caves. Similar to the other drawings, they showed others who drank liquid from the odd-shaped bowl.

Kim stood incognito at the back of the room to watch the proceedings. Julie sat on the floor next to Barge on a brown bearskin rug that gave the participants a comfortable place during the ceremony. Centered against the far wall was a marble tower that rose fifteen feet from the floor. It was made of symmetrical stones precisely fitted together to create the ancient pillar. Barely a visible seam could be detected in its craftsmanship, narrow at the top with a notch cut out on the right side. A channel of smooth, cup-shaped stones cascaded over each other and spiraled down around the tower to carry whatever might flow out of the top to its destination; a triangular-shaped stone bowl. Inside the bowl was a stone ladle waiting to be utilized.

The bowl looks like the same one as in the ancient drawings.

It was evident to Kim that The Offering would involve something that would geyser up out of the tower and then fill the bowl. It sat empty, gleaming in the faint candlelight, waiting for the delivery of whatever precious resource was to be produced. Barge and Julie sat beside each other, facing the tower as if they always sat in those predefined places. They were waiting for the other two members of Marshera to join them.

She gently pushed back the deerskin divider to enter the room. A tiny waif-like girl with white hair appeared. Behind her was Julie's brother, Charlie. Julie waved to them and they sat beside her, completing the half circle.

Julie turned to Kim and waved her over to introduce them, "Creen, this is…." Creen interrupted, "Kim, yes, I know. The person who saved you from drowning."

"She has ESP and bad manners," said Charlie.

Kim couldn't believe how tiny and pale Creen was. *She's almost transparent!* "Sorry, I don't hug," Creen said. "We are both pleased to meet each other." She quickly turned and sat on the rug.

"You met my brother, Charlie," Julie said. They briefly hugged. "Sorry I disappeared on you," he said. "Ashun and Winger took me with them. Anyway, thanks for helping out my sister and being a hero and all." Kim immediately detected his sarcasm toward her.

"It is the time!" Barge's voice boomed loudly. That was her cue to recede to the back wall and observe.

Immediately, all four joined hands and began to chant strange phrases at a low volume.

“Nebisata, your Blue Water… Wikusanta, Wikusanta”

"Give us life, your sons and daughters… Wikusanta, Wikusanta”

With eyes closed, they sat on the bearskin rug and chanted the phrases repeatedly. Holding hands, they swayed side to side and chanted as Kim heard a low gurgling sound come from the tower. She watched in amazement as steam began to billow out of the top.

Their mantra was repeated again and again, "Wikusanta, Wikusanta." More steam billowed out of the cone as the gurgling sound became louder and higher in pitch. They switched from holding hands to putting their arms around each other's shoulders. Louder each time, they hailed for their Blue Water. Their swaying became more exaggerated, "your blue water… Wikusanta."

Kim wrapped her arms around herself as she nervously watched them singing and swaying. "Give us life now… sons and daughters, Give us life now… Nebisata…"

What is Nebisata?

And then it happened, as steam billowed from the tower, a blue, foamy liquid emerged to crest the top of the cone and fill the upper reservoir. It spilled out through the notch to flow down into the circular chute. The hot, blue liquid moved down around the cone, leaving a steam trail behind as it slid over the cool stones. The liquid snaked around the tower as it had done every day for a thousand years before, ending its journey by splashing into the stone bowl and filling it to the top.

Their chanting and swaying transitioned to joyous applause and cheering. The gurgling ended as the last few drops of foamy blue elixir filled the mortar.

The chamber went utterly silent. Barge looked to Charlie. "It is your turn today." He immediately sprang to his knees to stir the ancient ladle clockwise. Steam rose up as he cooled the liquid. Charlie brought the ladle before his face as he closed his eyes to gulp down the potion. Smiling, he lowered it back into the bowl to refill it and gently handed it to Creen. She consumed the steamy liquid as Charlie had. The consumption was followed by Julie and, finally, Barge. He lifted the bowl to pour the contents into the ladle, brought it to his mouth, and drank it in one swallow. Then he carefully set the ladle to rest inside the bowl to be used the following day.

All four of them stood up and formed a group hug. They went to Kim and gathered around her. She wasn't sure what they would reveal, but she had to ask some questions.

"Why do you drink it?" asked Kim. Their faces had become red like they had sunburns from a day at the beach.

"It's The Offering, the Nebisata," Creen answered, already aware of Kim's question.

"What does it do for you?"

"The Blue Water keeps us alive. After several years it cures us completely," said Barge.

"Keeps you alive and cures you from what?"

"We all have terminal illnesses," said Barge. "The Fountain of Life keeps the illnesses we were born with away. Without drinking from the Fountain, we all would die from them. The Fountain of Life not only prevents us from dying, it permanently heals our chronic afflictions. There is just enough Blue Water for the four of us. The Offering is consumed from the sacred Patera, filled by The Fountain of Life, every day at four o'clock in the afternoon. That is the only time the healing water is offered. That is why it is called The Offering. We must drink The Blue Water as hot as we can stand it, every day for five years. After that, a resident is called a Penta, and they are completely healed."

"Then we are free to leave," said Julie. "But we can never go home again."

"Wait, why wouldn't you go home if you are healed?" Kim asked.

"To protect the secret of Marshera," Barge said. "If Normals learned about The Fountain of Life and its Blue Water, they would overrun Marshera. Everyone and anyone with any illness would lie, cheat and perhaps even kill to steal the healing Blue Waters. That is why Pentas must relocate far away from where they are known. They must also change their identities. If we returned to the homes we came from, the secret would eventually be discovered. People would ask how someone with a terminal illness was miraculously cured. The secret of Marshera would be revealed. Everything is pre-arranged well before a Penta has completed their five-year journey. Money is set aside in a trust by our founder."

Barge looked directly at Kim, "We have never revealed the secret of Marshera to an outsider before you. You must never reveal the secret to the outside world when you leave. If outsiders ask, you must tell them Marshera is a harmless hippy colony."

"Barge is a Decade," Creen blurted out. He's here for ten years but only has four more to go." Then she turned to face him and smiled, "He's also hiding something, but I'm not sure what. It's some secret that is hidden deep inside. I can sense it."

Barge looked at her with no expression and slowly shook his head.

"Is it the nature of your illness?" Kim asked.

"We don't discuss the illnesses that brought us to Marshera. That is private. We were all chronic and terminal when we arrived at this place. Marshera keeps us alive every day. The future is what we live for. The future is filled with hope. That is why each of us wears the sign of the lotus flower tattooed on the back of our necks. It is the only flower that rebirths daily."

“How did this place begin? Who built Marshera?"

"The ancients created this place. The caves, the Fountain of Life, and the garden beds were all built a thousand years ago. The last inhabitants before modern times were Abenaki Indians of colonial times. The cave drawings from the ancients told them and us how to use the Fountain of Life. Mother taught us the ways of the Ancients and then the Abenaki. Our chants are their chants.”

Julie joined the conversation, "Mother taught us the history of the Abenaki Indians. They had seen their villages dying from Smallpox and Measles, spread by Colonists. There were stories the colonists sometimes spread their diseases through infected blankets given to the Abenaki as gifts. They had no resistance to those diseases and began dying. So many moved north to Canada. But winter was coming. A young woman from one of the villages named Amassol accidentally rediscovered Marshera. It had been unoccupied for many decades. Amassol and her village moved into Marshera for the winter to hide from the Colonists. They planned to stay here until the spring and then move north to Canada to join other Abenaki natives. When they moved into

Marshera, some of the villagers had Smallpox and Measles. They gave the sick ones the Blue Water, and it cured them in months."

"But why didn't they have to stay here for five years as you all do?"

"Smallpox and Measles are infectious diseases, not genetic disorders," said Barge. “The Fountain of Life takes us five years to repair our DNA genome. As Creen said, I am what is called a Decade and require ten years to heal."

"Last question, why not give some of the Blue Water to scientists so they could analyze it and copy it? Millions of lives could be saved, couldn't they?" Kim asked.

"Mother told us a sample of the water was secretly provided to scientists to analyze and copy it without exposing Marshera. But it could not be copied successfully. The element that makes the water blue is not found anywhere else on earth. Also, according to the cave drawings, the Blue Water must be consumed right away, and hot, from the Fountain of Life. If it is not, the water loses its potency. That's why Marshera must be kept a secret," said Barge.

Kim realized that all her questions had been answered. It was all explained in the cave drawings and the secret of Marshera.

"I understand," she said. "All of mankind would find a way to get here to try to drink this fountain of youth. Then they would destroy it for some greedy enterprise," said Kim.

"It's not a fountain of youth," Julie said. "We age at the same rate as you, Normals. It's a Fountain of Life that cures the diseases we were born with."

"Normals? Is that people like me?" Kim asked.

"Yup, you're one of them Normals. And we hate Normals!" said Charlie.

"Charlie!" Julie yelled at him. He hung his head and went silent.

"It's okay," said Kim. "Fountain of Life, not Fountain of youth; got it. What is Marshera?"

"Marshera is the name given to this place by the Abenaki," said Julie. It was named after Amassol's mother. Instead of a medicine man, they had a medicine woman. She was the great healer of their village that understood the Blue Water and its healing powers. Marshera will always be a place of healing."

"The problem is that now Marshera is making us sick. It is something in the water, we believe." Barge said.

"Because of Rumbles the Dinosaur!" shouted Charlie.

"I think I can help you folks with that problem," said Kim. "Barge, we need to talk."

"She has a special test kit," said Julie. "It can tell us what is bad in our water."

"Then talk we must," Barge said. We cannot waste any time. Winter is coming, and we are almost out of food."

They moved out of the room and into the Common Room. Kim felt privileged that she had been trusted with all of the information contained in the secret of Marshera.

What the people of Marshera or Kim didn't know, was that their newly trusted friend would soon reveal their secret to the outside world.

Chapter 25
Blue Water

"You there?" She was afraid she'd lost him again. "Brad, I can …arely hear you. We got disconn…ed."

"Yeah, I'm here," said Brad. "You were telling me about this guy you met."

"Stop it please, Brad. Ther.. …othing going … and … know it."

Kim moved up the stairs closer to the Falls Room to improve the cell signal. It worked; they could talk with clarity by picking up another reception bar.

"Brad, the guy that helped me, Nick; he's a local. Stop being so suspicious."

"Hey, I'm not the one talking to strangers. Is he there in those caves with you now?"

"No, he is not here. Please stop making me feel guilty. I have enough on my mind."

"Now that I can hear you, why don't you tell me the whole story, Kim? I'm listening."

She told herself she would never break her promise to the people of Marshera. But he had a way of making her feel that she needed to confess.

This one time Kim and never again.

Brad was someone she knew and, more importantly, someone she could trust.

Kim told him everything.

"Let me this straight, this Blue Water geysers up every day, and they all drink it, and it cures their health problems? Sounds very far-fetched." He continued the guilt trip.

"It's true, Brad. They document their health improvements by months and years. After drinking the Blue Water from the Fountain of Life, they are healing and getting better."

"Why the hell do they keep it secret?"

"Think about it, Brad. With all the disease in the world and then the Covid-19 pandemic, if the secret of Marshera got out, all of humanity would descend on them. They tried to duplicate the blue water years ago, but it has a chemical in it that can't be copied. The other issue is there is only enough liquid for four people, and they have to drink it hot the second it comes out of the fountain. They can only save four lives at a time, and that time is five years each."

"All you need to do is get a sample to the lab, and they'd analyze it. Then they could duplicate it. I'm in the chemical business, Kim. Big companies can copy anything. If the Blue Water cures like you say it does, then Jesus, can you imagine the money we could make? Heck, we'd be billionaires!"

Kim felt a jolt of fear run down her spine.

"Brad, I'm going to make you swear to me again; you promised not to tell anyone about anything I am telling you right now. These people trusted me, and I promised them. You are the only one I've told, so you must promise me that you'll keep Marshera confidential. Promise me, Brad, right now."

There was silence, and Kim felt another jolt of anxiety shoot up her spine.

"Brad! Are you there? Hello?"

"I heard you, Babe. I won't say anything. I promise. See you in a few days. Love ya."

"Love you too," Kim said, relieved that Brad promised secrecy.

What did I just do?

***

Brad picked up the laptop nervously, attacking the keyboard to make sure he was still logged in.

Good, still in. Shit, this Blue Water presents a ton of options. First things first!

Moving to Kim's favorite chair, Brad navigated around the computer's directory, looking for the folder. Laughing, he blew by the one marked Recipes. He was about to download a valuable recipe named NSO's. The folder had been opened many times, but not recently. *API Formularies; there you are again, old friend.*

He double-clicked on the folder, and Brad's smile turned to a grimace when the password prompt appeared. Hmmmm, again? Not a problem. He set the scrap of paper with the passcode on the keyboard and accurately typed the password. His pinky depressed the enter key.

INCORRECT PASSWORD. The phrase stared at him from the middle of the blue screen.

"What the…?" He entered the characters again, this time with meticulous precision.

INCORRECT PASSWORD

"Jesus Christ, no, please." He tried three more times before accepting reality. Her work folder, *API Formularies*, now required a separate password that was different from the one allowing access to the laptop.

"Fuck's sake!" He yelled and threw the laptop across the room. Luckily it hit the back of the couch before it bounced down to land on the floor upside down.

Fishing a pack of Marlboro Reds from his coat's inside pocket, he lit one up and leaned against the quartz countertop to stare blankly at the white cabinets. He reached inside the lower cabinet and pulled out the Beefeater. Filling a tumbler halfway, he took a long draw followed by a drag on his cigarette. He stared at the white cabinets across the room. It was the first time he'd noticed how bland they were.

They lack character, just like me.

He had to conjure up a plan B. Brad knew he was good at inventing lies and scenarios to get what he needed. It was a standard operating procedure for job titles like sales representative or attorney. He just had to create something to get that password for the API Formularies folder.

Kim, Babe, I think you must have accidentally saved the cookie recipe in the API Formularies folder. Can I have the password, Babe?

He rehearsed it, speaking it out loud, and then tried it again in the empty condo.

It'll never work, idiot. She trusts you, but she isn't stupid.

Motionless, he kept staring at the white cabinets, frozen in fear. Flicking the ashes into the sink, Brad exhaled a cloud of smoke. Pfft, the ciggie fell into the empty tumbler, extinguished by gin residue. He hadn't slept much after the news about his mother. Shuffling back to Kim's chair, he fell into it and closed his eyes.

In his dream, he became invisible, a handy superpower when you're a thief. He found himself in a scientific lab where there was one bed, and lying on it was his mother, sleeping peacefully. Standing over her was Mr. Chang in a white lab coat. Brad stood motionless against a pale blue wall, watching them. *What the hell is he planning on doing to her?* There was a portable tray with several syringes spread across a clean white cloth. Mr. Chang spoke to her in a low voice, almost a whisper. Brad ambled toward them and carefully listened.

"We test every painkiller drug that we manufacture, Mrs. Parkland. The procedure will consist of me injecting several different drugs into you, one at a time. You are of advanced age, and therefore you will overdose and die; of that, there is no doubt. The good news is that the data we collect from your autopsy will help us perfect the drugs. The use of your body for experimentation and testing is of particular interest to your son. It will also count as payment toward the debt that he owes."

"Wait! I tried everything!" Brad walked toward them as Mr. Chang looked up and around the room, squinting to see where the voice came from.

"Please don't hurt her! Please!" Brad begged him.

"Bradley, I can hear you," said Mr. Chang, looking up toward the ceiling. "You shouldn't beg needlessly. It is unbecoming of you. You have nothing of value to offer me in exchange for your mother's life. Begging will not help save her."

"But I do have something to offer! I have a better solution," said Brad.

Mr. Chang honed in on the direction of his voice. His face looked puzzled.

"Hear me out, Mr. Chang; I have stumbled on something remarkable. There is this special water, it is blue, and it bubbles up from underground in a cave once a day. It is rare and only available in one place in the world. Here's the good news, it's close by."

"Tell me again why I care about blue-colored water, Bradley?"

"You care because the water can heal people that are dying from all kinds of deadly afflictions and diseases. It's located in a mountain cave in New Hampshire, and I can get you some. Then you can send it to China and have the lab make a copy. It will be a thousand times more valuable than any synthetic opioids, Mr. Chang. You don't need to experiment on her. You don't!"

Mr. Chang looked up at the bright surgical lights from overhead. The lights reflected off his glasses, giving him the appearance of a robot. "I can hear you, but I can't see you, Bradley."

"This is because there is no substance to you. People who take money in advance and fail to pay it back have no substance. It's like they're invisible. You haven't had substance for a long time. Your mother can't see through you, and neither can your friends. But I see right through you, don't I, Bradley? So if you will excuse me, I will now proceed to give your mother her first injection."

"But I really can deliver this time, Mr. Chang! Kim has access to the Blue Water! She will do anything for me. This is a real thing, and I can get you a sample! Then you can duplicate it. Do you see the possibilities in this scenario? You sell the disease, and then you sell the cure! The cycle then repeats itself over and over. Your people in China can copy and reproduce anything you once told me. Give me this chance Mr. Chang. Give me this one chance to get you the Blue Water first. Then you'll have leverage over the entire planet! We won't make millions; we'll make billions! What do you have to lose?"

Mr. Chang continued staring motionless at the ceiling. "We?"

"I mean, you; you can make billions. You can make a fortune with this Blue Water."

He lowered the syringe to the table. "You were once a great asset to us, but now you have become a liability. Perhaps this is your last chance to square yourself. I'll give you twenty-four hours. Get me a sample, and we will test it to see what the blue water consists of."

Brad's eyelids popped open as he bolted upright in the chair. Momentarily frozen, he leaped up and found his phone to call Mr. Chang. The phone rang several times as he wiped his forehead with his shirt sleeve. No practice was needed now.

This time he knew exactly what to say.

Chapter 26
Wild Horses

He'd been dead for over a day when Nick found him. There was some nasty shit that went down in Falluja but nothing like this. Overnight stays in motels were necessary when he delivered an Arabian for Gus to a horse stable as far away as Litchfield, Connecticut. Then he'd head home. It had been one night and many miles logged when he finally rolled up the gravel driveway late that afternoon.

Tired from the drive, Nick lumbered into the barn and stood staring like a statue.

Hanging by the neck from the main carrier beam was the man who had raised him, loved him, and taught him everything he knew about horses.

Gus was putting on a cringe-worthy display. His tongue was thrust out with teeth clenched around it. White foam circled his mouth, leaving a milky residue. Scrape marks surrounded his neck where the rope was cinched. Maybe he desperately tried to undo the noose, changing his mind too late.

Jesus, Dad, what you do to yourself?

After a while, Nick cut him down. He noticed his giant hands balled up in tight fists like he'd been in a final brawl with the Grim Reaper.

It was a sight that no son should ever see.

Almost five years after Gus had taken his own life so brutally and strangely, Nick still didn't understand why. Like most suicides, those closest never see it coming. He must have been in pain, he thought. But from what? He never showed any signs.

I guess we're all actors at heart.

Everyone puts on a front. Everyone wears a mask to hide their true self. People create many kinds of masks and façades to hide what really burns and churns inside their souls. Nick thought about his father wearing a confident mask of authority and stoicism to cover up some unknown deep-seated pain. If so, he wore it well. What confounded him was the light he'd seen in his eyes when he was around his Arabians. There was no hiding it. He loved their show and strength. The sheer spectacle of equine poetry in motion as they held their tales high and galloped about so smoothly, their floating gaits and shimmering black coats. Hadn't that been enough?

Nick tried to stop asking himself that question because there were no answers.

Dead men tell no tales.

***

It was 5:30 AM, and Nick was bored. He held the reins and mindlessly walked Cracker in endless laps around the pen as part of his training. The exercise didn't help his ankle, still tender from the run-in with that nasty pig, Elvis. He had hoped that scaling the wrong four thousand-foot mountain while fighting off black snakes and wild pigs would dissuade Kim from her goal of finding a girl who he believed was just fine. They'd saved her life. Wasn't that enough? Now she wanted him to take her to Wildcat and the hippy colony. He had other priorities.

Cracker was almost ready to be under saddle at two and a half years old. Most breeders of Arabians, or "Arabs," as they were called in horse circles, waited until their colts turned three. But he needed to push the envelope and sell this stallion now. The loans that his father had left him were sizeable, and he barely kept up with the payments to Milt Logan's bank.

The market for Arabians fluctuated wildly, but recently he heard it was strong. There was hope that Cracker would fetch ten or even fifteen thousand. It wouldn't surprise him. He was a magnificent animal. Maybe the finest Arabian they'd ever owned. But how much would be left over after his costs? Stud fees, veterinary bills, feed, stabling, and tack; it all added up. The meager profit wasn't worth his time. It was time to get out; he kept telling himself. He did it to honor his father's legacy. Besides, it was all he knew.

Unhitching the reins, he walked ahead of Cracker four more laps around the pen. This time they would go in counterclockwise circles as he talked to him, building trust between horse and man. As they lapped, Nick stopped talking to the animal and returned to the past.

Nick and Gus battled fiercely off and on when one day, out of the blue, Nick announced that he intended to join the Marine Corps to fight for his country. Gus opposed him from the start. Wanting to protect his only child, he never let up. Stubborn to a fault, his father even refused to see him off when he shipped out to boot camp at Parris Island. The training was a thirteen-week test that Nick had always wanted. He'd passed every horse riding test with flying colors, but what about this one? Nick graduated at the top of his class, receiving the Honor Graduate Award. He was then sent to an Infantry Training Battalion, where they turned him into a warrior. He further tested his toughness, requesting to be sent to a heavy war zone in Iraq. Nick wrote to his DI: send me into the middle of the shit. They granted his wish. In the middle of the shit is where he landed. The Battle of Fallujah was a month away, followed by Operation Phantom Fury. Ten thousand US Troops waged heavy combat for two months. Five hundred men were wounded when it was over, and ninety-five became casualties. Nick saw intense action, evading bullets, mortars, and IEDs throughout both battles.

He never suffered so much as a scratch.

He felt invincible until one day his company was pinned down on a sand dune west of Halabsa. The IED exploded under them, causing their Humvee to roll, landing Jake Terrel, Nick's best friend, out in the middle of enemy fire. Guns popped off, leaving sand explosions all around, preventing them from saving his life. Nick wouldn't have it and ran out in an erratic pattern, dodging gunfire to get his friend. He succeeded in dragging him to safety as rounds whistled past his head. He couldn't believe his luck; he survived without a scratch again.

Inevitably, fate trumps luck. Nick became careless. He stood up at the wrong moment, and Juba, Iraq's famous sniper, sent one straight through his gut. Blood spurted up in the air from his belly. The pain was indescribable. Nick was almost gone when the Black Hawk Medevac got him out of there. He was given three surgeries in Germany. They shipped him back home when it was determined he was strong enough. He and his father hadn't talked since he left for basic training. Throughout the nine-hour flight, Nick wondered, *what can I expect when I get home?*

He found out fast. His father was frantically concerned for his son's life. Gus provided the most loving care he had ever shown his boy. When Nick returned to the hospital for follow-up surgeries, Gus held twenty-four-hour vigils, sleeping at the hospital, refusing to leave. The heroic veteran would have to endure five more surgeries to live a normal life again. He got through all of them. Still, frail six months later, a Purple Heart and a Bronze Star Medal were awarded to him. One day after recuperating for so long, Nick returned to being Nick again. He jumped on an Arabian named Comet and rode through the trails for hours.

The ordeal brought both of them closer together to be more adult friends than father and son. Nick began taking on more of the responsibilities of running the ranch. Gus still had yet to involve him in all the financial details but promised he would, eventually. It would all belong to Nick as Gus headed toward retirement. And just like that, he was gone. Nick was the only one left in charge. He still had a lot of questions but no one to ask. And that became a problem.

***

"Well, look who's back in town," Walt lumbered over, holding two large coffees.

Nick finished his lap with Cracker and headed over to him.

"What's up, Walt?"

Tilting his head, he looked strangely at him. "Looking like you got a limp there, son. Donnybrook at the Risin Son? Or did you get kicked by that there horse of yours?"

Nick took a long pull off his coffee, "More like a kick from a wild pig."

"Say what? Where'd you run into a wild pig?"

"You don't wanna know ol' man," said Nick.

"Nah, you're pulling my leg. That crazy horse you got there must've nailed you. Hey, don't be embarrassed; it happens. If I had a nickel for every time a nag kicked me in the face, I'd be living in Miami Beach by now."

"By the look of your face, you should own Miami Beach."

"I couldn't go there if I wanted to. The wife would never talk to me again."

"Your wife died years ago, Walt."

"Exactly my point!" Walt yelled out, laughing. “You fell for it!”

Nick rolled his eyes. "Fuck off, you old shit-kicker."

"Ahhh, yes, his inner Shakespeare doth emerges."

"Whatever. Have to work Crack for another hour. Makin a few grain deliveries around the area later," said Nick.

"Alright, I'll be behind the shed on the tractor," said Walt."That job ain't gonna finish itself." He lumbered away in the other direction.

"Hey, old man!"

"Ya?"

"Sugar cubes."

Walt placed four of them in his dirty palm and returned to the project.

It was time to walk Cracker in counterclockwise circles, followed by unbridling and commands. The horse learned almost instantly. This animal had depth and intelligence behind its chocolate-brown eyes.

He stopped walking and felt around for the sugar cubes in his pocket. It was a calculated risk but what the hell. He walked into the barn and out with the saddle and pad.

Gus would usually do this part. Nick had learned by watching him. "It takes a special touch when dealing with an unbroken colt," Gus said. "You develop it with time and practice." His father hadn't realized that Nick was born with the touch.

The saddle pad was brought out and shown to Cracker as Nick looked him in the eye. His voice was the calm and confident voice of the alpha. "It's just a pad Crack. Not gonna hurt you, buddy." He brought the pad close to his snout and held it for him to smell. The horse flared his nostrils and blinked with approval.

Cracker stood still as Nick flopped the pad on his back where the saddle would go next. He gently raised and lowered his hind leg showing a reaction to the foreign object. Nick walked around in front of the horse again, where Cracker could see him and feel safe. He produced a small sugar cube from his palm and held it under the horse's mouth. He gobbled it up, smacking his lips in enjoyment. Patiently, Nick kept within the horse's eyesight for several minutes. He continued to talk to him as the alpha, calm and in control. If there was such a thing as a horse whisperer, Nick had watched his father do it for his entire life. Now he would take over.

Over to the fence, he picked up the saddle and walked with it while showing it to the horse and speaking softly to build trust. It was quiet out; the only sound came from Walt on the tractor behind the barn. Cracker stood motionless, looking at Nick as he held the Freedom Arabian Saddle under his arm. "Gonna offer you the saddle just like the pad, Crack. Ain't gonna be nothin'." Nick slowly moved to the black stallion's side and swung the saddle up on top of the horse. Cracker made the same movement with his rear leg, only more pronounced. He whinnied, raising and lowering his head and snorting loudly through his nose. Nick went back in front of him and stroked his neck in praise as he offered another sugar cube. Cracker gobbled it down as he had the first.

"Atta boy Crack. Walk in the park," he said, stroking his neck. "You're ready, buddy. You are so ready."

Nick looked up into the sky, "You seein' this?"

The horse adapted to the saddle so well. A voice inside Nick's head said, *go for it*. He tightened the cinch straps underneath and made his next move, sliding his left boot in the stirrup to mount Cracker. Walt came back and watched in amazement. He ran over and opened the gate just as Nick said, "Let's really see if you're ready! Hiyaaaaah!!"

They shot through the gate like a fighter jet and pilot taking off with afterburner engaged. They were a blur as they flew through the field and headed down a trail at full speed. It had been too long since he'd had the time for this. He was flying again, that feeling of freedom. Just man and horse, the wind rushing at him caused tears to stream down his cheeks. The only sound he heard was Cracker's galloping hooves. Standing in the stirrups, he leaned forward and maneuvered the stallion around fallen trees and ditches. It was like Cracker had already ridden this trail a dozen times. He flew over and around obstacles like he was an Alfa Romeo, showing off his silky smooth gate. Nick reached his hand down to feel the horse's neck muscles expand and contract as they zoomed around the loop. Finally deciding the test ride was over, Nick guided him back to the ranch and inside the pen.

Dismounting, Walt asked, "Was that half as fun as it looked from here?"

"Twice as much!" Nick responded with a smile as he picked up his Stetson off the post and dusted it off.

Undoing Cracker's saddle, Nick unclasped the cinch straps only to have his phone ring out from his pocket with Fall Boy singing again,

So light em up up up, light em up up up, I'm on fire! He stepped back and pulled out the phone to read it.

Cracker erupted, rearing back on his hind legs to kick Nick in the shoulder. He flew backward to fall flat on his rear end while his phone landed in the dirt. Saddle and pad fell to the ground as Cracker squealed and galloped to the other side of the pen. Standing motionless, the horse seemed to be saying, after that ride, how dare you not focus all your attention on me!

"Getting the message y'all not a fan of Fallout Boy!" Nick yelled to him as he rolled over on his side to rub his shoulder and pick up his phone.

It was a message from Kim.

Hi Nick, How's the ankle feeling? I have news. I'm actually in Marshera! Right? Long story - went on tour w/ Wildcat Off-Road Playground place and guy knew where a secret entrance to Marshera was. I made it there and they let me in. Julie's here - She's seems Ok. Need a huge favor. They're having major problems with drinking water here. Making them all sick. I have a water test kit at my Mum's from school. Could you stop by and get it? She'll have it ready for you. Now for the huge part - Can yu bring it to me here at Marshera? Know I'm asking a lot Nick. I will pay you that one fifty I promised. If yu say yes, she's at 29 Post Rd. Let me know if you can do tomorrow? Thank you if the answer is yes! Kim.

Nick sat on the ground, shaking his head as he stared at his phone in wonder. So much for dissuading Kim from her goal of finding Julie. He wondered if she was flirting with him to get the test kit or if she was feeling the same thing as him.

Bring the test kit, Nick. Why not?

He looked up at Cracker sauntering around the pen. "Time to put you back in your stall."

Nick typed his reply and sent the message, *Okay*.

Chapter 27
Everybody Wants To Rule The World

The word scarce is defined as a lack of sufficient supply of an item required to meet its demand. The item is typically a commodity, such as food, water, oil, or money. Closely related, the word rare is defined as an item not found in large numbers and, therefore, of interest. Examples of rare items might include the corpse flower, an albino alligator, or a parking spot in downtown Manhattan. The words scarce and rare are often used interchangeably. Whether something is scarce or rare can be argued. A third and more important variable can settle the argument - demand. How strong is the demand for the item that is scarce or rare?

If an item is in high demand and the item is scarce and rare, its value will surely be high.

An example of this rare economic condition was a giant meteorite composed of a rare element not found anywhere else on Earth. That same meteorite was buried ten feet deep on the side of a mountain in rural New Hampshire, thus making it scarce.

The element that the meteorite was composed of was in urgent demand by an international organization named ITER and a certain middle eastern country, making the meteorite scarce, rare and in high demand. Therefore its value was not only high; it was priceless.

The meteorite, or space rock, as others sometimes called it, was composed of an element that originated far away in the cosmos. The element was known as Continuum (symbol NU). A certain Dr. Conti and his team discovered the meteorite and element in the nineteen eighties. At the time, the space rock was an exciting discovery, but there was little interest in Continuum. It was scarce and rare but lacked demand and thus had no value. Decades later, demand for Continuum arose. The scarce and rare element was a crucial, final component required for constructing the Holy Grail in power plant technology, the world's first fully functioning nuclear fusion reactor.

A nuclear fusion reactor was the answer to save the planet from the effects of global warming. Nuclear fusion was a far superior technology to all other forms of power generation. All the other greenhouse gas emitters, such as gas, coal, and hydro, were obsolete. Even solar and wind solutions contributed only ten percent to the power grids around the world. Then there was nuclear fission, used to build reactors of past and present and known for creating deadly radioactive waste or the potential for meltdowns. There was always a concern about reactor accidents that could spread deadly, radioactive clouds as they did in Chernobyl, Fukushima, and Three Mile Island.

Nuclear fusion power was the solution for the future, eliminating all other types of toxic power plants. All that was needed to power the fusion reactors would be readily available hydrogen isotopes derived from elements of deuterium and tritium.

The process of fusing hydrogen atoms to create a mega-powerful reactor had seemed simple enough on paper, but it was close to impossible in the real world. In simplified terms, a fusion reactor was a mini sun held in place by a magnetic field that resided inside a metal chamber. If scientists could create this condition, the benefits would be plentiful amounts of green, sustainable energy that would last as long as a star.

Several countries had tried to build experimental fusion reactors, but none were successful. The United Kingdom's JET series, Russia's T-15, USA's TFTR, and Japan's JT-60 were all fusion reactors that crashed and burned. The biggest obstacle was building a reactor chamber that could contain the incredible power of a mini sun. After years of trial and error, Russian scientists perfected a design that could do the job. It was called the Tokomak reactor chamber. With this milestone accomplished, thirty-five countries created a multi-nation consortium named ITER (International Thermonuclear Experimentation Reactor) to develop and build a working nuclear fusion reactor. It would be located in southern France. Funding for the project was in the billions and supplied mainly by the larger counties involved: China, the USA, Russia, Japan, South Korea, and the European Union.

As scientific tests continued, the consortium discovered a new problem. The fusion fuel, tritium, was not stable enough to start and power the reactor. They had to find a fuel to replace tritium for long-term, sustainable operation. The fuel would need to be similar to tritium but more robust and stable.

The fuel they needed was called Continuum. ITER's scientists were made aware of a large deposit of Continuum in rural New Hampshire. When they were ready, they would give a green light for its extraction.

While ITER was perfecting its reactor design, a foreign nation was building its fusion reactor from plans that one of their scientist-moles had smuggled from the ITER consortium. The blueprints and schematics required to construct the reactor were provided to its top scientists to complete their reactor well before ITER's was even started. They would be the first country to achieve fusion power when their reactor was completed. The entire world would see this as a crowning achievement, proving that Iran was now a dominant nuclear superpower to be reckoned with.

Armin Ahmadi, Iran's President, had been informed for years that due to sanctions from the West, their country's power grid was failing and unable to supply their energy needs. They needed new power plants. His scientists and advisors informed him that standard nuclear fission power plants were a thing of the past. They unanimously recommended building a nuclear fusion plant instead. The output of just one nuclear fusion reactor would generate ten times more power than several nuclear fission reactors. Once completed, their country would be self-sustaining and never need the outside world again.

There was another benefit.

The hydrogen atom had many uses. Iranian scientists knew that two hydrogen atoms combined with one oxygen atom would yield water, a necessity for all life. In contrast, if they combined four hydrogen atoms and no water, they would achieve nuclear fusion and the ability to produce a mega-ton H-bomb powerful enough to obliterate a small country or a city like New York. They would now be the most powerful and self-sustaining country on the planet. Iran's leaders delighted at the thought of launching nuclear missiles at strategic targets to knock out global power grids and retaliatory weapon systems. At the same time, their country would reign in self-contained isolation.

They would no longer fear unbearable sanctions from the West. Iran would now be the country that would be feared.

Iranian scientists made President Ahmadi aware of the one missing link they would need to finish the mammoth project; Continuum. They had to have the only source of Continuum on the planet. After the negotiations were finalized, the price tag of fifty billion was agreed to, and the up-front deposit of ten billion was paid. The secret operation to excavate the Continuum meteorite began.

The construction of the full-scale nuclear fusion reactor had been started. When the Continuum arrived, it would be installed for the reactor to start up. Their friends from Triad brokered the deal. They would be the middlemen between a Swiss mining company named Chromel International and the nation of Iran. The lead time required for the meteorite's extraction would be one year. By year's end, the reactor would be built. They would be ready for the delivery of the Continuum.

President Ahmadi was pleased with their plan.

For once, time was on his side.

Chapter 28
Help

The Hydro-Blue Dodge Ram pickup slowly made its way up the long driveway to 29 Post Rd. The driver killed the engine and walked to the front door of a white cape with front dormers and a green roof. Kim's mother appeared wearing a navy blue sweater and a warm smile. She invited him in.

"Hi, I'm Jennifer Moreno." She reached out her hand, "Nice to meet you."

"You as well, Ma'am," Nick gently shook her hand.

"Please come inside. It's certainly nice what you're doing for Kimmy. I'm a bit afraid for her, but she's intent on helping this young lady and her friends. Once she sets her mind to something, well." She shrugged her shoulders.

"Yep, I guess she wants to test their water there at the hippy colony. Area's untouched by people, so heck, it should be the cleanest water in the state," said Nick.

"Well, this is what she studied at university, and I know she'll be excited to use her training to help them out if she can. She told me you're a horse rancher."

"Yes, ma'am, Breed Arabians and sell 'em off once they're trained. Usually one or two a year."

"That sounds really nice. Just you? No family to help out?"

"No, ma'am, just me and the horses. Oh, and there's Walt. He shows up now and then and does small projects. Comes and goes, you know." Nick looked down and smiled.

"Sounds nice. Well, I still have a lot to do and put away around here. I'll let you go with her test kit. It's the blue case next to the door."

Mum looked at Nick and took his hands in hers, "Please keep her safe. Kim's all I've got, and she means the world to me. You're a good boy. I can see that. It's nice to know some good boys are still left in the world."

"Yes, ma'am."

The truck roared to life with the test kit sitting on the passenger seat. Her parting comments about him being a good boy stayed in his head and made him smile as he backed out of the driveway.

Nick pulled into the Hungry Bear coffee shop and put it into neutral, letting the engine idle. He rubbed his face with both hands and looked at himself in the rearview mirror, not recalling bags under his eyes before. His phone vibrated with an incoming call; "Jesus, not now!" He hit the decline button and then typed his text message to Kim.

Got the kit. Need a little break from the ranch. Let me know if you and the hippies need a hand fixing the water problem. Got some experience.

***

The directions provided by Kim by way of Barge were all Nick needed to navigate his ATV to the meeting place. He knew the territory well.

This time, Kim would lead as they made their way up the steep incline to the top of Wildcat Mountain. They would hike a different route to Marshera and stay outside the tunnels. Skinny and treacherous, the trail would lead them under Wildcat Falls to the secret door Barge showed Kim.

The path became rock-covered and wet, preventing footprints from being detected. Nick's breathing became heavy. His endurance was challenged by Kim's test kit that was strapped to his backpack. Pulling a red bandanna from his pocket, he wiped his forehead and pressed on.

A shroud of churning water cascaded over their heads as they inched along the wet ledge. Water sprayed their faces wet as Kim turned back to Nick and yelled to him to watch his footing. Not more than five seconds later, Kim's sneaker slipped on a wet rock, and she slid off the trail's edge, headed to certain death. She screamed and grasped for a small tree to hold her teetering on the edge as rocks and dirt fell down a hundred-foot drop below. Her grip was wet, and her hand was slipping. She had seconds. *This must be how I end.* Her fingers slipped off when out of nowhere, a hand slapped around her wrist and pulled her up onto the path and safety.

"Going somewhere?" Nick shouted. She was in his arms again and pulled away.

"I should practice what I preach!" Kim said.

Nick smiled, "Does anybody?"

"That's the second time you've saved me!" Kim yelled.

"Might even be the third, but who's counting?" said Nick.

They tread carefully on the slippery path a little further before arriving at the hiding place to enter Marshera. Kim found her way to find the moss-covered boulder tucked into a crevice. Nick watched in amazement as she felt along the bottom of the giant rock to find a notch to put her hands on. Kim pulled the massive stone, and it rotated open, revealing a brightly lit cave.

"C'mon! The door will close on its own."

They stepped inside the entryway below the Falls Room, looking for Barge.

"Follow me up the stairs," Kim said.

They climbed up and turned a corner to enter the Falls Room. Nick looked in amazement to see a river of water flying through the room and then shoot out of an opening to become Wildcat Falls. Standing in front of them stood the giant man, Barge. He had two towels slung over his shoulders. With wet faces and sopping hair, they put the towels to use.

"Welcome, I'm Barge," he said. They shook, and Barge's giant hand engulfed Nick's.

"Howdy, partner."

They followed Barge down the stairs, through Marshera, and into the common room. Creen and Charlie sat together on the stone couch. "Please sit and rest," Barge said.

Kim could see the lotus flower tattoos on the back of all their necks for the first time.

"Where's Julie?" Kim asked.

"She will be along shortly," said Barge.

Nick pulled the towel from drying his head to look at the surroundings. He couldn't believe what his eyes were taking in.

"This is a cave?"

"What do you think?" asked Kim.

"This isn't the hippy colony that everyone in Crawford thinks it is," said Nick.

"This is the real Marshera," said Kim.

Julie came into the room and walked straight to Nick to hug him. She was speechless, but her actions revealed all he needed to know. She was grateful beyond words.

"Sure am glad to see you're feelin' better," said Nick. "Good thing that river's so damn cold, ain't it?"

Julie hung her head, embarrassed. "Let's just say I'm done with rope swings."

Everyone laughed until Creen looked up and shouted a warning, "Mr. Rumbles is awake again!"

A tremor faintly vibrated across the floor underneath them.

"What's she talking about?" Nick tried to whisper to Kim. He could sense the floor tremor increase and wondered what he was feeling.

"What she means is hold on!" Kim shouted.

The floor, walls, and ceilings began vibrating badly. Barge had to drop to his knees.

Rubble and rocks fell from the ceiling as everyone covered their heads and ducked for cover. After several minutes the vibrations abruptly stopped

"Whoa! What the hell?" Nick looked at Kim and then at the others in the room.

"They're getting worse," said Creen. "Because of my sensitivity, I can feel the vibrations sooner than the others. I'm Creen, by the way."

"I will address the vibrations and tremors shortly," said Barge. But first, I want to introduce Nick Caldwell to everyone. As we all know, Nick helped Kim save Julie, and now he's brought Kim's test kit to help her determine the cause of our water problems. Kim will analyze our water with her test kit. She and Nick will stay the night in the two extra bedrooms."

"My senses tell me they will stay more than just one night," said Creen.

"If they help solve our water problems, they can stay as long as they want," said Barge.

"Do they know where Mother went?" asked Charlie

"Nobody knows where Mother is or why she disappeared," said Barge.

"Mother? Rumbles?" Nick whispered into Kim's ear through her black hair.

Kim whispered, "Mother was their caretaker. She left to investigate the tremors that we just felt but never returned. They're kids, so they think the tremors are coming from a dinosaur named Rumbles sleeping in the caves and then waking up."

Barge looked directly at Kim. "As we all know, the vibrations and tremors have become worse. Our water and vegetables are poisonous. Yet we cannot leave Marshera before our time for healing is complete. Kim believes the cause of the vibrations and pollution of our water and food is probably due to an underground earthquake or even a volcano inside the caves. The vibrations may be why Mother never returned to us from her journey. If her test kit reveals what she thinks the problem is, I would like to ask Kim and Nick to go with me down the same tunnel Mother took to find the source of our water pollution problems."

Barge turned to them, "Will you two help us?"

Nick responded, "What you're talking about is some reconnaissance mission down a dark tunnel that'll be dangerous as hell. Do I got that right?"

"Basically, yes, you do," said Barge.

"Count me in, partner," said Nick.

"Count me in, too," said Kim.

"I'll come!" Charlie yelled. His guilt for not being there to save his sister was obvious.

"No, you won't," said Barge. "It's too dangerous. The four oldest will go. We will find the source of our water and food problems and return safely to Marshera."

"No! I'm going," Charlie demanded. "I can handle it. I could have saved Julie if Ashen and Winger hadn't stopped me. Now, these two get all the credit for saving my sister when it should have been me!"

"My decision is final," said Barge. You will have your chance sometime in the future, Charlie. Now It is almost time for The Offering. I will see you all in the sacred chamber."

"The Offering?" Nick turned to Kim.

"You'll see in a little bit. I didn't want to tell you until you arrived," said Kim.

She turned to Julie, "That reminds me. I want to test all of your water sources. Will there be some residue of the Blue Water left over after The Offering so I can test it with my kit?"

"Sure, there's always a little left in the bottom that you could have," said Julie.

During The Offering, Nick stared in awe at the strange ceremony, just as Kim had. He asked Kim why the four residents received their daily doses of hot Blue Water. She explained the DNA correction and the long-term cure for their afflictions. In the end, Julie brought the cauldron over. They poured the residue into a small test beaker that Kim produced. From there, they proceeded to the cafeteria with the sample. Kim was anxious to see what was actually in Marshera's water, blue or clear.

Kim plugged in a USB cord to interface the test kit with the mini laptop that accompanied it. Nick watched her set up the test and concluded the equipment must be expensive. The test kit held various bottles, test tubes, and beakers. Kim took a small beaker to the faucet and filled it with water. She added several drops of liquid from one of her bottles to the beaker, swished it around in a circle, and then dropped a digital probe into the water. After thirty seconds, the test kit made three beeps. Kim watched for the readout on the mini laptop. Her eyes focused as she used her index finger to read through a results table.

"And?" asked Julie, waiting along with the others patiently.

"I'm seeing significant levels of toxic materials like heavy metals, VOC's and a couple of carcinogens that this kit can't identify. There are also trace amounts of hydraulic oils and even some Methanol too."

"Are these chemicals strong enough to affect the purity of our water and vegetables?" asked Barge.

Kim looked up at him from the laptop, "There's more than enough toxicity in this water to cause harm to any living animal or plant."

Next, she tested the Blue Water in the test tube using the same process.

"I see the same toxic pollutants as the clear drinking water. However, the percentages are significantly lower. There is an additional chemical compound here that the kit can't identify. It's not toxic, but I've never seen anything like it."

"How dangerous is the Blue Water?" Barge asked.

"The levels are higher than the safe levels where they should be but not as bad as the drinking water I just tested."

"Altogether, the tests show me several partial answers about the source of the pollutants."

Julie stood quietly, listening to their conversation. "The water from the Falls Room. What about that?"

Charlie reacted and stood up, "I'll get some! I can do it!" Barge looked down at him and gently smiled, "Of course, you won't. I'll be right back."

"C'mon!" Charlie shouted as Barge went under the cabinet and found a metal cup and some string. In a moment, he was gone, heading towards the Falls Room.

"Why doesn't anybody let me do anything around here?" Charlie shouted.

"You're just a kid; relax," said Julie.

"No, I'm not!" Charlie shouted back in frustration. He stared at Kim. "This is all your fault!" Charlie ran out of the area in tears. For the first time, Kim felt her anxiety trigger. *Am I causing more harm than good?*

Barge returned with his arm and shirt sleeve dripping wet and holding a half-filled cup of river water. He showed it to Kim. "Enough?"

"Plenty," said Kim. She poured the water into a clean beaker and dropped the probe into the cup to look at the mini laptop screen for readings. Kim only took twenty seconds to look up at everyone and proclaim, "This is the purest water I've ever tested. Not a trace of pollutants."

Barge summarized, "So, we see seriously polluted water from our well, less so from The Fountain of Life. But the river water is crystal clean and unpolluted. What would your conclusion be?"

"No conclusions yet. I have a theory. I hope it's wrong, but I don't think so. I believe our trip down the tunnel will provide all of the answers we need," said Kim.

"That may not be the only thing our trip proves," said Julie.

"What do you mean?" asked Nick.

Julie looked at Kim, "The Forbidden Tunnel is the one that Mother went down."

"It's also the one from which she never came back."

Chapter 29
Burn Down The Mission

"How long has it been since you've been down this tunnel?" Kim asked. The darkness enveloped them until the flashlight's beam came on to illuminate their way. She was behind Barge, the leader, followed by Julie and Nick.

"I've never been down the Forbidden Tunnel before," Barge said. "No one has, except for Mother."

"Then how do you know it leads to the source of the tremors?" Kim asked.

"Mother told me," Barge said. "She also found an old map left by the Abenaki that lived in these caves. It detailed all the tunnels."

"The only person from Marshera that's ever been down here never returned and is now presumed dead," Kim said. *Just great!* She could feel her anxiety begin to increase. It was one thing to bravely volunteer to go on the reconnaissance mission but another to actually do it.

I've had my fill of tunnels lately.

The tunnel offered what Kim thought it would; dank, dark, cold, and full of cobwebs. The flashlight reflected off their intricate weaves of silk as Barge swiped them away. The one's he missed streamed across Kim's face and tangled in her hair.

"Do you guys hear the plink of dripping water? I hope we don't have to cross any boiling rivers. One per lifetime's enough for me," Kim said.

A rat scurried along the wall, and Kim jumped to the other side, letting out a hooting yell. Her anxiety was well within the caution zone.

"Jesus, I never want to see another cave ever again when we're done here!" She kept a watchful eye on the ceiling, looking for any sign of bats.

I've had enough of them too!

They could feel light tremors reverberate under their feet, causing Kim's nervous system to call for a red alert. She placed her hand on her chest to feel her heart pounding. She wanted to break into a sprint to use up the adrenaline flowing through her body. A pang of nausea caused her mouth to water from the omnipresent smell of rotten eggs. Anxiety level now in the danger zone. Red alert!

"Anybody know what that smell is?" Julie asked everyone. "It's giving me a headache."

Barge sighed. "We don't know what causes the smells or where they originate from. They seem to be stronger inside this tunnel."

Suddenly a massive tremor hit with a shock that caused them to grab onto the walls to stay upright. The tremor paused for a moment. Before they could recover, a succession of stronger, earthquake-like vibrations shook every tunnel surface. Silt and dirt came down on them. A large rock released from the ceiling, slamming onto Barge's shoulder. He moaned and dropped to his knees. The flashlight left his grip and went out, casting them into blackness.

"Barge!" Julie yelled and crawled to him in the dark as Nick searched for the flashlight.

Silt, dirt, and rocks kept raining down on them as the tremors continued. Barge, Julie, and Nick hunched over to cover their heads with outstretched fingers, hoping another rock bomb wouldn't hit them. The quakes and vibrations reverberated over and over for several minutes and then abruptly stopped. Then a low-pitched droning resonated throughout the tunnel.

Nick found the flashlight and flicked it on to see Barge's face twisted in pain as he rubbed his shoulder, trying to recover. He rose to his feet, determined to shake off the hurt.

Nick scanned the area with the light looking for Kim. It landed on her, lying motionless on the ground.

"Kim!" Nick yelled and got to her first. He kneeled beside her, "Hey you, you alright?

Shining thc light all over her, he looked for injuries but saw none.

"She's conscious," Nick said. His military experience came back to him. Lightly, Nick touched his fingers to Kim's neck to check her pulse and then leaned down to her mouth to listen for her breathing. Her eyes were squeezed tightly shut. Anxiety status: overload.

Nick looked at Barge and Julie, "Seen this before; she's in the middle of a panic attack."

Kim knew her mind was consumed in a raging storm, but there was nothing she could do about it. Already feeling claustrophobic, the tremors and darkness triggered her into an overload condition. She entered a cycle of fear and panic. The tunnel represented her life, constantly crashing down on her. If only she were a turtle, able to retract into her shell where it was safe. The other tunnel had given her obstacles she could see and overcome. There was at least some control. Here in this tunnel, she had no control over the roof caving in on her. Scared witless, she hyperventilated, feeling sure she was about to die.

Nick received his PTSD training in boot camp and then experienced it first-hand during battle. When the bombing began, you had to find a hole to jump into. The foxhole is at least a temporary safe place for soldiers to shield themselves from mortars, shrapnel, and bullets zipping by. Explosions went off all around them, and no one knew whether a mortar shell would land on top of them or not.

Sometimes they'd look over to see the foxhole next to them blown wide open and filled with black and red. Body parts, internal organs, and blood would be smeared across the blackened sand. Whether it was due to nature or nurture, a few guys couldn't deal with the stress. Their minds lacked their own fortification, and like a foxhole, they imploded. Nick was one of the fortunate ones. He was built to be a soldier, mentally as well as physically. The added benefit being he had yet to be in battle as long as some others. When a couple of his guys couldn't handle what they'd seen, he was there for them.

Laying down next to Kim, lightly he kept his hand on her back to maintain a connection to the outside world. He could feel her body tremble as she tried to fight through it. The ground was cold against his skin as he listened to her breathing in short, shallow breaths. The untrained might instinctively tell a person suffering from a panic attack to calm down or not be nervous. They may try a little tough love and ask them to be stronger. None of these strategies would work. Training and experience taught him this would only push the sufferer deeper into their hellish world. He would let her come back to reality on her terms. Gently, he stroked Kim's back and waited for her to return to their world. "We're all right here," he said softly.

"Not going anywhere, Kim. The tremors are all done, and we're all gonna keep you safe, darlin'. Try to take some deep, slow breaths through your nose, then let 'em out your mouth. You'll be alright." Nick kept his hand gently on her as a lanyard to the outside world.

The others remained silent, letting Nick be the voice to guide her back. He could feel her shaking subside as she recovered from the attack. Kim rolled over to lie on her back and breathe deeply. Her chest rose as her lungs filled with fresh oxygen. She held her breath for a beat and then slowly exhaled. Deep breathing repeated while her eyes remained shut, slowly taking a second deep inhale and then another. After two more breaths, Kim blinked her eyes open to see Nick lying next to her and the others kneeling behind him in the dim light of the flashlight.

They care about me. They're like my family.

Kim managed a smile and saw their worried faces change to smiles too.

Barge asked, "Kim, are you feeling okay?"

"I am fine. Let's keep going." She stood up and brushed the silt from her clothes. "As the saying goes, what doesn't kill me makes me stronger."

"Kim are you sure?" asked Julie.

"Hundred percent."

"Okay, you guys heard the lady. Let's skedaddle," Nick said.

Fifty yards passed, and the droning hum grew louder, filling the tunnel with noise pollution. The tremors that came and went were mild. Kim was grateful that none were as bad as the first one. She still had an underlying fear that they would all be crushed to death. Having faced her lowest lows, Kim began to feel like a survivor. She had survived a lot in the past few days and felt tougher. Things were changing inside her.

Survivors were tough because they had to be. Sick and tired of being the pleaser and getting pushed around, she knew she had to change to save Marshera. She also needed to save herself.

She began walking faster and took the lead position with no one questioning her.

The inky black foreground beyond the flashlight began to change to gray. They were getting closer to some light source. As the gray became lighter, the droning grew louder. The path through the mountain had been flat, but now she could feel her legs ache from the uphill ascent. The gray began turning brighter as the tunnel curved left and right. Then Kim realized their trek had taken them clear through the mountain to the other side.

" I wonder why we haven't seen Rumbles yet?" Julie said.

“Or any geological activity that you mentioned, Kim,” said Barge

“If my theory is correct, we should have our answers in a few minutes,” Kim said.

As they climbed uphill, the tunnel took a final turn to the left. Straight ahead, there was an opening that revealed a blue sky. It was a portal to the outside world. A warmness filled Kim’s body, and she felt a sense of relief. Checking her watch, they had traveled for forty minutes and hiked three miles. The droning was at its loudest now.

The tunnel opened up, expanding into a small cavern to quell Kim’s feelings of claustrophobia. She was the first to reach the opening; the others were behind her. Crawling up to the opening’s edge, a growth of shrubs and bushes partially blocked their vision but helped hide them. They gathered to look down on the outside world and see what was happening.

None of it was good.

Down below them was a large landing, a man-made shelf that jutted out from the mountainside and spanned half the length of a football field. Construction workers in hard hats moved around the area. A large blue metal frame was set up horizontally and attached to the side of the mountain.

Inside the frame, was a large cylinder with sharp cutting blades that protruded outwards. A giant opening had already been cut out of the mountain's granite exterior. The workers had to make it deeper with the boring machine. Fifteen crew men moved about the area, getting ready for the procedure. One appeared to be in charge. Well over six feet five and rail thin, he wore a yellow hardhat in contrast to the crew's blue one. He spoke into his two-way radio. "One final push Mac; you ready?"

"Ready to go, Tom," came the reply.

"Let it rip."

The operator pulled several of the machine's levers to engage the boring cylinder as the crew applied their gray earmuffs. A loud whining overtook the area, telling Kim of the source of the noise they heard as they came through the tunnel. It reminded her of an airliner revving its engines for takeoff. The industrial borer's cylinder was four feet in diameter and twenty-five feet long. As the cylinder began spinning, the apparatus in the blue metal frame slowly inserted it inside the mountain to drill the existing tunnel hole even deeper. Water gushed out of the cylinder as it cut into the mountain. All four felt the cave vibrate as silt and rocks fell behind them. The opening in front of Kim comforted her from suffering another panic attack. The machine hammered and bored deeper, creating a noise that was deafening. Kim and the others put their hands over their ears to shield them from the decibels. Diesel exhaust spewed out; its black cloud flooded the area and funneled into the cave, causing them to cover their noses and mouths with their shirts. The ground and walls vibrated with a violence they had never felt.

Chunks of chewed-up rocks combined with a nasty mess of sludge and mud spilled out of the borer and onto a motorized conveyer belt. The belt dumped the mess all over the side of the mountain, creating an ugly scene. The machine bored and drilled for fifteen minutes before it finally stopped.

"Okay, that's as far in as we gotta go," Tom said into the radio. He changed a button and spoke into the radio again, "Terry, get the Frack ready."

The boring drill retracted, giving ample space for the second operation. A large truck backed up to the hole in the side of the mountain. Several large hoses were unwound from a spool and connected to metal rigging assembled inside the man-made cave.

"Start it up!" Tom ordered through the radio."

Several of the crew entered the opening, and a higher-pitched noise began from the machine. Replacing the diesel exhaust, the stench of rotten eggs permeated the air. The second machine started its operation as torrential amounts of water ran down the side of the mountain.

"Why are the Normals drilling holes inside our mountain?" Julie yelled over the noise.

"I have a theory," Kim yelled back.

They hunkered down in the cavern, enduring the noise, vibrations, and wretched smells of rotten eggs. It took another thirty minutes for the secondary operation to end. The operator backed out the machine's injection nozzle from the newly created channel they had created. Workers gathered around to insert a cylinder with large rubber hoses attached to the end of it. The operator sounded a signal for the workers to clear and then shot the cylinder into the opening to stop at its predetermined location. They overheard one of the crew talking to his coworker.

"Okay, that one is in place. What we got, like three or four more?"

The coworker responded, "Yeah, four more, and then it's time to pop the damn thing outta there once and for all."

"Thank Christ," said the first one. "Can't wait to get out of this place and back to civilization."

Bleeeeeeeeeeeep! The sound of an air horn was heard from the digital safety sign that stood to the side of the operation. It displayed *an ALL CLEAR* warning to the crew to let them know when there would be explosives to blast additional holes in the mountain. The air horn also sounded to start and end the work day. It was quitting time. The workers quickly shut down the operation and put their tools away in the tool crib. The tall guy they called Tom jumped into a golf cart and drove out of their site down a winding dirt road.

All four from Marshera stood up and brushed the silt and dirt from their clothes. It was time to assess what they had just witnessed.

"Looks like they're after something. Got boring, and then hydraulic fracking operation going on inside the mountain," Nick said in a low voice. "Must be a shit load of gold or silver in this here mountain. I never heard of miners using fracking to go after precious metals, though."

"Don't they typically use fracking to remove natural gas?" Kim whispered.

"Yeah, but that ain't what they're doing out here," Nick said. "This has to be costing them a small fortune to get whatever they're going after. They got a boring machine, a fracker, and explosives. Must be some kinda ore. All I can think is that they're using fracking 'cause it lets them drill at weird angles to go after the stuff that's hard to reach."

"What is fracking?" Barge asked.

"It's a fairly new mining technique," said Nick. "Let's the miners drill at angles to get ahold of natural gas deposits that regular drilling can't reach. The machine pumps millions of gallons of water mixed with sand and nasty chemicals at high pressure. The water cuts through underground shale rocks until they can get to the gas. But they ain't after gas here."

"Fracking causes pollution and other problems; true?" Kim was connecting the last pieces of the puzzle.

"Yeah, huge problems with fracking contaminating the underground water supply and people's wells. My dad knew all about this stuff. The problems are from the miners dumping the fracking wastewater into nearby rivers and lakes. Even the gas they find underground gets mixed in with the water supply, causin' shitloads of health problems. Some guy on TV was running his kitchen faucet and held a match to the water. It actually caught fire! There's been small earthquakes going off at some fracking sites too. A lot of people been protesting against it."

235- The Canaries

Kim had listened to Nick explain fracking to them and reached her conclusion.

"Okay, guys, I have enough data to tell you what I'm certain is happening here. The fracking; it's the reason Marshera is sick. It's poisoning everything; your water supply, vegetables, the Fountain of Life, and most importantly, your bodies. Your bodies are being polluted as you try to heal them. Even using alternate methods for water and vegetables, you're breathing secondhand diesel exhaust. Many of the chemicals Nick mentioned are what I saw in the water test. There are a few I couldn't identify, though."

"So the tremors shaking rocks from our ceilings, the pollution of our drinking water, our food, and Blue Water are all due to this thing that the Normals seek to dig up?" Barge asked.

"Yes," said Kim. "The tremors and vibrations are from the Boring machine and any explosives they may use too.. The pollution of the water is from fracking; it's seeping into your well and wherever the Blue Water comes from."

Barge rose and paced back and forth in the cavern, pounding his palm with his fist. "When you said our problems may be from natural causes, it seemed logical. I never believed that stuff about a dinosaur. The truth is, we didn't know what was causing the problems. But now we do. The Normals and their machines are killing us for reasons we do not even know, although I'm sure some form of greed drives it."

"As they say, follow the money," said Kim.

Julie looked up at Kim, "So there isn't a dinosaur?"

"I'm afraid not, Hon," Kim tilted her head and smiled at her.

"Oh darn, wait till I tell the others; they'll be so sad," said Julie.

As they whispered, Nick unpacked his binoculars to survey the mining operation. He turned the zoom lens dial and focused through the trees on a tan-colored trailer in the distance.

"Looks like that manager, Tom, is going home. He was inside the trailer, but now he's stowing some gear in the back of his pickup."

"Can I have a look?" asked Barge.

"Sure." Nick handed the Steiner Binoculars to him, and he raised them to his eyes. Barge turned the ridged wheel with his index finger until he had a razor-sharp image.

"Yes, the supervisor is about to get into his pickup. Wait, some woman just walked out of the trailer. She's leaving too. She looks like an Oriental girl," said Barge.

"Let me see, please," Kim said.

As Barge handed the binoculars to Kim, she scolded him, "It's an Asian woman, just to let you know. Calling someone from the East, an Oriental, isn't used anymore. It's just Asian."

"Why's that?" asked Nick.

"Oriental is an antiquated term that gives people visions of us carrying incense or hitting a gong or something. It promotes a racist image of Asians," said Kim.

"I think I understand," Barge said. "You know this because you are an Asian?"

"Yes, but I don't have to be Asian to know that word is dated," Kim said, raising the Steiner's to have a look. She adjusted the lens, having already used them two days prior. A clear view of the woman was visible as she stood outside her car, looking down at her phone.

"I'll be damned," said Kim.

"What?" asked Julie.

Keeping the binoculars pressed to her eyes, Kim said, "Last Friday morning, an Asian Woman rang the doorbell at the condo where I live with my boyfriend, Brad. She was trying to sell me on Christianity. She was all pushy, so I slammed the door in her face. She wanted to speak to Brad too."

"And so?" said Nick.

Kim lowered the binoculars and handed them back to Nick.

"That's her."

"Serious?" Nick said. "He focused in on her. "Yeah, well, she is an Asian woman, and you know, many people think all Asians…."

"Stop!" Kim cut him off. "What am I going to do with you two? We do not look all alike. Anyway, that's her. She's dressed more business-like than last Friday, but that's definitely her."

"Maybe just a coincidence," said Nick.

"I hardly think so," said Kim. "I'll have to figure out why I've seen this random woman twice in the same week at two different places five or six hundred miles apart."

"Well, now that we know the story here, let's be moseying back to Marshera," Nick said.

Kim was feeling outraged and pissed off. Who was this sneaky little person ringing her doorbell and now involved in this operation that was killing the people of Marshera?

"Nick, you served in the military in Iraq, you said, right?"

"Yeah, like I told you before, in The Gulf War; why?"

"What's that term the military uses; search and destroy mission? Have you ever been on one of those?"

"All the time. What's your point?"

"I noticed the crew didn't lock the tools up after putting them away. Maybe you can show us how to use their tools on a search-and-destroy mission. We wreck all of their machinery and stop the tremors and pollution. Does everyone agree?"

"Yes, I agree with Kim," said Barge. His face was red with anger.

Nick looked at them. "I don't know about destroying private property; not a smart idea. If we got caught, it wouldn't be good, and you know, Search and destroys' were fine in the desert against an enemy of our country, but this here's expensive machinery, so it's not a great idea. We should probably let the cops know, and they'll handle it."

"Serious?" Kim looked at him strangely. These jerks rip out the side of Wildcat Mountain for whatever greedy reason and, in the process, contaminate the water supply and the people living in Marshera. And you give me private property? Also, didn't you tell me the cops in Crawford are useless?"

He stared at her face, filled with intensity and emotion. For once, he had no aw shucks, cowboy comebacks loaded in the chamber.

"I guess we search and destroy the shit out of this place right now," Nick said.

Kim's expression changed from anger to a smile.

They instantly became the most destructive saboteurs anyone could find. No longer a search and destroy mission, it became a scorched earth mission. The toolbox was opened, and Nick pulled out gloves and safety glasses for everyone. Next were the tools of demolitionists; sledgehammers, pick axes, and hacksaws. The noise of metal on metal and smashing glass bounced off the mountains to echo across the valley. Kim and Julie took hammers and broke windows, while Nick and Barge used twenty-pound sledgehammers to destroy instrument panels and controls. Barge found a sharp utility knife and slashed all the hydraulic hoses to the fracking machine. Then he slashed tires and anything else that could be cut with the blade. When they were finished, the area resembled a war zone right after a battle. There was smashed glass and puddles of red hydraulic fluid seeping from gashed hoses. They stood and admired their destruction, wiping their faces, wet with sweat.

"No more tremors?" Kim asked.

"No more tremors," said Barge.

"No more Rumbles," sighed Julie.

"We better get out of here pronto," said Nick.

"I know a trail back to Marshera that goes around the mountain instead of the way we came. It will take longer, but at least we will be outside instead of inside that tunnel. Just follow me," said Barge.

"Wait!" Kim shouted. "We've stopped the source of the tremors. We should take the shorter route back to Marshera. If I can handle it, I know you guys can too."

"Nick looked at Barge and Julie, "Tunnel?"

"Tunnel," Barge said.

"Tunnel," Julie agreed.

As they marched toward the tunnel, Nick hoisted a wooden box onto his shoulder.

"What's in the box?" Kim asked.

He turned to her, holding it securely with a gloved hand, and smiled. "ANFO; it's an explosive like TNT. Always good to have some around the house, just in case."

Kim was the last in line to crawl through the hole to the Forbidden Tunnel. She paused and turned to take in the view. Above the carnage and destruction, orange cotton candy clouds floated effortlessly across the twilight sky. Patches of mist had settled into the valleys of neighboring mountains, and Kim's face formed a smile. The natural beauty of the fall mountains added to her joy. They had courageously made the dangerous trek through the tunnel to discover the source of Marshera's problems and then took the only action that made sense.

Those kids were here first, you bastards.

Chapter 30
Everybody Hurts...Sometimes

The text message said, *Call me ASAP*. The high that Kim felt after their success in stopping the miners by destroying their equipment was erased when she read his words on her phone. To her, they weren't nice words. They were alarming words. She always did this to herself. Whenever she received any incoming information that was unexpected, it was immediately classified as a threat, and her brain would release a stress hormone called cortisol to flood her nervous system and switch on feelings of fear that would consume her. Excusing herself from the celebration, Kim moved towards the Falls Room, where there was a chance for a bar or two of cell signal. Kim whistled a familiar song and practiced deep breathing as she walked.

"Hey, Brad."

"Hey Babe, how's everything going? How's everything going at that cave place? How's… uh… what's her name?"

The signal and reception were surprisingly strong, even with only one bar.

"It's going good. It's hard to describe over the phone, but this place was in danger from a mining company on the other side of the mountain causing major tremors and other stuff. The floor would shake so badly you couldn't stand up sometimes. They were drilling and fracking, causing all kinds of problems here. Anyway, I'll tell you all about it later on. What's her name is Julie. I don't have much time right now, so what's up with you? How's everything going on your end?"

"Everything's great here. Hey, do you remember when we first got together like two years ago when your roommate moved to

California with no notice to pursue a career in acting? We'd been seeing each other for six or seven months, and you were worried about affording the rent by yourself. I said why don't you come and live with me because my condo has plenty of room. You were really stressed with your anxiety problems, and after you moved in, you were happy again. I remember groaning when I saw all the stuff you owned and how we had to put some of it in storage. And now we've been together happily for a while, and it's been great…."

"Brad, what's your point? You're going on and on herc. It sounds like you're building up to something, reminding me about how you saved my life. I had a few other options before you asked me to move in, but that's ancient history now."

Brad stood up and paced the floor, not expecting her to snap at him.

"Well, I don't know about the term saving your life, but I did bail you out of a major jam, and so I need you to work with me on something to get me out of a little jam too. I need you to return the favor."

Kim let out a sigh of exasperation, "Go on?"

"Do, you remember I told you a few weeks ago the numbers are down for everyone this year? Sales are just down with the whole pandemic and all. Management keeps reminding us that we're lucky even to have our jobs still."

"Brad, I wish you'd get to the point. What do you want?"

"Okay, well, I'll get to the point and save you some time. I keep returning to the last conversation we had about that Blue Water those people are drinking. You were saying that it cures their diseases. I've been thinking, so hear me out. If you could get me a sample, like a small sample that nobody would miss, it would do us a lot of good. No one needs to know from where the sample came. You know my bud Paul's a chemist with Monsanto, and he can copy anything, so like..."

"Brad, you didn't tell Paul about Marshera and the Fountain of Life, did you? Tell me you didn't tell him about the Blue Water!" Kim was frantic and wanted to kick herself for betraying Marshera's trust.

"No! Of course not! Listen, I'm the business guy in this relationship, and I'm telling you we're looking at millions, Babe, maybe billions if what you're telling me is true. More importantly, it would help numerous people on our planet if we could make this stuff available. Who are we to play God and deny millions of sick people a cure? Oh, and speaking of sick people, I have something to tell you. My mother's got something; they don't know what it is, but she's going in for tests, and it looks serious. And don't forget your mother just beat cancer, and what if she falls out of remission in the future? Think about our own families. Know what I'm saying, Babe?"

There was a very long silence. "You still there?"

"Yes, Brad, I am still here. Listen, it's a moot point because they told me that someone tried to analyze the Blue Water and tried to copy it years ago, but it can't be copied. There's a unique element in the water that my test kit couldn't identify. I don't know if a scientific lab would, either. Plus, these people who take it say it has to be consumed hot as soon as it bubbles up out of the earth at the same time every day. So drop the whole idea, Mr. Businessman. And don't say a peep. You swore to me you wouldn't. You know, I was happy five minutes ago, and now I'm triggered. What do they think is wrong with your mother?"

"Oh, sorry, Babe. They don't know yet. That's why they're testing her from head to toe. Kim, hon, please just listen to reason. I'm sure it was years ago when they tried copying the blue stuff. They've made huge advances, so it's worth another try, Babe."

"That's it, Brad! I do not want to discuss it anymore! I have to go. Just drop the idea. We'll get through your job situation together. If there's a downturn in sales or they let you go, we'll figure it out.

Don't we always? I'll give you a call when I'm headed home. Love you."

The dynamic between them had always been one where Brad played the alpha male, and Kim accepted him bossing her around with insults and condescending remarks. She let them roll off her back as he made fun of her anxiety and silly rituals. He hadn't been like this in the beginning. But when he sensed her weakness, it was like blood in the water, and he would come at her again and again, chopping her down. Was he a narcissist? She wasn't sure. All Kim knew was she was sick and tired of his up-and-down treatment of her. The problem is the narcissist who thinks he is superior doesn't like being stood up to by someone he believes is inferior.

"Wait for a second, Kim! And don't you dare hang up, you little bitch; unless you want to see your clothes, furniture, and laptop in the driveway getting soaked by the rain. You had better get me a sample of that blue shit those people are drinking. Or you can find a new place to live too. After all the nice shit I've done for you…"

Click!!

It had only happened once, and compared to what she read other women had gone through, it seemed minor, but who knows how far he would go someday? He had shoved her, supposedly by accident, but she knew there was some malice behind his actions. It started within the past year, and she couldn't fathom why. He profusely apologized after she locked herself in the spare bedroom and cried. Therapy was promised as he begged her to forgive him through the door. But treatment never came.

They were on thin ice lately with Brad's behavior. She had no time for his games. There were lives in the balance. Julie and the kids of Marshera had accepted her into their world and lives. She wouldn't let them down.

***

"I can't reach her, Mr. Chang. She's in the mountains where there's no cell signal. I've left her voicemail messages. I think I have to go there and meet her face-to-face. Then she'll give me the sample right away."

There was a silent pause. "Mr. Chang, you still there?"

"Yes, I am here, Bradley. Please get in touch with Ms. Chen. I believe you two already know each other."

“She will see to all your needs.”

Chapter 31
We're Working It

The nutty smell of freshly brewed coffee permeated the inside of the tan-colored trailer. A white box of pastries sat next to the coffee maker. All this and the comfort of a warm shelter couldn't distract them from the feeling that failure was now inevitable.

"Looks to be the hippy colony people from what I could make out on this surveillance video," said Tom.

"Let me see," said Lee Chen.

Tom had the video camera hidden in a nearby tree to spy on the crew to ensure no tools or equipment was stolen. He also wanted to listen to them in case of any security leaks. The video on his phone showed Kim, Nick, Barge, and Julie smashing, cutting, and destroying the mining equipment with his worker's very own tools.

"I've warned those fucking guys before about locking that damn tool cage!" Tom said as he kicked the trash basket sending it across the room spewing trash on the floor.

Lee Chen watched next to him, taking in all the images. "Do you know any of them?"

"There's two of them I recognize. We've spied on them over the past year. The big kid's name is Barge. I don't know the young girl's name, but she lives in the Hippy Colony. No idea who the adult girl and the tall guy with the curly hair is."

Eyes squinting, Lee Chen could feel her blood pressure rise as she watched Kim and her friends laugh while they destroyed the equipment.

They're laughing as they ruin my life.

"I know who the adult girl is. Her name is Kim Moreno. I'd love to pay her back for this stunt as soon as possible."

"We've got some serious damage that's been done to all machines," Tom said.

"How long?" she asked.

"How long what?" said Tom.

"How long until you can get the operation back up and running? What else would I be asking about?"

"It's too soon to tell. I'll have to assess the damage. It'll take a while."

"Mr. Foulke, we don't have a while! If we miss the deadline, heads will roll, and I do mean literally. A chain of events is scheduled to occur once you extract that meteorite. So, again Mr. Geologist, figure out how to get those machines running!"

The carnage committed by the Marshera reconnaissance team had been effective, causing the completion of the project to come to an abrupt halt. Tom sat upright in the office chair with his arms crossed, rocking back and forth, wondering how he'd fix everything. He turned around to look at the wooden shelves containing replacement parts covered in dirt and grease. Drill heads, augers, pistons and hydraulic hoses were available, but who knew if they were the right parts and if they had the time to install them?

Lee had only been onsite for a short time, sent by her boss because he believed in her. Along with the assignment came the innuendo of returning only if the job was completed on time with perfect execution. Now, those bastards had dropped this mess in her lap.

"So, tell me, Mr. Geologist, how do we finish the extraction of that multi-billion dollar meteorite? I'm here to get this project done on time. How do you recover from your dumb-ass guys not locking the god-damn tool crib?"

Tom looked at her with intensity in his eyes.

"Right, you've been sent here to make sure this project is completed on time. You show up at the eleventh hour to claim hero status, but do you know what we've been doing for the last year? Let me tell you quickly because time is of the essence, Ms. Chen."

"The first item on our little to-do list was for my team to build a road up the side of a mountain. Easy stuff; all we had to do was cut through dense trees and brush to wind it back and forth up to an elevation of four thousand feet. Then, we brought in dump trucks by the hundreds with solid fill to construct a hundred-and-fifty-foot-long ridge where we could start the mining operation. Next, we used specialized equipment called ground penetrating radar, it's like an ultrasound, to pinpoint the meteorite's exact location. Oh, but it only got easier. We then began clearcutting and removing all the trees, vegetation, and boulders from above the meteorite so excavation could begin. "

"I get your point, Mr. Foulke. You don't need to..."

"No, wait, I'm not finished. With the ridge built, we brought in the boring and fracking equipment, but first, we had to blast through the granite with a shitload of ANFO explosives. After the borer cut the cavity deeper into the mountainside, we fracked out numerous micro-channels that encircled the meteorite to accommodate a hundred explosive charges with wireless detonators." Tom was standing now and preaching to her like a minister selling a sermon.

"Enough, Tom!" Her comment fell on deaf ears.

"At the time of the meteorite's extraction, the wireless charges will be armed and simultaneously detonated, forcing the meteorite out of its crater to roll a short distance down the side of the mountain into an area that we also created. It's filled with a bed of soft sand to cushion the asset's landing. And then, finally, a thirty-five-foot long flatbed semi-trailer with a crane will lift the space rock on board to be transported to a sea freighter docked in Portsmouth, New Hampshire. The freighter will have only one item on its manifest sheet; a meteorite worth fifty billion dollars. Before the ship begins its journey to Iran, they will remit the balance of forty billion dollars, due. When they take delivery, their country will be the first with a nuclear fusion reactor and the most potent mega-bomb on the planet! That, Ms. Chen, is a condensed version of the year-long struggle we've dealt with!"

“Congratulations on your efforts, Mr. Foulke. You have been paid handsomely for them.”

"We are near the final extraction phase, Ms. Chen. Suddenly, all my equipment is severely damaged. You want to know when we can finish the operation? My answer is that it will take me some time. Of course, I see the urgency of the situation! How in God's name could I not!" Tom was sweating and breathing heavily as he flopped back into the chair.

There was a knock on the trailer. Two men from Tom's crew were there to rush him up to the mining site to inspect the equipment further. He stood up and looked at her. "As somebody once said, I'll be back."

Two hours later, Tom was back with a list of parts needed to fix the machines. Making calls on his phone to parts suppliers, he inquired about any options for new or used replacement parts. His voice was desperate, pleading with the man, begging him to save his life.

As she listened to his calls, Lee Chen's phone rang. The caller ID required she talk in private outside in the cool fall air.

"Hello, Mr. 524," Lee answered.

"Good day, 213." Mr. Chang answered.

"To what do I owe this honor, sir?"

"You are using your encrypted phone with the latest software update, 213?"

"Yes, I am; always, sir," she replied.

"Good. I received your message. Provide me with an update on the situation there."

"Of course. We are dealing with a setback due to some vandalism from a few locals that live in the caves. We hope to have everything under control and running again soon."

"Excellent. I knew the operation would be in good hands once you arrived. I am glad you called me. There is something else I need to discuss with you. I received an inquiry from our business associate, Bradley. We discussed an item that may be of interest to us."

"I am listening, sir."

"According to our friend, there is a blue-pigmented water that people in the caves of this Wildcat Mountain consume. This water is alleged to have certain medicinal qualities that could prove beneficial to us. He tried to convince me that he could reach out to his love interest, a certain Kim Moreno, to utilize her help in acquiring a water sample. If this water possesses the properties he describes, our people on the mainland would like to analyze it for obvious reasons."

"Hmmm. Interesting; how can I assist you, sir?"

"As you may have ascertained from our recent meeting with Bradley, he needs to be more reliable in delivering on his promises. Therefore I would like you to add this item as a deliverable. I want a sample of this blue-pigmented water for analysis. I would not rely on Bradley to come through. He has proven himself unreliable. Consider what other alternatives you may have besides him. It would be best if you acquired the sample before the extraction of the asset. The asset, of course, is still your top priority. Can you accomplish both tasks for me, 213?"

"Of course, sir. I will begin this task as soon as…Oh, okay, I see Brad is calling me on my other line as we speak."

"Then I shall let you take his call. I was about to tell you he is on the way to you. Gather whatever helpful information he has, and then do what you want with him"

"Understood, sir."

She looked at her phone and pressed the button to take Brad's call.

"Hey, Brad, what's up?"

"I had a call with Mr. Chang."

"I know, Brad. I just spoke with him."

"So if you spoke with him, you know I'm on the way to you. I need your location."

"I will text directions to you after we finish our call."

"Okay, I'm boarding a flight from Baltimore to Manchester, New Hampshire. Where exactly are you?"

“I am in a region that is called the White Mountains of New Hampshire.”

“Huh? What are you doing in the mountains?”

“I will tell you when you arrive, Brad.”

“Alright, I'll rent a car and drive up to your location. Not sure what time I’ll get there.”

"Before you go, Brad, you should know I'm sitting in a trailer here at Wildcat Mountain. On the opposite side of the mountain, there’s a hippy colony where your girl Kim is staying. Tell me, how do you plan on getting a sample of this blue water from her?"

"What? You're at the same mountain as Kim? How did this all come about?"

"I'll explain it all when you get here. Answer my question, Brad. How will you get this sample of blue water from your girlfriend, Kim?"

"How? Like I told Mr. Chang, I can sweet talk her into getting me some. I just have to talk to her face-to-face and turn on the charm. After I get the water, he will let my mother go."

"The reason I ask is we have Kim on videotape with another male whose name is Nick, I believe. They appear to be very good friends, if you know what I mean. It appears that she is with him now. Are you and your girl Kim even a couple anymore?"

There was a long pause on the phone. "Yes, dammit, we are still a couple. She said on the phone, he was only helping her out. I'll put her on a guilt trip, and then she'll give me a sample of the blue water. It works every time."

"We shall see Brad. I'll text you the directions. Call from the car when you're en route."

In the trailer, Lee Chen saw Tom running both hands through his graying hair.

"Have you calmed down enough to have a conversation about status, Mr. Foulke?

"Yes, I have. Here's where we are. Most of the important parts we need to get the fracking up and running won't be available for a few weeks. That's the bad news. The good news is I can steal most of the ones I need, like hydraulic hoses and a pump, from the Boring Machine. Repairs take time, and it's time we don't have."

She stared at Tom with a dual expression of anger and worry. "So what do you propose?"

"What I propose is to use the ANFO explosives in the meantime to blast out the areas behind the meteorite that will allow us to frack out the last channels for the four remaining explosives. Then everything will be in place for the extraction. We are going to lose a day, but we'll still have the meteorite out several hours before the trailer arrives to take it away. The damage they did to the machines is making us cut it really close."

"Will the blasting so close to the meteorite damage it?"

"That's a good question that I don't know the answer to. The meteorite is made of pure Continuum. It's an element not found on our planet. We have never measured its hardness."

"Let me rephrase the question. In your professional opinion as a trained geologist, will a limited amount of blasting destroy the meteorite?" She leaned forward, her hands on his desk.

"Dammit!" he slammed his fist down. The bang engulfed the trailer, and she jumped back. "I am a scientist! I don't have the data to answer you. We have no time and no options!"

Startled, Lee Chen shouted, "You will have to take your chances on an educated guess! After all, you're the scientist!"

Tom stood up and took in a deep breath to calm himself. "You're right; I'm the Geologist. I'll calculate what I believe is the right amount of explosives required to finish the job without damaging the meteorite. When we push the button to extract it, the goddam rock might come out in fragments. Either way, it's on me. Those people in the hippy colony will be getting some payback, though. If they think they felt vibrations and tremors before, they ain't seen nothin' like what's going to happen once we start blasting!

"I couldn't be happier," said Lee Chen. "Blast your heart out; just don't hurt the asset."

Chapter 32
Bridge Over Troubled Water

The people of Marshera rejoiced and celebrated the destruction of the mining equipment. There would no longer be deadly pollution poisoning their water and food. The earth-shaking tremors that traumatized them were now officially gone. Sitting in the cafeteria, they discussed what needed to happen next. All were present; Barge, Julie, Creen, Charlie, Nick, and Kim.

"We have resolved the source of our water and food problems," Barge said. "But now it is time to get organized. We still need a new water source. Without clean water, we die, and winter is coming soon."

"I'll state the obvious," said Kim. Marshera has all the crystal-clean water they need, just gushing through the Falls Room. There must be a way we can access that water supply. I know it's on the other side of Marshera and too far from the beds in the Lightroom. I know it's dangerous for fear of falling in the river and going over the falls, but it's the only logical solution."

"Mother was strict with us about the Falls Room," Barge said. "She taught us from day one to stay away from there. No one is allowed to go up there without another person, and for good reason. It's too dangerous."

There was a period of silence as they brainstormed possible options and solutions.

Nick looked to Barge, "The river that cuts across the Falls Room; it's at a higher elevation than we are here, right?"

"Yes, by at least ten to fifteen feet. Why?"

"I'm thinking about a siphon," said Nick. "If some hose were lying around, I could weigh down one end with a rock and lower it into the river. Then I'd start a suction through the other end of the hose to bring the clean water to this side near the well. All we need is for the hose output to be lower than the input. The water will flow continuously, but that's okay. We can build a watershed to hold clean water. We did the same thing when my platoon helped out the Army Corps of Engineers with a village outside Basra in Iraq. We tapped into a stream, and we ran a hose downhill to feed them clean water. "

"Just one question," said Barge. "What is a watershed?"

"It's like a pond of clean water for drinking," said Nick. "You know, a reservoir."

"Why don't we put the clean water into the well?" asked Barge.

"We don't know how long it'll take for the well to be clean again," Nick said. "Probably shouldn't mix the clean and the polluted water together. We can move your water pumps from the polluted well into the bottom of the watershed and have Marshera back in business."

"Nick's right about not mixing the clean water with the polluted well water," said Kim. "It can take years for a polluted well to become clean again."

"Pretty sure there is some plastic hose in the storage area out back; not much, though, said Barge. “If memory serves me right, there is only one piece. It’s about ten or fifteen feet long. It’s way too short to make it to this side, so that idea's out. "

"Do you have any flat pieces of wood lying around," Nick said.

"What are you thinking?" Kim asked.

We could build an aqueduct and direct the water from the hose to this side of Marshera.

"We have no wood," said Barge.

"Damn!" Kim said.

Another period of silence ensued as Kim tried to brainstorm a solution; so did the others.

"The drawings!" said Kim. "The drawings I saw in the cavern on my way to Marshera."

"What about them?" asked Julie.

"Something you said to me yesterday, Julie. It was when you gave me the tour of Marshera. You told me the drawings on the cave walls were instructions."

"That's true. They are."

"One of the drawings showed several women and men building a canoe. They made it out of long branches and tree bark for the skin. The drawing showed them collecting roots, limbs and tree bark from the ground. They tied the bark to the frame with the roots. Why couldn't we use the same principles to build a canoe but instead leave it open on both ends to form a channel? You know, like a pipe cut in half? I know it probably sounds crazy," Kim said.

"It's actually brilliant," said Nick. "Doesn't have to be fancy. The water will trickle slowly down the aqueduct into the watershed."

"I know where there are many fallen birches in the woods not far from here," said Barge. We have a rusty, old hand saw in the storage room. I can bring it to cut some long branches for the frame. Shouldn't take me too long to gather everything."

"While he's gone, We can dig the trench for the watershed. Best to collect some flat stones for the bottom of it, too," Nick said.

"This thing's happening!" Kim said enthusiastically.

At Barge's direction, they formed teams. Barge and Charlie went to collect the bark, branch, and root materials while Kim, Nick, and the others used kitchen utensils to dig the hole that would become the watershed. Nick and Kim then searched outside and collected flat stones to line the bottom. They opened up a crevice separating the wall between the Falls Room and Marshera's living area to allow the hose to transport clean river water to the aqueduct.

Barge and Charlie returned with ample amounts of long branches, roots, and birch bark; they peeled off fallen trees. While Barge and Nick cut the branches to even lengths, Kim researched online how to heat the roots in water to strip them into twine. The twine was like a strong string that held together the framed branches and the overlapping birch bark. Kim, Barge and Nick created several half-pipe channels that flowed into the succeeding one to drain the freshwater into the new watershed. Support stilts using excess branches were fastened to the aqueduct with root twine to hold each section in place above the floor.

Nick calculated the necessary watershed size. The hole only needed a five-foot circle three feet deep to provide enough water for Marshera. Julie would call their new watershed Little Pond as she and the others arranged the flat stones across the bottom. The hollow reservoir sat empty, thirstily waiting for clean water to find its way down the makeshift aqueduct they'd just created.

The project continued throughout the day, with no one taking time for lunch. The only break was The Offering at four PM. By seven PM, everything was done, and it was time. Barge, Julie, Charlie, and Creen circled the Little Pond waiting anxiously to see a trickle of water dance down the aqueduct. Nick and Kim made their way up the rock stairs to the Falls Room. The last step to be completed was the dangerous task of connecting the water supply to the fast-moving river. After tying a rock to the end of the plastic hose, Nick lowered it into the river. Taking the output end, Nick started the suction to draw the water, and they watched the liquid work through the plastic tube, inching its way to his mouth. Nick pulled it away from his mouth and crimped the hose to stop it temporarily. He set it down into the birch bark aqueduct. Once the crimp unfolded, clean water would flow into the Little Pond.

"Why did you stop it from flowing?" Kim asked.

Nick looked at her and smiled, "Your honors."

Kim smiled at Nick as she stared at the plastic tube waiting to be released. Pangs of attraction swept over her, and Kim realized she was falling for him. More than once, she and Nick had worked together as partners, giving and taking as partners do. She kept comparing Nick to Brad. There hadn't been another man besides him for so long. Loyalty was a value she held in high regard, and she accepted Brad for his faults. But his faults had become unacceptable. She knew they had to end their relationship after his verbal abuse on the phone. Kim could feel he was up to something, but she hadn't had the time to figure it out yet. Now, Nick had given her the honor of turning on the fresh water. He put her first. It wasn't something she was used to.

"Now?" her voice cracked a little.

"Now," Nick said.

Kim unkinked the plastic to see the pure water that would give life back to Marshera slowly wiggle its way down the white bark-lined aqueduct on its way to the watershed.

"Yes!" Nick clenched his fist and pumped it.

"Yes!" Kim leaped up and wrapped her arms around Nick. He equally returned her embrace. The emotion she'd held back for the past few days overtook her. She had been through so much, saving Julie's life, the harrowing experience of finding her way to Marshera and helping to save everyone living there. She had never felt so much purpose in her life. Kim pulled back and kissed Nick deeply and warmly on his lips, feeling no remorse. It had been coming. They both knew it. When the kiss ended, she felt happy but not embarrassed.

Okay, I may be a tiny bit embarrassed.

"I should apologize for surprising you. It's an emotional time."

"No apologies needed after a kiss like that," Nick chuckled.

"Well, thank you, you know, for your kind words of support."

"Sure thing, darling." Oops, wait, I know. "You're not my darling."

They laughed until he blurted out an awkward question.

"How long you had 'em"?

Kim answered his question with a question, but she knew what he meant. "Had what?"

"The panic attacks, like the one you had in the tunnel the other day."

Kim picked up a small stone and began playing with it. She hadn't discussed the attacks with anyone but her therapist. "They started a few years after I lost Grace. I have them off and on depending on stuff going on in my life. Sometimes there's no reason; they just happen."

Then he shocked her with another question, "Is that why you take the pills?"

Kim was thrown back. "So you know, huh? Well, now I'm embarrassed right down to my core. They help me return to my baseline when I'm peaking, which is hard to explain. I need to quit; keep telling myself I'm going to."

He builds me up, and now he tears me down!

"Seen Marines, tough as nails, have panic attacks and take all kinds of drugs to deal with them. They were shell-shocked cause a shell blew up the guy next to them. It affects people differently. Some guys can't move on past the thing that spooked 'em. Anyway, you ain't alone. Lotta people deal with stress for different reasons. You losing your sister and all, I get it." He rested his hand on hers, and she felt sensations shoot up and down her body.

That's a little better, Nick.

For the first time, Kim realized Nick was far more than a smart, aleck, laid-back cowboy. He picked up on her panic attacks. She had succeeded in hiding them from others with her acting performances or managing them with various painkillers.

"Let's head down and see if that pond is filling up," he said.

"I'm more than happy to end this conversation," Kim said, smiling at him.

Standing in a circle around the Little Pond, they watched a steady stream trickle out of the makeshift aqueduct. Their smiles were clear evidence of unanimous approval. Creen reached out and held a plastic cup under the water to fill it up.

"Hi, guys! Come taste; it's good!" said Creen.

Both Kim and Nick took turns drinking the fresh water. Both agreed, it was clear and clean. Free from pollutants, their drinking warer was again, pristine.

"Still got some stuff to do to finish the project," said Nick.

"Such as?" Kim asked.

"Need to hook up a second siphon hose so the water doesn't overflow the sides of the watershed. I actually found a second piece out back that I can wrangle into use. I'll siphon off just enough water to keep it full and send it down the old well. That should help clean it up too."

"Why do all that?" asked Barge.

"That's how a watershed works," said Nick. "New water in, old water out. It's always changing over. This setup may be temporary, but it beats drinking poison fracking water."

"There is one more concern," said Barge. "The Blue Water; it's not currently clean. Will it poison those of us that drink it daily?"

"My educated guess is that drinking the Blue Water would harm you and the others over an extended period," said Kim. "But, we have stopped the source of the pollution. Over time, the Blue Water should cleanse itself while the toxicity levels drop."

Kim made an announcement while everyone rested and took turns drinking the clean water. "Now that we have resolved our water problems and have clean drinking water, we need to repot every plant that provides food to Marshera. That means every bed in the Lightroom. Every plant and fruit tree will need fresh soil and clean water to produce healthy produce again. I can manage the project, but I'll need help."

"I'll help out. The siphon hose shouldn't take long," said Nick.

"Everyone will help," said Barge with an authoritative voice.

"Can we be all done for today?" said Creen." I will need to rest if there is a lot of work tomorrow. I don't do well with physical labor."

"Yes, creating a new water supply is a big accomplishment," said Barge. "Tomorrow, we will replant the vegetable and fruit beds in the Lightroom. We will be self-sustaining again."

"Now that we destroyed the bad guy's machines pretending to be Rumbles. They were bad, right Kim?" Julie asked, sounding childlike.

"Yes, they were. There's no need to worry. We shouldn't be hearing from them again," Kim smiled and put her arms around Julie to hug her. She looked over to see Nick's face filled with worry and mouthed the words, "what's the matter?" He shook his head to dismiss her concern.

Creen reached over to refill her cup with fresh water, "If the truth is there's no such thing as Rumbles the dinosaur, then what happened to Mother? Barge gets angry whenever I say someone killed her, but I feel it inside. She is no longer alive."

They had all formed a deep connection to Mother. She taught them and loved them. They were *her* children, and she, *their* mother. Every day there was hope she would emerge from the tunnel that she last disappeared in. Now they knew there was no hope of seeing her again.

"We officially don't know what happened to Mother," said Barge. He went to Creen and gave her a gentle hug to comfort her. Julie began to weep with the same realization as Creen. She went to Barge, and he wrapped both girls in his arms while they sobbed.

It was a momentous day in Marshera. All four of them had come there with terminal illnesses. They were to live there for five years, drinking the healing Blue Waters from the Fountain of Life. Gradually they would transform as their DNA mutated and repaired. Their illnesses were going away. They were healing. If given a chance, the Fountain would heal them, saving them, as it had done for their predecessors throughout history.

The next day they rose at dawn. It was Kim's turn to be in charge. She would utilize her botany education to manage the project. She was getting her hands dirty again, and it felt good.

The beads of perspiration on Kim's skin mixed with water droplets as she carefully led them down the slick path under Wildcat Falls to where they would retrieve bucket loads of the catalyst for all living plants; dark, rich soil. It was packed with nutrients and, best of all, no harmful chemicals. Legs, arms, and backs strained as each person carried every type of container they could find to lug the heavy, moist soil up the path and into Marshera. They made the back-and-forth trips so many times, a seven-foot-tall mound was created in the middle of the Lightroom. Then they could change out each plant's soil.

The first day of the project was productive. The repotting had begun. After The Offering was over, everyone dispersed to various rooms in Marshera to rest. Kim sat alone in the quiet of the common room with a piece of paper detailing everything that needed to happen over the next day. Lost in thought, she closed her eyes and meditated for a while, deeply breathing and relaxing her body and mind. Julie sat down next to Kim and snuggled up to her.

"What are you thinking?" Julie asked.

"I was meditating for a while. Then, I was thinking about my sister, Grace," Kim said.

"Is she home where you live?"

"No, she's no longer alive. We lost her ten years ago, but she's alive in my heart. I just wish she was here to see all we've accomplished. She would love you guys."

"I didn't know," Julie said. "I'm so sorry your sister died. I wish I could've met her. But at least I have you."

Kim put her arms around Julie and held her. "Yes, you most certainly do, my dear."

Later on, in bed, Grace came to visit Kim in a dream. She woke up, not returning to sleep until three in the morning.

The next day continued with the tedious chore of repotting and replanting every single vegetable and herb plant. Then came the fruit-bearing trees. It all went according to plan. The grueling work continued nonstop on every bed in the Light Room. Kim made sure that everyone wore plastic gloves from a box she found in the cafeteria to prevent any absorption from pollutants soaked up by the contaminated soil. Fresh water from the aqueduct provided plenty of irrigation for the freshly repotted plants.

Kim took in a deep breath and smiled. *Rejuvenated plants for rejuvenated people*. It was a mammoth job, but the teamwork had gratified her. Charlie argued with her and opposed her on several tasks. Several times he quit only to return to work again. Everyone had unbridled enthusiasm and energy to fix their damaged food source. Kim and Nick worked side by side as they helped perform the backbreaking work on the larger fruit trees, potatoes, beets, and carrots that grew underground. Each plant had to be shaken out to remove all the tainted soil from the plant's roots and then repotted with new earth.

Julie walked by as Kim and Nick were laughing and remarked, "I think there's more than just fruits and vegetables growing around here!"

The group worked from sun up to sun down, digging, planting, and watering. By day's end, they had almost finished. Every plant had been re-potted in fresh, untainted soil. The botanical healing process could now begin.

It had been two long and arduous days. After The Offering, everyone took turns taking warm showers and turned in early. There was a little more to do the next day, and then they were done. Exhausted, by nine o'clock, everyone had gone to bed.

The saying goes that it's easy to fall under the spell of assumption. Everyone noticed how closely Nick and Kim worked together during the project. Yet they still needed to establish something. What happened that night was unexpected by even them.

Lying awake in her bed, Kim was restless. She couldn’t sleep in the unfamiliar location. There was so much that had happened. Intense with emotion, Kim's mind felt like a Christmas tree, all lit up. Two days of crushing physical labor had been rewarding in several ways. Now, some reward was due for all that she had done. Wanting to be held and feel secure, she desired someone strong yet gentle who wouldn't judge her for her unpredictable actions. Moments later, Kim slid under the covers and wrapped herself around Nick. He was warm and lean; she was soft and smooth. He returned her gesture with strong arms that pulled her close to him. It was two in the morning, and they felt good together; they felt right together. Caressing each other's young bodies with wandering hands, Kim and Nick shared wet, passionate kisses.

And then they made love.

They lay together naked under the blankets, warm and satiated when they finished. Their passion complete, now was the time for awkward conversation. But for some reason, it wasn't.

They talked like they had been lovers for years. "Brad and I haven't been together …like we were for a long time," said Kim.

"Why not?" Nick asked.

"I'm not sure. He's been acting strange for the last year, saying there's a ton of pressure from work. He works in sales but hardly ever leaves the condo. Working from home gives him time to always be on my case. Been an ass to me more times than I care to admit. For some reason, I've been putting up with it."

"That sucks. Why don't you move out?"

"I've explored that but haven't dared to go through with it yet. Lately, I've become closer to pulling the trigger and moving in with a friend. He can sense I've been unhappy and tries to make up to me with flowers and gifts. Then I forgive him like an idiot."

"What about you?" Kim asked. "No cowgirls for a cowboy around this place?"

"Had a thing with Chrissy from the Son, you know, Bill's daughter, the bartender. It only lasted a few months and then died out last year. She says I've been down in the dumps ever since Gus died; probably right."

"You never totally get over it," said Kim. "I blame myself for Grace dying and then live with the guilt. I forgive myself, and the loop begins again."

They connected on various things and talked into the early morning hours. Their conversation flowed as they joked back and forth; Kim giggled loudly and covered her mouth to avoid waking the others. It became apparent to Kim that they were very compatible. But, there was no talk of a potential future either.

Marshera was almost fixed. Kim assumed she would return to Mum's and Nick to his ranch and horses. Then she was supposed to head back to Maryland. But his condo wasn't her home anymore. Brad and she were over as far as she was concerned.

Why not move up here to New Hampshire and live with Mum and see where this goes?

The next day, Marshera replanted the remaining vegetable plants into their beds. Nick made a few minor tweaks to the freshwater supply, and the project was completed.

The noises heard in Marshera had returned to normal. Kids were playing chess, checkers, and various board games. Laughter and arguing were heard throughout the cave again. It was the sweet sound that had been missing for a year. Kim joined in on any of the games she was asked to play. She felt grateful to be asked but, at the same time, worried. Without even talking to him, Kim had figured out why Nick had been concerned.

The reconnaissance team had seriously damaged the machines and the operation. But after spending all that money, Kim wondered and worried. Would they give up? Would they pack up and head home?

Are Marshera's problems all over, or are they just beginning?

Chapter 33
Shake It Off

Topaz sat and read another threatening message from her. He knew he had to reply but needed to tread carefully. Of course, her ultimate loyalty was to the company. Sure, they had feelings for each other. It started as an occasional hookup, but then emotions became involved when it became a regular thing. Now he had been ripped off. It wasn't only his ass on the line; it was hers too. He had to buy time and find that bastard. The trouble was, that bastard had entirely disappeared. *I'm evaluating my options. Right now, they suck.*

Lee Chen was startled when her phone vibrated with his reply. He'd gone dark, and she'd feared he was gone. Then she would be the one in deep shit. But at least now he was communicating.

She messaged him back: *There are options. If you take my call, we can discuss this. We are more than just a hookup. I care about you, and I don't care about many. I can't help you unless we talk.*

He read her message and shook his head. Then he replied. *I know where your loyalty lies. It's not with me. It can't be or your ass is in a sling. Have to find that MF that got me and get it all back. I put the word out on the streets, Waiting for an answer. Then we can talk. My ass is in a sling until I get it all back.*

She fired back in a desperate attempt. *No! This is still in my hands. I can help you. Don't wanna see you hurt. Come up here to me in the mountains. We can fix this thing. Last chance, call me right now and discuss.*

He shook his head, swiped left, and then pressed delete.

Chapter 34
You Shook Me All Night Long

Creen kept staring at the board, trying to determine her next move. The match was at the classic endgame stage with only three pieces left. In chess, it was known as *the opposition.* Julie's king and pawn were staring down Creen's lone king on the board's light-colored squares; advantage, Julie.

Although no official timer was on the table, an unofficial one was ticking inside Julie's head. "Time's up; make your move already."

A few spectators had wandered into the cafeteria to stand over their shoulders, making Creen nervous. Julie took a step closer to checkmate by moving her king to C3. All Creen could hope for at this point was a stalemate. She reached over and dragged her king backward in retreat to C5. "There," she said, looking at her.

Julie rolled her eyes and moved her king diagonally to C7, pushing Creen further into a corner and controlling the board. In five more moves, it would be checkmate.

Nick and Kim sat on the table's long bench side by side. Everywhere they went, they seemed to be side by side now. With hips touching, they didn't attempt to hide the obvious. They had the confidence of a couple that radiated love.

A vegetarian lunch had been prepared for all with the meager supplies available. It would be at least six weeks until the re-potted gardens produced edible vegetables and fruit. The game finished with Julie, the winner. Now everyone would eat. The joking and teasing began amongst them. It was harmless and helped ease the tension. Every minute with no tremors put their minds more at ease as life returned to normal again.

Kim was curious and asked a question about something.

"Do you all refrain from eating meat?"

"We are vegetarian and vegan depending on the person's preference," Barge said.

"Why? If you don't mind me asking?"

Barge swallowed his food and spoke with a hint of reprimand. "We live by the Golden Rule. The rule tells us to save lives and never take one. That goes for any living creature, not just people. We practice what we preach."

Sensing an awkward moment, Creen quickly changed the subject. "We all need a trip to a hair stylist, she said. "Everyone's looking shaggy."

"We still have the clippers and scissors from when Mother cut our hair," said Charlie. "Why don't we buzz all our heads?"

"Sounds good; let’s start with you," Julie said.

"I agree; let's buzz the guys!" said Creen.

"My aunt was a hairdresser and taught me a few things years ago. I could give the guys a trim if necessary,” said Kim.

"It's official, Kim, if you can style hair, you're our new Mother!" Creen said.

"Should we ask Nick to stay as the Father?" asked Charlie, giggling.

Nick hung his head and smiled as everyone laughed openly. It was a good feeling to laugh again.

Creen looked up to the ceiling and then at the others.

"Did you feel that?" she said, looking at Julie.

"Did I feel what?" Julie answered.

"The vibrations, the tremors like we used to feel," said Creen.

"No, I didn't feel anything. Julie said. Those are done now. We broke their stuff."

"I felt it too," said Kim, looking over at Julie's plastic cup of water. A small ring appeared. Then another, and then a third.

"Dammit, all!"

A shuddering series of thuds shook the floors and walls, reverberating massive shockwaves throughout Marshera. Each thud felt like the hammering of fists into their chests. They grabbed each other in panic as wave after wave of tremors left them stunned. Plates and silverware bounced across the table and slid off, shattering on the rock floor. Creen let out a high-pitched scream as Charlie grabbed her hand and pulled her under the table with him. Julie followed her brother as Kim, Nick, and Barge ran around collecting dishes about to smash. Then they joined the others underneath the table, seeking shelter from the storm.

Hale bombs of rocks, silt, and stones fell from the ceiling to land on tables, counters, and floors. Picture frames fell off walls. Their cherished memories came crashing down, breaking into pieces.

Kim felt her anxiety ratchet up to the danger level. *Is this when the entire ceiling drops down and crushes us all?*

In tears, Julie crawled over, and Kim wrapped her in her arms. She held her tightly to ease her terror, although she was equally terrified. The dampness of Julie's tears seeped through her shirt as the shelling continued.

"But we smashed their machines!" Julie's muffled voice came through Kim's embrace.

"They must've fixed them!" Kim yelled over the noise. "I don't know anymore!" She and Nick clasped their hands together. Charlie rubbed Creen's back as she whimpered and moaned. She kneeled with her forehead against the floor; her hands covered her head.

"It ain't from fracking. Miners are using explosives now; from what I remember, they have plenty of them." Nick said. He felt the buzz of a text message from his phone as he looked at Kim and Barge," We need to do another recon as soon as this is over. See what the hell they're doing!"

"Agree!" Barge shouted back as Kim nodded her head.

The terror continued for ten more torturing minutes. A total of fifteen minutes had elapsed, when it finally stopped. An eerie stillness hung in the air as dust floated down from above. They stayed under the table for a while. It was safe there. They had to be sure the barrage was really over. After several minutes, Kim heard a quiet conversation between the two kids. Then there was a little laughter; it was over for now.

Nick read his text; *Couple guys come round here looking for you, son. Saying you owe them some green. One had a gun tucked inside his coat. You borrowing money from somebody besides Milt Logan? I was getting here and told them I don't know nothing cause I don't. Where are you? They gone for now. Call me, Walt.*

Everything was so different now. When Nick was young, time was as slow as molasses. Days, weeks, and months took forever. Even when he rode their Arabians with wild abandon, time seemed infinite. Now time was in scarce supply. There was no time to ride anymore. There was only time to worry.

***

Their trip through the Forbidden Tunnel was made in rapid time.

This time, Kim felt stronger, although she didn't object when Nick took her hand and held it throughout the journey. It was just the two of them; the others stayed behind to pick up the pieces.

Nick pulled Kim back and stopped their progress. His flashlight reflected off a wall of rubble and rocks that blocked their passage. "What the hell we gonna do now?" Nick said.

"This is bullshit," said Kim.

Climbing to the top of the rubble, she pulled a rock off and let it roll down onto the floor. "How do you eat an elephant?" she turned back to look at Nick. "One bite at a time!"

As the rock came rolling down, Nick jumped out of its way. He got the message; get it out of the way! Twenty minutes and a few scraped knuckles later, the wall was removed, and they made their way to the end of the tunnel. As they approached the opening, faint voices were heard. One of the them sounded familiar.

A sliver through the bush that covered the cavern revealed a clear view of the man that Kim had lived with for the past two years. Standing next to him was the foreman, Tom. Facing him was the Asian woman who rang her doorbell. Kim now had the answers to her questions; Brad was one of the bad guys.

"What's the point of bringing Brad and me up here, Tom?" asked Lee Chen. I've already seen the ugly hole you guys hacked out of this mountain."

"That ugly hole has allowed us access to your precious meteorite. With my mickey mouse repairs to the Fracker, I hope to add the last micro-channels that encircle it. Then we add the last of the explosives for the detonation scheduled for this weekend. For security purposes, twenty armed guards will be here before the asset's extraction," Tom said.

"That's what the plan calls for, Tom. Thanks for the status report. Brad and I have a ton of things to do, so we'll head back to the trailer."

"Wait!" Tom's powerful voice cut through the air, causing them to stop and turn around.

"We are going to detonate over a hundred charges simultaneously. That's a massive amount of force. According to my calculations, the explosion will cause that ugly hole to implode as the meteorite emerges from its crater. At the time of detonation, every cave, tunnel, and cavern at this elevation will also implode. That includes the hippy colony. That place they call Marshera will experience a cave-in. Every person and everything inside that cave will be crushed. Am I making myself clear? Anyone left inside will die."

"Oh, my God!" Kim whispered to Nick.

"Shhhhh, let's hear all of this."

Lee Chen paused to process the information she just received.

"The people from the hippy colony," she said. "They're collateral damage."

"You're not serious," said Tom.

"I'm dead serious. This meteorite must be delivered on time. Failure is not an option. I couldn't care less about some hippy colony that won't be missed for who knows how long. This is a business transaction worth billions, and our organization has already spent millions on it. The delivery of the asset must take place on time."

"Miss Chen, I am being paid handsomely for managing this operation. I always wanted to come back here and excavate that meteorite. But I never agreed to kill innocent people. The explosives will not be detonated until I know the hippy colony has been safely evacuated."

"We don't have time for evacuations, Tom! And I don't need Mr. Chang's permission to do anything it takes to deliver that asset! And I do mean anything!"

"Not sure what you mean by anything, but if one hair on my head gets touched, there'll be no detonation," said Tom calmly. "I'm the only one with the codes to blast out the meteorite."

"Stop being naïve, Tom. You know you're going to detonate the damn charges. Who paid the millions for everything here: the mining equipment, the workers, the payoffs to local officials, and your salary? Triad and Chromel are going to get a return on their investment. Trust me, I'll see to that," she said.

"No matter the circumstances or who is paying the bills, I'm not a murderer, especially when it comes to young kids, Miss Chen."

They stared at each other, and tempers escalated, "Okay, Tom, you win. I will have Brad get in touch with his girlfriend Kim, who we spotted on the video destroying *your* equipment. He will inform her that they have to evacuate or die. Do we have an agreement?"

"That's all I ask. No one should get hurt or die for a giant, blue space rock," said Tom.

She turned to Brad, "Text her first and tell her they need to evacuate."

"Understood," said Brad.

"Okay, we're done here, Tom. Why don't you take the cart back to the trailer and complete your final preparations? I need to speak with Brad about our plan to relocate those people from the hippy colony once they're evacuated."

"Okay, I'm off," said Tom. He shuffled over to the electric cart and coasted down the curved road back to the tan trailer leaving a cloud of dust behind him.

Brad was just about to send the text message when she grabbed the phone out of his hand. "You can't tell her about the detonation or that they need to evacuate."

Brad stood dumbfounded, "What the hell? You just told me…

"I was telling Tom what he wanted to hear. I'm going to let him get everything in place, and just before he asks for verification, I'll come up with a reason for him to push the button."

"That sounds risky. He said he wouldn't push the button unless there's an evacuation. Why don't we just let them evacuate?" Brad asked.

"Look, Brad. You need to make a choice here. Who's team are you playing for?"

"I'm on your team, but I've been living with Kim for the last two years."

"Yes, I know. But what do you think will happen if we tell Kim and those other people they have to evacuate? I'll tell you what they'll do. Nothing! They'll know we wouldn't ask them to evacuate because we're concerned about their safety. They will lock down and stay put right where they are, refusing to leave. Tom won't detonate the charges to blast the asset out of the ground. Then we're both screwed."

"I see your point," said Brad.

"Right, there's no other way."

"If doing this frees my mother and gets her back home, then the hell with Kim and her friends. But if we crush the hippy colony, it could be considered murder."

"We'll be long gone; I'm not worried about it."

"There's one more thing, Lee. If I could talk to Kim and tell her to evacuate or she and her friends will be killed, she would owe me one and probably give me some of the Blue Water for Mr. Chang. I need to deliver a sample to him in exchange for my mother's freedom!"

"No! Do not contact Kim. You talking to her isn't in the plan, Brad. You will help me on some projects and I will contact Mr. Chang to free your mother."

Kim and Nick sat in a state of shock. Kim had to stomach that the man she once was in love with was willing to let her die.

“My God, it’s a giant meteorite they’re after,” Kim said.

“That’s gotta be one hell of a special space rock they’re diggin’ up,.” Nick said.

"The two questions I have are when exactly are they going to detonate all those charges and how do we stop them?" said Kim.

"He said this weekend. It’s Thursday, 5:15 PM. We need a military plan of attack," said Nick.

"You have something in mind?"

Nick smiled at her, "Yeah, I got something that’ll stop those muleskinners for good."

"What the heck’s a mule… Never mind, let's go!" As they began to run, Kim grabbed Nick's hand. She tripped over a rock to tumble onto the ground, yelling as she fell. Nick helped her to her feet, and they ran back to Marshera through the Forbidden Tunnel.

A guard named Alexander Baez had arrived onsite early. He was known for being sharper than the others and was within earshot of Kim's voice when she fell. He climbed up the embankment and found the entrance to the tunnel. His flashlight revealed footprints in the dirt. They were fresh. Reversing direction, Alex crawled out of the opening.

"I’m headed down to the trailer," he said to a nearby guard. “I found something useful.”

Alex had found something very useful indeed.

Chapter 35
For What It's Worth

Julie and Creen sat next to each other on the Common Room couch with a blanket covering their legs to keep them warm. Engrossed in a half-finished game of checkers, Charlie and Barge sat on the floor across from each other. All were waiting for Kim and Nick to return and tell them what they had discovered on their trip to the mining site.

Upon arrival, Kim and Nick informed the people of Marshera of the grim news. Lee Chen would crush them to death, and a cave-in would destroy Marshera. There were less than forty-eight hours to figure out a solution.

"This is devastating news," said Barge. Marshera, our healing place for the sick, will be destroyed. The Fountain of Life, our Blue Water, the Lightroom, Wildcat Falls, and the wonder of these caves that the Ancients discovered so long ago. They will all be gone after the explosion. I still can't believe their careless, evil deeds."

"Speaking of the Blue Water, I've put the last piece of the puzzle in place," Kim said.

"What do you mean?" Barge continued pacing the floor.

"Tom, the foreman called the meteorite the giant blue space rock. Not only did we learn they are mining a meteorite, but it's also a blue meteorite. The Fountain of Life yields hot blue water that you consume daily. My test kit couldn't identify the blue element in the water. Blue water and a blue space rock? The meteorite must be the secret to Marshera's healing powers. It's no coincidence."

"Seems logical, but how can you be sure?" Barge asked.

"I just did some research on my phone. There are all kinds of stories online about this meteorite. It is composed of a rare element that is not found anywhere on earth. It crashed and buried itself underground on Wildcat Mountain around a thousand years ago. In the eighties, a professor from The University of New Hampshire named Dr. Conti led an expedition and discovered the meteorite. It's made of an element called Continuum. The water from Wildcat Brook gushes right through the center of this mountain. It's a rare phenomenon in nature that causes something called a water gap. The water circulates over the meteorite, absorbing the Continuum. Then it's superheated and forced up by the geyser into the tower every day at four PM to flow from The Fountain of Life during The Offering. Do you see what's happening? The water that heals you is created from the Continuum meteorite that the miners want to rip out of the earth. The Continuum saves your lives and the meteorite is the only source of it on the planet."

"So we've been drinking space water? That's so cool," said Julie.

"Yes, you have. You've been drinking space water with incredible healing powers," said Kim. I don't believe these people know of the meteorite's healing potential. Continuum must have some other properties in its unique composition to make it worth billions. Even if the miners could extricate the blue meteorite without imploding Marshera, removing it would mean the end of The Fountain of Life's healing powers."

"We need to attack to save Marshera," said Barge. "It's the only way."

Low-level tremors and vibrations reverberated under their feet, reminding them time was running out. The miners continued to loosen the last rocks that held the meteorite to its earthly bond.

"We don't have much time to plan the attack," said Nick. "A nighttime attack will be our best chance to defeat them. The problem is they've got twenty guards with guns coming, and we have, well, we have no guns. The other thing is when will they detonate? Tom the foreman said this weekend but we have to find the exact day and time."

"There is one thing you may be forgetting," said Kim. "You stole that ANFO explosive."

He looked at her and smiled, "I haven't forgotten about it. The ANFO will be part of the battle plan. But first things first. We need help. We need warriors."

Nick turned to Barge, "Can Ashun and Winger help us, and do they have any friends?"

"Perhaps," said Barge. "But we don’t have a way of contacting them. They live in the woods with no means of communication."

"I know where they live," Charlie blurted out.

"Excuse me? Nobody knows where they live," said Julie.

He bowed his head, realizing that he'd accidentally revealed his secret. "Sometimes, I sneak out when everyone's asleep and walk the trails. One night I saw Winger hunting for food, and I followed him. Then I saw where he and Ashun lived. It's a great big treehouse high up a huge tree." Everyone glared at him with surprised faces.

"Ya, I know. I shouldn't be doing that," Charlie said.

Barge stared at Charlie, "We will discuss this later, Charlie. You and I are going to this treehouse to find Ashun and Winger to get their help."

"We seem to be missing one obvious solution," said Kim. "Why don't I call Lieutenant Jacquard from the Crawford Police Department? I mean, after all, he is the police. He said I didn't have enough information to file a case to find Julie, but now I have something far more important to report."

"Don't!" Nick yelled. "I've ignored the truth long enough, and that stops today. I told you that everyone in Crawford has a look-the-other-way attitude. We don't ask and we don't tell as long as the businesses thrive. But everyone knows that the cops in town are paid off by Chromwell, the Swiss investors that bailed us out years ago. The meteorite is what they want. It must be worth billions to them. We overheard Lee Chen tell the other guy that town officials had been paid off to look the other way."

"You mean Lieutenant Jacquard too?" Kim asked. "Now I know why he could have been more helpful."

"I don't know about Jacquard. My dad told me once that he might be the only clean cop in town, but other people think differently. Thing's this, you all call the cops, and some of them will come up here and help the bad guys kill us, so they ain't exposed for being dirty."

"We can't go to the police because of what Nick said. Therefore, the only option we have is to stop the miners from blasting out that meteorite," Barge said.

"I'll create a battle plan to beat these bastards," said Nick. "I can do this."

"They teach you this stuff in the military academy or something?" Kim asked.

"No, they didn't. In basic training, we received some battle strategy information. I've read a ton of books on my own. I'm a student of famous battles and their strategies; been into this stuff for a long time."

"You've read books on war but never planned out a winning battle?" asked Barge. "That sounds concerning."

"No I haven't, but I have this one mostly figured out already. Every battle is won before it is ever fought, said Sun Tzu. We'll copy what they did at the Battle of Saratoga. First, create a diversion and confuse the guards and the miners. In the meantime, we carry out the plan as we divide and conquer. All this stuff will set up the final part of the battle plan that will finish this thing for good. I have to check a few logistical things first."

Barge turned to Charlie, "You can find Ashun and Winger's place again?"

"Oh yeah, I'm good in the woods. I never get lost."

"Alright then, let's go and get back before The Offering. Meet me outside under the Falls in ten minutes."

Nick found a large piece of paper that he would use to create the battle plan. It would have all the local terrain and trails around the mountain with steps needed for victory. They had to know each of their responsibilities. Then he began walking toward the Falls Room.

"Where are you headed?" asked Kim.

"Have to take the trail to the top of the mountain for a bit to look at a few things; all part of the plan. Be back in an hour."

"Okay, be careful," Kim watched him walk away and for the first time, accepted him as hers now. They belonged to each other, and she knew there would be no going back to the life she knew in Maryland.

The others remained assembled in the Common Room as Kim returned and sat with them. Julie asked Barge to discuss the origin of the Blue Water. "I wonder why Mother never told us about the space water."

"Mother never knew about the space rock or where the Blue Water came from. Nobody did. Before you came to live here to be cured of your afflictions, the mountain's owner was told of The Fountain of Life and doubted its healing powers. He visited Marshera, saw the cave drawings, and spoke to the Abenaki that lived in the region. They told him of their ancestors and how the water healed their smallpox and measles in colonial times. The owner became a believer and had Marshera converted to a newer facility that could heal four children at a time. They would be selected by a secret lottery of limited candidates based on their severe afflictions and if they were well enough to live here for five years away from their families. After this place was modernized to the way it is now, I was the first to live here and begin the healing process."

"We didn't know about this," said Charlie. "Who is the owner?"

"The owner of the mountain was a billionaire. He died several years ago, but he left an endowment to keep this place running for a long time into the future. He gave me everything, but he couldn't provide me with life until I came here. That is what he wanted for me before he died."

"So you knew this stranger?" Julie asked.

"I not only knew him, I loved him. He was my father."

Chapter 36:
Take A Chance On Me

Thought you would come to the mountains and see me. How can I help you if you keep hiding? You know they'll find you unless we talk first. You're not one of my regular workers, I don't have to tell you this. I've called, but you don't answer. I'm not a chaser. There's something between us that's more than physical. You should use that. Hiding out won't make the problem go away. It'll only make it worse. This is my last message to you, Topaz.

We can fix this, but first, you need to come in from the cold. You are Topaz, remember? You're my Rock of Gibraltar. Contact me now, or I will forget what we have and be forced to take drastic measures. If my two people find you before I hear from you, they'll make your life very uncomfortable. Call me now, and let's fix this. - Lee.

Chapter 37
Amazing Journey

"Almost there," said Charlie. "I promise." He panicked as he searched for familiar landmarks in a forest where everything looked identical. The last thing he wanted was to blow it with the man he regarded as a father figure. Pushing his short legs as hard as he could, his lungs struggled for air. The respiratory affliction he was born with hampered his progress.

"I've never been down this trail, and we've been hiking it for almost an hour. You said it would take half the time. So, are we lost?" Barge barked out to him.

"No, I'm sure it will be coming up soon. It has to be," Charlie said. His head continued to swivel, as his mind tried to recall the way, wondering if, in fact, they were off track.

"I know I'm being tough on you, Charlie, but we are pressed for time. We have to figure out how to save Marshera."

Sensing forgiveness in Barge's voice, he decided it was time to ask the question that had been bothering him.

"Need to ask you something, Barge."

"Quickly, what is it?"

"When the battle begins, can I fight with you and the others? I'm sick of being the little kid that always stays behind. I wanted to do more exciting things now."

"Exciting things?"

"Things like the journey through the Forbidden Tunnel that you guys went on."

"The journey through the tunnel was dangerous, Charlie. Creen could never go on those missions. She's far too delicate. I needed someone reliable to watch over her."

"But when will it be my turn to be an explorer or a fighter?"

"What do you call what we're doing now?"

Charlie expanded his chest as he tried to breathe enough air before speaking. "I think I'm on this mission because you need me to show you the way to the tree fort."

"Everyone serves a purpose in contributing to the greater good, Charlie. What you're doing for Marshera today is of great value. The others could not lead us to Ashun and Winger's home."

"That's right. Kim can't do this! She doesn't know the way here. Only I do!"

"Do I detect a problem with you and Kim, Charlie?"

"Ever since Kim showed up, I've been treated lousy. I'm sick of her bossing me around too. Also, she's a Normal, and we don't like them. I wish she would just leave!"

"We judge all people individually, Charlie. To do differently would be prejudiced. Do you remember Mother teaching us the history of racial bias? It affected all races, especially my ancestors of African descent. Not all Normals are bad. We are careful to keep our distance, that's all. Besides, adults from any race are considered Normals."

"I forgot about all that stuff," Charlie said.

"Without Kim and Nick, we wouldn't know the cause of the tremors that frightened us or what made us sick. She and Nick helped us identify the problems and then fix them. Now they're helping us defend Marshera. It would be nice if you were thankful they are helping us, Charlie. "

"I'm not thankful for her," Charlie said.

"Something tells me this is about redemption. You previously informed me that you were upset because you didn't participate in saving your sister Julie's life. Is that why you are angry?"

"I don't know what that redemp…word means," said Charlie.

"Redemption is when you make up for something that you did wrong or think you did wrong. But you didn't do anything wrong. Ashun and Winger prevented you from trying to save Julie so you wouldn't get hurt. They were doing what I asked them to do."

"I guess some of that is true. But I'm still ready. Kim gets to do stuff, and she's not even one of us. I'm ready to do stuff too. I was ready when Julie needed me, and I'm ready now."

"You say you were ready to save your sister, but you don't know how to swim, Charlie."

Why can't Barge see I'm growing up? I'm not the little boy that came to Marshera three years ago with his sister. I'm ready to be tested and prove I'm a man.

The trail turned radically left. Charlie stopped and looked straight up at a giant elm tree that seemed as tall as Mount Washington.

With heads tilted back, they gazed at the tree fort that Barge guessed was fifty feet up the tree. It was no ordinary tree fort, more a full-size house between the branches. Barge's voice echoed around the trees as he called up to Ashun and Winger. Unfortunately, after several attempts, no one yelled down from the elevated dwelling.

"We came all this way, and there's nobody home," Barge muttered.

"Maybe they're asleep?" said Charlie.

"Then we have to find a way up there to awaken them, said Barge. "But I do not see any ropes or ladder."

"And there are no branches to climb up until halfway up the tree," said Charlie.

Frustrated, Charlie plunged into the dense brush to check the other side, desperately trying to find a way. He crashed through branches as twigs snapped under his feet, searching for a solution to their problem. He crawled under a limb to emerge into a narrow clearing.

That's when he saw them.

"Hey Barge, come towards my voice. Think I found something!"

Barge made his way through tangles of branches to stand beside Charlie and take in the strange sight. A single row of twenty trees with no limbs stood before them. The tops of every tree were cut straight off, giving them the appearance of uncarved totem poles. The heights started low and gradually became taller until they reached the tree fort, fifty feet off the ground.

"It's a row of tree poles!" said Charlie, excited he'd found a way to the destination.

The good news was the poles were fairly close to each other; the bad news was they would both have to maximize the nerve and balance needed to scale the row without falling. If they failed, there would be serious injury or even death.

Barge was quiet as he stared at the column of tree poles, "Is this our only option?"

"Only one that I see," said Charlie.

He walked to Charlie and rested a giant hand on his shoulder. "You said you are ready. Lead the way."

Charlie smiled ear to ear, "Okay!" He turned and jumped onto the first pole.

"One thing," said Barge.

"What?" asked Charlie.

"Don't fall."

Charlie looked ahead at the row of twenty wooden columns, each escalating in height. Here was his chance to prove himself.

The obstacle course they faced was simple. It would require precise footing and balance to step from tree to tree. Like most tests, it was easy to start but then became more challenging to finish. The first five trees were close to each other, and Charlie crossed them quickly with short hops. The next few were further apart, each one taller than the previous. After traversing from tree to tree, Charlie looked back to see Barge behind him. Then he looked down. They were twenty feet off the ground, but it looked like a mile to him. Charlie realized at that moment that he was deathly afraid of heights. Standing paralyzed in fright, he stared down and imagined the outcome if he plummeted to the ground.

"So far, so good, I guess," he yelled to Barge nervously.

The wind picked up. Nearby branches swayed and rustled as the pole he stood on moved and swayed. Charlie outstretched his arms and bent his knees as his tension increased. He did not want to go any further. He wanted to turn back.

"Barge, I'm not feeling good."

"What's the problem, Charlie?"

"I just found out I'm afraid of heights."

"Everyone is afraid of heights. Just go slow and remember one thing."

"What's that?" asked Charlie.

"Don't look down."

You wanted to show you're grown up. Get going, and don't look down.

Carefully Charlie hopped to three more tree poles. After the last one, he couldn't help himself and peeked down again. He was thirty feet high and perched on a wavering tree pole.

What was I thinking? I'm not ready to do this!

Down below was an array of jagged rocks. A deep chill ran through his core. Another gust of wind slammed into his side, and he knelt on the flat top. Feeling like he was about to vomit, Charlie's mouth became watery. He spit and watched the liquid drop down and splash on the rocks. *There were five more tree poles? Or is it six?* It seemed impossible. He wanted to stay where he was.

"Go on, Charlie." Barge's voice boomed as he stood defiantly on the pole behind him with arms folded. Charlie's eyes were closed. He barely opened them to look back.

"You're doing fine. Finish the job." Barge said sternly.

Again he rose and mustered the will to finish. Carefully hopping from one column to the next, he never looked down. *Forward progress, one at a time.* He was a wreck but managed to gut his way through the last few tree poles.

Charlie was the first to step off, then Barge, landing on a deck surrounding the tree fort. Charlie cheered out loud and pumped his fist. They had made it.

Like a house, the fort had an actual door, but it was locked. Barge's fist pounded to create a thundering sound. No one answered. Charlie stood behind him and looked in wonder at the small gray house with an A-frame roof and windows on the sides.

After several attempts, it looked as if their risky trip down miles of trails and crossing tree poles fifty feet high was a waste of time. Barge looked for a rope to lower themselves down.

Then Ashun flung open the door.

She stood with her mouth gaped open and hands on her hips. A shock of jet-black afro hair sprang from her head. "I can't believe you guys are standing on my porch!"

"We need your help," said Barge.

"What brings you two here? How can we help?" said Ashun.

"Is Winger here?"

"No, he's deer hunting; not sure what time he'll be back. Is everything alright at Marshera?"

"Everything is not alright at Marshera. A lot has happened since you brought Charlie and Julie back to us."

Barge explained how Kim and Nick came to them and helped them discover what was causing the tremors and the poisoning of their water and vegetable beds. The most important information was that a final detonation would crush Marshera and anyone inside in a day or two; they weren't sure of the exact time yet.

"This is very scary." What will you do?"

"Kim's friend, Nick, served in the military. He is creating a battle plan for us to attack the miners and stop them before they detonate the explosives. It's going to be a first-strike attack, and Nick said we need you and Winger, along with any other warriors you can find to help out. Me and Charlie came out here to ask for your help. Will you and Winger help us, Ashun?"

"You better believe it! I can't believe what I'm hearing!"

"We can't thank you enough."

"Wing and I don't usually go over to that side of the mountain, but still, I can't believe we never spotted a mining operation," she said. "They must be well hidden. The nerve of them digging into *our* mountain for some rock they plan to sell for money. The Normals only care about one thing; money. I know Winger will be as pissed off as I am. Wildcat Mountain, the Falls, and Marshera are all sacred Abenaki land. How dare they!"

"We are glad you can help us. Everything is happening so quickly."

"We will always help our friends from Marshera," said Ashun. "And we will protect our sacred land. Do they have guards, and if so, are they armed?"

"Yes, they do. We overheard there will be twenty, and we can safely assume they'll be armed with rifles and pistols. It will be dangerous."

"We've got no guns here, only bows, arrows, and blow guns. We can reach out to our Abenaki brothers and sisters in the region, but we're cutting it close. They won't have much time to get here."

"You two don't have a phone or any way for us to communicate with you," Barge said.

"Not to worry, we will get as many friends to help as possible. Not sure if they'll be warriors, but probably better than nothing. What time do we attack?" Ashun asked.

"The battle plan's unfinished. We believe it will have to be no more than forty-eight hours."

"Understood; what time do you want us to meet you at Marshera?"

"Say seven PM?" Barge said.

"We will be at Marshera Sunday at six thirty to understand the battle plans and get into position," Ashun said. "You're quiet, Charlie. How's it going?"

"It's going great." His shaky voice told her something different. "I like your tree fort. Can we see inside?"

"There's no time," said Barge. "We must return to Marshera. Then we will finish the battle plan with Nick and Kim. See you, Winger and hopefully some friends soon."

“Again, thank you, Ashun."

She led them around to the far side of the deck and showed Barge and Charlie the platform that would lower them to the ground.

The hike back to the caves of Marshera was a quiet one. Charlie was excited that he was given a chance to lead the way when they scaled the tree poles, but he'd had a breakdown. With Barge's encouragement, he finished. But it hadn't been easy.

I may still be a kid, after all.

Chapter 38
Don't Let Me Down

This is my final message to you, Topaz. I'm done asking. My people will burn your house and kill anyone and anything on the property. You know we're capable. Sick of you not returning messages. Call me now or else. L.

Topaz knew she meant business. He had evaded her for too long, and their relationship only got him so far. A reply needed to happen now. The plan had been to find Luscious and bring back the money. Then he'd contact her. But Luscious was gone, off the grid. A phone call to his contact in Providence was made to discuss their mutual friend. He found out about Luscious losing the digit for gambling away company money on a basketball game, of all things.

"Not going to give you my bullshit secret decoder ring number. You know who this is"

"It's about time you called me Topaz. I heard what happened," she said.

"It's going to suck for Luscious when I find his ass. I *will* get you every penny back."

"Luscious did you no favors, Topaz. He paid back everything he owed us. Then he and his family disappeared. He solved his problem and made you my new one."

"Like I said, I will find him and get the money back. It's taking some time."

"What if I told you I have a thing I need done that'll solve your problem?"

"Such as?"

"How long would it take you to come to me in Crawford, New Hampshire."

"I'm closer than you might think. Why?"

"Listen to me carefully..."

***

Nick didn't feel like getting out of bed and leaving her warm body, but he had to. It was fortunate that she slept so soundly; he need not worry about waking her. It all seemed so natural now between them. In a short span, they had felt the unmistakable chemistry that couples in love always do. The way their bodies fit together and how the first touch of their naked skin exhilarated each of them. It was all so new and fresh. Simpatico. There had been a few others before Kim, but each night as he drifted off to sleep, he could honestly say to himself, *I'm in love for the first time.*

Life is full of tasks we resist, like waking up early to walk the dog, driving the kids to school, or facing someone you dread facing. But he had to take care of business.

Everyone was asleep at two o'clock in the morning. That was a safe assumption. They trusted that he would be too. But he wasn't. Everything had been carefully prepared and safely hidden ahead of time. They wouldn't miss it. The procedure would take at most an hour or two. He would be back in bed with her before anyone woke.

Then they could be together, and he'd be done with her for good.

He navigated through the tunnel toward his destination. The tunnel was familiar to him by now. The dank smell made his stomach turn. For the first time in his life, he was nervous.

Emerging in silence, he waited in the shadows. Only one light was on in the mining area; attached to a tree, it shone bright like a moon. Minutes later, she appeared as a silhouette, casting a striking figure. He watched her look for him. Her tousled hair in the breeze and the outline of her body reminded him of why he had found her so irresistible. Slowly he came into her view.

"If it isn't my Topaz. Finally, he appears."

"It's nice to see you again, Lee."

"So polite and formal; nice *to see you again*. I guess I deserve to have my ass kissed a little. I've been kissing yours, texting you with no answer for days."

"I don't care who's kissing whose ass. I brought what you wanted."

"It's not for me, lover. How much did you get?"

"It's close to a cup's worth. I put it in a sealed beaker from the test kit."

"Is it really blue, or is that folklore?"

"It's as blue as the ocean."

"Yes, but is it as blue as your eyes? Good work, Topaz. You used to do good work."

"What's with the attitude?" he said. "You might as well call me by my real name now."

"Protocol is Protocol, Topaz. That's how the organization wants it. Keep it professional."

"Why don't you all just say who you are instead of hiding behind fake names, numbers, and companies? Why don't you say that's how Triad, the Chinese Mafia, works?"

"Careful now, Topaz. You never know who's listening."

"Like your sniper friend? I imagine he's out there somewhere with his crosshairs me."

"Yes, I imagine he has you in his sights. So tell me, how is life hiding out in the hippy colony?"

"They aren't hippies, just for the record. They're sick kids that are trying to get better. At least they were until you guys started polluting their water and food with fracking and drilling. Now you're gonna set off a ton of explosives all at once and cause a cave-in. That'll kill them. That ain't right even by your standards."

"The mining activities were all needed to extract the meteorite. Except for the final detonation, that's coming shortly. As far as the hippies getting sick or crushed, I say, *zhè jiùshì rénshēng*, such is life. Enough small talk. Let me have the Blue Water."

"First things first. Does this square us? Does it wipe out my debt?"

"I don't know, Nick. You lost a lot of our drugs and our money. I will tell Mr. Chang that you delivered the Blue Water, but in the end, if the water is worthless, so were your efforts."

"That's not what you said on the phone. Talk about bait and switch. By the way, I didn't lose the drugs and money. Your guy, Luscious, stole them."

"You're the one who got rolled."

"You can convince him, right? Mr. Chang knows I'm also a good earner and dependable because you said you told him. Plus, there's us."

"I don't know, Nick. What is *us*? Just because we hooked up now and then for sex, does that mean there's an us? Maybe we're just two animals that need to fulfill biological functions. I didn't see it as anything more than that."

"You could have fooled me."

"Maybe I did, Nick. Besides, a little birdie told me you have a new girl now. You've been feasting on Brad's leftovers."

"She ain't with that asshole anymore. They're all done."

"Is that so? So defensive; is this love for you, Topaz?"

The conversation went silent. Nick reached into his pocket and gave her the container of Blue Water.

"So, where do we go from here?"

"Yes, Topaz, where do we go from here? Let's discuss the present and the future. You're hiding out with Brad's girlfriend, Kim. Oh, sorry, you're fucking Brad's girlfriend, Kim. You're also helping out the people in Marshera. I'll use their stupid name; what the hell. You're probably looking for a way to protect them, but there's only one way you can. Tell them to get the fuck out of that cave immediately, or you'll all die."

"You're ain't gonna get them to leave Marshera. They gotta live there and drink the Blue Water every day to heal. They would just as soon die then leave. I've given you what you wanted. Tell Mr. Chang that squares us. This cowboy's outta here." Nick began walking towards the tunnel to head back.

"I'll let you know when you're done, Nick," she said. Just like I did with Gus."

Nick stopped dead in his tracks and turned to stare at her.

"What did I just hear come out of you? Is it true, or are you making shit up, Lee?"

"Actually, I haven't the time to talk any further. My friend has his AR-15 aimed at you, so I suggest you leave now. Go back to your friends and tell them to evacuate right now or they'll be crushed. I'll let you know what Mr. Chang says." She turned and walked away, disappearing into the blackness.

***

"They say that love is blind, and lovers cannot see. The pretty follies that they commit."

Kim stood before him as he emerged from the Forbidden Tunnel. Her hands were on her hips, feet spread apart with eyes focused as she quoted the Bard.

"Well, ain't this a nice how do ya do?" Nick said.

"I should have seen right through you, Nick Caldwell, you traitorous bastard. Or should I call you Topaz?" All of Marshera stood in unison behind her, faces grimaced and tired by the early morning hour but more so by their trust being broken. The cave was silent enough for a pin drop. She didn't care to hear his case; the jury had already convicted him of high crimes and treason. He decided to give his defense whether she or they wanted to hear it or not.

"Y'all think you're Gods or something; that's what I think."

"What on earth are you trying to sell us, Nick?" Kim asked.

"Tell ya what I think. Marshera should've given a sample of that Blue Water to the outside world long ago so they could figure out what it's made out of. Yeah, I know it's supposedly been tried, but I ain't convinced. If them scientists could copy it; they could make some more for other sick folks. But instead, y'all are playing God by keeping it a secret. Only God can decide who lives and dies. What I did was a good thing in the end. I did your dirty work for ya'll, so now you don't have to. That's where I come out on this here thing."

"We trusted you with the secrets of Marshera," said Barge. "As far as your previous statement goes, scientists tried to copy the Blue Water years ago but failed. It can't be copied."

"Right, there ya go again. Time to give it another try," said Nick.

"The problem is if the outside world is unsuccessful, our secret will be revealed, and then the mobs will descend on this place. They will want to drink the Blue Water from the Fountain of Life as we do. Marshera will be destroyed," said Barge. "The Blue Water is why the secret of Marshera must be kept intact."

"Yeah, but what if they *can* copy it? Millions might live. "

Kim interrupted them. "Nick, you have to leave Marshera right this minute."

"Why's that, Kim? Thinkin' if ya get me outta here, I won't tell all these nice people about your opioid addiction? That's right; she's taking pain pills left and right; she got a whole bottle full in her bag. Guess it's alright to take illegal prescription pain pills when you're perfect. Do you know what you are, Kim? You're a dang hypocrite!"

"Hypocrite? Tell me now, Nick, what have you been secretly delivering in those giant bags of horse grain that are stored in your barn? You don't need to tell me; I already connected the dots. You're a drug dealer and a liar. My secretly taking drugs to manage my anxiety is a far cry from your secret, now, isn't it?"

"It's all the same!" Nick fired back. "The bean pot's callin' the tea kettle black! I may be a drug seller, but you're a drug user. You're also a hypocrite!"

Kim's face was red and twisted. Her eyes were welled with tears and pain. "Get out, Nick! Just get out now!"

Lowering his head, Nick marched into the bedroom to grab his backpack and head for the door near the Falls room.

"But don't we need him?" Julie yelled out as tears ran down her cheeks. "He was making the battle plan because he was in the Army. Can't we give him another chance?"

"No, Julie, we can't. He betrayed our trust. He must leave."

"I agree with Kim," said Barge.

"But he saved my life! Kim even said so!"

Kim came to Julie and hugged her tightly. It was a dark moment as everyone became even more frightened than before. They had hours until the roof caved in on them, and now the architect of their defense was caught sleeping with the enemy.

The stone door closed with an echoing thud as Kim sat alone. She had just ripped away the man she was meant to be with. Tears dripped off her jaw. She didn't even try to wipe them.

What the hell have I done?

Chapter 39
You Belong To Me

Three loud taps on the door from the muzzle of a gun snapped their heads toward the alarming noise. Lee Chen motioned her head, and Brad unlocked the door, holding a pistol. She pulled the knife out of its holster that rested behind her jacket and held it down inside her sleeve.

"Who is it?" she barked out.

"Alexander Baez, one of the guards. I discovered something you will be interested in."

"Enter!" she commanded.

A young Asian man dressed in camouflage and tactical gear entered the office. Brad closed the door and locked it.

"Ni shi shei?" Lee shouted at him.

"I would rather speak English," he said. My Mandarin is not so good."

"Then tell me who you are and what you want! Quickly!"

"After you left the site, I heard a noise; it was a woman yelling. I hiked up a nearby hill nearby where you and those men were talking. At the top, I found an opening behind some bushes that led to a tunnel. There were footprints inside from two people. I could smell their odor too. They must have been listening to your conversions."

"Could you locate this tunnel again?"

"Yes, without a problem."

"Interesting," She turned and looked at Brad. "This presents a timely opportunity to us."

"What do you mean?" said Brad.

Ignoring his question, she turned back to the guard, "You've done well identifying this tunnel and reporting it to me. What is your name again?"

"Alexander Baez."

"Return to your post, Alexander Baez. We will be up on the ridge to see this tunnel shortly."

Brad locked the door again and turned to her. "What opportunity?"

"The tunnel that he discovered must lead to the hippy colony. Tom and I suspected a secret passage through the mountain they took to destroy the equipment."

"And we care about this because?"

"When I met Nick, he told me those people would never evacuate the hippy colony. I have a mission for you and your new friend, Alexander Baez."

"And what mission would this be?"

"The Chinese have a saying, *Luàn zhōng yì yǒujī.* Translated, it means, Amid the chaos, there is always opportunity."

"Still not getting you," said Brad.

"You will later tonight."

***

As they moved through the tunnel, they discussed what defenses might be in place. They might expect booby traps, barriers, and fake floors. As the end of the tunnel approached, they crept, listening to the rock fragments crackling under their feet.

In the dark surroundings, Brad thought of his mother. She'd always been his biggest cheerleader and told him he could become anything he wanted. How had he become this?

This little caper was going to be it, he decided. It was time to play it straight, he told himself. They'd do their little deed, settle his debt with Mr. Chang and then say bye-bye. Other changes were coming too. Kim was gone; he knew that he'd lost her. No surprise; the relationship had been slipping for some time. It was time for Brad Parkland to renew himself.

Brad and Alex executed the plan to perfection. The booby-traps and other defenses they worried about never existed. They just slipped into Marshera during the early morning hour and took her. She resisted mightily, but Brad restrained her, wrapping her in his arms while holding the towel in place. Alex injected 3.5 mg of Midazolam into her arm. The thrashing and kicking ended within twenty seconds. She became as limp as the towel that muffled her screams.

Alex carried her back through the Forbidden Tunnel, fireman style. Like a ragdoll over his shoulder, they made their passage back to emerge into the dawn sunrise. Julie's arms and long hair dangled down her captor's back. Brad looked at the lifeless girl with disdain. It didn't sit well with him. They were dealing with a young girl. She was innocent like he used to be. The sunrise pierced around Whiteface Mountain, blinding Brad. Maybe that was what he had been suffering from for the last year he thought, momentary blindness.

Julie was brought to the trailer and locked up in a spare room as Lee Chen's prisoner. She would now reach out to Marshera to negotiate a deal. The terms were non-negotiable. Julie would be returned to them just as soon as they evacuated Marshera. Proof that all inhabitants had vacated the caves would be all that Tom needed to push the button and detonate the charges. The meteorite would be extracted, making them all very rich.

***

Kim woke up in a fog, her knees pressed to her chest with arms wrapped around them. She hated rising this way with only three hours of sleep. How would she and Marshera win this battle without Nick? She wiped the sand from her eyes and blinked them open. Feeling weary, she stretched her arms and legs out to complete her morning routine of deep breathing and yoga to maintain mindfulness. Her room was quiet, located away from the other bedrooms.

Tip-toeing quietly through Marshera as the others slept, Kim pulled aside the curtain door of Creen's room. She was still asleep under a pile of covers. Next door, the covers that Charlie kicked off his bed were put back on him by her. Finally, to Julie, their connection was like the one she'd had with her sister Grace. Julie's bed was empty, her covers strewn across the floor. A stray hand towel lay on the blankets. Wearily, Kim shuffled to the bathroom. It was unoccupied. *She's not in bed or the bath, so where then?* Kim relieved herself and then continued her search, knowing she would find Julie quietly reading somewhere in Marshera as she often did.

Where is my little tiger lily?

She checked the couch and chairs in the Common Room but came up empty. Worry began to build inside her. Her pace quickened as she erratically searched and re-searched every room. Barge's room; he was snoring but all alone. The Offering room, Cafeteria, and lastly, The Falls Room. They were all empty! Julie had no reason to leave Marshera now that the food and water situation was fixed. Back to Creen's room again. Wait a minute! The Light Room, why didn't she think of it before? It made perfect sense. Julie liked to check on the progress of the plants they had repotted. She searched in and around each of the vegetable beds, but there was no Julie to be found.

The hand towel!

It wasn't one that Kim had seen before. It was a strange green color. She ran back to Julie's room and grabbed the towel to smell it. There was a hint of ammonia and a medicinal smell she couldn't identify. When the obvious hit, she dropped to her knees in pain.

“Dear God!...No!” Kim shrieked at the top of her lungs in anger. Losing Grace all those years ago exploded back into her head as she screamed in pain, realizing the obvious. Barge, Creen, and Charlie came running into Julie's room.

Kim moaned over and over in tears. "I said I wasn't going to lose another one!”

“And now I have!"

Chapter 40
She Said She Said

Kim wept uncontrollably, blaming herself for Julie's abduction. They gathered around her for support, but she couldn't help thinking back to her sister Grace. She had never stopped blaming herself for Grace's death all those years ago. Now it was Julie's turn.

Dammit to hell, I've failed again!

"How do you know it's that Chinese woman we saw before, this Lee Chen?" asked Barge. What if it was Nick? He might have returned for revenge. Besides, how did they know about the Forbidden Tunnel?"

"I don't know," said Kim. "I don't know what to think. Maybe Nick told her about the tunnel when he was with her. I'm so confused right now. I know he cared about Julie, and I can't see him harming her."

"Why don't you message him?" said Creen.

Kim looked at Creen and then the others. Blinking through tear-covered eyes, she barely saw them nod with approval.

It was at that moment a realization came over her. There were three men in her life who she had loved and trusted. All three had let her down. First, her father. Did he kill her sister and then disappear in guilt? Then the two men she had fallen in love with, Brad and Nick. Both had betrayed her. Her scientific mind was trying to calculate conclusions, and the one Kim arrived at was that she had relied on men far too often. It was time to rely on one person and one person only; Kimberly J. Moreno.

This moment had been the last straw. It wasn't going to be the straw that broke her back; it would be one that made it stronger than ever.

"Where's my goddam phone?" She wiped her eyes with the palms of her hands and then tucked her hair behind her ear.

***

Tom stood in the half-opened doorway, towering over Lee Chen and Brad. "We have a little more work left to create the final channels to place the explosives. We managed to jury-rig the fracking machine by stealing parts from the Boring Machine. Thing is a mess but good enough to finish this project. The final blast's last explosive charges will be in place right on time."

Lee Chen looked straight at him, listening while Brad sat by her side, typing on a laptop as if he were her assistant. Her eyes darted toward the locked room next to them, where Julie was lying unconscious from an unhealthy dose of opiates.

"Time?" she asked.

"Still a go for tomorrow night at nine PM," Tom replied.

"Excellent, that will keep us on schedule with some cushion for when the truck arrives at midnight to get the asset," she said.

"Don't forget about evacuating the hippy colony," said Tom. "As I said before, the meteorite doesn't come out unless I have verification those kids have been moved."

"It will be done, and you'll have verification before the detonation."

"How will you get them to leave? I don't want to get ready to push the button and have you tell me you couldn't get them to leave. They should already be out of there."

"I have the leverage to get them to leave, Tom. Don't worry about it. It will be done soon!" Lee's face became flushed with anger. She wasn't used to being questioned.

"Carry on with your work, Tom. You'll have your proof."

Tom refused to give in, "I'll need documented evidence of their safe removal. A time-marked video or Facetime from an iPhone before the blast will do."

"Seriously?"

“I have trust issues with this operation. Before I joined last year, I heard the story about the hippy colony caretaker who came snooping around here. She suspiciously disappeared.”

"What you heard about the caretaker disappearing took place before both our times. Let's talk again in a few hours; by then, the status will have changed."

"Very well. I look forward to finishing this operation and getting home to my wife and kids."

As soon as Tom closed the door to leave the trailer, she turned to Brad. Before she could speak, Brad did first. "When are you going to message Kim that we have the girl, and they have to leave the hippy colony?"

"I want to speak with her, face to face. Contact her and arrange a meeting after everyone at the mining site has gone home."

"You're shitting me, right? Let me talk to her. I want to tell Mr. Chang I flipped her so he releases my mother."

"Set up the meeting with me and only me, Brad."

"Are you going to kill her?"

"Let's see how it goes."

***

Kim stood alone in the Lightroom and marveled at how well the plants and trees were returning now that they were given clean water and untainted soil to grow in. The leaves were a vivid green, and the vegetables were plump. A text message appeared. It was from Brad.

Kim, I'm being asked to set up a meeting between you and Lee. She wants to discuss a deal for returning Julie to you. But you have to meet with her first. Can you be at the mining side in two hours? PS- Only you- no backup or else.

She stood motionless, read the message repeatedly, and then laughed out loud. Brad, who always treated her like a subordinate, was now Lee Chen's errand boy. Of course, she had Julie. It was obvious what Lee Chen wanted in exchange for releasing her. Anxiety and fear began bubbling up inside her anticipating the meeting. Walking amongst the plants, she touched their leaves and then leaned down to smell the beautiful scent of fresh vegetables. Stay in the present, don't catastrophize, she told herself. But all she could think about was Julie being held captive.

Tell her I'll meet with her, Brad.

***

Kim emerged from the tunnel, and looked for her. Barge pleaded with her to let him tag along in secrecy for backup, but Kim declined. It would be better if they talk one on one. The rain had just stopped, and wet rocks gave off an earthy petrichor that reminded her of Maryland. Carefully she rounded a corner to see her. It was all because of this Lee Chen, this disturbed woman, and her associates that she and Marshera had suffered so much misery. They had turned everyone's life upside down. And now she had Julie.

Lee Chen was dressed as she always was; a business suit with a tight-fitting pink top and stiletto high heels that were inappropriate for the location.

How vain could a woman be to dress all frilly in a construction zone?

She stood arrow straight, smoking a cigarette as Kim approached her. For once, she was anxious but but not paralyzed with fear. The new Kim was cynical, tougher, and ready to battle.

"I am here. Where is Julie, and what do you want to release her?" Kim said.

She turned to Kim and tucked her black hair behind her right ear. "You get right down to business, don't you?"

"I'm busy, so let's get this over with."

"Yes, let's. I am aware that you and your hippy pals have been spying on our conversations. Therefore I realize you are aware that we will extract the meteorite soon. The only thing that stands in the way of completing our operation is…."

"The collateral damage. Yes, we overheard. You want us out of Marshera. Or should I say the foreman guy wants us out. Otherwise, you'd be fine with us being crushed to death. Or tell me, is it just me you want dead? Because ever since the first time I saw you standing outside my front door posing as a Christian, you've been nothing short of satanic."

"Don't get edgy with me, Kim. You've been nothing but a pain in the ass to me too. I haven't forgotten you slamming your front door in my face and sabotaging our equipment. I should stab you in the eye, but I need you to do something for me first."

"God only knows how many people's lives you've ruined. Starting with Nick, you have something hanging over his head, and that's why he stole the Blue Water. He may have given you a vial of it, but the Blue Water can't be copied, so good luck with that. He is now banished from Marshera. Then there's Brad. You've got him by the neck too. Now you've taken Julie."

"And I assume you want this dear girl back in one piece. Am I right?"

"Yes, she is dear to me, and I want her back. If there's a shred of goodness in you, then give her to me right now, or you'll be sorry."

"There is no goodness. I'm the bad girl."

"No argument here."

"I suggest you calm down and stay in your good girl lane Kim. You're punching over your weight class. If you want that girl in the trailer, you'll have to satisfy one condition first."

"Fairly certain I know what that condition is." Kim looked away in disgust.

"You guessed it. You and your friends leave Marshera within two hours."

"And if we don't, we'll be crushed to death from the blast that will free the meteorite."

Kim took note of Lee Chen's momentary slip-up, revealing where Julie was.

"Exactly," Lee Chen feigned a hint of a smile.

"Did you forget that we overheard your conversations? The foreman said he wouldn't detonate the charges unless we safely evacuated Marshera. It sounds like we should stay put," said Kim.

Lee Chen snapped back at her, "Did you forget who we have in custody?"

"Then what we have is a standoff," Kim said.

"Trust me; we will find a way to get you people out of there eventually. By the time we do, your Julie will be living in China and working as a comfort woman, a Xing Nuli; what you would call a sex worker. There's no standoff. I have all of the leverage. So get your people out of that cave, and we will release your friend."

Kim shuddered at the thought of Julie in the situation she described.

"There is a bigger issue here, Ms. Chen," said Kim. "Marshera needs the Meteorite. Its unique geological composition is what creates the Blue Water you so desire. The mountain water runs over and around the Meteorite, and then it's super-heated in an underground spring. Every day at four PM, a geyser inside Marshera produces just enough of the Blue Water to heal four kids after they drink it. If that blue Meteorite leaves here, you've signed the death sentence of those four young people. Marshera is not a hippy colony. It's a self-contained recovery colony that has healed people for a thousand years. Now you people want to crush it to extinction."

"Yes, the Blue Water they all drink," Lee Chen said. "If this mysterious water that I now have a sample of heals as you say it does, we will copy it and make more billions."

"Let's assume your scientists can copy the Blue Water and sell it to cure people of their fatal illnesses. Won't that be enough? You and your people will make trillions, not billions. I am imploring you to stop the removal of the Meteorite so that these young people continue to heal. It will be the ultimate win–win scenario."

“But you just told me the Blue Water can’t be copied. I wish you would make up your mind, my dear Kim. It doesn’t matter; the Meteorite is extracted at nine PM tomorrow and sold for fifty billion dollars. The Blue Water is a bonus if it heals. To get the girl back, clear everybody out of that cave immediately or be crushed to death. Oh, and I will need you to send me video proof you have vacated."

Kim stared at Lee Chen, wanting to rip her apart but suddenly felt a strange sense of déjà vu. It was a peculiar feeling that she couldn't put her finger on. "You know we have some things in common; we're both young and in our twenties. We've had to fight for our place in this male-dominated world. We are both of Chinese heritage. So I appeal to you, woman to woman, Chinese to Chinese, do not do this. Give Julie to me and leave the Meteorite in the ground where it belongs."

"Chinese to Chinese, right? Only one of us is Chinese; you are American. While you grew up an adopted brat in a warm, supporting home, I was raised in a dirt poor hut in the middle of China with horrible parents and a brother that raped me."

"Warm supporting home? Adopted brat? My baby sister died in her crib right next to my bed. I loved her like I'll never love anyone ever again. I blame myself for her death every single day. Then my father left, never to be heard from again. I live with PTSD, I'm in psychotherapy, I run, I swim, and yes, I'm addicted to Oxycodone. Every day was a struggle until Julie, and the Marshera kids came into my life. I used to be a naïve, scared girl, but I've had to toughen up over the last five days and fight my inner demons. And I have conquered them. Ten years ago, I lost my baby sister Grace, and I guarantee you, I'm not losing another one."

"Interesting coincidence, said Lee Chen. I, too, lost my baby sister when I was young. I called her my Perfect One. She was ripped away from me in the middle of the night. My mother told me she died, but I figured out years later, she was given up for adoption. My parents needed a big strong boy to farm the land and care for them when they became old. Because of China's population control laws, families in our region could only have two children. My parents already had a girl, and that girl was me. Because of me, they gave my perfect sister away, and, like you, I've been blaming myself for losing her ever since that day. So one day, I escaped that dirty little Ganzi village in Hunan Province. I made something of myself. That's who I am today, so don't give me that poor me shit. You just found your confidence, but I had to earn mine years ago. You don't want to know how I earned it. Trust me; I'm tougher than you'll ever be."

Kim stared at her silently with a puzzled look on her face. "You grew up in Hunan Province? "

"Yeah, but I got out of there. What the hell do you care?"

"Your sister, what year was she adopted?"

"In ninety-six, okay? Time to end this discussion."

"I had a weird feeling when we first met in Maryland and then again now. My adoption paperwork says that Hunan Province is where I was born and lived until I was adopted in March 1996 at two years old."

There was a long pause. Lee Chen was processing Kim's information. "Your birthday; when is it?"

"The nineteenth, March nineteenth," Kim said.

"Your right shoulder, show it to me," she demanded.

Kim turned sideways and slowly pulled up her sleeve to reveal a birthmark on her shoulder. It was a perfectly shaped crescent moon. Lee Chen stared at Kim while she pulled up her right sleeve to show her the same exact birthmark.

Lee Chen could barely speak. "Jesus Christ, you're my baby sister."

Chapter 41
I'm Over My Head

"You look scared, Kim," said Barge.

"There are several reasons I should be."

A long pause hung in the air. Barge waited for the bad news while Kim tried to decide if she would tell him the woman threatening to kill them was, in fact, her sister.

No, I can save her. There must be some good.

"The meteorite is all they want; they'll stop at nothing to get it. The detonation is on for nine PM tomorrow night. If we stay here, Tom, the foreman, won't detonate. But then Lee Chen will send Julie to China to be sold as a sex worker. She offered that if we vacated immediately, she would release Julie. But why would we believe her? She can't be trusted."

"Bastards!" Barge yelled out as he stood up to pace again.

"Some good news, though, Lee Chen revealed Julie's location in addition to the detonation time. She's inside the trailer at the bottom of the hill. Rescuing her has to be part of our plan."

"Absolutely." Barge stared at Kim with a strange look on his face. It was the first time she had ever seen him scared. "We need to blockade the tunnel; protect ourselves from ambush. We'll put all those rocks and boulders back in place and then whatever traps I can create. There can't be any way they can get to us."

"Then we need to piece together the details of Nick's battle strategy," said Kim. "My concern is we don't have much time to figure all this out!" Kim was frantic, realizing that everything had to come together in short order. How could she lead them to victory against such overwhelming odds?

"What the hell do I know about battle plans, Barge?"

"About the same as me, I imagine, next to nothing."

Kim smiled at him, "I know it looks hopeless, but I must tell you how much I appreciate your friendship. You've been so helpful and inviting since I came here." She leaned over and hugged him. "No matter what happens, I love you."

"Our feelings are mutual. You've helped us so much."

"I won't mention you slamming the stone door in my face when I first arrived; a minor oversight!"

They both shared a hearty laugh that was desperately needed.

"Alright, Let's get going. I'll lay out Nick's battle plan on the table and try to make sense of it. Why don't you and the others blockade the tunnel while I try to figure out his plan." Kim said.

"I'm on it," said Barge as he made a beeline for the tunnel.

Kim took the large roll of paper containing Nick's battle plan and unrolled it, lying it on the cafeteria table. She weighed down the corners with various utensils, holding it in place. The plan included a drawing of the area near the dig site, nearby mountains, access roads and trails. Kim added the trailer where Julie was a prisoner. Nick had created a sequence of steps numbered one through five that needed to be executed for success.

Step one of the plan showed the locations of Ashun, Winger, and any friendly forces they brought. They would create a series of diversions while steps two and three began. The plan showed Barge and Kim moving in opposite directions on their separate missions. But there were only a few details written down by Nick. The battle plan was a rough sketch, a first draft. Kim would have to figure out the rest to fill in steps four and five on her own. But there was so little time left. *Dammit!*

Kim saw that step five occurred at the top of Wildcat Mountain above Marshera. But how and what was to take place? If she could figure out the final step, the preceding ones would fall into place.

Over and over, she reviewed the battle plan hoping to figure out all the steps. Nick had scribbled a few arrows, but his notes made no sense. She put the pieces together to mostly understand steps two, three, and four. They consisted of hers and Barge's missions. However, the final step had yet to be detailed. Whatever was to happen would occur at the top of the mountain. All she could fathom was that the top would be a perfect place for a sniper. She remembered Nick had been badly wounded by a sniper in in battle. He had drawn three stars overlooking the mining site. A sniper could shoot the guards and perhaps stop the explosion from there. *Nick must have planned on being the sniper using his military experience. But we don't have any rifles? Was he going to go home to get his army rifle and come back?* The high ground was advantageous but seemed too far away from the mining site. Plus, the angles the shooter had would be restrictive. The sniper theory made no sense!

Kim realized she was running out of options and time. She needed help. Having to call Nick made her cringe. One of Mum's famous sayings came to mind; don't bite your nose to spite your face. Sadly Kim had done precisely that. The simple fact was that banishing Nick without thinking it through may have written all of their eulogies. If he was here, they could finish the plan. His military experience during battle would also be invaluable right now. A flashback popped into her head. Kim recalled Nick carrying the wooden box filled with explosives on his shoulder as he looked back at her and flashed his boyish grin. That's when her heart skipped a beat. He was gorgeous. Why had he betrayed her? She had fallen for him hook, line, and sinker, only to be betrayed.

Nick said the case of ANFO explosives would be part of the battle plan. That's it!

Kim stared at the map from all angles and concluded the explosives were a false lead. There was no way to throw or fire them from any projectile toward the enemy. That theory also made no sense.

Complete and total fatigue had set into every cell in her body. Kim's brain was struggling to solve problems. And she had a lot of problems.

She picked up her phone and stared at the screen, not able to muster the courage to call Nick, so she texted.

Hey Nick, Ya I know – bad form texting you. But we're in trouble & I need you to call me ASAP! Please! Your battle plans are not clear. Do it for Julie and the others, not for me. Call me!

Kim stared at the phone's screen, hoping to see a return text, but none came. It had been a long and incredibly stressful day. Drained both physically and emotionally, she tried calling him. The phone weighed a hundred pounds. It went to voicemail.

She leaned back in the chair, ran her fingers through her hair, and took a long deep breath. I need just one damn minute. She closed her eyes and rubbed her temples. What the hell have I done to these people? I can't win this. I'm not a soldier.

Into her purse, she retrieved the plastic bag. Out came a pink pill from her work stash. *There's no other option. I have to function. I have to.*

She downed the pill, chased it with water, and then placed her head on the unresolved battle plan.

In five seconds, she fell sound asleep.

Kim lifted her head from the table to see him standing before her.

"Cody, how did you get in here?"

He laughed loudly, "You know me, I'm everywhere."

"I can't talk to you right now. I have to reach Nick. He has to tell me the rest of the plan."

"You will not reach him, my dear. He is preoccupied at the moment."

"How do you know? Did you see him?"

"In a way, yes, I saw him. He will not talk to you now. He may never again. But fear not, for you already know the plan."

"No, Cody, I do not know the plan. I'm missing some of the details and all of step five, the most important step."

"You only need to look inside yourself for the answers, Kim."

"You don't understand, Cody! Nick served in the military, and he understands battle strategy. He started the plan, but then we had to ask him to leave because he betrayed us. He betrayed me just as I was falling in love with him. Why is it that those who I love are taken away from me? Do you know what the problem is, Cody? I'm damaged. I was damaged the day my Gracie died, and I'm still damaged now!" Kim sobbed into her outstretched fingers.

"That is exactly right, Kim. You are damaged."

"What?" Kim pulled her hands away. "You didn't have to agree so fast."

"I agreed with you because we are all damaged in our own way Kim. But you move forward and work through your deficiencies to reach your goals. You keep telling me that you need Nick, but you don't. Yes, you are damaged, but you will still succeed despite it. You always have and always will, Kim. All you have to do is believe in yourself. Who dove into the icy cold river, pulled Julie to safety, and then gave her CPR until Nick arrived to help you resuscitate her back to life? Who made her way through the bat-filled tunnel and crossed the scalding river to locate Marshera? Who used their education and tools to identify what was killing the people of Marshera? There is no need to answer. *You* did, Kim. It was you, my brave one. When unsure what to do, look deep inside yourself for the answers. Believe that you will solve any obstacle that prevents you from achieving your goal. The answers are already there inside of you, Kim."

"You think I am special? You think I can do this?"

"I know that you can. Go with your gut, and all will end well."

"I'm still not buying it, Cody! This is all feel-good affirmation crap because I've been racking my brain trying to find the answer to this battle plan, but I can't. So I need clarification as to what I should do next. I need help. I need Nick!"

"I must now depart from here, but before I do, I will leave you with two Abenaki proverbs that we all swear by. They will guide you to the answers you seek. The first one is about mother earth. Take only what you need. When you are done, leave the land as you found it. As you prepare to wage battle, remember the second. There is no death; there is only a change of worlds."

"Farewell, Kim."

She bolted upright from a dead sleep to look around the room.

"Cody?"

It must have been a dream. But it was so real.

A feeling of guilt washed over her. While the others toiled, she carelessly slept. Kim looked down at her watch. Okay, it'd been only fifteen minutes.

Cody had planted a ray of hope inside her.

I must believe in myself. I've solved problems before, and I can solve this one too!

Refreshed and energized, Kim repositioned the map again and stared at it intently. The corners continued to curl up, and the utensils were too light to hold them down. Kim pulled some loose National Geographic Magazines from a tall stack at the end of the table to weigh down the corners. What am I missing?

She grabbed her phone to call Nick again but stopped herself.

Stop it, Kim! This one's on you! Cody's right. Find the answers yourself!

Kim began talking to the map out loud, "Take only what you need and leave the land as you found it. Well that doesn't apply to Lee Chen and her friends. Cutting huge chunks in the side of this mountain and then blasting out a meteorite that's been resting under the earth for thousands of years."

She circled to the other side, walking around the map from an opposite angle. Her leg bumped the table's edge, causing several magazines from the stack to slide onto the floor.

Kim ran over to pick them up and plop them back on the pile.

Looking at her watch, a jolt of fear came over her. There wasn't much time left until the battle began. She needed to find Barge and see if Ashun and Winger were in Marshera and brought some reinforcements.

Think, Kim! Dammit, think!

There was one key area at the top of the mountain overlooking the dig site where Nick had drawn three separate stars in three different locations. Each star was circled to show its importance. Kim leaned over the table from the side, arms spread open as she stared intently. There was movement from the corner of her eye; yet again, several magazines slowly slid off the top of the pile and back onto the floor. This time, half of the stack was scattered all over.

"Jesus, I do not need this!"

She hurried back over to pick up the pile of magazines to put them back on the stack. She froze and stared at the last magazine in her hand. It was an old issue. National Geographic, September 1982. Kim stared at the cover, then at the messy pile of magazines. She ran back to the map and smiled. The three stars made perfect sense now.

Take only what you need. When you are done, leave the land as you found it.

"Of course!"

Chapter 42
Homeward Bound

According to the record books, the fastest time ever recorded by a racehorse was 43.97 miles per hour. The chestnut filly was a thoroughbred named Winning Brew. Kentucky Derby racehorses average 37 – 38 miles per hour, making the record that much more impressive. Nick heard tales of the horse and was pretty sure Cracker could beat that record if given the chance.

There was time to ride him now. That was the good news. Having lost the only woman he'd ever loved was the bad. Riding was a nice distraction that helped him manage his ruminating over his actions that led to losing her. To say he missed her was an understatement. He ached for her from a place deep in his soul. No matter how many ways he justified his recklessness, he couldn't pardon himself.

I blew it; lock, stock, and barrel.

They'd accomplished so much in a short time and loved with such intensity. Then there was Marshera. He was mostly a loner; Nick had suddenly been needed by a group of kids trying to survive the selfish and greedy actions of a multinational corporation that forgot its values. Kim had needed him, too, but the truth was, he had needed her more. What bothered Nick the most was Kim thinking that he had planned on using her all along to steal the Blue Water. His back was against the wall, and it became the only chip he had to bargain with.

Now he knew what people meant when they said losing someone they loved was like having an arm amputated. Kim had been amputated from his life, but inside his heart, she was still there.

Nick let out a long exhale as he fed Cracker and then put him back in his stall. Where the hell was Walt anyway? He appeared out of thin air and then disappeared just as quickly.

Nick set up shop on the other side of the barn, next to the bench grinder. He picked a horseshoe off the pile to grind down its sharp edges and surface rust. The anvil and hammer pounded and flattened the half-moon making it useable again. After finishing a dozen pairs of shoes, Nick shut down the grinder and slowly tinkered around the bench area, cleaning up and putting tools away.

The black Crown Victoria was sparkling clean, making it appear out of place on a horse farm as it slowly moved down the dirt driveway. When it came to a stop, two men stepped out wearing dark sunglasses and suitcoats with white shirts and ties, making them look as out of place as the vehicle they arrived in. They weren't bankers or financial people. The two men were looking for only one person; the proprietor.

Nick heard the car, walked out of the barn, and circled around the side. He met face-to-face with two people he was hoping to avoid, Boris and Dimitri Volkov.

"Hey, Nick, where the fuck have you been?" Boris' English was more broken and edgy than in the past. “Me and Dimitri getting a little tired of coming out here every week to kick your ass. Weren’t we just here a few days ago when you said you’d meet us, and then you blew us off? Did you not learn your lesson, Nick?”

He stood silently, staring at them. His eyes darted to Boris’s brother Dimitri, standing in his periphery, smoking a Camel. "What do you guys want? I squared things with your boss."

Dimitri, small and wiry, was born with a condition called fast twitch muscles. Fibers transmit brain signals to muscles at lightning speed. The kick was a blur, delivered to Nick's lowest rib. It crippled him. He fell to his knees and screamed out in pain. That was just the beginning.

Boris was the bigger brother and decided to join the party, "We never got the memo."

They took turns wailing on Nick, kicking and punching him repeatedly until he was close to unconsciousness. Lying on the ground, he bled as he writhed in pain.

Boris turned to Dimitri and pointed his chin to the car.

"Get it."

Sensing his master's attack, Cracker whinnied and banged against the stall door. Nick lay horizontal on the dirt, fighting for a gulp of air as Dimitri hurried back with the wooden board and Tanto knife. They would be the ones to perform the ritual this time, not Lee. After it was done, they would present it to her as a gift. The process was the same as with Lucious, but there wouldn't be a need for a Chinese pistol to be held to Nick's head. He was as weak as a kitten. Boris slid the knife's edge into the board as Dimitri extended Nick's pinky finger while he held his hand in place. The linen cloths were wrapped around the hand, and the men took their positions. In a minute, Nick would be one digit lighter.

Grabbing a handful of curly blonde hair, Boris lifted Nick's head. "You get only one chance, Nick. Where's the money and the dope? Tell me!"

Nick could barely speak, "You two sidewinders probably know better than me."

He dropped Nick's head and nodded to his brother Dimitri.

Nick wanted to fight them off. It was no use. They would cut off his pinky finger, but he would live. Disfigured, yes, but hey, he knew he deserved it. You play with hornets until one day; you get stung.

Nick moaned in pain as drool and spittle drained from his lower lip. The hand was held in place; Boris raised the knife in the air and looked at his brother to smile.

Chuck Chuck…Boom! The Winchester 1897 twelve gauge pump action shotgun exploded, blasting a corner off the barn, sending splinters and wood into the air. The deafening explosion reverberated across the field. Both brothers hit the deck, lying flat in the dirt.

Chuck Chuck … Boom! The weapon exploded again… Boris heard the round hiss by his head. The attacker advanced on them and fired again.

Chuck Chuck … Boom! A plume of gravel showered Dimitri as the shell exploded into the ground beside him. "Don't kill us!" He yelled out, covering his head.

Chuck Chuck … Boom! Walt was positioned in a military stance, five feet away from them. The shotgun was pointed at Boris's head. He looked up to see Walt snarling behind the gunsight, his finger resting on the trigger.

"I'll cut you in half with this thing. Get the fuck away from that boy."

"Hey, that boy owes us money, a shitload of money! We're just here to collect it," Boris yelled as the echo of the gun faded in the distance.

"Don't give a fuck who you think owes you money. Both of ya get the fuck out of here."

Dimitri stood slowly, the shotgun barrel now aimed directly at his face. His movements were careful, never turning away from Walt as he and his brother retreated from the barn. As they crept toward the car, Dimitri darted back to retrieve the knife and board lying on the ground.

Chuck Chuck …Boom! The board splintered into a thousand pieces as the Volkov Brothers jumped into the air and broke into a sprint. They dove in the black sedan and flew down the dirt-packed driveway.

The silence told Nick it was over. Walt went to him and kneeled by his side. Nick slowly pulled himself upright to lean against the barn. He rubbed his ribs, moaned, and squinted at Walt through the blood in his eye. Walt pulled out a handkerchief and held it on his bloody nose.

"Where'd you learn to shoot like that, old man?"

"Indochina; nineteen seventy-two. How are you feeling?"

"Sore as hell, motherfuckers got me good. Kicked the shit out of me."

"Those two Russkies looking for money from you?"

"Yeah, they think I owe their boss."

“Think? Well, do ya?

“No, I don’t.”

"Ain't Milt Logan's giving you a line of credit if ya needed it."

"Yeah, but it's, like, not enough. Long story. Vietnam? You never told me this."

"You never asked."

His phone vibrated, and Nick grimaced. He gritted his teeth as he rolled on his side to pull it from his pocket and read the text. The message lifted his spirits.

Please! Your battle plans, not clear. Do it for Julie and the others…

He smiled; there was an opening, a chance for redemption. A chance to get her back.

Now, she needed him too.

329- The Canaries

Part Three

"True courage is being afraid, and going ahead and doing your job anyhow, that's what courage is."

General Norman Schwarzkopf Jr.

Chapter 43
Billion Dollar Baby

Barge entered the cafeteria, now a makeshift war room with Ashun and Winger in tow. He had just spoken to their Abenaki friends, who volunteered to fight the intruders that had defaced their mountain to steal its treasures. They left to go to the hiding place in the trees, waiting for the battle to begin.

A mandatory meeting had been called for all to attend. Kim had decoded Nick's five-step battle plan, and they needed to discuss the details. Everyone needed to know what their role would be. They sat at Marshera's cafeteria table as Kim unrolled the battle plan's instructions that covered all five steps. Only after the risky execution of steps one through four could they achieve the final step five. Then they would stop the destruction of Marshera, once and for all.

After individual roles and actions were reviewed, questions were asked and answered. The time was seven twenty. There were only ninety minutes to stop the meteorite's extraction that would end Marshera and their lives. No argument was given by Charlie when Barge asked him to stay with Creen inside Marshera. Kim and Barge, the only ones with cell phones, would communicate with each other throughout the battle.

The decision by all to go down with the ship was unanimous. The kids from Marshera had entered the healing program requiring they drink the Blue Water from The Fountain of Life every day. There was no turning back. Missing a daily dose would cause an immediate and irreversible decline in their health, resulting in death within a year. Even if the battle plan failed, they would die trying to stop the miners from crushing Marshera to remove the meteorite that saved their lives.

Before they adjourned the meeting, Barge informed everyone of a final issue to settle. To save Marshera, they would need to break the Golden Rule. The rule was taught to all of them starting on day one. No matter what, the Golden Rule was never to be broken. *Marshera is a place to save lives. Those who come here to heal must never take one.* Theirs was a place that gave life. To take life was the unforgivable hypocrisy that all that Marshera stood for. The battle plan, if successful, could result in fatalities. Barge was their defacto leader and arranged for a vote to make a one-time exception to the rule of Marshera. The vote was unanimous in favor of defending their home. There was no way around it; tonight, they would have to kill to survive.

Ashun and Winger left to take a position in the trees with their friends as everyone in Marshera hugged each other tightly before the battle began. Kim was included and never felt as loved as she did at that moment. They all prayed for the safe rescue of Julie. Their love for one another was pure and dedicated. Sure, they fought and disagreed often, but above all, they cared for each other. All of them experienced a unique camaraderie from living together in Marshera for years as part of a group of healing children whose lives were about to change forever.

Kim went to her room to text her Mum. She needed to tell her that she loved her and give assurances that her return home would be in time for dinner after wrapping up a few loose ends. The dangerous mission she was about to undertake was omitted.

See you tomorrow, Mum, unless I get myself killed first, Kim said to herself.

She texted Brad to get Lee Chen's numbers before she sent a second text.

It's Kim your newfound sister. I'm reaching out with love. We have both been grieving the loss of our sisters but look what life has handed us. A second chance! There is still time for you to do the right thing. There is good in your heart. I can tell because you're my sister. You came from a tough childhood, and you did what you had to do for survival. But as sisters, we can begin again together. We can learn from each other. Don't crush Marshera, please! One chance in a million is what we have. Let's take advantage of it! Meet me halfway, my sister. I'll always be there for you. I promise. The tattoo on your wrist is in honor of your sister. That's me! She's alive and asking you to come to the bright side. Join me, sister. Please

Your Perfect One, Kim.

When she came out of her room, Kim wiped the tears from her eyes and decided she was ready to battle. Surprisingly, Charlie approached her without warning and wrapped his arms around her for the longest time.

"I'm sorry I've been so mean to you. You're just trying to help."

"It's all right, Charlie," Kim said. I know what you're feeling."

"You got my sister back once before. I sure hope you can again. Please get Julie for me. Please!"

"I'll do everything I can to get her back to you, safe and sound."

***

At the dig site, the miners were ready for the extraction. They were prepared to end a year of drilling, boring, and blasting to extract what one called "the Billion Dollar Baby." Twenty guards armed with Kalashnikov AK-47 assault rifles would protect it. They stood in gray coverall uniforms, spread around the rock ledge to cover all angles of the site from any potential threat. The detonation would happen on schedule at 9:00 PM. Anyone even approaching the area would be killed immediately.

***

"Ninety minutes until detonation."

The monotone voice bellowed out a safety warning. The air horn sounded from the digital safety sign as it displayed the countdown. Tonight there would be a final, mammoth blast to free the meteorite. The last message the safety sign would broadcast would be the *All Clear* announcement to warn everyone on the ledge to clear far away from the concussing shock wave of one hundred explosives detonated simultaneously.

Ashun and Winger were in place, poised at the top of a tree along with Achachak, Keem, and Niben. A pureblood Abenaki woman, Niben was as fierce a warrior as anyone who lived. Their quivers were fat with arrows waiting to be launched. Each warrior loaded two into their bows. The enemy was about to receive an extra surprise; Ashun soaked half the arrows in kerosene ahead of time.

"Light 'em up," Ashun said, touching the lit torch to her flammable arrow before handing it to Winger. Ten arrows, five burning hot, were pointed with their tips in a precise heading toward the star-filled sky. She asked the question, "Ready to take back our mountain?"

"Hell ya," Niben said in her nastiest voice.

All five raised their bows with strings drawn back to their ears in the ready position. Their hands were shaking from the string's resistance. They couldn't hold on any longer.

Softly, Ashun gave the word - "Fire."

Five bow strings snapped; their sounds resonated through the trees. The arrows silently pierced into a graceful arc, each one reaching its apex, cutting across the face of a brilliant moon to descend on the unsuspecting guards below.

Without hesitation, they reloaded with ten more arrows and again pointed them to the heavens. There would be no mercy tonight.

"Fire."

Snap, snap, snap, snap, snap!

Had their aim been true? "Wait for it," Winger said, holding his hand to his ear.

Distant voices shrieked out in pain, “Ahhhhhhhh! Shit! I'm hit! Run for cover! It went through my fuckin arm!"

The dig site had turned to carnage.

The warriors nodded and resumed the attack, launching ten more and then another ten.

Fires and confusion broke out around the dig site as the guards ran for cover. Both miners and guards were afraid to extinguish the fires or else risk getting impaled by more incoming death. Some dove under the mining equipment, seeking protection, while others ran behind nearby trees.

"Now we move," said Winger.

Step one – Create distraction and disarray. Progress report: Underway.

"Somebody! Anybody! Tell me, what the fuck is going on?" Lee Chen screamed over the walkie-talkie while hiding under a tree near the side of the ledge. Tom had just left to help the men put out fires around the site.

"Alex Baez here; our guys are getting hit by arrows fired from the woods. I've got a few down that are wounded."

"Who the hell are these people with the bows and arrows?" She yelled at him.

"One of my men told me there's a small population of Abenaki Indians that live in these woods," said Baez. They consider the hippy colony and Wildcat Mountain their sacred place. They're going to defend it, but it's nothing we can't handle."

"You had better show them who owns this place tonight. Your guards have assault rifles; all they have are bows and arrows. Get some men into the woods to find those fuckers and end this shit! Do it quick, Alex Baez!" she screamed into the device.

"I'm on it! Baez out."

He shouted at three of his men and pointed in the direction where the arrows came. "You, you and you; head down there and start spraying the trees." His men sprinted full speed towards the forest, opening fire as they ran. Their assault rifles lit up the night, popping off bullets that flashed like fireflies shooting randomly into the woods. The rounds ripped through trees, severing branches and splintering wood as they sought human flesh.

Brad guarded the Forbidden Tunnel. If anyone from Marshera were brazen enough to emerge, he would shoot them without question. Lee Chen crackled over the com, "Brad, you must've seen the arrows launched at our guards from the woods. Has anyone tried to come out of that tunnel? Kim must be behind this. I should've killed her last night when I had the chance! Over."

"Nobody's come out of the tunnel," Brad said. I saw the guards get nailed by the arrows. I hid inside the cave before I got one through the head. Wait, I can hear gunfire from the trees."

"Right, Baez sent some men into the woods. They'll find whoever's launching the arrows and shoot their asses off. Keep me posted if you see anything. Kim and her hippy friends have to be the ones behind this. I didn't think they would go on the offensive. I'll have to counter; out."

***

With step one in process, Kim began her journey down an overgrown trail barely visible in the dark. It would take her through dense trees and vegetation to rendezvous with her goal of rescuing Julie. Equally nervous and determined, she was aware that this one was on her alone. There would be no Nick to help out this time. With the moon her only light source, Kim squinted, trying to locate the trail. Feeling as if she would become lost any second, self-doubt seeped inside again. So many things could go wrong. Suddenly, her mission seemed impossible.

I'm going to find my way in the dark around to the other side of Wildcat Mountain, through the woods to a trailer that a guard probably protects with a gun. Then I rescue Julie?

The sulfur smell from the rifles caught a breeze and wafted into Kim's area, telling her step one of the battle plan was working. Checking her watch, Kim noted she was on schedule. The next part was what made her anxious. Step two in the battle plan was a lot to ask of her, but she would do it without hesitation. Her body wanted the pink pills she had stored in the cave, but she would play this one straight. Dopamine and adrenaline were her drugs of choice tonight.

Feeling confident, Kim jogged for a while down the trail until scattered clouds floated overhead, covering what little ambient light the moon had left to offer. She slowed to walk carefully, trying to see the her way in the dim light. Then she stopped.

The trail was gone.

A chill ran through Kim's spine as a cold air pocket came out of nowhere and wrapped around her body. Progress thwarted; she faced a wall of thick shrubbery that blocked any forward movement. Kim kneeled to the ground and decided to risk exposing her location by turning on her flashlight. Crawling around the area, she pointed the light in all directions.

Except for turning back, there was nowhere to go. The confidence she had felt instantly switched to panic and insecurity. It overtook her. Kim was sure she had followed the exact trail from the plan.

I knew it! I have no sense of direction. Who did I think I was, Amelia Earhart?

Kim turned off the flashlight and sat quietly on the ground, feeling hopeless. The feeling engulfed her. They all had their jobs to do, and she had now failed at hers.

I should have snorted some of the pink. I'm too edgy!

Thoughts of her newly discovered sister seeped into Kim's consciousness. Lee Chen had such a different childhood than her. Her sister, she thought, was certainly evil but she was also filled with confidence. She would've already solved the problem and gotten back on track by now.

But if she's my sister, we share the same DNA. There's some of her inside me and there's some me inside her. If Lee Chen can figure out a way to get out of here, why the hell can't I?

Defiant, Kim told herself to imitate her big sister and show some swagger. As evil as she was, Lee Chen was, at this moment, her inspiration. *If I can just convince her to be inspired by me to do good, I think I can save her!*

Kim put her hands in front of her face and burrowed straight through the thick brush like an animal. The thorny branches snagged her sweatshirt, like fingers holding her back. Steadfast, she crashed against the forest, blazing her own trail.

That's what my sister would do, and dammit, that's what I'll do too.

***

A half mile in the opposite direction, Barge took the trail that ran under Wildcat Falls and around to the west side of Wildcat Mountain. On his shoulder was the case of explosives that Nick had stolen. He was a big man and the only one that could take on step three. But even the biggest of men wouldn't be crazy enough to attempt what lay ahead. The bulky wooden crate weighed more than a hundred-and-twenty pounds. He needed to carry it up a steep trail for the length of a football field until he summited the peak of Wildcat Mountain.

With the crate upon his shoulder, Barge scaled the steep terrain covered with gullies, gravel, and boulders. He felt strong and purposeful as the uphill slog began. After progressing forward, Barge stopped to wipe his sweat-filled brow while taking in the brilliant view of the cosmos-filled night sky. Time was crucial, and he hoisted the crate back on his shoulder and resumed the trek. Another thirty yards were eaten up; halfway there. Abruptly, he stopped and set the crate down to stare in disbelief.

The Germans have a word for it; Steilhang. It means the steepest of mountain slopes. Greater than a thirty-degree slope is considered a treacherous ascent for hikers. Barge looked up at a forty-degree slope to the top. He'd gone a hundred yards, leaving two hundred more to go. The trail forward was a wall that shot straight up to the stars. All he had to do now was lug a back-breaking crate filled with explosives up it.

Lord, give me strength.

He would do it. His dedication to Marshera and its people was boundless. They were his family, and he had been chosen to protect them. Barge took a deep breath and grunted as he hoisted the crate onto his shoulder.

Let's get to work.

Chapter 44
The Eye Of The Tiger

"Seventy minutes until detonation …"

The five Abenaki warriors anticipated the chase and moved to a new location, evading the hailstorm of bullets that hissed by their heads. They knew the terrain well, running silently through the forest as their ancestors did. Once there, they would go back on the offensive and launch another round of arrows at the dig site.

The guards stopped at the tree line to listen for movement. Rafael called Baez on the walkie-talkie radio, "No luck, sir. They're deep in the woods, so we're headed back."

"For Christ's sake, follow them into the woods!" Baez screamed into his radio."

"Sir, there's no trail or nothing. We don't want to get lost. Think we've scared them off anyway," said Rafael.

"Don't move an inch. Read off your coordinates to me. I'll come out to you," said Baez.

"But sir, they're gone."

"Not an inch; do you hear me? Now give me the coordinates."

Like Ashun and Winger, Baez was also a tracker. He sprinted out to join the guards in two minutes time.

"Follow me," he said.

Like a laser beam, Baez's LED flashlight pierced through the trees, entering the thicket of dense overgrowth. When they arrived where their enemy had last been, he aimed his light down to the ground for a closer look. A broken twig and footprints in the pine needles were all he needed to pick up the trail. Baez moved quickly like a bloodhound sniffing the way as his men tried to stay with him.

Winger led the warriors to their next destination and climbed up an oak tree to an opening in the branches where they could launch another salvo toward the enemy. The full moon was gone, but they knew where to aim. Doubling each of their bows with arrows again, they pointed to the sky. Again, Ashun called it, "Three, two, one…release." The arrows took flight to inflict pain on anyone in their way. Waiting to hear screams, they listened, but none came.

"They must have found shelter," Achachak said too loudly.

"Or we missed," Keem said.

"Shhh!" whispered Niben. "Remember, we stay silent."

"Reload and release!" Ashun barked out in a loud whisper.

Ten more arrows fed hungry bows that spit them out into the sky. Again they waited for feedback. A single guard screamed out in pain, "I'm hit!"

"We got them now!" Keme laughed loudly, not caring about their pursuers.

Then the shit hit the fan.

Baez and his guards unleashed their deafening AK-47s on them. Their rifles exhaled shells as they unloaded armor-piercing bullets into the tree, ripping through anything in their path. Niben screamed as all five scrambled further up to avoid the shots. Ammunition whizzed by them while they looked for a way to cross over to a neighboring pine tree.

Suddenly, Keem yelled, "I'm hit!" Blood spurted from his gut.

A second later, he went limp. His lifeless body bounced off limbs and crashed through branches as it plummeted to the ground.

When the sickening noise was over, they knew he was gone. Ashun found a sturdy limb from the adjacent tree, and they crossed over to hide behind its massive trunk. Ashun looked around, "Wait! Where's Winger?" she whispered.

"Don't know. I'm sure he will find us," said Niben. "We better move again."

"No, I won't leave here without Winger." A stray bullet cut off the branch above her, and she recoiled.

"He may be down, Ash!" said Niben. Another bullet ricocheted and ripped into her arm. "Ahhhhh!" she screamed as her hand gripped her arm. Blood circled her fingers as Ashun climbed over to help her to a safer location higher in the tree.

Lee Chen's voice came over Baez's radio, "Have you taken out the arrow shooters?"

"Found them in a tree. One's down, a couple wounded, I think. They're still in the trees, but we'll keep shooting till they're down for good."

"So we're clear?" asked Lee Chen.

"Shouldn't be long. Yeah, you're clear, over."

"Let me know when you've got all of them. I'm out."

Baez and the guards continued to fire up into the trees as Winger lowered himself to crouch on a branch behind them. Empty shell casings and blue smoke hung in the air as each man fired up the tree wanting to be the hero. He loaded the dart into the barrel of his blowgun. The tip had been dipped in taipoxin, a venom from the Bolivian King Cobra Snake. A new type of dart was being used. It had a smaller head, designed to penetrate the epidermal layer, deliver the toxin and then drop to the ground, all in a matter of seconds. There wasn't enough poison to kill them, but they'd be paralyzed for an hour. Winger wrapped his legs around a thick branch and let his body dangle upside down. He aimed the eight-foot barrel at the shooter closest to him. As Winger watched him blast away, he waited for his opening. With the guard's neck exposed, Winger filled his lungs until his chest bulged. He exhaled a ferocious force through the tube. A rush of wind, and the dart zipped out of the tube to land in the middle of the guard's neck, injecting the venom before it fell to the ground. The guard slapped the area, thinking it was a bug bite. Seconds later, he lay face down in the pine needles. Winger reloaded another dart and aimed at the next guard.

***

Barge searched for motivation to accomplish the herculean task of clawing his way up the steepest mountainside he had ever seen while carrying the heavy case of explosives. He found it by calling back to the memory of the hardship his ancestors endured every day of their lives living in antebellum slavery. It was the eighteen-thirties, and his family was considered property. They worked for a master in the sweltering southern heat, cultivating and picking cotton, tobacco, or anything else grown by the plantation. They dug ditches, built roads, and even entire houses by hand. And all for zero pay. Those that stepped out of line were publically beaten or flogged as a reminder to the others. Often, family members were sold off to various plantations splitting his ancestors apart. Some women were raped and impregnated by their masters or their help. The atrocities were endless. Barge was in hell for sure, but this needed to be done this one time to save Marshera from those who would plunder its resources and take away their freedom to heal. His ancestors had to endure a living hell every day of their lives. He could endure this hell for one night to honor the memory of his family of the past and his family of present, Marshera.

The outline of the mountaintop was visible now. Barge was almost there. His shirt had changed from damp to plastered against his skin. The wooden case of explosives felt like it weighed a thousand pounds, and every muscle and fiber in his arms, back, and legs screamed in pain. His left hand braced against the rock, the crate under his right; he planted one foot after another to close in on his destination.

As Barge climbed, there was another struggle that raged inside his head. Everyone in Marshera agreed there would be a one-time exception to the Golden Rule. They would need to break it to save the place where they lived and healed. But the writings on the walls of their cave and the Golden Rule were what he lived by. *Marshera is a place to save lives. Those who heal here must never take one.* To Barge, the Golden Rule was his gospel and his religion. He was proud to have lived his life in obedience to its promise. He would be the one that would have to kill all those souls to save Marshera. *Can I be a mass killer? Can I?*

When the time came to save Marshera and kill others, he was torn as to whether he could or not. And that was going to be a significant problem.

The black outline of the ridge came into view. The trek had been backbreaking, but he had done it. Every muscle and joint in his body was on the verge of failing.

As Barge crested the top of the mountain, he felt his reward. A lovely breeze swept across his sweat-filled face. He set down the crate and closed his eyes to take it in. It seemed like the best feeling he'd ever felt in all his life. A dry area was found on the bottom of his shirt, and he wiped the sweat from his face to feel new again.

Step three was complete. He had made it to the peak with the explosives. Step four was on deck. The case slung on top of his right shoulder; Barge marched toward his destination, the mammoth rock formations along the edge of the mountain that overlooked the dig site. He told himself there would be no meteorite extraction tonight or any other night. That was if he could accomplish step five. If he could, Marshera would be safe again, perhaps for all time.

The immense rock formations Nick had put stars next to on his battle map came into view. They were the size of houses and looked down over the dig site like angry parents watching their children misbehave. With a flashlight in his mouth, Barge's bare hands pried the lid off the crate to see the contents for the first time. Twenty large bags were filled with gray, explosive ammonium nitrate crystals and twenty wireless blasting caps. A wireless distribution box and a black carrying case labeled detonator were also included. Following the instructions left by Nick, Barge handled each of the bags carefully as if they were newborn babies. He slowly submerged five wireless blasting caps inside five bags of crystals. After sealing the bags tight, he tucked each one into a deep crevice of each rock formation and then covered them with sand and rocks to compact them. The wireless distribution box was centered on the ground to let the operator detonate the charges individually or simultaneously. Powering it on, he smiled to see all the LEDs flash green. Before Barge moved away to a safe distance, he noticed a black button on the distribution box marked *M/O*.

Safely away from the blast zone, Barge unpacked the detonator from its carrying case and began arming it. Inside the case was a slip of paper left by Nick. It had the detonation code. Barge entered the numbers and selected all five charges to explode simultaneously. Cell phone in his hand, he was excited to text Kim and update her on his progress.

If Kim and the others arrive, she may have the courage to push the button.

And then he saw the millions of stars again.

They weren't the brilliant stars in the night sky above him. The stars he saw were the kind that occurs when the skull is hit by a blunt object causing the occipital lobe's visual cortex to shake violently. The brain immediately sends out electrical impulses that result in the recipient saying they saw stars. Barge slumped down to the ground, knocked out cold.

"Miss Chen, this is Sahara Nunez. I came to the top of the mountain like you told me to. Someone is up here with an electronic device. I knocked him unconscious with my rifle. Let me know how to proceed."

She stood by, waiting for a reply from her boss.

At the moment, Lee Chen was preoccupied.

***

The latest salvo of arrows had landed on the dig site but wounded only one guard. The blast would still go off as planned. Tom had returned to join Lee under the tree for a status report.

"We're still looking good, Tom. Just some locals from the area. Baez has it under control."

"Excellent, we have a few blasting caps showing red. My guy needs to fix them. Should be a go to push the button and extract the meteorite on time at nine." He began booting up the detonator, with lights showing green and red as it went online.

"Perfect," Lee Chen said.

Tom looked down and began flicking all of the switches on the detonator. "Oh, and as we discussed, I still need proof that the hippy colony has been evacuated."

She hesitated before answering him, "It's all set, Tom. The hippies are all out of there. Push the button when you're ready. Let's finish up this project and get out of here."

Tom stopped arming the detonator and looked at her. "You'll have to excuse me, but I don't trust anyone. A video or live feed is what I need. Otherwise, no detonation. I told you before, I'm not murdering civilians."

A voice came through her walkie-talkie, "Miss Chen, this is Sahara Nunez. I came to the top of the mountain like you asked. Someone is here with an electronic device. I knocked him unconscious with my rifle. Let me know how to proceed."

She turned down the volume on the radio and stared at Tom.

“Who the hell do you think is attacking us Tom? Are you clueless? It’s the hippy colony!”

“You told me earlier it was some local Indians and your guy Alex had it under control. Look I don’t know or care. I’m not arming the charges or pushing the button to detonate until I have proof the kids from the Hippy Colony are out of harm’s way. End of conversation!”

Her mouth formed into a perverse smile as she reached into her pocket and pulled out her phone.

"Okay, Tom. I'll make the call now." She pressed one button on the phone.

"Hey, it's me. You in position? Good, yes, cell signal's weak, but this will only take a minute. I need that live feed right now. Call me back and face time so we can see them live "

She stared at Tom, showing no emotion waiting for the callback.

"Thanks. I'm not trying to be a pain in the ass, but a quick verification is all I ask. A bunch of kids doesn't need to get killed, right?"

Her phone vibrated, and she pressed the green accept button to see the live feed. "I'm here. Can you see them?"

"Yes," she said. "Hold on," Lee Chen turned the phone and held it up to Tom’s face.

He froze in horror as he looked at the phone's screen. Tom expected a live FaceTime feed of the inhabitants of Marshera, evacuated safely outside from their cave. Instead, he stared in shock at a visual of his two young sons swinging on their backyard swing set, laughing playfully. His wife was taking turns pushing each one from behind. The phone camera pulled back to reveal an obese man with curly black hair holding a Remington AR15 assault rifle with a long-range scope attached to the top. "I can pick off the mother now, Lee. Let me know how to proceed."

"You, sons of bitches!" Tom shouted. "I should've known from the start. He fought his feelings of wanting to hurt her physically. "That guy walks away from them, or there's no extraction. Understood? He leaves this second!"

"You have it backward, Tom," she said. "You push the button and extract our space rock, or he picks off your wife, the mother of your two kids, first. Then he takes those kids and hands them to a guy we know in Los Angeles. They'll be sold to a Taiwanese broker. Lots of demand for young boys these days."

His fist clenched tightly as his face filled with rage. Tom wanted to attack her, but he feared for his family. He came to his senses. "You lying bastards. How do I know you won't kill her and take them anyway after you get your meteorite?"

"Seriously, Tom, do you think we want the Chula Vista local and CHP on a manhunt for two small kids? Your family will be safe as long as we get what we want. We get the meteorite, and you get your family. Oh, and you never have to see us again. End of story."

"What about those poor kids in the hippy colony? We can't just let them die!" he said.

"I told you before, Tom. They're collateral damage. Those kids are our canaries in a coal mine. Do you remember what happens to the canaries, Tom?"

"Of course I do. They die."

"Exactly, Tom. Because canaries are expendable. They're just little birds that no one cares about. You need to get real. Those kids were spying on us, and they've seen our faces. If you think it's smart to let them live to identify us and tell their tales of what happened here, you're more naïve than I thought."

Tom realized she was right. He had lost the fight. "My man Valdez is finished fixing the blasting caps. One last thing I want is verification my family is safe and proof your guy is miles away before I push the button."

"You'll have it," Lee Chen said.

"May God forgive your soul for what's about to happen."

Chapter 45
Climbed a Mountain And I Turned Around

"Forty minutes until detonation …"

The image was barely visible through the darkness and the trees. Ugly metal trailer; it didn't belong in this beautiful wilderness. Kim hid in the shadows and prepared for what she had to do next. In what kind of shape would she find Julie? Could she be moved? *Focus Kim!* The light inside the trailer allowed her to see him through its little windows. She felt her stomach tighten from anxiety. Soon it would be time to attack.

The guard was big, over six feet tall, with a shaved head and a red face. *What if they moved Julie and she isn't here?* Kim remembered to use logic. There would be no reason for a guard unless Julie were in there too. Lowering herself to the ground, Kim crept to the corner of the trailer, knowing he wouldn't see her as long as the inside lights stayed on.

Removing the spool of black wire from her backpack, she attached an end to the frame and circled the trailer's perimeter, unspooling the wire while pulling it tight. The wire that was in the crate of ANFO explosives would be put to good use. She couldn't believe how daring this was. Somehow, she had found her inner confidence again, maybe because she had to. It was time to execute the plan. She would get Julie out of this shithole.

The wire secured, Kim had one more item left to do. She cut off another length, tied it around a bush across from the trailer, and brought the other end to the corner where she hid out of sight. *Can I actually do this?*

Anger overtook her, and she said to herself. "You bastards think you can sneak into our house and take my Julie while we sleep?"

She reached into her backpack and pulled out the weapon. She held it tightly in her hands, ready to use. Desperate times call for desperate measures. Stepping up the three stairs to the trailer door, she pounded on it three times and dashed back around the corner. A moment later, the door was yanked open from the inside. The guard's bald head poked out to look from side to side with a scowl. Hiding around the side of the trailer, Kim pulled on the wire, causing the bush to rustle.

He took the bait.

Gun drawn, he tried to run down the stairs. Instead, his foot caught the wire, sending him head-first into the bottom step. His gun slid across the dirt as he lay unconscious on the ground. Kim had hoped the fall would've knocked him out, not requiring her to do what needed to be done next. She ran to him and dropped to her knees. With two quick movements, Kim pulled down on his belt, exposing the upper part of his rear end, and then plunged the arrow into it. Winger had soaked it with curare and given it to her. His leg kicked, and he swung his arm around in reaction. She backed away; thirty seconds later, he was out.

Kim leaped to her feet and flew up the trailer steps.

"Julie!" Kim yelled as she ran from room to room, looking for her. "Julie, where are you? Answer me!" The back room door was locked at the far end of the trailer. Her body was flooded with adrenaline as she pounded. "Julie, open the door, honey! It's me, Kim!"

Jesus, she must be unconscious.

Wild with panic, Kim ran around the trailer, looking for anything to get the door open. A broken hydraulic piston was sitting on the wooden shelves filled with heavy metal parts. She grabbed the oily piece and began wailing on the door knob. The part was heavy as hell, but she had the strength of five men right now. Wham! Wham! Wham! The knob broke off and rattled across the floor. Kim slammed her shoulder against the door, and it flung open.

She burst into the room to find Julie sitting in a metal chair with her wrists zip-tied behind her back. Her head was slunk down, eyes shut tight. Kim lifted Julie's face to see her skin was pale and cold.

Dear God, please don't tell me!

"Julie, can you hear me!" Kim shouted directly into her face with no response. Clammy skin and a limp body could only mean one thing. She was near an overdose.

Plunging her hand back into the backpack, Kim frantically looked for the wire cutters. Her hand was shaking as she cut the zip-ties and slid Julie out of the chair to lay her on the floor. "Julie, wake up" she yelled, inches from her face as she gently slapped her cheeks.

Julie partially opened her eyes and looked at Kim to force a half smile.

"You're going to be alright," Kim said as Julie fell back unconscious, still sedated. Pinching her nose, Kim gave Julie CPR, breathing fresh air into her lungs and then pushing in on her chest. After her condition improved, Kim lifted her upright and yelled again. Wake up! Slowly, she was coming out of her drug-induced coma. Kim leaned her against a wall.

"I'll be right back."

She ran into the small kitchen and turned on the cold water to wet a towel. With the cold towel in hand, Kim turned to run back. She stopped dead in her tracks. He stood there towering in the doorway. Blood trickled down his face from the gruesome gash.

I'm so screwed.

Frozen, Kim stared at him in horror. He was a giant, but she noticed something. His eyes were glassy. The bloody hand gripping the door told her something else. *He's still feeling the drug.* Injured and drugged, the guard still knew his job. He charged at Kim like a bull. She stood in terror, a deer in headlights, not realizing she'd suckered him into a last-second fake. Ducking under his flailing punch, Kim tried to escape, but the giant tripped her, and she stumbled to the floor. He reached over and grabbed her shirttail, bringing his fist down and slamming a blow to her back. Kim screamed in pain as she struggled to get free. His hand was a vise, dragging her across the floor to him where certain death awaited. Reacting on instinct, Kim began kicking furiously with both legs. One kick caught him square in the nose, and he released her shirt in agony. Up on the countertop above was a metal coffee pot. Springing to her feet, Kim grabbed it and swung it wildly, missing on the first few tries until she nailed him directly in the head. The impact made a sickening clang as her attacker was knocked unconscious. Loose zip ties on the counter were used to secure his wrists and ankles. Standing up to return to Julie, Kim looked down at him. "You lost to a girl."

She ran back to hold the wet cloth on Julie's face.

"Did they inject or make you take it in pill form?" Kim asked her.

"The pills; they made me take them, or they kill me."

"Do you think you can walk? We have to get out of here."

"I don't know. I'll try."

"Last question," said Kim. "Do you think there will ever be a time when we can just hang out without me giving you CPR?"

Julie smiled from the corner of her mouth and whispered, "Probably not."

Arm in arm, they moved down the stairs and out of the trailer. Kim spotted the trail that led up the hill to Wildcat Falls and the entrance to Marshera. They limped along as Kim texted Barge again. *Hey, need a status report? Are you set up and ready to push the button? I got Julie and headed back.*

No reply.

***

He was hanging upside down and aimed at Baez. With the other guards down and out, he readied the killing dart that contained three times more poison than the others. It would only take thirty seconds for Baez to die.

To kill the snake, you must cut off the head.

Winger filled up his lungs to launch the deadly projectile. Suddenly Baez stopped firing. He looked down to change the clip on his rifle and saw Winger a second before he fired the dart. Baez held up his gloved hand in self-defense, and the dart stuck to his palm before it fell to the ground.

Did I get him?

There was no time to see if the venom did its job. Winger scrambled to right himself and bolted up the tree. With no shots fired, he wondered if Baez was without a weapon or dead.

There was no time to find out. Winger had to find Ashun and the others.

***

"Twenty minutes until detonation …"

The young recover quickly. It's just a fact of life. Kim had brought some water from the trailer. Julie's strength was returning. Picking up the pace, they made good time. Kim was worried; why hadn't Barge replied? Something was wrong. Had he succeeded in placing the explosives where they belonged, or had something gone wrong? She and Julie approached a fork in the trail. One way was the quicker to the top of Wildcat Mountain. The other way would take Julie to Marshera.

"Are you strong enough to make your way back to Marshera? I need you to get Charlie and Creen outside to safety in case we don't stop the miner's detonation. It will crush them! I can't connect with Barge, and I'm panicking!"

"Yes, I'm feeling better now. I can make it," said Julie.

"Are you sure?"

"Yes! Now go find Barge!"

Kim took off like a shot.

"Wait!" Julie yelled to her.

Kim ran back. "What's the matter?"

Julie threw her arms around her, holding her tight. "Be careful. I love you."

"I love you too."

Blinking away the tears, Kim flew up the path toward the mountaintop. Several reasons crossed her mind for why Barge hadn't contacted her; none of them were good. She rounded the corner of the narrow trail and saw the silhouette of a man. He stood in the middle blocking her. Was it a guard, or maybe it was Barge? She kept running until she saw who it was.

Brad.

He stared at Kim as if he had been expecting her. His right hand was holding a gun that pointed straight at her chest.

"Going somewhere, Babe?"

"Shit! Move aside, Brad. I have nothing to say to you anymore."

"I don't think so, Kim. I'm supposed to report on anyone in the area," Brad pulled a radio from his pocket.

"I'm in a hurry! And when did you start carrying a gun? Are you going to shoot me with that thing?"

"You never know what to expect from people, Kim. Some people betray you and fall for a cowboy. Who knows what I might do? Payback's a bitch."

"You've got your wires crossed, Brad. Pretty sure it's you that betrayed me. Hacking into my laptop, or at least trying to, so you could sell my company's formulas to God knows who. Is that why you asked me to move in with you? Then you tried to talk me into stealing the Blue Water from the Fountain of Life. Yes Brad, I can put two and two together."

"The other day, I asked you for a favor, Kim. They took my mother, and that Blue Water was the only way to get her back. After all, I've done for you, the one time I ask for something, you throw me to the wolves for a girl named Julie that we don't even know. I'm the man you loved, remember? You can't replace Grace with Julie. You do know that, right? What's done is done, Kim. You can't go back in time."

"What's done is us, Brad. I was thrown into this whole mess after saving Julie from drowning. These bastards you're involved with had her held hostage. She almost overdosed. Thanks to you and your friends, Marshera will be crushed when they detonate their charges. Are you happy? Stop worrying about yourself for once, and maybe be concerned with those sick kids. Consider what you could have been and what you've become, Brad."

He stood in silent defiance.

"What would your mother think of you at this moment?"

She walked around his left side, but he blocked her way.

"Nice speech Kim but former girlfriend or not, I can't let you pass."

"That girlfriend you lived with is gone, Brad. I have a purpose in life now, and for once, it's not serving you. So if you need to shoot me, go right ahead."

Kim felt a vibration under her feet. The ground began to tremble as a strange rumbling grew louder. She worried that the charges to free the meteorite had been detonated. The ground vibrations grew stronger and stronger as she heard something crashing through the forest.

The thumping...Something familiar about this....

"I'm not going to shoot you, Kim. But I can't let you go either. I have a job to do ...."

Elvis, the feral pig, burst out of the thicket as if shot out of a cannon. Somehow he had wandered to new surroundings in his never-ending search for food. The pig made a beeline straight for Brad. "No," was all he could muster in disbelief as it slammed into his side. Bam! Brad's body contorted and flew through the air to land on his back in excruciating pain. Barely missing a beat, Elvis kept on going, snorting and rumbling into the distance. Kim ran to him, "Are you alright? Anything broken?"

"No, I don't think so," Brad said in anguish. "He nailed my hip; it hurts like hell."

She put her hand on his cheek and then brushed his hair back into place.

"I have to go. I'll come back for you later. You'll be okay." She took off running at full speed toward the top of the mountain.

Lee Chen's voice came through the radio speaker, piercing and loud, "Brad, what's your status? Seen anything strange going on? I've been trying to reach the trailer, but there's no answer. Need you to head down there immediately and ensure the girl's still secure."

Brad crawled to pick up his radio and pushed the button, "Haven't seen anyone. I'll head over there now."

Old flames still flicker long after the fire is out.

***

Cracker flew down the trail at full gallop, lit only by a flashlight and a billion stars. His rider needed to reach the top of Wildcat Mountain as fast as possible. The destination required far more power and agility than his ATV could provide. The horse was his best option, being the strongest stallion he'd ever ridden. Still raw and untrained, he was also the craziest. Soon, the horse's strength would be tested. Voicemails from Kim told him she needed help. He didn't care what she thought of him at this point; this was his chance to get her back.

They arrived at the base of the mountain trail. Nick looked up the vertical angle.

“Jesus Christ, I don't know, Crack.”

Nick pulled on the reins to hold him back as Cracker raised up on his hind legs and whinnied like a race car revving its engine. "Alright then, you crazy bastard, let's go!" Nick let off the reins. "Hiyaaaaah!"

Cracker jumped through the air like a gunshot.

The horse thrust himself up the steep grade, grunting and puffing as his powerful legs pushed, slipped, and dug toward the summit. All the time, Nick wondered how much time they had before the end of Marshera. It was all his fault. He'd been shooting himself in the foot all his life, and now was no different. Cracker bucked and snorted as he climbed up the impossibly steep grade. Nick leaned so far forward that his face was buried in Cracker's mane.

They crested the top of the mountain and rode straight to the rock formations along the ridge. Nick dismounted Cracker and turned on his flashlight to see the central signal distribution box. Its LED's blinked green, ready to go.

Good! He was pleased that Kim and Barge had figured out the plan's details.

Now to find the detonator. But where were they?

Nick turned his head to listen to the warning off in the distance.

"Ten minutes until detonation ...."

"Jesus Christ, somebody's gotta blow these charges!" he yelled to the empty sky.

Nick jumped back on Cracker and rode around the mountain top, looking for either Kim, Barge, or the detonator.

"Hey, guys! Where y'all at?" He called out to them.

They passed the solar panel array that provided electricity to Marshera, but no one was seen. Continuing to roam around the mountaintop, they turned left at a rock pile, and Nick saw the blinking yellow light. He jumped off Cracker to see Barge lying on his side unconscious.

"Hey man, you alright?." His words were a waste of breath. Barge was still out.

Nick felt for his pulse and vital signs. They were normal. He decided to finish setting up the detonator in time to set off the charges. He rebooted it until all five lights showed the wireless connection was green and good to go.

"There's no time like the present," Nick said and hovered his finger over the ignite button. He heard a boot crunch on the gravel behind him. Before he could react, two bullets slammed into his side like a hammer hitting him twice. A second later, the wounds burned like a hot poker had been shoved inside him. He yelled out in excruciating pain and fell over on his side to feel blood spurting out his ribs. The dark figure of a guard stood above him. It was a woman.

She aimed her rifle at the detonation box and fired six rounds. Chunks of plastic and metal scattered everywhere, and Nick's hope of saving Marshera from destruction was rapidly ending; so was his life. She would move the muzzle back to him and finish him off, so he tried an old Army trick. Holding his breath, he opened his mouth to let saliva run out onto the ground. Eyes staring off into the distance, he faked his death the way he'd seen it happen for real in battle. She moved the gun's muzzle over to Nick's head and stared.

"Fuck it." She turned around and walked away.

Kim reached the crest of the mountain and vomited from exhaustion. Gasping for air, she staggered toward the rock formations she remembered from the map.

Where the hell is Barge?

Semi-delusional from exertion, Kim saw a cliff jutting up into the night sky and ran to it, hoping it might be the one. But it wasn't. Disoriented, she yelled out, "Barge! Where are you!"

We're not going to make it.

"There was a noise to her left that sounded like a horse whinnying. She detoured in its direction, not even knowing why. "Cracker buddy, what are you doing here? Where's Nick?" She rubbed his muzzle and looked around the area. Cracker snorted and bobbed his head in approval of her affection.

"Warning! Five minutes until detonation. All personnel must clear the blast zone!" bellowed the robotic voice in a low monotone.

Cracker walked by her side as she wandered around in fear looking for Barge or Nick. Why are men never around when I need them?

The feeling snuck up on her again; hopelessness. Hope was evaporating, and all they had worked for was about to be lost. Almost defeated, Kim was lost too, wandering around the mountaintop with a horse while they ran out of time. She stopped walking and saw the faces of Charlie, Creen, Barge, and Julie float through her mind. Then came Grace.

No! Dammit! I will NOT give up!

She turned to Cracker, fighting tears, "Help me find them."

Somehow he could sense her feelings by the tone of her voice. He walked in a different direction, and without question, Kim followed him.

A detonator shot full of holes was smoldering. Lying on the ground next to it, was Barge and Nick.

"Jesus Christ, no!" she screamed and ran them. Barge was semi-conscious and groggy, slowly coming out of it. He looked over at Nick lying in a pool of blood.

"Probably too late for poor old Nick," he said with resignation.

Kim unzipped her backpack to pull out a small safety kit. She yanked it open and frantically applied gauze and tape to save the man she loved.

"Help me, Barge! Open some more gauze and bandages!" She ripped Nick's shirt apart to expose a bullet hole leaking blood on the ground. Barge regained consciousness and helped her clean the wounds and then patch them with white gauze pads and tape. The gauze turned red as fast as they applied it. Nick moaned in pain. He was somewhere between unconsciousness and death.

She grabbed his chin with her bloody fingers, "You are *not* going to die tonight, Nick Caldwell!" Her voice was strong but shook with nervousness.

He moaned in pain as they kept adding gauze and tape. Kim could see where a bullet had gone into his side and come out the back. That wasn't the problem. The second wound was closer to his abdomen and bleeding. The bullet was still inside him, doing damage.

What happened next took place so fast, it was impossible for Kim to comprehend. They heard a footstep come out of nowhere behind them. Kim and Barge looked up in unison.

Alex Baez stood looking down at them with a rifle pointed at Kim's head. Radio raised to his face; he called her. "Ms. Chen, it's Alex Baez. I'm on the summit as you ordered. Got the girl and two men from the hippy colony. What are your orders?"

The radio crackled with her voice, "Kill them both. Do the girl first, and make sure you put a two in her."

Kim couldn't believe what she had heard. *Did she read her text? How evil had her sister become?*

Baez placed his finger on the trigger and pointed the rifle at Kim's head as Barge scrambled to shield her. Looking around Barge, Kim stared straight into the killer's eyes with defiance. All her fear and anxiety had disappeared. There was a calmness. She was ready for death. She had been for a long time.

At the last second, Baez changed his mind. Barge had to go first. He moved the weapon to point it at Barge's head. Kim covered her eyes, not bearing to see her friend die.

A loud shot rang out.

"You fuckin bastard!" She screamed through hands that covered her face.

There were footprints and movement. A second shot exploded. Then a third and a fourth shot echoed across the mountaintop. Kim was afraid to look. What had just happened? She hadn't been hit. Did he shoot Barge again and again? And now it was her turn?

Kim yanked her hands down to open her eyes. Baez's head was pointed to his chest as he toppled face-first to the ground. Standing behind him in a cloud of smoke was the killer.

It was Brad. A moment later, he fell over backward, flat on his back.

Kim yelled in shock, not believing what she had just seen, "Brad?"

She ran to him to see the bullet wound in his stomach. Barge came over with the medical kit, and they began applying bandages and tape on the wound.

"This is the Final Warning! One minute until detonation. All personnel must clear the blast zone!" bellowed the robotic voice in a low monotone.

Kim looked at Barge, crazy with panic. "He's still alive, but we have to detonate the charges. There's only a minute! What can we do?"

"The detonator's destroyed. The only way is to push the M/O button on the distribution box. It's the manual override. But whoever does that will die from the blasts!"

"Barge, we're going to lose Marshera!"

"Look!" he pointed behind Kim.

Nick was limping and staggering away from them toward the rock formations.

"What are you doing, Nick? Come back, or you'll be killed!" Kim yelled out to him.

"I'm already dead," Nick yelled back. "Take care of them kids, Kim."

"Please, Nick! I'm begging you! Come back, and we'll find another way!"

"Ain't no other way." His voice and his image faded to black in the night.

Suddenly she felt all alone in the world. The man who she had fallen deeply in love with, the man who she was meant to be with, was walking to his death. Kim wanted to run and stop him, but her gut told her not to. There were others she needed to save now.

"Alright, I will," she called out faintly.

Kim couldn't hold it in, "I love you!"

There is no death; there is only a change of worlds.

Ten, nine, eight, seven, six, five,

The five explosions came fast, one after another, with devastating shock waves. Five thuds from the detonations shook the ground so hard they knocked Kim and Barge off their feet. She sat up off the ground, trying to see into the distance.

It had begun. The boulders and giant rock formations shattered into billions of chunks that ran down the mountainside, starting a chain reaction. The explosions had done exactly what they were supposed to do. A monster landslide ensued.

A tidal wave of rocks, boulders, dirt, and trees roared down the side of the mountain like a tsunami. Tons of earth engulfed everything in its path, instantly devouring it and then covering what it consumed with new earth.

Tom stood in shock, watching the crush of the mountainside rush straight down at him and the dig site, knowing they would all die. There was no running away. They deserved this fate for their sins. They had defaced and raped this mountain in the name of greed. They had polluted and poisoned the mountain's clean water and hurt sick kids trying to heal. Their caretaker had been murdered and disposed of by the crew. Mother Nature had her final say. So be it. He thought about how hard his death would be on Victoria and the kids. He would miss them.

The wave consumed them, and after they died, everything went dark for infinity.

The entire mining operation and all the equipment were buried under hundreds of thousands of yards of dirt, rocks, boulders, and trees. A gigantic mushroom cloud of silt and dust engulfed the entire area dropping visibility to zero. It drifted through the trees to dry the blood spilled that night. Now the mountain could begin to heal again. So would the people who lived inside the caves. Marshera would continue, and so would its people.

Take only what you need and leave the land as you found it.

Chapter 46
Funeral For A Friend

"We need to slow down the bleeding, or he dies," Barge was applying bandages and pressure on the bullet wound. Brad's body insisted on leaking out his blood.

"We're out of bandages, Kim. There's a large medical kit in Marshera's cafeteria. It has gauze bandages, tape, and pain pills too. We have to stabilize and then get him to a hospital."

"I'll run down and get it," said Kim. "I have to check on everyone and make sure they're alright after the avalanche. Be right back."

She flew down the mountainside, worrying if Brad would die. For reasons Kim couldn't understand, she still cared about him. The man Kim had truly loved just died. It didn't seem real yet. She kept hoping Nick would walk back and stand over her shoulder, making his cowboy euphemisms again. *Why did you leave me?*

Running down the mountain required careful footing, but it was much faster than climbing. At the bottom of the downgrade, Kim flew down the trail toward the hidden entrance behind Wildcat Falls. She opened the stone door to find Creen crouched down, sitting on the floor. Her face was in disarray, paralyzed with fear.

Kim sat down with her and wrapped Creen in her arms, "It's okay, honey. It's all over now. The bad guys are gone."

"But, I'm afraid,"

"Afraid of what?"

"There's death inside Marshera tonight. I can feel it coming, Kim. It's strong."

"No. Honey, the people that wanted us to die are what you're feeling. But they died instead. Where's Julie and Charlie?"

"I think they went in the Falls Room. Julie said she would come back and get me once everything was safe. But she never did!" Creen shivered with fear.

Kim took off her sweatshirt and wrapped it around her. "It's going to be alright. You sit here and rest. I'll be right back."

The river's noise grew louder with each step up the rock stairs. Kim could feel the loose sediment, shaken from the ceiling, during the avalanche under her feet.

"Julie, Charlie, you guys alright?" Fear grew inside he as she made it to the top step. Her fists were closed into tight balls; nails dug into her palms with the apprehension of looming danger.

Where are they?

Kim crept slowly into the Falls Room and froze in terror.

Julie was standing with an arm wrapped around her neck and a hand covering her mouth. The other arm held a pistol pressed against her head. The person holding the gun was Lee Chen.

Kim's heart pounded against her chest. Terror and tears filled Julie's eyes.

Lee Chen shouted, "So this is the way it'll work. She and I walk leave here, and she stays with me until my people pick me up. Then I let her go. You interfere, and I'll put two in her head."

"Where's Charlie?" Kim shouted.

Julie tried to wriggle free and shook her head. Lee Chen's grip tightened, and she stared at Kim. "He didn't make it."

"You little bitch."

"Enough! The kid kept trying to save his sister. You'll get the same if you don't turn around and leave."

"What'd you do with him?"

She motioned her head towards the raging river.

That little boy went over the falls. Kim felt a primitive, murderous desire to kill her sister. It came from a place deep within her. Conflicted, she also wanted to save her.

"You heard me. Turn and leave, or I shoot you, and then I shoot her," Lee Chen said.

"Julie stays here. You don't have enough bullets in that gun to stop me. It's over; we won. So, I want you to let her go and surrender."

"Surrender? I guess you're trying to get you both killed. I'm the one holding the gun."

"Yes, surrender," Kim said. "Did you read my text message?"

"Yes, I read it quickly, but I was busy, as you might imagine."

"Right now could be the turning point in both our lives," Kim said. "We should come together as sisters and help each other. Fate brought us together for a reason. You were devastated when you lost your sister, but she is standing right in front of you, trying to save you. So I'm begging you, please! Put down the gun, and I swear I'll be there for you."

Lee Chen shook her head. "Yes, of course, I see an opportunity for us, but it's far too late for me. I am fully formed, and I like who I am. Like I told you before, I'm the bad girl."

"But we share the same DNA, Lee. Together we are stronger."

"I've made it this far by not being sentimental. I won't start now. Goodbye, Sis." She pointed the gun at Kim and cocked the hammer.

Julie was waiting for her window. When Lee Chen moved the gun from her head and pointed it at her friend, she had it. Raising her leg, she stomped down on Lee Chen's foot with all her might. She screamed in pain as the gun went off with a deafening explosion. The bullet ricocheted off the ceiling as Julie tried to wrestle away from her. Kim was already on the move. Running full speed, she dove through the air and landed on both their bodies. Julie was thrown aside as the gun skidded across the floor. Clenched together, the sisters wrestled and clawed at each other on the ground, trying to gain the upper hand.

Lee Chen had the advantage. She had fought other women and men during her days in the Japanese Yakuza. Physically stronger, she overpowered Kim getting her in a chokehold. Kim's face turned red and distorted. Her larynx was becoming crushed as she fought for air.

"Charlie was a beautiful boy, and you killed him, you murdering bitch!" Kim reached back and jabbed her finger into Lee Chen's eye, escaping her grip. Without stopping, they came at each other and fought again. But the older sister dominated.

"You're losing, little sister. I'll be leaving with your girl soon."

Kim screamed out, "Over my dead body!" They rolled over, clenched together, and dangerously close to the torrent of water that flowed to the falls.

Lee Chen broke away from Kim and stood up to scan for the gun. Her head whipped side to side, but the weapon was missing. Reaching inside her jacket, she pulled out her Tanto knife.

Kim sprang up and caught her breath. Bravely, she raised her arms, ready for more combat. Her only thought, she was not leaving here with Julie.

With the Tanto knife above her head, she came at Kim with its pointed edge headed for her face. Kim grabbed her wrist at the last second and squeezed tight, the knife inches from her face. There was nowhere to retreat; the river was directly behind her. They fought for control of the knife; neither one giving an inch.

"Careful little sister… I know how to use this thing," Lee Chen said.

"Give yourself up!" Kim shouted. "I will help you!"

"I'd love to talk, but you've got to go." She broke from Kim's grip and shoved the knife forward as Kim raised her hand in defense. The blade stabbed straight through her flesh like hot metal through butter. Kim screamed out as blood spurted and streamed down her forearm. Lee pulled the dripping knife out, ready to plunge it into Kim's chest.

Julie had found the biggest rock she could throw and flung it with both hands. It arced through the air with flawless precision, smashing into the middle of Lee Chen's back, knocking the knife out of her hand, and thrusting her into Kim.

Both sisters toppled over - right into the raging river.

"Julie!... Help!" Kim screamed out as they both flowed towards the falls.

Kim began swimming harder than she ever had in her life. Her arms were a blur as she windmilled them against the onrushing current and tried to steer herself to the riverbank. Desperate, Lee Chen grabbed Kim's ankle and hung on like an anchor. She may have been the older and tougher sister, but she had never learned to swim.

Frantically swimming upstream, Kim fought a losing battle. Then her sister's fingernails dug into her ankle as she pulled herself up Kim's body. Lee Chen was dragging them both toward their deaths. Kim kicked Lee Chen in her hand and face until she let go. "No! No! No!" Her grip on Kim was broken.

Free from her sister, Kim tried to swim to the riverbank. Her muscles depleted, she resigned herself to going over the falls and her death. Suddenly, her right hand came down and slapped against something unexpected; another hand. Water filled her eyes and nose as she looked up to see Julie's outstretched arm. Their hands locked in place. Julie tried to pull her to safety, but she weighed only ninety pounds. Kim began dragging her backward over the riverbank and into the river.

"Let go of me!" Kim tried to shout, her mouth filled with water. Julie wouldn't unlock her grip on Kim's hand. The river dragged them toward the falls and their deaths. Then Julie saw it lying on the ground; Lee Chen's knife. As her body slid, she grabbed it with her free hand and stabbed it into the dirt. They stopped, but there were seconds until Julie's strength would fail.

Kim saw it protruding out of the water, a rock. She kicked and paddled towards it. Julie screamed as her grip slipped off Kim's hand, "I'm so sorry!" Julie yelled out as Kim lunged to her right, barely catching the rock. With her last bit of strength, Kim flung her other arm around it, thanking Mother Nature for all rocks.

Suddenly, Lee Chen came out of nowhere, having latched onto a branch growing from the riverbank. She crawled up Kim's body again, digging her fingernails into her legs to drag herself out of the river's suction.

Kim yelled out in pain, holding to the rock. Her strength gone; she had a moment of hope. *Maybe she wants to be saved?* Grabbing Kim's clothes, Lee Chen was at her sister's waist. Kim looked back, and her heart sank. Lee Chen held a sharp rock above her head. Julie screamed from above. Kim looked up at her outstretched arm. Reaching down, Julie gave Kim the knife.

"Told you I was stronger than you, sister," said Lee Chen, the jagged rock about to damage Kim. Devilish in appearance, soaking wet strands of hair streamed across her face. Kim knew there was no hope of saving her now. *A tiger never changes its stripes.*

"Maybe you're stronger," said Kim." But I have something you'll never have."

"Julie!"

Kim swung the blade around and impaled her sister's shoulder. Blood spurted out as Lee Chen screamed hideously. She released her hold on Kim, to be sucked backward by the river, and disappear through the opening to plunge over Wildcat Falls.

Julie pulled Kim onto terra firma and safety. Soaked to the bone, Kim shivered as Julie tended her wounds to stop the bleeding.

They sat side by side, feeling like they belonged together.

Kim turned to her, still catching her breath.

"You….. saved…my life, young lady."

Julie smiled, "Figured I might owe you one by now."

There was a quiet moment as they listened to the roar of the river echo throughout the room. Marshera was saved, but some of the people they loved had died.

"Kim, I don't know the right words," said Julie. "Your sister, she's gone. You just found her, and then you lost her. I'm so sorry."

"I still can't believe it. I lived in grief from losing a sister all my life, yet I had one all along. She was an evil sister. I desperately wanted to save her, but I had to let her go to save us."

Kim's eyes filled with tears that ran down her cheeks. "Charlie, oh my God. Our beautiful Charlie. You lost your brother. I'm so sorry. I loved him," Kim cried, and Julie wept with her, "Me too."

Julie put her head on Kim's cold, wet chest without a care in the world. She sat up, looked at Kim, and wiped her eyes, "Hey, you know what? I lost my brother today, but I gained a sister."

Kim smiled at her lovingly, "So did I, Julie. So did I."

Chapter 47
What Is And What Should Never Be

It was an unhappy happy ending for the Volkov brothers. Heavily stocked with weapons, they fought a twenty-man SWAT Team inside an upstate, New York shack until their bloody deaths.

Mr. Chang's New Jersey company, NAIL, was raided by the FBI. He was apprehended in Hong Kong and extradited to face numerous felony charges in The United States.

Lt. Jacquard worked with the State and Federal investigators and prosecuted several state officials and police officers who took bribes and Chromwell for its illegal business practices.

Ashun was wounded from Alex Baez's rifle. Her's and Niben's wounds were mainly superficial. They were both treated and then released at the local hospital. Niben returned to live off the off-grid somewhere in the New Hampshire wilderness. Ashun was released to Winger to do the same. They would use a variety of herbs and ointments to aid her healing as Winger waited on her in their shady tree house.

After being medevacked to the hospital, Brad's bullet wounds required surgery. He was in critical condition but pulled through. As soon as he was released, he made sure his mother, recently released from captivity, was transported safely back to her assisted living facility. He sat down with her to confess everything and apologize for his involvement. Barb didn't believe a word of his story, telling him terrorists had kidnaped her and that he had rescued her.

Kim went home to Mum's house and told her everything. She told her about Nick and how they had fallen deeply in love with each other. She told her of how he heroically died to save Marshera.

A few days later, Kim left Mum's house and promised to return in a few hours. There was a meeting to be held in Marshera. Barge requested her attendance. She had a vague idea of what the meeting might be about. To get back out to Marshera, Kim called Wildcat Off-Road Playground. She asked for Cody, but the person that answered the phone said he was new and didn't know who Cody was. Kim wanted to thank him from the bottom of her heart. Cody had given her confidence and determination when she was ready to give up.

Just as she was about to leave, Mum called her back into the kitchen and asked her to sit down. She had some rather bad news for her daughter. Mum's text to her in Marshera about a clean checkup wasn't accurate. The truth was that her cancer was no longer in remission. There would be more rounds of chemo and radiation required. Her mother's outlook was grim, to say the least.

Kim was devastated and wanted to stay with her. Mum said not to fuss. It only made her feel worse. Then Kim thought about her upcoming meeting in Marshera and had an idea.

***

Kim stepped inside the same office, expecting to see Cody. Instead, the dirty blonde mechanic who had been disassembling an engine was now sitting behind the desk and still smoking a Marlboro cigarette.

"Hi, is Cody in by any chance?" Kim asked.

"Who?" he replied.

"Cody, you know the owner? I think he said his last name was Metalak or something."

Dirty blonde smiled at her and then looked bemused. "Ain't no Cody round here, lady."

"What?" Kim was confused and looked around the office. “He gave me a tour and rode out to Wildcat Falls a few days ago. You know, Cody? Native American with long black hair?"

"Ma'am, there *is* a Cody Metalak. But he don't own this place or work here. Cody Metalak was a famous Abenaki warrior a long time ago. There's a plaque in Crawford that has all kinds of stuff about him. The guy was legendary; hunter, fisherman, and warrior. Fought the British and the French. Killed a lot of 'em protecting his village. Lived to a hundred and twenty supposedly. He's buried about ten miles north of here off route 145."

Kim tilted her head and stared at him dumbfounded. "You have no one here named Cody? I'm sure he drove me out to Wildcat Falls and then came back to visit me. He helped me, and I want to thank him."

He lit up another Marlboro and leaned back in the chair to carelessly blow a plume of smoke towards her, "You can keep on askin' for Cody Metalak all day long, lady but the only place you gonna find him is buried in the cemetery off 145."

Frustrated, Kim told Dirty Blonde she had called for a ride out to Wildcat Falls. A ride back would be needed too. He would be well compensated and was happy to oblige.

Back to her car, Kim retrieved bags of food for her friends at Marshera. Kim sat motionless in her driver's seat and thought about Cody. She was bewildered. *Was Cody a ghost? Or my guardian angel?* He had felt like an old friend from the first time they met. She couldn't put her finger on why. He spoke as she did and even had the same mannerisms. She peaked in the rearview mirror, and that was when it hit her.

Oh my, Cody was me?

***

The meeting at Marshera was held immediately after The Offering. During the session, Kim sat in the back and thought of Nick and how much he had sacrificed for her and Marshera. The damage from the avalanche to Marshera was thankfully minor. After The Offering and a discussion led by Barge, a vote was held that had to be unanimous. It was, of course.

Kim was invited to become Marshera's new caretaker. She would be their new Mother. The position was paid by a trust fund set up by Barge's multi-million dollar father years ago. They asked her to agree to stay for at least three years before moving on. Kim heartily accepted the position on one condition. Mum was fighting cancer and would come to live in Marshera to take Charlie's place. Barge, Julie, and Creen all happily accepted Kim's terms.

Before she left for the ride back on the ATV, Barge came clean to all. It was time, to be honest. There was no such thing as a Decade. He had been living in Marshera for fourteen years and would have to stay there for the rest of his life. He had a rare form of leukemia and would only be kept in remission by drinking The Blue Water from the Fountain of Life daily. He had grown to love his life in Marshera, never wanting to leave. Barge's father owned Wildcat Mountain and had paid to modernize the cave-dwelling years before by adding alternative, green energy sources while updating the living arrangements. At Barge's request, his father left Marshera to be run by him and the caretaker, who would now happily be Kim.

Kim decided to test Marshera's water before she left. To her delight, the levels of toxic chemicals in the Blue Water had dropped significantly and were now safely in the green zone. The watershed water was still clean, pure and safe to drink. A final test was performed on Marshera's well water. It still showed unacceptable levels of contamination. They would try again in six months.

And so Kim went home to Mum to tell her the good news. They would be Cave-Mates for the next three years. Kim explained the plan to Mum. The Fountain of Life would cure her cancer.

"So, Mum, how do you feel about living in a fancy cave for the next three years and then walking out completely healed?"

"And you will be there, my darling daughter?"

"You know it!"

"Wherever you go, I go!" Mum smiled for the first time in a long while.

***

The baby was delivered inside Marshera, along with a doctor and midwife beside her. A healthy 7.2-pound baby girl named Nicole Grace Moreno was held and adored by everyone. She came into the world precisely eight months, and two weeks to the day they saved Marshera. Now they couldn't wait to take turns helping Kim take care of the new addition to Marshera Family.

Not even a month after Nicole was delivered, Kim received a surprise phone call from Walt, who worked at the Caldwell Ranch. He told her that the ranch had been sold and the new owners wouldn't be horse ranchers like Gus and Nick were. They still had Cracker, who loved to run wild out in the nearby fields. It had been too painful to sell him. He wanted to find the right place for the beautiful Arabian but was hitting a dead end. Kim had an idea. She made a call to Tanya, a friend from work. Following her passion for horses, Tanya left the company to work for the National Park Service in Assateague Island, Maryland. There are over three hundred wild horses that live on the island, mostly the wild Chincoteague breed. Tanya said Cracker would fit right in and adapt perfectly. She arranged for Cracker to live there if transportation could be provided. Walt was beside himself with joy. "No wonder Nick fell for you!" He would happily transport Cracker down to Maryland to let him run free with all the other wild horses for the rest of his days.

***

It was coming up on the first anniversary of Kim being Marshera's new mother. Barge stopped by her room one day to say hello to the mother and child. Kim was playing with Nicky and admiring how perfect her little nose was. Barge, of course, agreed.

"Just wanted to make sure you two are alright."

"Everything is better than alright, Barge. Mum's doing great. So is everyone else."

"You ever get nervous raising a kid inside a cave?" he asked.

Kim lifted Nicky above her chest to watch her giggle, "Are you kidding me? Not in this cave. I have you, Mum, Creen and Julie. I have my family! And that's all she and I will ever need. Besides, C'mon now, Barge, me get nervous?"

Kim and Nicole lay on the bed as she thought about how her life had drastically changed in the last year. *I was so low until that day when I dove into the river and found Julie.*

She went back to playing with Nicky to bring joy to both their faces. She saw Nick Caulfield in her indigo-blue eyes as she lowered her back down to hold her and whisper to him, "Wish you were here to see this but you're off riding with Gus now, aren't you? Ride on cowboy."

What did the future hold for Nicole Grace Moreno? It was anyone's guess, but Kim knew one thing. Somewhere, somehow, she'd be riding Arabians.

***

Café' Tournon was a place she frequented often. Sitting discreetly at an outside table, she wore dark sunglasses and a black fascinator. The pan-fried escargot had just arrived, but that was just the entrée'. Tartare de boeuf would be followed by mousse au chocolat and cappuccino. The snails eaten; her fingers clicked around the smartphone's glass. Then she received a call.

"Good afternoon, 213. My plane just landed. You are at the predefined location?"

"Yes, 651; I am here."

"You have the item, of course?"

"Yes, I have the item. It never leaves my person." She looked down and slid the vial of blue liquid out to look at it, then quickly put it back and closed the zipper shut.

"Excellent, 213. Expect me within the hour."

She lit up a Clope, took a deep inhale, and smiled with the comfort of knowing they still respected her.

Someday soon, many more will too.